To Pay
the Ferryman

To Pay the Ferryman

Ferryman

PAT BLACK

Polygon

First published in 2025 by Polygon, an imprint of Birlinn Ltd.

Birlinn Ltd
West Newington House
10 Newington Road
Edinburgh
EH9 1QS

www.polygonbooks.co.uk

1

ISBN 978 1 84697 679 7
eBook ISBN 978 1 78885 717 8

British Library Cataloguing-in-Publication Data
A catalogue record for this book is available on request from the British Library.

Typeset by 3b Typesetting, Edinburgh

For Jamie

Aylie

1

There are rivers in all of us, Detective Inspector Lomond reflected. One day they run dry.

He swirled the coffee in the polystyrene cup, watching his reflection dance. It was a notoriously horrible blend, and always came as a slap in the face. Exactly what Lomond needed after the post-mortem.

He waited for Chick Minchin in the usual room, a clean place decorated with fresh flowers that reminded him of similar spaces in hospitals where people were made to wait for bad news. He avoided the chairs and leaned against the far wall underneath a painting of the Bridge of Orchy. His posture had barely changed in the past six or seven minutes. For unusually long periods of time, he hardly blinked. Anyone who had been watching him and did not know him would have thought this behaviour odd, and worth noting.

He knew the name of the person he'd just seen opened by the pathologist, had looked at the digital faces she presented in life, just before he had seen the final reality. The inspector was well used to the process by now. He had learned a long time ago not to compartmentalise, but to go with the anger and disgust, the repulsion, to lean into it; to let its hard edges and ugly textures sharpen his focus. The trick was never to show it. In the immediate aftermath of the grim clinical business, it took a little time for Lomond to come back to a normal state, and he liked to do this alone.

The door opened, and the pathologist appeared. Minchin was a schnauzer of a man with mostly grey hair who had suited his moustache but had bowed to decades of good-natured peer pressure by shaving it off within the past year. His shirt sleeves were rolled up and fastened by silver garter clips, and he crossed the floor fast, stopping close enough to butt noses with Lomond, if he wished. This prize-fighter's approach could be unsettling if you didn't know Minchin, and sometimes even if you did.

The pathologist folded his arms and sniffed at Lomond's coffee cup. 'That's not the good stuff you're drinking. That's the machine rubbish, isn't it? They swapped the machine six months ago. It was bad before; it's a war crime now. Not fit for human consumption. You should have come to me for the good stuff, Lomie. Wee place round the corner. My treat.'

'Bad coffee can still wake you up.' Lomond sipped at his drink and shivered. 'At least it's hot.'

'Weather still crap?' Minchin squinted through the blinds. 'Silly question?'

'Silly question.'

'You'd suit a hat, you know. It'd complete the picture. And it'd keep your ears dry.' Minchin grinned.

'What's your news, Chick?'

'Cause of death was the wound to the throat. Killer's right-handed. Probably grabbed her by the chin, pulled it back. Happened fast. Considering what he did and how he did it, it was quite a clean job. *Whoof.*' Minchin whipped a hand across his own throat. 'Right across the carotid, through to the other side. Didn't sever the windpipe. Instant loss of blood pressure. But here's the thing – she wasn't dead when she went in the water. Reflex action.' The pathologist drew in a quick breath. 'Took water into her lungs, seconds after the killing stroke. Alveoli were burst, but not in a pattern that indicates drowning. Throat wound killed her.'

'So she had her throat cut, then went in the river straight away. How long was she there?'

'I'd say thirty-six hours.'

'Saturday night.' Lomond nodded. 'Any idea how far she might have drifted?'

4

'It's hard to say, Lomie.'

'Sexual assault?'

Minchin bit the side of his mouth. 'No sign of it that I noticed. Wouldn't commit to an answer, though. We'll wait and see what the tests show. No bruising elsewhere, or defensive wounds.'

'Could we have lost any evidence with the body being in the water all that time?'

'It's possible, but she wasn't in there long enough, really. The body was in good condition, considering.'

'Seems like she was executed.'

Minchin was not an altogether serious man, and certainly not a quiet man, but he could be coy when it came to giving opinions about anything other than the science and the hard facts – something he could sign off on. Not on this occasion, though.

'You've got a daftie out there, Lomie. It's the cleanliness of it. "Ritualised" is the word I probably shouldn't use. Where'd they find her?'

'Runner spotted her from the riverbank. Saw the hair first. Wasn't sure what he was looking at, to begin with.'

Minchin grunted.

Lomond's small dark eyes were restless. 'You remember the Daisy Lawlor case? The lady of the lake, the papers called it. Hitchhiker. Went from festival to festival. Bit of a hippie. This was the mid-nineties.'

Minchin frowned. 'Rings a bell. I was in Fife at the time, mind. Unsolved, wasn't it?'

'I worked on that case. Similar. Very similar. Naked girl, left in water. Had her throat cut. Not as broad or as vicious a stroke as this. But she had a few other injuries. Two in the back. One in the abdomen. Throat was cut, probably post-mortem. They weren't sure if the other cuts were made pre- or post-mortem. Water was used for disposal.'

'I'll have a look at the files, Lomie.' Suddenly, the pathologist grinned.

'What's so funny?'

Minchin shook his head. 'Early nineties, yeah?'

'*Mid*-nineties,' Lomond said, pointedly.

'Must have been when you were Baby Officer Lomie, Strathclyde's finest. In uniform.'

'And?'

Minchin snorted. 'I just can't picture you in uniform.'

2

Detective Sergeant Slater sat at the back of the briefing room, with a notebook open on his lap for form's sake.

He had chosen to sit beside Detective Sergeant Smythe. She was in a relaxed pose, her hands folded in her lap, one leg crossed over the other. Her notepad and pen lay on the seat beside her.

'When'd you get the call?' Slater asked her.

'Same time as you, I guess.'

'I'd actually gone to the gym, for once. Psyched myself up and everything. Gave myself a target. Then, wallop, call came in.'

Smythe said, 'Never a good time, is there?'

'Say that again. Aw, look . . . his royal highness must be on the team as well.' Slater nodded to the left-hand row of seats, where Myles Tait sat with two or three other officers. Slater often remarked that Tait had the look of a tailor's dummy brought to life, but this was to ignore a good head of hair and fine, chiselled features. He was, Slater supposed, a guy whose gym time never got interrupted. Tait locked eyes with Slater for a second or two; neither man acknowledged the other openly. Tait turned back to his colleagues and made a remark, and they all laughed aloud.

'Sounds like fun over there,' Slater said. 'Comedy night in here, eh?'

'Try to grow up a bit,' Smythe said sharply.

Slater bristled but said nothing. There was some movement at the head of the lectern; a door opened, and voices carried through. The briefing room display screen flickered into its pale blue half-life while a cursor danced in the corner.

'You'd never guess it,' Slater remarked, 'but Lomie doesn't like doing these. He says it's like pulling teeth.'

'That is a surprise,' Smythe said. 'He comes across well enough.'

'Suppose that's the trick.'

Lomond carried a ring-binder which he put down on the lectern. He had taken off his overcoat, and Slater noted with some surprise that his boss had lost a bit of weight.

'Afternoon, everyone,' Lomond said, gazing out across the officers assembled in their seats. The presentation screen now showed a tall, slim, smiling girl with long blonde hair. She was on a night out, grinning into the camera. The face of the friend who had her arm around her shoulders was cropped out.

'Aylie Colquhoun,' Lomond said, 'twenty years old. From Castlemilk, former student at Strathclyde Uni. History and politics. Had some interest in joining the Scottish Greens. Dropped out last year before her second-year exams in May. Lived in Garnethill, shared flat, short-term lease. Had done some modelling work; we don't know where she was working now. Found near Easton Wharf, but most likely entered the water somewhere east of there. Her throat was cut. According to Minchin's report, she was placed in the water immediately after she was killed, sometime after eight p.m. on Saturday night. She might have drifted for miles.

'First, we'll check all available CCTV around bridges and known entry points where a car might have easily accessed the river without being seen. From there, we'll liaise with the media and find out if anyone saw anything suspicious.'

Smythe raised her hand. 'Sir, did she enter the water naked?'

'Looks like it. Should go without saying that we won't be giving out any of these details to the press, on or off the record, but past experience tells me I should say it anyway. Twenty-year-old girl found dead in the water, suspicious circumstances, nothing else for now.'

Once the briefing was over, Slater joined Lomond in his office. 'We out and about now, boss?' he asked.

'Absolutely. I want to talk to her mother first.'

Slater looked surprised. 'Thought we'd have given her the news already?'

'Aylie was twenty – she can't be long out of the family house. Mother is in Castlemilk. No other relatives. I want to start at the beginning, find out what she was doing with herself.'

DS Smythe joined them. She had radically altered her fair hair in the past week – it was shorter now, though not brutally so. Slater didn't realise she'd been summoned until she said, 'Sir?'

'Ah, Cara,' Lomond said. 'Thanks for coming. I'll need you to check something separate for me. It might be to do with the case, but probably not: just something we have to check out. I want to make sure we get it right.'

If she was taken aback, she didn't show it. 'Understood, sir.'

'I'll be in touch within the hour.'

She left the office, and Slater said, 'I thought Smythe was tagging along with us, gaffer?'

'She will be, but not today.'

'Side mission, eh? Secret squirrel stuff.' Slater smiled. 'Should I feel threatened?'

'Ach, you can if you want.'

'I've every right to be, I suppose. She is brilliant.'

'Yep.' Lomond nodded readily. 'And normally I'd want her along for a death knock. I guess I'll have to make do with you.'

'Now I feel threatened *and* slighted, gaffer.'

'C'mon. My car. Try not to crack any jokes. Seriously.'

★

Irene Colquhoun lived in an eight-in-a-block with verandas at the front in Castlemilk. She was two floors up, in a two-bedroom flat with stark white lace curtains in the window.

While Lomond and Slater waited for a reply at the security door, a man appeared at an identical entrance in an identical block right across the road. The door slammed back, and the

9

man – stout, thickly muscled, anywhere between twenty-five and forty, paunchy and bald – glowered at them.

'What you looking at?' Slater growled.

'What?' It was the instant reaction of the guard dog to the postman. The man started across the road, clenching and unclenching his fists. 'What did you just say, mate?'

Utterly unfazed, Slater strode towards him with his warrant card out. 'Yeah, hello. My name is Police Scotland. What's your name? Can we be friends forever?'

The man withdrew, sullen and muttering, his fists still clenched. He made a great show of banging the security door behind him; any neighbours who were not invested in Lomond and Slater's presence by this point had certainly taken a stake now. Some brazenly appeared at their windows, some lurked like wraiths behind blinds and curtains.

'Idiot,' Slater said, biting the side of his mouth. 'I'm going to find out exactly who that was and . . . I tell you . . . file a wee note to myself!'

'Try not to get into a scrap, Malcolm,' Lomond drawled, a tad reproachfully. 'Remember we've got to drive out of here after this.'

'Animal kingdom, isn't it? Always the same in these places. Fort Apache. They don't know you, so they want to kill you.'

'That's a bit unfair. I grew up on a housing scheme.'

'Would that fact make us more dead or less dead?'

A voice came out of the intercom, startling them both. Lomond had been about to press the button again. 'Hello?'

'Is that Mrs Colquhoun?' Lomond asked. 'We're with the police. I spoke to you on the phone earlier.'

'Oh, mammy, daddy,' she said. Then the buzzer sounded, letting them into the building. 'Mammy, daddy. Come on up.'

*

Mammy, daddy. That was all she said at first, over and over. Every fresh utterance jarred the two men as much as the weeping.

10

They grew stern with the repetition; in a way it calmed their own nerves, steeling them.

Irene Colquhoun stood against the mantelpiece, wringing her hands. On that shelf were pictures of the blonde girl, at all ages. No one else appeared in the photographs: only that same beaming, beautiful face.

'Please sit down, Mrs Colquhoun,' Lomond said. He placed a hand on her arm. 'I can't tell you how sorry we are about what's happened.'

The dead girl's mother allowed herself to be led to the couch. She was only in her mid-forties, but seemed older – as did the flat, Lomond realised. The net curtains, the floral print wallpaper, even the crocheted throw on the back of the leather settee.

Irene was still in a state of shock – jittery, full-beam shock, not the withdrawn, quiet kind. She was blonde herself and had her daughter's hazel eyes, long, thin nose and prominent cheekbones.

'Can't take it in. Can't take it,' she said.

'Is there someone around who can help you today?' Lomond asked. 'I don't like the idea of you being left on your own here.'

'My sister's coming. She's in Huntly. She'll be down. Her and her man. Sometime soon.' She clutched her hands, fingers working the knuckles, like a surgeon preparing for an operation. Perhaps they were in want of a rosary. 'Mammy, daddy. Did she suffer? Can you tell me that?'

'She didn't suffer, Mrs Colquhoun. We're pretty sure of that. She might not even have known anything about it.'

'You're not lying?'

'I would never lie about something like that,' Lomond said gently.

'Mammy, daddy.'

'Do you take a cup of tea, Irene?' Slater asked, a touch too brightly.

'Tea . . . what?'

'I'll make you a cup of tea,' Slater continued. 'You probably

11

don't like people poking about your kitchen. I wouldn't like it either. But I'll tell you a secret . . . see my gaffer, here? You trust him with the tea, you'll regret it. Now me, I've got the gift. Lots of milk, no milk, two sugars, one sugar, a half sugar, dark brown, too milky, trench warfare – pick a shade, say the word, and I'll sort it for you.'

'Sure. Just in the kitchen. Tea stuff's beside the kettle. Wee tin for the tea bags. Coffee if you want it. There's a mug stand.'

'Perfect. Milk? Sugar?'

'Just milk.'

Once Slater was gone, Lomond said, 'I absolutely hate doing this. It's the worst thing in the world. Seeing you like this. Having to see people suffer. I absolutely hate it. I say that from my heart.'

'Can't be easy,' Irene said. 'Can't be easy, that. Coming to folk's doors. The two lassies from earlier, who took me to ID her, they were lovely. Couldn't have been nicer. Wanted to stay for a while.'

'I'm so, so sorry, but I have to ask you a couple of questions.'

Irene's face drooped. 'It's OK. You have to ask. You need to catch him. Whoever did it to my lassie.'

'I'll lift him, Irene,' Lomond said. 'You'll see him in court. You'll look him right in the face, I promise you.'

She nodded.

'Did Aylie say she was in any danger? Did she mention anything to do with boyfriends, anyone like that?'

'Aylie was a closed book. I didn't know much about her. As an adult, like. She lived with me . . . but we didn't get on. She was a teenager two minutes ago, near enough. She was just a girl.' Irene's intonation was blank, but her fingers dug into Lomond's forearm.

'When did you last see her?'

'Christmas. She was around for a couple of days. It was just me and her, though. She made a point of it, since her granny died. I know it's boring for her. I head out to clean in the mornings, that's my job, but that's it. Nothing else. I like to stay in and watch the telly. Homebody. She was out and about, total opposite. She doesn't take after me.'

'She's not been home since then? Christmas?'

Irene shook her head, and a tear dripped off the end of her nose. 'Not in this house. I saw her on her birthday, in the town, not too much after that. January baby. We went out for a buffet. One of those Chinese places. All you can eat, you know? She barely ate a thing.'

'She was clever, eh? History and politics, wasn't that the subject she was doing?'

'I think so. She should be in her last year now. Stopped it, though. Never said why. I was looking forward to putting her graduation photo up there with the rest.' She gestured towards the mantelpiece, garlanded with images of the dead girl.

'She told you how she was getting on?'

'Just bits and pieces,' Irene said. 'Going to uni in Glasgow, and I never knew a thing about it. Her course. Then she just drops in that she's out of it. She was always like that. A mystery.'

'How about work?'

'She said she was fine . . . took twenty quid off me, plus money for a taxi as well, when I met her. But she told me she had something – work in a pub, she said.'

'How about pals?'

'She did have friends – clever set at school. Tricia Mayweather. Marianne Henderson. They were her mates. The ones you would want your daughter to be friendly with. But they all moved away for uni – Trish was at Aberdeen, and I think Marianne got in at Sussex, of all places. Aylie hadn't spent much time with them since school . . . To be honest, I didn't keep much contact with her either. You never got much out of her.'

'When was the last time you spoke to her?'

'January. Like I said. Her birthday.'

'You hadn't spoken to her in ten months?'

Irene shook her head. 'Just messages on the phone.'

13

'Does she still have a room here? I'd like to take a look, if you don't mind. It can tell you a lot about a person, especially the young ones. My lassie's about the same age as Aylie – I know the score. A mystery at the best of times. You sometimes feel like you're living with a stranger.'

'Oh God, aye,' Irene agreed readily. 'The teenage years, especially. Mammy, daddy.'

'I'll be quick. And I promise I won't be taking anything out of the house. You can come with me if you like. Or you can check if DS Slater's tea is as bad as his patter.'

'I resent that,' Slater called out from the kitchen, in a mildly exasperated tone.

*

The bedroom hadn't been dusted for a while – possibly since the last time it was slept in. Lomond noted the grubby patina coating the top of the dressing table, where deodorants, hairbrushes entwined with golden strands, and more toiletries stood to attention in a ragged line before a long mirror. There was a pile of paperwork to the side. Lomond's keen eyes picked out the date on a bank statement, left at the top of the haphazard pile.

There were posters of pop stars – a little out of date, Lomond thought, and perhaps a little young-skewing for an older teenager. In contrast, over the bed was a print of Audrey Hepburn in her *Breakfast at Tiffany's* dress, batting her lashes in black and white. A large print of the New York skyline dominated the wall, with postcards stuck in the frame. Most of these were from Malaga, though there were some from the United States, including Las Vegas's neon outline. Lomond picked one out and studied the writing on the back.

'Was Aylie into travel?' he asked Irene.

'Oh aye. That's what she wanted to do. The big dream. World tour, backpacking. But she never had the time or the money.'

Lomond tucked the postcard back in the frame, then studied the back of another. 'These are all from Gordon – that's her dad?'

'Aye,' Irene said shortly, with a grimace. 'Don't be fooled. He's never here. Had nothing to do with her. Postcards and a cheque in an envelope at birthday and Christmas – that's been her lot since she was three.'

'What does he do for a living?'

'No idea. Last heard of in Malaga. A bar or something. Best place for him. And he sent those postcards, aye, but never sent an invitation to her, to get her over there. Even though she was desperate to go.' Irene's eyes widened. 'Christ, I don't know if he even knows . . .'

'We'll handle that for you,' Lomond said. 'You don't have to worry about that.'

'I just don't know what to do . . . I don't know what to say. I'll have to tell my work. I don't how I can cope.'

'Your sister will be here soon. I'm so sorry, Irene. It's rotten. Absolutely rotten. I wish I didn't have to do this. I wish this wasn't happening to you. It's the worst.'

Lomond pointed to the picture of Audrey Hepburn in her black dress. 'God . . . I thought that was a photograph. It's a painting or a drawing, is that right? That's some talent, that.'

'Oh aye. She was an artist, definitely. Wish she'd done that, really. That was a talent and a half. I think she called it "photo-real" . . . She had the gift, that's for sure. Off her dad's side, I guess. I couldn't draw you a bath.'

'Is that Aylie's signature, there? In the corner?'

'It is. She loved her art. Never picked it up past third year at school – no idea why. Think she wanted to do politics, go into that. She thought she might be prime minister one day. But she had an amazing eye . . . Here, look at the book. This is her stuff.'

Irene picked up a large photo-album sized volume. It was filled with sketches and dress designs, faceless models in what

15

appeared to be fifties style fashions. Ra-ra skirts, bobby socks, headbands. There were some rare splashes of colour – one red torrent in particular running through the kind of dress Jackie Kennedy had once worn with distinction particularly jarred Lomond – but by and large these were pencil sketches, black and white. This was not an area of Lomond's expertise, but it seemed to be the work of a sure hand.

He paused at one image detailing underwear: brassieres, stockings, girdles and knickers which seemed to complement the fashions in the preceding pages. Every leaf was decorated with the signature on the Audrey Hepburn sketch – an A, transfixed with an arrow.

'Incredible,' Lomond said. 'I would have thought she was into fashion design, not history or politics.'

'That was a wee fad she had, right when she left school. Burlesque, they called it . . . I didn't like the sound of it. She did club nights, when she was too young to go to them herself. Helping out on the doors and stuff. Think she told me she was getting into photography at one point.'

Lomond made a quick note. 'Do you know what the club was called?'

'No idea. I went mental at her when she told me. I was daft to do that. Never heard anything else about it from her again.'

Lomond paused before a portrait shot of the dead girl, a glossy photograph inserted into the album. Even in black and white you could tell that her skin was flawless. The eyes were frank, with a little mischief in them. The type of nose that might twitch when she smiled. Lomond would have sworn this was a professional photo, and he would also have sworn that the girl in the picture was in her mid-twenties, not her mid-to-late teens.

'When was the last time she stayed the night?' he asked.

'As in stayed here? In her room?'

Lomond nodded.

'Ah . . . I think . . . maybe about two, three years ago.'

'Wouldn't she have still been at school back then?'

'Yep. Moved out before she left school, actually.'

Lomond frowned. 'Moved where? Into halls at uni? A shared flat?'

'I think so,' Irene said. 'Like you said. Teenager. They don't tell you much.' She even managed a chuckle.

'How about bills, paperwork?'

'You're looking at it, right there. She'd come back for the odd bits and pieces. Not recently, though. She told me "I never met a bill I couldn't outrun".'

Lomond stared at the dead girl's image. The composed, confident features were a dreadful juxtaposition with the face as Lomond had first seen it in the flesh, under the bright lights of Minchin's examination room. When Minchin pointed out the ruin of her throat, clogged with grime. When he exposed the final grim secrets of her heart, her lungs, what had still been in her stomach, her bowels: even her brain.

Someone had taken this girl, as she was then, and with one single sure and confident stroke they had made an end of her, then pitched her into the water. Perhaps they'd shoved her; perhaps they'd kicked her between the shoulder blades. Perhaps she had been kneeling. And that had turned the girl in the photograph into the girl Lomond knew, the one on the slab. The one whose rivers had ceased to run.

Lomond cleared his throat. 'Thanks for this. I can't know what it cost you. Thank you.'

'Whoever did this . . .' Irene said, shaking her head. 'Take him away, will you? Lock the door on him.'

'Whoever he is, wherever he is – I'll have him. That's a promise.'

★

'Mammy, daddy,' Slater muttered, without a trace of humour, as they emerged from the security door. 'She's got no one, really. Totally on her own.'

Lomond fished out his phone. 'She's got a sister in Huntly. But she'll have to wait until she arrives. Staring at the walls. I don't think she's even organised anything for the funeral. I'll get someone on to that, to help her out. Hopefully, the sister can step in.'

'Nothing else we can do,' Slater said quietly.

'Not for her, no.'

'Weird one, though. The situation, I mean.'

'Yeah. Didn't seem to know anything about her own daughter. Fell out, I'm guessing.'

'And her daughter moved out when she was *school age*. That bedroom was more like a shrine. Dust was thicker than my ma's Christmas cake. And my ma doesn't scrimp on the icing. Boyfriend?'

'Maybe. I feel like we don't know any more about Aylie Colquhoun than we did this morning. We're going to, though.'

'Anything new?' Slater nodded towards Lomond's phone.

'We've spoken to Aylie's flatmates. All solid alibis, it seems. Two had been on holiday for a week, the other was working on the rigs. Aylie had a job – worked at Mr Mojo's.'

Slater frowned. 'That name's kind of familiar, but I don't know why. Why is it familiar, gaffer?'

'You tell me, Malcolm. Why is it kind of familiar? Also . . . do you have a hanky or something on you?'

'Eh? What for?'

Lomond pointed to the car. On the passenger door, slashed in broad black strokes from a marker pen, were two words.

OINK OINK

3

Lomond and Slater cracked open the lids of their coffees. Slater took a sip, misjudged it, and scorched the roof of his mouth and tongue.

Content to wait a little and sniff at the rising steam from his cup, Lomond gazed at the Clyde, and the imposing block of flats across the water. They were at their favourite berth, a coffee kiosk by the Clydeside, tucked into a leafy nook near some metal benches.

'Aylie worked in Mr Mojo's, eh? I remember now – I was in there once.'

'Oh aye? Mr Mojo's, eh?'

'It was a stag do.'

Lomond would not look at him. 'A stag do. Right.'

'Aye . . . Tommy McDonagh, guy I went to school with . . . hardly spoken to him since school, in fact. Think it freaked him out that I became a polis. Anyway. We ended up in Mr Mojo's. Wasn't my idea, I just went along with it.'

'Sure.' Lomond took a sip of coffee from the cardboard cup, trying to hide the smile that threatened to break ranks on his face. 'Couldn't have been down to you.'

'Well, it wasn't my party. I wasn't the best man or anything. Not my shout.'

'You did all you could, Malcolm.'

'They had lassies from all kinds of places – Ecuador. All over.'

'Ecuador seems very specific,' Lomond mused.

'Anyway, at midnight, they made them all take their tops off. As a freebie-type thing. I didn't know where to look.'

'Really?'

'In a manner of speaking. Anyway, Tommy McDonagh decided to get his top off as well. Place went nuts. But I think some of the lassies disliked him taking the attention, and things kind of went south . . .'

DS Smythe appeared from the foliage, startling both of them. 'Sir?'

'Hi, Cara. Get you a coffee?'

'No thanks. Just had one.' She smiled at Slater. 'You were in the middle of saying something?'

'It's fine. We can pick it up later,' Slater said.

Smythe turned to Lomond. 'I spoke to the workmate on the phone.'

'Oh aye – workmate at Mr Mojo's, you mean?'

Smythe nodded. 'Interesting one – apparently, Aylie Colquhoun was due to work on Saturday night, but she swapped shifts with the workmate for the Friday instead.'

'She know why?'

Smythe shook her head.

'Think we'd best head out there and talk to her,' Lomond said.

After a pause, Slater said, 'Maybe we'd better talk to all of them. You know. We didn't know she worked there till today. Something's bound to turn up there.'

Lomond and Smythe shared a look. Then they both burst out laughing.

Slater's face was pink. 'Well . . . just saying . . .'

'You think *we're* going over to Mr Mojo's? A *strip club*? *That* Mr Mojo's? That one you went to for a stag do?' Lomond could barely get the words out. Smythe covered her mouth with her hands and turned away.

'Well . . .' Slater straightened his jacket collar.

'You and me? In a strip club!' Lomond was still laughing. Even the bored woman at the kiosk looked up from her phone for a moment, smiling. 'Away and have a talk with yourself. We'd come out cross-eyed. This one's women only. Cara's going. She'll pick up everything we would miss – which would possibly be everything.'

'See you back at the office!' Slater snapped. He put the coffee to his lips, forgetting about the nuclear temperature, flinched, and then hurled the cup into a rust-rimmed bin close to the bench.

Once he was gone, Smythe said, 'Have you ever seen him embarrassed? I've seen him angry, but never embarrassed.'

'Ach, I shouldn't make fun of him. I'll pay the penalty for it, don't you worry. Slater's too wide to take a slagging for long. How'd you get on with the side project?'

'A blank, so far. I've got a paper trail to chase up tomorrow. I'll crack on with Mr Mojo's. Anything turn up at the mother's place?'

'Just more mysteries, to be honest. Aylie's work is the main line to follow. I'll let you in on what I have in mind once you've got back to me later on, see if things add up.'

★

In the café of the Centre of Contemporary Arts, DS Smythe spotted Nerine Guzman from a long way off. She was hunched over her phone, chin close to the table. Even seated, Smythe could tell she was tall and long-limbed. Her muscled neck and shoulders marked her out as a dancer – perhaps even a ballerina. She had curly hair drawn back into a tight ponytail, with loose strands falling across a pretty, freckled face. Brown eyes looked up, startled, as Smythe stopped at the table.

'Excuse me – are you Nerine?'

'Oh, you're the policewoman.' She spoke with a distinct accent. She was second generation, Smythe knew, her parents having come from the former Yugoslavia just before it broke up. 'I thought you would be wearing a uniform.'

'Afraid not – plain clothes for me. Can I sit down?'

'Of course.' Guzman straightened up. The word was statuesque, Smythe thought. She stopped herself from squaring her shoulders to match the stance.

21

'I'm so sorry to have to speak to you in these circumstances. It must be a terrible shock, losing a workmate this way.'

Nerine gestured helplessly. 'What can you say? It's unbelievable. She was killed, is that right? Murdered?'

'We're still awaiting confirmation, but – yes. Off the record, someone killed her.'

'I spoke to her three nights ago. We swapped shifts . . .' Nerine shook her head. 'It's a shock. I broke down and cried when I found out. Then I locked the doors in my flat. Horrible, you know? I had my boyfriend with me, but I didn't want to go out for a whole day.'

'Were you good friends?'

'I hadn't known her long, but we got close, yes. I'd been round her flat . . . helped her decorate her room. She hadn't long moved. Complained about the colour of the paint on her walls. It was only magnolia, I said. What's the problem? Magnolia is everywhere. She said, "That's the point!" She wanted pistachio. That's what she was like. She pushed for it, they agreed – the landlord. The mess it made of my clothes.' Nerine shook her head. 'Means absolutely nothing, now.'

'Exactly how long had you known her?'

'Since she came to work at Mr Mojo's. She was a good dancer – popular. That blonde hair, the boys loved her. But she was nice. Younger than she looked. I was a bit of a big sister for her, I guess. We talked a lot. She was talented, you know, creative. Designer. Wanted to design her own clothes. A performer, too. Taught herself. Why she did politics at uni I'll never know. She said there was never a path for her to do design. So she taught herself.'

'You say she was popular – did she have any regulars at the club? Anyone who got a bit too fond of her?'

Nerine sighed. 'We've all got our fans. And we do have men who come in often. Regulars, as you say. Mostly they're harmless.'

'Mostly?'

'Some get a bit too attached, and we have to get the boys in to move them on.'

'Ever any trouble?'

'There's trouble now and again. Drunks. Guys who want a bit more than a dance. Stag dos are the worst.'

Smythe thought of Slater, wondered what his face would look like in Mr Mojo's darkened corners. 'Any trouble you can remember around Aylie?'

Nerine shook her head. 'No . . . well. There was one man. Older. Or he looked older, anyway. Bald. Quite heavyset. Nice looking but not fit. He might still have been in his twenties, you know the type. Sometimes he'd appear on a Friday night, still in his office clothes. Suit, collar and tie. Not an expensive suit. He took a real shine to Aylie. He tipped her quite a bit. One time she tried giving it back to him – "No, that's too much," she said. That was the kind of girl she was.'

'You know his name?'

'She talked about him as Colin . . . something like that. I never danced for him, so I don't know for sure.'

Smythe was already taking notes. 'So he had a thing for her?'

'Definitely. He didn't seem like one of the weird ones. I've had a few of them. He was kinder, respectful. A lot of the regulars are respectful. They adore us, I would say. You know how some men get. Hopeless.'

'Would you say Colin was well known among the managers?'

'Definitely. When he finds out what happened, poor man . . .' Nerine's hands flew to her face. Then she broke down. Smythe's hands covered hers. 'Sorry,' Nerine said, voice creaking. 'It's so hard to believe . . . Did she suffer? Was it a pervert who did it?'

'Again, off the record . . . she didn't suffer. We're quite sure of that. It's a strange one. I can't say any more, but I can put your mind at ease on that point.'

'Thank God.'

'What else can you tell us about Aylie? Was there a boyfriend?'

Nerine shook her head. 'No. I think there was someone she knew at uni. But that ended after her first year – or second year? I think the boy took off for somewhere else, another university. She started work at Mr Mojo's just before she dropped out. The money was decent.'

'Cash in hand? There's no record of her working at Mr Mojo's officially.'

'I don't know anything about that,' Nerine said, far too quickly. 'I pay my taxes.'

Smythe waved her other hand. 'I'm not interested in that. It's more Aylie I'm concerned with – as a person. And her movements. What was she like to work with? You said she was creative.'

'Oh . . . you've no idea.' Nerine opened a slim black handbag and brought out a tissue, which she dabbed at her eyes. 'She wanted to create and choreograph her own performance. Burlesque, you know? I think she'd done club nights. The fifties, that was her thing, you know? Costumes, very Jackie O. She had a whole performance worked out, a routine. "Hey honey, I'm home", she called it. As if she was waiting for her husband to get back from work. She was always looking for a set, a sort of fifties show home. She wore this beautiful underwear, like . . . not vintage, but vintage style. She was so into it. That's where Shea spotted her, the boss. Persuaded her to give Mr Mojo's a try. She thought he was smitten, but he tried that act with me, too. And the rest of the girls.' She grinned. Smythe saw that she had a cute gap in her front teeth and thought, *That seals it. A model*, definitely.

'She seemed to have a passion for design, vintage clothes.'

'That's for sure.'

'She still do the burlesque performances? Club nights, cabaret, that kind of thing? They used to do those at the Chancellery, I think.'

'That might have been the place she started – but she hadn't done those performances for a while. Too busy, she said. She had some work lined up, here and there. In fact that's why she wanted to swap shifts. You know. She was meant to be in on Saturday but swapped me for my Friday. Is that . . . when it happened?'

'We're not sure exactly. We'll know in a few days.'

'God . . .' Tears spilled down Nerine's cheeks. 'Poor girl. So beautiful. And funny. She was tough, you know? A tough kid, from the streets. Tougher than I ever was. She was the real thing. But vulnerable, in a way. I wanted to look after her. She was only twenty.'

'What was the reason for her not working on the Saturday?'

'She had another gig.' Nerine lowered her voice. 'Something on the side. It was starting to work out for her. It was a way for her to work on her performance. Seemed to be going really well . . .'

'Whereabouts was this? Another club night?'

'No, she worked from home. Cam work.'

'Say that again, please – cam work?'

'You know. Video camera. Online stuff. At home. Performing. You need me to fill in the blanks? She was doing it from home. The dances. It got the money in.'

'She was working for herself? Or for another outfit?'

'I don't know – it could have been a do-it-yourself job. You can turn yourself into your own industry now, your own brand. She told me it was classy. That was the word. Said it let her try out her personal routines, try new stuff. She said she was paid well for it. There was a name . . . My something or other. She had a gig booked for the Saturday night. That's why she swapped . . . That's why she died, I guess.'

Nerine Guzman paused, then. Her face was blank. The dreadful finality of it, and the guilt to come, snatched the expression off her face.

Smythe felt her own eyes water at this desolation. She blinked to control it.

'No,' the policewoman said, underlining her last note, 'that wasn't why she died at all.'

4

Back at the office, Lomond sipped at his coffee.

Slater sat down at the desk opposite him. 'No word on CCTV yet, gaffer?'

'Nothing,' Lomond said. 'It's not out of the question that the body came a long way. I've asked the Humane Society to get back to me about tidal patterns.'

'No decent tips?'

'A couple that haven't checked out. One mentions "a lassie waiting for someone" at a bus stop near her flat, but it was only a nosy neighbour who reckons the girl had dark hair. Aylie was blonde.' Lomond rubbed at his eyes and yawned.

'Thoughts so far?'

'How do you mean?'

Slater sat forward and lowered his voice. Unconsciously echoing Chick Minchin, he said, 'Looks ritualistic, doesn't it? Weird. No sign of sexual assault?'

'Minchin said it didn't seem like it, but they're still doing tests. We don't know for sure. Body in the water – it changes things. Means you don't quite get all the evidence you'd like.'

'Guy knew that, eh? Whoever did it. Knows the form.'

'We are definitely dealing with a daftie,' Lomond agreed.

'Random?'

'Too soon to say, Malcolm. Way too soon. Boyfriends have done worse.'

'We'll get a lead. The clothes, for a start. Unless he made her take them off first.'

'I think he . . .' Lomond paused, collected himself and ended the line of thought. 'We'll see. Minchin didn't notice any other obvious wounds. Nothing that suggested she'd been on her knees. Nothing that suggested she'd been harmed before it. Nothing to suggest she tried to protect herself. Or had time to.'

'I'm thinking . . . and I'm just making a suggestion, before you shoot me down . . . he made her kneel, cut her throat, then removed the clothes. They're probably in flames as we speak. Buttons in a grate. I reckon we need to find a car. He surely used a car to transport her. We'll get him,' Slater affirmed. 'Quick as you like. Don't sweat it. How about her mobile?'

'Switched off. Last ping was in the outskirts. Can't triangulate it.'

'Travelling by road?'

'Possibly. There was a footpath running along the side of the road where her signal cuts off. It was heading out into the sticks. No witnesses.'

'Calls?'

Lomond sighed. 'Annoyingly, no. Nothing on the log. Calls to friends at Mr Mojo's – a couple to Nerine Guzman, arranging the shift swap. Possibly some chat via an app, some instant messaging. Harder for us to get to. Red tape. We'd have to find the phone to be sure. And even then, we can't be positive.'

Smythe came in. Out of the three, she looked the least tired, though she had arguably had the busier day. She nodded at Slater and pulled out a seat. Slater sat up straight and edged his chair away slightly.

'Anything?' Lomond asked.

'Loads,' Smythe said. She pulled up the cuffs on her jacket and rested her hands on the desk. 'First, I got hold of the manager at Mr Mojo's. Quite a tight ship – professional, so far as these places can go. Not quite a sticky carpet kind of shop.' She glanced, quickly, at Slater, then continued: 'She was shocked, tearful on the phone. Gave a couple of officers a statement. She confirmed what Nerine Guzman told me – that Aylie worked on a casual basis, cash in hand plus tips. She did well, earned well, was well liked by the punters and the other girls who worked there. She didn't know about the cam stuff.'

'Cam stuff?' Slater asked.

'Yeah – according to Nerine, Aylie made some money on the side doing stuff on cams.'

'Webcams? Sex work, you mean?'

'No, that wasn't it. She was a performer – burlesque, outfits, choreography. She had an act: fifties housewife, I think, is the best way of describing it.'

Slater snorted. 'Yeah. A fifties housewife who takes her clothes off. Gotcha.'

Smythe frowned and compressed her lips in irritation. She refused to take the bait. 'We don't know what it means. Nerine Guzman said it was a performance. She seemed slightly in awe of Aylie, but I don't know whether grief is doing that or sympathy . . .' She shook her head. 'We'll need to see what kind of stuff she was doing and who she was doing it with.'

'They're taking her computer apart now,' Lomond said. 'Laptop was found at her flat – plus what looked like a home studio to me. Blackout curtains, photographer's screen, light meter. Professional kit. Plus costumes, the kind of thing you're talking about. Vintage clothes – a collection of them. All packed away in plastic. A portfolio of photos – again, not amateur stuff. It won't take long to find out what the platform was, who took them, that sort of thing. And from there, it won't take long to nail who did it.'

'There's the problem with the swapped shift,' Slater said. 'I think that's the flaw, surely. The night she was killed, she was meant to be working.'

Lomond nodded. 'She changed it quite suddenly. Short notice. There's nothing on her wall calendar or in her online organiser to indicate what the issue was. But there's no doubt in my mind that finding out where she went is the key. It's the line to follow for now.'

Smythe asked: 'Boyfriends?'

'Flatmates said she hadn't brought anyone back for months,' Slater said, riffling through his notes. 'None of them really knew what she did for a living. Nice enough, bit of a stranger, intriguing lifestyle but didn't mingle. They thought she did bar work, worked nights at a club. And she might have done. Landlord didn't ask questions, either, so long as the rent came in. She didn't introduce them to any boyfriends, but she'd only been there eight months. And some nights she didn't come back at all. She seems to have earned cash in hand. Rent got paid. Nobody asked questions.'

'The flatmates definitely ruled out?' Smythe asked.

Lomond nodded. 'As far as I'm concerned. Out of town. Loads of witnesses. Time-stamped pictures on social media. Solid alibis.'

Slater continued: 'She hadn't had a serious boyfriend since the end of her first year at uni, it looks like. He's out as well. Seems she pined after him, according to her friend at uni. Not clear who dumped who. Seems she wanted him back. We took a statement – Jennifer Curran, the pal. Said she faded out in her second year, late nights. Uni was incidental. Then irrelevant. Aylie'd been disillusioned with the course. Said she'd taken the wrong journey in life. Said she wanted to be a designer, work in theatre.'

'Theatre, performance, design,' Lomond said, making a note to himself on his pad. 'Clothes. The cam work. This is what I can't get past. This is what I need to find out. It's what's making me most curious.'

'There must be something on social media,' Slater mused. 'I had a look on Facebook, but she hasn't updated her personal profile in months. Looks like she hardly updated it anyway. One or two photos at Christmas, with her mother at the flat in Castlemilk. No sign of her performance stuff on the personal profile – I would have thought she would have had a second account, but no. I'm guessing there must be another account somewhere, though, for her sex work stuff. People who do the cam work have to put themselves in the shop window, so to speak.'

Smythe cleared her throat. 'We're making an assumption here about sex work, and I think we need to be careful.'

'It's a reasonable assumption,' Slater said.

'No, it isn't. If it turns out you're right, I'll happily accept it. But this doesn't sound like regular cam work. She had an act at the club, apparently. She liked to wear the vintage costumes, including the underwear, when she performed for customers. Management indulged it. She was popular. I think there's a bit more to it than just sex. On her side, anyway.'

'Cases like this, it's always down to sex,' Slater said. 'You can dress it up any way you want, you can attach any sort of artistic, critical, look-at-me hoo-ha, label you like. End of the day, eye of the beholder, cam work is for the benefit of perverts. A pervert killed her. I don't want to go down the wrong path here – it might turn out to be an ex-boyfriend or a creepy punter at Mr Mojo's – but whoever did it was motivated by one thing, and it wasn't big fancy skirts and baking cookies.'

'Any theories in particular you want to share?' Smythe asked, a little tartly.

'Flick?'

'What?' Lomond sat up. His tone of voice drew attention from around the office, a sudden shriek of feedback.

'Is it Mr Flick?' Slater asked warily. 'It's something we'll get asked, anyway. Whenever something like this crops up. Is there a possibility?'

'Not a chance,' Lomond said. 'Mr Flick was a mutilator. This guy did it clean, or as cleanly as you could.'

'I'll see if there's any pattern that fits in,' Slater said.

'You can try. I wouldn't waste your time.' Lomond changed the subject. 'Anything else come up on the other thing, Cara?'

She frowned. 'Well, yes, and no. It's weird. First, there was the throat wound. That's similar, though just one side of the neck. Carotid, done from behind.'

'Whoa.' Slater raised a hand. 'Want to tell me what's going on? Is this another one? If it's part of the investigation, I want in on it, gaffer.'

Lomond pondered a moment. 'There was an unsolved case. About twenty-five years ago. When I was in uniform.'

'What, the Lawlor girl?' Slater said. He shrugged. 'Well-enough known case. What's the secrecy?'

'Yes. Daisy Lawlor.' Lomond drummed his fingers a moment. 'She was found in the pond at Rafferty Landing. Big country house in Lanarkshire.'

'You weren't first one at the scene again, were you?' Slater asked.

Smythe tutted at the tastelessness of the question, but Lomond answered, his tone unchanged: 'No, but I did work at the scene. And I did see the body. Naked, placed in water. Similar wounds. Not identical, though.' His brow was troubled for a moment, then he turned to Smythe. 'That's why I asked Cara to check whether any of the details match up while we talked to Mrs Colquhoun.'

Slater shrugged. 'Fair enough. Not sure why you had to go secret squirrel, though.'

'The secret is . . . well, Cara'll tell you,' Lomond said, nodding at Smythe.

'The secret is the secrecy itself,' she replied. 'Rafferty Landing was owned by the Earl of Strathdene. Ancient family, ancient house, ancient money. Daisy Lawlor was found in the pond at the back of the house. Her throat had been cut, but just at the carotid, and done post-mortem. The fatal wounds were delivered to the back, from behind, before the throat was cut. Daisy was full of ecstasy and drink. There was no sign she had been sexually assaulted. She was from a middle-class family, but they hadn't had much contact with her for a while. She was reckoned to be a free spirit.' She nodded to Lomond, who acknowledged what she was driving at.

'Sounds familiar,' Slater said.

'She wasn't from the area. She was thought to have been hitchhiking, heading for the A82, going west, but first of all she was going to a festival. Meeting up with schoolfriends. This was all pre-internet, pre-mobile phones, remember.'

'Bit of a stink about the earl, wasn't there?' Slater asked. 'I'm going by what I've read over the years.'

'He was never linked to the body,' Smythe replied. 'He had a lot of land out there – a big enough estate for people to camp out in, which it seems they did, over the summer months. There was a heatwave that year.'

Lomond nodded. 'Yep. Boiling. Hottest summer I could remember. That didn't help, either. With the body.'

'So there were squatters, ravers, travellers, all staying on the estate. The old earl was a tolerant guy. Too tolerant, it seems. The body was found a couple of days later.'

'Who got pulled in for it?' Slater asked.

'This is where it gets murky,' Smythe replied. 'Or murkier, anyway. It seems that the earl was away the weekend Daisy Lawlor was killed. And his son was holding a house party.'

'I didn't know that,' Slater mused. 'I'm sure I cross-referenced Daisy Lawlor a couple of times when we were investigating other cases.'

'That's where the secrecy comes in.' Smythe's eyes brightened at this point. 'There was an interdict made in the case, banning any mention of the earl's son anywhere in media coverage. He's not mentioned much in our notes, either, except to say that he'd been eliminated from inquiries. Several travellers who were heading for the west coast were pulled – it seems she got onto the estate with them – and there was one good suspect, someone who'd been in and out of jail. But there was no evidence to bring, and we never charged anyone for it.'

'Who's the son?' Slater asked. 'What am I missing, here?'

'Torquod Rafferty,' Lomond said. 'I haven't kept much of an eye on him, but he was a suspect, that's for sure. He dropped out of the inquiry – he had a solid alibi, and there was nothing to tie him to the body. Same with three other friends he had invited over to stay that weekend. He had a party on the Friday night. On the Saturday, Daisy Lawlor was killed, and her body was dumped in a pond at the rear of the estate, close to the gates and the camp site where the travellers had stayed.'

'Torquod Rafferty and the other friends were staying at a hunting lodge on another estate, about thirty miles away, on the Saturday night,' Smythe continued. 'There was no evidence at the lodge that Daisy Lawlor had ever been there. And there was a solid alibi for the four of them who were – Rafferty, his best mate, and two girls who were staying with them.'

'Cover-up stinks,' Slater said, nodding. 'I can see why it rankles.'

'How long is it since you looked in on Torquod Rafferty?' Smythe asked the inspector.

'I have to confess, it could be ten, fifteen years – the time gets away from you,' Lomond said.

'Well, he's been busy, sir. And he's changed his name. And renounced his title. This might shock you.'

Smythe had a Sunday supplement from the previous weekend under her arm; she raised it and pointed to the photograph on the cover. A handsome man with clear, pale blue eyes and thick eyelashes, wearing a blue-grey suit, tieless, with the shirt collar open. He had a pale yellow inflatable rubber ring around his middle, with a gormless duck face protruding around about where his navel would have been. On top of his head was a frogman's mask, with a snorkel trailing by his ear. He held an open umbrella, and the face was stoic, mock-serious, but very handsome, if a little pock-marked.

Lomond started forward, took the magazine, and gazed at it incredulously. 'You're joking!' he cried.

5

As if in a dream, the boat sheared through the Clyde. It looked more suited to the Caribbean or Monaco – somewhere where the sky and the water would have shared the same tangy blue of a child's felt-tip pen. There it might have been at home, but here it only denoted power, from the razor-edged trim of the hull to the easy growl of the engines that Lomond felt through the soles of his feet.

There was one man at the wheel on the deck, and he waved to the assembled press pack by the Clydeside.

Torin MacAllister's straggly fringe was already the subject of mockery – both gentle and savage – among caricaturists the length of the UK. Flying away from his fine clear brow, it simply looked . . . Lomond sought another phrase, but in vain . . . windswept and interesting. The rest of the face was fine, clear and chiselled. In spite of some rain earlier, there was no sign that he was in any way soggy.

'No life jacket,' Slater said, at Lomond's ear. 'Can we lift him for that?'

'Don't know if it's essential on a private boat.'

'I'll check, though,' Slater said, flipping open his phone. 'Bound to be regulations.'

'Let's talk nice to him first.'

MacAllister looked relaxed even as he performed a spin in the middle of the waterway. For a delicate second or two, Lomond thought the pilot had overcooked it, and the vessel lurched to starboard, threatening to capsize. But the issue soon righted itself, and MacAllister punched the air imperiously.

'Tart,' Slater remarked.

Some of the press corps by the waterside cheered as he performed one more turn before bringing the boat to a berth on the quay by the water's edge. The landing stage in the foreground was pale blue shot through with white waves, and a banner and bunting all in the same colours and a full marquee had been set up on this platform. The campaign slogan was written across the top of the tent: *The fish that swam.*

Two men at the dockside helped tie up the vessel. There was a strange tension when MacAllister cut the engines, then trooped down the stairs towards them.

'I'll be delighted if he falls,' Slater said, clapping enthusiastically along with the cheering crowd.

'Bit noisy, this bunch, for a political stunt,' Lomond said.

'More plants than the Botanic Gardens, gaffer. Are there really that many Tories here? This city? Seriously?'

'Better believe it,' Lomond said. 'This guy's going to the top. So they tell me.'

'So a paper told you, you mean?'

A man in a duffel coat tested the mic once or twice, then addressed the waiting press pack and the supporters. 'Now, without further ado, the man who's going to take West Ochilbank in Westminster – the face of the future, Torin MacAllister!'

'Torin MacAllister my arse. Who's the guy in the Paddington Bear get-up? We know him?' Slater asked.

'That's Donald Ward.'

'Artist?' Slater squinted. 'Won a portrait prize or something? Looks like they found him under the Kingston Bridge.'

Lomond shrugged. 'Well . . . he's an artist.'

'What's the connection with Rafferty?'

'They've been friends since the year dot,' Lomond said. 'Since primary school. Or your nearest dreaming spires, available for only one full mortgage per term.'

'Meaning he was there at the party at Rafferty Landing where that lassie died?'

'Yeah. Him, MacAllister-stroke-Rafferty, and the two lassies.'

'All cleared?'

'All cleared, and subject to an interdict once they were cleared.'

'Torin MacAllister,' Slater said again, as if trying the words for size. 'Torin ...What I don't get,' he muttered from one side of his mouth, 'is the name. I get why he'd want to change Torquod. Why would you then go to Torin?'

'Sounds nicer. I quite like Torin. Could see myself calling my son that, if I'd had one. Torquod, though . . . Kind of sounds like a mouthful of marbles, you know that way?'

'Torquod,' Slater said, trying it out in a strangulated voice. 'Yeah, a bit.'

'Also sounds like Torquemada.'

'I didn't expect the Spanish Inquisition.'

'No one expects the Spanish Inquisition,' Lomond responded dutifully.

'It's just . . . Torin? I could see if he went for Tommy or Terry or something like that. But, instead, it's Torin. He's gone from very weird to kind of unusual. Why bother at all?'

'Still quite posh, but Celtic, in a way. He's coy about his connection to the earldom – although he's given that up to take a seat at Westminster. Or so he hopes.'

'He's not got a chance, has he?'

'Very high approval ratings. Takes a nice photie.'

'In the name of God, why? A Tory, here? When was the last one that was elected first past the post in Glasgow? Seventeen-canteen? The age of the dinosaurs? Surely, he's had it. Regional list at Holyrood is one thing; you don't actually have to win anything to get in there. This is different.'

'We're going to find out.'

'Hi everyone,' MacAllister said, grinning at the applause and the flashbulbs that tracked his every gesture, completely at ease. 'And thanks to the weather, for not drenching us. I'm here to formally announce my campaign for West Ochilbank.'

This time there was longer, sustained cheering. Lomond noted that Donald Ward was the lamplighter for this applause, turning around to make sure everyone saw him clapping his hands. *What if they all stop?* he wondered idly.

'So I'm running the campaign you can see above me here – *The fish that swam*. It's centred on Glasgow's most shamefully under-utilised resource: it's about ten feet away from you, and you'll get wet if you jump in it. We may not be able to restore these banks to their former glory, when Glasgow was the workshop of the world, but there's something we *can* do. Something Glasgow does very well. We can party. The leisure potential of the city of Glasgow is vast, and its river is untapped. That's why I'm going to put forward an investment plan that will benefit the constituents of West Ochilbank. One that will attract pubs, clubs, a new maritime heritage centre focused on the shipyards, restaurants, a new marina in the city centre, and opportunities for water sports and pleasure boating.'

'How about Captain Nemo and the *Nautilus* while you're at it,' Slater said, a touch too loudly. This drew some notice and one or two definite dirty looks. One tall man in dark glasses and a beard focused his attention on Lomond and Slater and kept it there. Lomond met his gaze coolly.

'So,' MacAllister said, 'join me by the waterside for a fish supper on us, and I'm happy to take any questions from the good people at the front . . .' He picked out a young woman with long red hair, standing beside a hunched TV cameraman. 'Yes, Stella?'

'Hey,' Slater said, 'she's with the big guys, isn't she? Sky or the BBC, I forget which.'

'Think she's jumped the dyke into national news now, but I'm not sure who she's with. And that's your signal, right there. That's how you know MacAllister's going places. Look at the attention he's getting for this.'

'Holyrood too small for him?'

'He's got the ambition. He's got the background.'

'And he's got the accent,' Slater said. 'Right kind of Scot, isn't he? Definitely the right type of Glaswegian.'

'You mean he doesn't sound like one?'

'You get the star prize, gaffer.' Slater nodded towards the man with dark glasses and the beard, who was staring brazenly at them as he approached. 'Hey up. The Feds are here. Let's split.'

The newcomer got taller and broader with every approaching step, as if he was in the final stages of transforming into the Hulk. He could have been a doorman in his long dark woollen coat, buttoned to the neck, and a pair of smart, heavily dubbined boots that gleamed like wet coal.

'I'll do the talking, Malcolm,' Lomond said. 'By that I mean you don't do any of it.'

'Hi,' the man said. His voice was raspy, but not rough – the kind of voice that you heard on commercials. 'You here for the launch?'

'Not especially,' Lomond said, still smiling. 'Great trick with the boat, all the same.'

'That's nice. If you're not here for the launch, can I ask you a favour?'

'Sure.'

'Try not to distract the man on the stage? You're talking very loudly, and it's rude to interrupt.'

'We can't help it,' Slater said. 'We're very satirical people.'

The man dipped his head a little and gazed over the edge of his glasses with some amusement. 'Do you think you might satirise yourselves somewhere else? Like, far away?'

Lomond sighed. 'We're policemen, in fact. DI Lomond, Police Scotland. This is DS Slater.'

'*Charmed*,' Slater said, with a ghastly grin.

The big man chuckled. 'Sorry, lads. You'll have to excuse me if I don't fall on my arse.'

'You what?' Slater said.

'I clocked you were police within seconds. You might as well have had a blue light on top of your heads.'

'And we want to speak to your gaffer,' Lomond said. 'As soon as he's done here.'

'Mr MacAllister is an extremely busy man, most of the time.'

'Less of your cheek,' Slater snarled. 'When he's done pressing flesh, take us down to speak to him.'

'Do you have an appointment?'

Slater simply blinked in pure astonishment for a second or two. 'Are you actually looking to get lifted?'

'Why – have I committed a crime?'

'This is important,' Lomond said evenly. 'Something to do with a dead girl in the water. You might have heard about that.'

Just for a moment, the amusement dropped from the big man's gaze. 'When I say busy, I mean very busy,' he said. 'Like, busy for days on end.'

'He'll make time for us,' Lomond said. 'You lead the way. Take us over to him and introduce us as soon as this is wrapped up. Quick as you like.'

The big man sighed and nodded.

They followed him down towards the adoring crowd behind the press corps just as it broke into a huge laugh after the prospective member of parliament for West Ochilbank gave a one-word answer to a tortuous question from a broadsheet journalist. Lomond smelled the fish and chips, the salt and vinegar, prepared in cones for the journalists by over-dressed servers from a kiosk set up next to the marquee, waiting for the press conference to end, and his mouth watered.

Screaming, the seagulls gathered above.

6

Lomond and Slater waited by the side of the platform while the big man collared the former Torquod Rafferty, diverting his attention from the red-headed woman with the TV camera. Rafferty's grin barely faltered as he bent his head to listen to the other man. His cool blue eyes flicked towards the two detectives. After a brief nod, he straightened his suit jacket and strolled over.

'Gents,' he said, flicking his fringe back from his forehead before extending a hand. 'What can I do for you today?'

Lomond shook the hand. 'I'm Detective Inspector Lomond, Mr Rafferty. This is Detective Sergeant Slater.'

Rafferty strode with some confidence towards Slater. The latter didn't look at all pleased with the contact or the familiarity, but he was impelled to take the hand when it was offered. The man was in good shape: not as tall as he looked at the podium, but broad and muscular, with a trim waist and clean-shaven. He was slightly pock-marked, but it seemed to enhance his face, in the way it would with a character actor or a villain in a western. His thick eyelashes were long for a man's.

'I hope I'm not in trouble,' he said. 'Heck of a way to finish up my campaign on day one.'

'Perhaps we could go somewhere quieter for a conversation?' Lomond suggested. 'I'm aware you're a busy man. I understand from your office that your next event is at Finnieston Crane, in a couple of hours.'

Now Rafferty looked less certain, and lines took shape across his brow. 'This sounds serious.' Even as he spoke he looked over Lomond's shoulder and waved, turning up the brightness on his smile. The red-headed journalist, who had turned round to scrutinise the scene, waved back with equal fervour.

Then, quick as a flash, Rafferty turned the wave into a thumbs-up. Further away than the red-headed journalist, sitting on a park bench close to where Lomond and Slater had viewed the press launch, the artist in the duffel coat returned the gesture. Lomond caught all this on the periphery of his vision; no one paying idle attention to the detective would have suspected he had clocked any of it.

'We just want to talk to you about a number of things, Mr Rafferty.'

'My name is MacAllister, Inspector. Am I assisting in your inquiries, then? That's how you put it, eh?'

'Exactly. And we'll stick with Rafferty for the time being, if you don't mind.'

'Well, before I decide, I wonder if I could see your warrant cards?'

Slater presented his, holding it very close to Rafferty's face. Rafferty held his ground, then whipped the card out of Slater's hand.

Cheeky devil, Lomond thought.

Slater fumed while Rafferty turned the card over in his hands before saying, 'Looks clear. You know, there are fakes of these all over the place. Wide-os everywhere. Satirists. People trying to con you. Video bloggers, you name it. Budding maniacs and prowlers and sex pests use them to get up to all sorts.'

'Only thing we know about maniacs is catching them,' Slater said, snatching his card back.

Lomond held his card up for Rafferty to look at, but the candidate for West Ochilbank smiled and waved it away. 'You're good, boys. Hey, the first question's from me: how are your sea legs? Fancy a quick trip on the boat? I can guarantee you we'll have some privacy.'

Lomond prepared to demur, but Slater got in there first, a

41

change coming over his face. 'You're giving us a shot on your boat?'

Rafferty nodded. 'So long as you promise not to stage a mutiny.'

'How about life jackets?' Lomond said. He was seeing once more the overbalanced boat as Rafferty had guided it through a figure of eight, too fast, too tight on the turn.

★

Rafferty kept the boat at an idle pace, although the wind and the spray still whipped into the three men's faces as the detectives stood at either side of their pilot. Lomond had never known before now if he got seasick, or if he was simply thinking about being seasick, or indeed if there was a difference between these two states; either way, he felt a sensation that stopped short of nausea but was a long way off simple butterflies as the engine growled and the solid lines and embankments of the Clydeside quickly withdrew behind them.

The Squinty Bridge twisted above them; once they'd re-emerged into the grey light, Rafferty slowed the engines to a mild purr. 'What can I do for you, then?'

'You may have heard that a young woman was pulled out of the water yesterday. This water. The Clyde,' Lomond said, unusually hesitant as the deck rolled slightly under his feet. 'She was twenty years old. No one knows what happened to her.'

Rafferty looked shocked. 'Where was this?'

'The body was found a mile or so due east.' Lomond pointed over his shoulder.

'That's appalling. I'm so sorry, I hadn't read anything about it. Suicide?'

Lomond shook his head. 'We're fairly certain at this stage that she was murdered.'

'God. Today of all days.' Rafferty shook his head.

42

Slater was about to pounce, drawing breath to ask Rafferty how he was equating his by-election campaign with someone being murdered; Lomond silenced him with a furtive gesture. 'It's unfortunate. I spoke with the girl's mother – I say girl; she was twenty. Anyway, her mother is devastated, as you can imagine.'

Rafferty shook his head. 'Murdered? Man. I *can't* imagine, now that you mention it. I can't imagine anything like that at all.' He glanced over his shoulder, looking Lomond in the eye. 'I wonder – why are you asking me about it?'

'Just wondering first of all if you'd seen anything,' Lomond said. 'I know you were out here over the weekend practising for your launch day.'

Rafferty shook his head absently, then smiled. 'Nah. Some kids threw stones at me, I remember that. From the Clydeside. When I was trying to practise the bagel.'

'Bagel?'

'He means the turn in the water,' Slater explained.

Rafferty smiled. 'To be fair, I think I'd have thrown stones as well, when I was that age.'

'Were you a bit of a tearaway at Fettes?' Slater asked. He pronounced 'Fettes' in consonance with 'sweeties'.

'It's "Fettes",' Rafferty said, without breaking stride or compromising his grin. 'And yeah, you could say I was a bit of a loose cannon.'

'I can believe it,' Slater said, picking at something on the chrome handlebars along the side of the bridge. 'Always the way – kids who have something to fall back on tend to be rebellious. In my experience, anyway. It's of no consequences to them, really, if they get expelled from Fettes.' He persisted with his unique pronunciation.

'Sorry, inspector,' Rafferty said, turning to Slater's superior. 'You were saying? About what this has to do with me?'

'Nothing. But there were one or two similarities that reminded me of something.'

Rafferty nodded, beginning to guess what was coming. 'Go on,' he said grimly.

'It reminded me of a case I was a part of when I wasn't long out of school myself. A girl, a little bit younger than the lassie who was found in the Clyde. She died at Rafferty Landing. A house you know well.'

Rafferty sighed. 'I've got nothing to add to what you must already know about that case. I didn't know a thing about the girl. She was killed by a . . . what would you call them now-adays? A member of the travelling community. My dad . . . he was lax. Child of the sixties. Great in his way. Well remembered. We used to get rock stars coming to stay. Writers, artists, poets. Singers. Big stars, even today. He knew them all, partied with them all. I could tell you some stories. But being like that meant he also opened his doors to people who shouldn't have been within a hundred miles of Rafferty Landing. The bad, as well as the great and the good. But no one who was there that night had anything to do with what happened to that girl. So, whatever you're driving at, I suggest you take it somewhere else.'

Lomond went on: 'The thing is, there's very little about that case to look into, at least where you're concerned. There was an interdict banning all mention of you. And three other people. One of them is helping out with your launch, in fact. Donald Ward, the man in the duffel coat, is that right?'

Rafferty said nothing, focusing on the water ahead.

'Extremely strange,' Lomond said. 'The interdict kept you out of the papers. Something of a blackout, I'd say. One or two journalists asked questions, but by and large they went with the line that the girl had been killed by travellers.'

'It's very easy to demonise travellers, gaffer,' Slater observed pointedly.

'So there's still some mystery over what happened at Rafferty Landing. Even after we think about the person who stripped that girl, knifed her to death, slashed her throat, and threw her in a pond.' He locked eyes with Rafferty. 'I saw the body, you know. When it was removed from the water.'

'That must have been a very upsetting experience for you,' Rafferty said. Then his expression softened. 'And if it makes you feel any better – if you have nightmares about it, so do I. Dad was never the same after that. None of us were. He learned a lesson he should have taken on board years before. He couldn't get over it – that something like that had happened on his land. That he opened his arms to people, only for them to do something like that. For a time he wanted to move away. A *bon viveur* was my dad, you could say that for him. Enjoyed his life. But that was the end point. My poor mother suffered more for it, quite honestly. My dad only wanted to take pleasure in things, whether that was art, music, culture or beautiful women. But he never wanted to cause pain. So for something like that to happen . . .'

'Why didn't he sell up?' Slater asked. 'I'm assuming he'd have made a few quid. Rafferty Landing is a palace, practically, isn't it?'

'He didn't sell it because generations of the family have lived there. Same reason I won't sell it,' Rafferty countered.

'Can you account for your whereabouts over the past few days?'

'Easily,' Rafferty said. 'I can have a full itinerary emailed to you within the next hour, if you like. I spoke to a lot of people – had to, to get this event running. I'll get someone to ping it over as soon as I drop anchor here, in fact.'

'That would be a big help if you could,' Lomond said. 'To assist in our inquiries.'

'Quite. Hah! Good one.' Rafferty grinned, entirely mirthlessly. 'So . . . if that's all?'

'Sorry to ask,' Slater said. 'You got a toilet on board this boat?'

Rafferty threw his head back and laughed. 'Subtlety is your watchword, my friend, eh? Yes, there's a toilet downstairs. And if you feel like having a nosy around down there, see if I've got some girls tied up or stuffed into the freezer, feel free.'

'Oh, I don't need to *go*,' Slater said. 'I was going to ask how they *work*. You flush it when you're at a quiet spot, maybe? Got to wait until high tide?'

Rafferty ignored this. 'I can take you back to where we started – or I could drop you off anywhere, in fact. Within reason.'

'Back where we started is fine,' Lomond said.

'Oh,' Slater said, 'can I ask, who's the big guy with the aviator sunglasses? Guy who looked like the baddie from *The Matrix*? He brought us over to speak to you.'

'That's Finn,' Rafferty said. 'Good pal of mine.'

Slater smiled sweetly. 'Finn who?'

'Sorry, I forgot. Police. Details. Gerald Finlay. Schoolfriend of mine. Helps with the campaign.'

'He works for you, you mean?' Slater made a note of the name.

'In a manner of speaking. It's not the way I like to think of the relationship.'

'But, clearly, that's what it is.' Slater capped his pen.

'Can I ask why you want to know?'

'Just curious, my man,' Slater said. 'I'm very nosy. Comes with the job.'

'I imagine that gets you into trouble here and there.'

'Mostly with the mother-in-law. She sees me as competition.'

Rafferty laughed and spun the wheel. The boat curved to the left, and Lomond clutched the railing, disliking the ultra-smooth texture of the stainless finish and its lack of friction, as if the entire craft might slither away from him and leave him in the water. As the river edged closer to him, he fancied it might want to grab him with dirty grey claws.

'Hey!' he cried out.

'What is it, gaffer?' Slater looked around, alarmed.

'Stop the boat a second,' Lomond said. He tapped Rafferty on the shoulder. 'Stop the boat, I said.'

'What's up?' Rafferty did as he was asked, arching an eyebrow.

'There's something in the water,' Lomond said.

Rafferty scanned the surface, shading his eyes, although the morning had turned gloomy.

'I can't see anything,' Slater said. 'Direction?'

'Eight o'clock, from where you're standing,' Lomond said.

'Yeah . . . I think I can see it . . .' Slater said, squinting. 'Nah. It's gone.'

'There's something in the water,' Lomond said, 'I'm sure of it. Floating. Take us over.'

'Sure. Eight o'clock, you say?' Rafferty restarted the engine, spinning the wheel.

Lomond focused on the slate water, kissed in threadbare patches by the white glare of the clouds above. Waves showed in negative in this light, black tongues lapping the broken white of the surface. Lomond wondered if the water ever looked blue, in any weather.

'There!' he said. 'You see it?'

'Hey . . .' Slater said, eyes widening. 'Isn't that . . . ?'

Lomond stepped to the side of the railings and peered over the side of the boat. He was aware of a curious dancing motion in the water, as if tiny fingertips were drumming on its troubled surface. Then there was a larger swell that lifted the boat alarmingly.

The water broke, and something massive surged into view. Lomond was aware of someone on the far side of the river calling out in astonishment, then an immense eye, staring at him from the turbid waters.

Then he fell in. Gloom; murk; in his nose, in his ears, the sodden roaring of his own immersion. The lifejacket propelling him to the surface. Then the awful touch of something much larger than him beneath the soles of his flailing feet, something of flesh and blood. Groping pathetically for something, anything: the boat too far away to clamber back on. Slater and Rafferty's faces, astonished. Then frantic movements. He raised his arms and cried out, unthinkingly.

47

As the lifebelt neatly hoopla-ed Lomond round the neck and dragged him through the water, he seemed to pass through a great huffing sigh, as if the sound was a physical barrier like the shower of vapour that became a rainbow in the air; with that great cough and snuffle came a stench of fish the like of which he had never smelled before.

Completing this farce, as he was dragged back towards the boat by Rafferty, came Slater's uncontrollable laughter. The detective sergeant could barely get the words out, but they sounded something like: 'Trust you to stick the head in a whale, gaffer!'

7

Lomond, clad only in his Santa-red dressing gown and a pair of slippers that had been tortured over a period of years by an old pet cat, sat alone in the bedroom, staring at his face in the dresser mirror.

Downstairs, he heard Slater and his wife laughing loudly as she showed him out of the house. Then Maureen knocked the door gently and came into the room.

She appeared in the mirror at his shoulder: tall and long-legged, her hair cut shorter than Lomond would have liked, but never would have admitted. 'You're knackered,' she stated. 'You need your bed.'

'I have to get back to the office. Can't really sleep.'

'Your boss told me that you're to have a night at home.'

'Which one?'

'Sullivan. She called me personally. Sounds like a radio DJ. Beautiful voice.'

Lomond's eyebrows knitted together. 'Oh God. Yeah. She sounds great. I bet she does.'

'Haven't heard you speak about her before.'

'A treasure. Chief Superintendent Sullivan. Looks great in a uniform as well. Gartcosh via Tulliallan. Anyway.'

'Yeah, anyway. So, Captain Haddock, after your Undersea Adventure I think you can have a night in your own bed.'

'My God, there's no privacy here, is there? I heard you and Malcolm having a right giggle. My career's finished when I get back to that office. I wonder what line he'll take? I'll be Captain Haddock, I bet. Or Captain Ahab. Who's that high diver? Guy who cracked his skull off the board one time?'

'Greg Louganis.'

'Him. That's what they'll call me. Place your bets.'

'Who's Whale Rider? Is he a superhero?'

'I've never heard o' him. Might be. Is that a film? Why do you ask?'

'No reason.' She placed a hand on the back of his neck. It was warm. He took a long, slow breath and relaxed his shoulders. 'What did you eat today? Stuff out of that wee van you go to? A muffin from the coffee shop?'

'Sure. I had a croque monsieur.'

Maureen spluttered at his attempted French accent. 'A croque monsieur?'

'It's like *une* toastie.'

'*Très bien!* I've put a big cottage pie on. I'm afraid you have to get dressed before you come down, though.'

'Well, I'm not in the habit of eating dinner in the nude, pet.'

'By that I mean wear something nice. A shirt and your good jeans. Not football shorts, no football strip, no terrible band T-shirt.'

'Why's that? We got company? I thought it was just Siobhan coming over.' Lomond's antennae twitched. 'She bringing a man?'

'Not a man. A lassie.'

'Eh?' In the mirror, Lomond had the benefit of seeing his own face at that moment, comically shocked.

'A friend. C'mon. Be presentable.'

★

Lomond just about remembered to tuck in his shirt before heading downstairs, where a hubbub of voices told him his daughter had arrived with her friend.

Siobhan stood in the doorway. She had inherited her mother's height, and the light, flyaway brown hair – subject of much anguish when the girl was in her teens. She was twenty-one now, and when she saw her father coming to greet her she smiled, all the angles and arches around her eyes and her mouth morphing into his as she did so.

'Hey,' she said. She heaved a video tripod against the wall and came forward to give him a hug.

'Hiya, tootsie,' Lomond said, patting her on the back. 'Need a hand?'

'Nah, we've got it here.' She pecked her father on the cheek, then turned to the front door. 'Well, maybe a *wee* hand . . .'

The girl who followed Siobhan through the front door was struggling a little with a huge video camera, surely more than a shoulder's load for anyone. She was a little taller than Siobhan, with a long, fine jawline that would have been severe had it not ended in a rounded, delicate chin. She was very pale, with short black hair that undulated across her ears and forehead in stylish waves and flicks. Her green-grey eyes settled on Lomond's with a little suspicion, even as he reached out to help with the camera.

'Ah . . . you're probably right,' the girl said, allowing Lomond to take the load. 'I could have smashed it on your floor. That would've been an introduction and a half!'

'Ach, you're fine. You should see me carrying the shopping.' Lomond grinned, and helped the newcomer ease the camera onto the floor. It looked new, even smelled new, with a cap fitted over the lens.

'You'll be Siobhan's dad?' The girl stuck out a hand. She was slim, with black leggings and a dark coat that sat low on her hips. Now he was closer, Lomond saw she had dark eyeshadow, a little gloomy but certainly striking. Fine white teeth appeared as she grinned. 'I'm Mint.'

'Minty! Pleased to meet you.'

'No, just Mint,' the girl said, still grinning. She had a strong grip.

'Mint. I like it,' Lomond said agreeably. 'Anything else to come in?'

'That's all,' Siobhan said. 'Sorry to dump it here – we've got some footage to review, if you don't mind. We'll ship it back out later.'

'No probs. You not staying over tonight?'

'Nah, we have to head back out.' Siobhan chased her fringe away from her forehead. 'Loads happening. You heard about the lassie found in the Clyde?'

Lomond's smile faltered. 'I know about it.'

'You working on that case?'

'Here 'n' there. You know how it goes. Anyway – cottage pie tonight, a big one – that good for you guys?'

'So long as it's not a meaty one,' Mint said, her hands on her hips.

'Ah, you're a veggie?'

'Yes, I'm one of *those*.' She grinned.

'Oh, not to worry. Eh, we'll definitely have something in that you can have . . . I'm awful sorry.'

Maureen said, at Lomond's ear: 'It's just as well I made a big *veggie* cottage pie. Not a shred of animal produce in it, and yes, I am including the milk I used to make the mashed totties. I'm Maureen, Mint. How d'you do? When you're all ready, the table's set. C'mon through to the dining room.'

★

Mint ate daintily, Lomond noticed, quick spear-thrusts with a fork. Knowing he was observing her and knowing also how he himself hated being scrutinised while he was eating, he looked away towards his daughter, who had scooped up just about all of her food already. He wanted to say 'Hope you've been eating all right at that flat', and 'Maybe we'll get in a shop for you next week' but decided not to. Siobhan had aged her way out of the zone where every utterance of his would be an embarrassment, but not too much beyond it.

Mint didn't live in Siobhan's shared flat, Lomond knew, having checked up on the other three flatmates before she'd moved in. One of the two lads living there had a record for disturbing the peace when he was fifteen, but then so could anyone, and he came from the sort of fishing town on the east coast where disturbing the peace was probably a legitimate cry for help. Siobhan had graduated in the summer, having lived at home to pursue a degree in English and history at Glasgow University. There had been a beautiful day on the quadrangle in July. And after that she had shocked him.

Lomond had thought that Siobhan's next step would be teacher-training college – she'd spoken of this before, and the pieces had all fit together. From even before she went to one herself, Siobhan had played 'wee school' with her dollies and stuffed bears – her as teacher, with a blackboard, calling out the class, often comically severe with her furry charges. This seemed a good, safe occupation, and would have fit in with her nature – sunny, on a par with Lomond's, a natural with kids.

And yet something had happened. She had gone for a film and television post-grad in another part of town, and declared she was moving into shared accommodation after saving her wages for an entire summer working behind the bar at the working men's club half a mile down the road. Lomond was still in shock. Maureen, knowing more – possibly knowing all – had made it happen as smoothly as possible. Now, a few weeks into her new course, here she was. And here was Mint, with her.

'You not hungry?' Maureen asked him.

'Oh, yeah, totally. It's great. You'd never know it was made with secret meat.'

'You been working today?' Siobhan asked.

'Yep.' Lomond blinked. 'Out and about with Malcolm. Long couple of days.'

'Malcolm – that's the guy who looks like a really stern teacher?'

'That's right.' Lomond chuckled. He preferred 'humourless Presbyterian minister' as a comparator, though this wasn't apt in terms of personality. Slater's hairless head and his lined, wiry, cycling-toned build and physiognomy aged him well beyond his years, while Lomond's softer lines took a few birthdays away from himself.

'Still thinks he's funny?'

'Oh yeah. Sometimes he even gets a laugh.'

Mint said, 'Did you say you were working on the case of the girl in the Clyde?'

Normally Lomond might have dissembled, as much to avoid awkwardness on a guest's behalf as to maintain operational security. Instead, he met Mint's frank stare and said, 'That's right.'

'Is it true about how they found her?'

There was a second or two of silence. 'I don't want to go all TV cop show on you, but I can't talk about that, for obvious reasons.'

'They said her throat had been cut.' Mint sliced a precise block of potato and popped it into her mouth.

Siobhan laid a hand on her friend's wrist. 'Dad's not really up for talking shop, I'm sure.' She turned to Lomond. 'I might as well tell you . . . we're working on that story.'

'How do you mean?'

'We're doing broadcast news as our first module. Well, we're looking to do a documentary, if we get the time . . . something long-form for our final project.'

'You working together?' Maureen asked.

'We're partnering on this assignment. Part of the brief. The wider documentary's for something after we graduate . . . which we might work together on as well,' Siobhan said. Lomond caught a hopeful tone in her voice that he didn't quite like. 'We've got a PD150 to take out on a job for the weekend. We're going to work on the girl in the water. But I promise not to bug you about it.'

'Well . . . sometimes journalists get a tip long before the police,' Lomond said. 'So if you do hear anything, let me know. Goes without saying.'

'They're saying it wasn't a crime of passion or a garden assault,' Mint said. 'They say she was slaughtered.'

'There's a very dangerous person out there.' Lomond sipped at his water. 'I'm happy to tell you that on the record.'

'They reckon it sounds like a maniac. I mean, not that it wouldn't be a maniac. You know, even if it was a crime of passion or a random assault. But this was like something planned, they said.'

'Who's they, if you don't mind me asking?' Lomond asked, a tad sharply. Maureen flashed him a warning sign, a slight change in the angle of her eyebrow.

'A journalist protects her sources,' Mint said, with the tiniest smirk.

'You must have had a long day, working on that case,' Siobhan said quickly.

'Yeah, a long couple of days, really. Anyway. Tell me more about this project. I can put you in touch with our media department, if you like – get you in with the press pack.'

'Already taken care of,' Mint said.

'We're just meant to cover the story, speak to senior policemen – not you, of course, I wouldn't do that.' Siobhan waved a hand in Lomond's direction. 'Straight journalism piece, TV news, editing the footage together. They want a fifteen-minute film by the end of next week. But we're doing a bigger project on the underground.'

'What – the Clockwork Orange? Govan, Ibrox, Cessnock, Kinning Park, that one?'

'No,' Siobhan said, joining Mint in an open laugh. 'The underground in the city. Artists. Poets. That kind of thing.'

'The darker side, too,' Mint added. 'That's my side of the partnership. Addicts. The homeless. Sex workers. That's more my bag. Siobhan will do the arty stuff, the culture you read about in the Sunday supplements.'

'That's kind of, but not totally, reassuring,' Lomond said. 'Just a one-year course, is it?'

'Yeah,' Mint said. 'But we're into the cinéma-vérité side of things, really. Want to do documentaries. Got some great ideas.

Producers recruit, sometimes, from our college. If the product's good enough. People have had ideas made for the telly from this stage. It could happen.'

'I thought cinéma-vérité was cinema. I mean, fiction?' Maureen asked.

'We want to blend both,' Mint said, gesturing with both hands. 'Documentary stuff, but arty. Real, gritty. Have you seen *The French Connection*?'

She had addressed this directly to Lomond, startling him a little. 'Gene Hackman? Yeah, course I've seen it. One of Siobhan's granda's favourite movies, in fact. The one and only DVD I ever bought him.'

'You'll know what I mean, then. Documentary-style. Raw footage is the best footage. That's what we're aiming for. That sort of intensity.'

'I have to say, *The French Connection* might give you a false sense of police work. In this city, anyway. I can't remember too many car chases. The ones I was involved in we gave up because it was too dangerous to keep going.'

'See? That's what I mean.' Mint clapped her hands. 'Even a police chase where they had to stop and let the guy carry on . . . that's what we'd love to capture. The reality of it. That's the stuff.'

'In terms of journalists giving us tips . . .' Siobhan narrowed her eyes. 'We did hear that someone's on the way.'

Lomond cocked an ear. 'Go on.'

'You know Ursula Ulvaeus?'

Lomond knew exactly who she was, and his stomach roiled for a moment or two. 'Pop star? No, actress . . .' He clicked his fingers, mock-confused.

'She's an activist,' Mint said. 'Very important public figure.'

'Oh, right, I think I know who you mean.'

'Mainly women's rights,' Siobhan said. 'I heard her speak at Glasgow uni last year . . . amazing speaker. She's considering standing in the by-election for West Ochilbank, but I gather she pulled out.'

'She shows up whenever a woman is murdered in the UK,' Mint said. 'Anywhere in the UK. She organises marches, holds rallies. She's busier than you might think. She's coming to Glasgow 'cause of the body in the water.'

'Got you,' Lomond said. 'I think I know the lass. Shaven-headed, that right? Sinéad O'Connor lookalike?'

'No, she's got silver hair, quite short . . .' Mint frowned. 'Who's Sinéad O'Connor?'

'Looks like I'll need to tip off the guys in uniform. And the girls,' Lomond added quickly.

'We're going to try and get an on-camera interview with Ursula. She's something else,' Siobhan said.

Mint laid down her knife and fork. 'I'd imagine she'd be a bit of a pain for the cops. Thorn in the side, like.'

'Absolutely not,' Lomond said, in complete sincerity. 'She'll give us publicity that we couldn't get with a front page or a press release or a ten-second soundbite on a camera. We're on the same side, us and the women's rights people. We want the same thing.'

'She might make you a bit busier than usual,' Siobhan said. 'What was it, forty thousand people at that rally in Hyde Park last year?'

'Closer to sixty thousand, I heard,' Mint said.

Lomond dug his fork into the snowy expanses of the cottage pie and forced himself to eat another forkful. 'It's all a help to me. But the protests sound stressful. You wouldn't believe it, but I like a quiet life.'

Maureen leaned towards him to murmur an aside. His phone cut her off; he got to his feet and turned from the table, phone at his ear. It was a landline number, from Govan. 'Lomond.'

'Gaffer, I'm sorry to do this to you,' Slater said. 'I know you were meant to have a night in and dry yourself off.'

'Spit it out, Malcolm.'

'We've found the car. Burnt out, six miles up the road from

one of the sites we looked at where Aylie Colquhoun might have been dumped.'

'Send me through the location. I'll meet you there as soon as.' He rang off. 'You'll have to excuse me, folks – I'm going to have to get into the Batsuit. Duty calls, villains to fight. Awful sorry.' He turned to Maureen, considering a moment. 'My spare suit . . . the one I wore to your Kendra's wedding . . . still in the spare room, aye?'

8

The wreck was a peculiar shade of orange. Lomond wanted to say 'ochre', but he wouldn't have wanted to call it in front of his colleagues – or anyone else – for fear of getting it wrong. The colour put Lomond in mind of the leaves as they would fall in the coming weeks, and from there he made a connection to hot chocolate, woollen gloves, and the fierce bright heat of the wood burner in his garden. All of these things were positive. Funny how a colour could trigger feelings in you, he thought, just a colour. A shade. Same with blood.

'Nothing left to pick at,' Slater said. 'Hardly even a frame. It's not a sketch of a car, now. It's not even an *idea* of a car.'

'There might be something to work with. A match head. Hair. Bit of stoor in the car, trapped in the gearbox. We've been lucky with these wrecks before.'

'Whoever did it used a lot of petrol,' Slater said. 'They were taking no chances.' He shifted his weight from one foot to the other. He had retracted his hands into the sleeves of his coat, having no gloves, and been taken by surprise by the shifting weather. They stood on a stone path, leading up towards a green valley where sheep still grazed. There were no stars, a huge bank of low cloud forming above the mountains blotting out the light. Around an hour before, Lomond had been at the dinner table, pretending to eat.

The burnt offering in the field about thirty yards away, still surrounded by forensic officers in white hazmat suits under the glare of portable lights, had been a Ford Ka up to a couple of days ago. This had not been apparent upon looking at it, but measurements had been taken of the breadth of the chassis and a clear impression of the tyres had been taken further down the single-lane path leading up into the valley, where the car had gone into a muddy dip. A registration number was a distant dream, for the moment. All around the wreck were the signs of an immense fire, the grass and earth scorched to black in a wide circle.

'Could just be a joyrider,' Lomond said.

'But you don't think so.'

'Who called it in?'

'Farmer. Runs a sheep croft. Think this is the time of year he gets ready to set the rams loose, you know? With the ewes. Sheep-banging season – what's it called? Tupping?'

'I dunno. I'm not local.'

'Anyway. Piece of luck that he came across it, really. Apparently, he'd no idea how long it had been there, didn't see any flames or anything. Nobody did. Got in touch with the community team and asked what he should do. First time he's had anything like that on his pasture. They had someone come over within the hour.'

Lomond sighed. His breath steamed up in the air. 'Might be nothing. We'll have to wait and see.'

'If it's a joyrider, they've gone to some effort to keep it hidden,' Slater said. 'God knows how much petrol they used to torch it. Must have had a canister.'

'If it's a joyrider.'

'So – just speculating here – what if the route this car would have taken to get here ties in with the last known ping of Aylie's phone? What if it's to do with our guy?'

'If it's our guy . . . then this is what I was worried about.' Lomond cleared his throat. 'It means that he's careful. Which means it was planned. All of it. Which means we might have a big problem.'

'He's dropped a clanger, though, gaffer. Surely. Trace the car, and we're on.'

'Could be,' Lomond said. 'There's a good chance that we're

looking at a mistake. We could be chapping his door the minute we trace the car.' He did not sound hopeful.

A plainclothes officer approached. She was short and thick-set, but muscular with it. 'Sir?' she said.

'Lorna – how you doing?' Lomond said. 'Got anything for me?'

'I've put out a call on the media for anyone driving along this road on Saturday night to check their dashcams. There are a few houses on the road leading to the turn-off – one of them belongs to the farmer. They're bound to have some CCTV – we'll be knocking on the doors soon to see if anyone has footage.'

'Excellent,' Lomond said. 'Any of the forensics guys got anything for us?'

'Nothing yet.' Lorna nodded at Slater and smiled.

'Hiya – McGillvray, is it?' Slater asked, smiling in return.

'It is.'

'Ah, smashing. I remember we've worked together on a couple of cases before,' Slater said. 'Glad you're with us on this one.'

Lorna McGillvray acknowledged the compliment with a nod, even a shade of embarrassment. 'Well – I'll head back to speak to the farmer now, sir. With a bit of luck, we'll get something to work with.'

'Cheers, Lorna – keep me posted.'

Once she was gone, Slater said, 'I remember her in uniform – does martial arts, I think. I saw her huckle a guy when we raided his flat. Dealer had an absolute fortune stashed in his house. As well as a katana blade – or something. Dunno where he'd been hiding it: seemed to have it in his hands like a magic trick. Tried to swing it at her; I think he picked the smallest one first, thought it was the weak point. She had it out of his hands and pinned him in two seconds flat. Wouldn't mess with her for all the overtime going.'

'She's good,' Lomond said. 'Amazing record. Bit like Smythe.'

'Smythe,' Slater said, the way a python might have said it.

'I realise you're not bosom buddies or anything. What's the score there?'

'I wish I knew.' Slater shrugged. 'It's a mystery. Maybe she doesn't like my face. I have no opinion about her face. She just comes across as cold. Absolutely not a problem. In fact, it's probably my problem. Maybe it's how she deals with things. Professionally, like.'

Lomond laughed. 'And you don't deal with stuff professionally?'

'Bad example. I just mean, she's got a barrier, and I can't get through. And maybe she doesn't want anyone to get through. It's just how she rolls, and this is how I roll. I get intae it my own way.'

'Whatever the score is, is it going to cause a problem?'

'Course not. We're a team, gaffer. I suspect she can't stand me, which isn't a crime. Just one of those things. I've had people who've rubbed me up the wrong way before. I'll have done the same to other people.'

'That's a decent assessment,' Lomond said drily.

'We all get on, by and large, and we all muck in. She's not on my Christmas card list, put it that way. But this isn't school. She's good at what she does.' Slater looked away as he said this last sentence.

'Too bloody good, her and McGillvray,' Lomond said. 'Probably running us before long. Some days I'd welcome it.'

'Ach, I wouldn't worry about that, gaffer. You'll be well retired by then.'

'Seriously. I don't want it to cause a problem, Malcolm.'

Slater bowed his head in mockery of gravity and grace. 'I'll consider myself warned. Anyway. How's things back at the house?'

'Fine,' Lomond said, with a sudden recollection of Mint's cocksure grin as she sat at his table, talking about murder while making a surgical incision in her vegetarian cottage pie. 'Why do you ask?'

'Just wondering if you had the space, you know?' Slater scratched his nose, disguising an impish smile.

'Explain, maybe? Space?'

'Yeah, radiator space. To dry your kecks out.'

Lomond closed his eyes. 'I'm going to suffer for this. Back at the office. Am I right? I'm going to suffer.'

'Gaffer, your underwater expedition is my secret, to keep unto the grave.' Slater crossed his heart, eyes closed, with a certain look of beatification on his face: a monk in a stained glass window, minus the tonsure.

★

Lomond blinked. The dolphin did not blink in return. However, it did appear to nod in the air conditioning, before turning coyly to one side.

Somewhere else in the office, the theme tune to *Flipper* played very loudly on a phone speaker, the treble distorted and especially painful to Lomond's ears.

'I think you'll find it was a whale, not a dolphin,' he said, with some dignity. 'You could have got the species right.'

'Do you know how difficult it was to find this here inflatable dolphin at such short notice, gaffer?' Slater asked.

'Not very, I'm assuming, given that we're kind of busy here,' Lomond replied testily. He swept the balloon off the table; its makeweight clattered to the floor. The effect of this was even more comic, the tethered inflatable now being at the perfect height for its large cartoon eyes to scan the desk.

DS Smythe pulled up a chair and sat beside Slater. She lowered her gaze and tried to avoid looking at the bobbing balloon.

'OK. What's new?' Lomond said.

'I went into the contacts file to find the SIOs on the Daisy Lawlor case,' Smythe said. 'I have to admit, I found it strange there weren't many records, given it was such a high-profile case.'

A silence followed; Lomond didn't fill it.

'So I found out that DI Toner and DS Whicklow were in charge of the inquiry.'

'Toner's dead,' Lomond said. 'Stroke. Died about three years later. In his chair, in fact. Cranhill Station. Cleaners found him one morning.'

'But I managed to get hold of Whicklow. Do you remember him, sir?'

Lomond shook his head. 'I spoke to Toner a few times. Decent. Drank a fair bit. Whicklow . . . Bit of a hard case, I remember. Didn't take to me, especially, but I don't think he ever really took to anyone. A polis, loved being a polis, wanted everyone to know it.'

'He didn't want to speak to me, sir. Said he had nothing to say about that case, and that I shouldn't contact him again for any reason.'

Slater clapped his hands. 'So . . . We contacting him again, aye?'

'Oh aye,' Lomond said. 'Let me think about it for a couple of days, and we'll talk to him then.'

'I also had a look at the case notes on what happened . . . Torquod Rafferty's alibi, in particular. Him, Donald Ward, and two girls went to a hunting lodge the day Daisy Lawlor died at Rafferty Landing. There's nothing on the two women. It's weird. You'd think they'd been cut out completely.' She shook her head. 'Seems strange that there'd be no details on anyone. It's an odd one. I'll dig a wee bit further, talk to some people. See what else I can find out about that.'

'Excellent. Thanks for that, Cara.' Lomond turned to Malcolm. 'Anything in regarding Aylie Colquhoun's computer analysis?'

'Yes,' Slater said, opening up a file on his laptop. 'Came in within the past five minutes.' He tapped on an app, and a PDF opened up with a list of web addresses. 'She was only involved in one streaming site. This is it, right here.' He pointed out one address in particular.

'MyGirl?' Lomond frowned. 'What type of site, exactly?'

'Nudes, mainly. But not quite X-rated stuff. No live sex, no penetration. Individual shows, live cams. Dancing girls, basically. Claes optional. Pays very well, per fifteen minutes. Before you start,' Slater said, cutting off Smythe as she prepared to speak, 'I'd say that it's quite a broad church. Seems that it has the type o' content that we spoke about before, given what her pal at the lap-dancing club told us. Performance. Costumes. Choreography. Pretensions of class, you could say.'

Lomond squinted at the web address. 'Not sure I'm following you.'

'It has people listed as "aerialists" . . . I think that's trapeze artists, that sort of thing. And there's naked yoga, obviously.'

'Obviously.'

'An all-nude version of *Swan Lake*, if that's what floats your boat. Naked ballet. Partially naked ballet. Good old mud-wrestling and wet T-shirts.'

'Sounds like porn to me,' Lomond said. 'Not sure I get the difference.'

Smythe cleared her throat. 'Well, it's only porn if you want it to be. Burlesque is a performance; it's not sleazy. It's got a long history.'

'Boutique porn, I think they call it,' Slater said. 'With all the scud you have online out there, piles and piles of it at the touch of a button, people are going to go for something that promises you a little bit of class. *Some* people, anyway. Something to lift it out of the gutter, I suppose. Makes it more digestible to middle-class people. Professionalised. If the BBC ever did porn, this is what it would look like. And it costs, too – so there's an attraction in that, sometimes.'

'Some would call it art,' Smythe said. Slater did not reply to this, though Lomond was sure he wanted to.

'Do we have any of Aylie's material?' Lomond asked.

'All of it,' Slater said. 'Seven films, well over an hour's worth. We can have a quick look at one now. Unless you'd rather be alone?'

'Just look at the start, maybe,' Lomond said. 'But if we've time, Cara, I want you and Lorna McGillvray to go through them. If it is boutique stuff and there are vintage costumes, then I want lists of the types of clothes, labels, where Aylie might have got them. That may be a link.'

Smythe nodded. 'I would guess with this kind of stuff they'll use tags, even a bit of advertising, telling people where they can get the costumes, the make-up, where she gets her hair done . . .'

'Shall we go for it, then?' Slater asked, finger poised over the mouse.

'Just a bit. Give us an idea. A flavour.'

Slater clicked on the link and sat back.

Lomond felt a knot of tension across his shoulders. Not so much to do with the idea of viewing something which had the hint of taboo about it – it was more to do with the sight of that face in animation. A face he had seen already, but not in life: a visage he had seen with a degree of intimacy that was denied to her mother or her lovers. But not her killer.

The audio was a slightly shrill ragtime tune led by the cornet, like Bix Beiderbecke. The tone was comic; not quite in the Benny Hill zone, Lomond thought, but not too far away. The colour scheme was loud, over-saturated shades, dominated by red. First of all, Aylie appeared, looking completely different from the photographs in her mother's flat. Bright red lipstick, a long, puffy skirt and her hair braided high, with a crimson cravat around her throat. Lomond felt earthed, jolted, by this garment, a lightning bolt transfixing him. He heard Smythe say, under her breath: 'Christ.'

Aylie stood in complete darkness as she ended a twirl. Then she beamed at the camera, clicked her fingers, and the rest of the scene changed. It was a kitchen with a long table, farmhouse style, and old-fashioned-looking but clearly expensive kitchen appliances hung from hooks in the background.

Aylie began to dance. It was energetic, rather than graceful.

There was no slow, sensuous movement – 'gyrations' was the word Lomond would have been embarrassed to say out loud – but confident spins and leaps, the skirt being the centre of attention, a constant cyclone of colour and shape. She had a wonderful hourglass figure – shapely legs, a large bust, tapered waist. But it was the clothes, Lomond thought; above all, this was about the clothes.

They sat in silence until she began to remove a pair of gloves, dropping them on the floor before placing her bare hand over her bright red lips with a mock-coquettish 'Oh!' gesture.

'That's enough,' Lomond said. 'That's what I thought, going by what you said. Let's find out if the videos are all like this.'

'This isn't as-live, is it?' Slater asked, watching Aylie slowly unzip the back of her dress before quickly pausing the video. 'I mean, it's a full performance, but it's recorded, not live. That's not the usual thing with live streams, is it?'

'I'll find out if she did any live streams,' Smythe said. 'I'll ask McGillvray to check the lower-level stuff on MyGirl, if there is any.'

'How about the site itself – the owners, where it's based?' Lomond asked.

'Glasgow, would you believe,' Slater said. 'Based right here. Hang on, there's a note from the guys who checked up . . . They said they had to dig deep to find out who actually owns it. Here we go . . .'

Slater clicked on a document. Their eyes crawled over the list of names.

Lomond saw it first. He gave a short, rasping chuckle. 'You have got to be kidding!'

9

The next day was clear, bright and sharp. But before the sunrise, Lomond and Slater were in the office.

Lomond took a quick call and made a note. 'Right. We know where he's going to be. You'll never guess where.'

'Big swimming pool project?'

Lomond frowned. 'How did you know?'

'I'm a detective as well, gaffer,' Slater said, in a hurt tone. 'Anyway. The baths – that's perfect.'

'How's that?'

'Well, I mean, given your new hobby. Your wild swimming.'

Lomond peered over his shoulder at the screen. 'Oh, very funny.'

'How you doing, anyway? Any chills, bugs, viruses, anything like that? Developed gills?'

'Ear's a bit dicey now you mention it, but that could just be from listening to you all day. Apart from that, fine. The Clyde's getting better, you know. Since the industry left it alone. Regenerating.'

'I suppose a whale being in there's a good sign for the environment. Any leads on your deep sea buddy, incidentally? Want me to put out a press release asking for witnesses?'

Lomond snorted, a decent impression of the sound the creature had made from its blowhole. 'A few folk saw it further down the river. It was on the news, I'm told. No sign of it since then.' He remembered it anew, with a sudden chill – the eye, scrutinising him with a quiet, alien sense of patience. And his sudden fear of being in the water with something that could have obliterated him.

'What time we on?'

'I'd go for nine o'clock on the dot,' Lomond said.

'Excellent. Time for a roll 'n' a coffee before we go, you reckon? Bacon and brown sauce, out the kiosk?'

Lomond brightened. 'I think that's in order.'

★

At nine o'clock on the dot, Lomond and Slater were shown through to an enormous hall. Light from stained glass windows was reflected and magnified off bright tiling in a kaleidoscope of colours. Every sound was a ricochet. A single white eye glowered down on the whole scene, a cupola at the centre of the building, its patina blue outcropping visible for miles around.

Lomond, who had slept that night, but not well, and not for long, stifled a yawn. Perhaps it was to do with the echoing expanse and the light, recalling a cathedral, putting him in mind of being bored in chapel in his youth. A smell of incense might have completed the scene. Certainly, the impression was helped by the sight of an insincere man dressed in black who approached them at some pace.

He was thin, with a high forehead and a dark shirt that suggested a Catholic priest who always refused a biscuit at funerals, his tastes running closer to Presbyterianism than he might have admitted. Despite his clear discomfort at the presence of two strangers, he flashed a quick, thin smile, the social equivalent of stropping a razor. 'Hi, gents. You're a bit early for the opening – I'm not sure who you're with?'

'We're with Police Scotland,' Lomond said, his warrant card in his hand. 'We want to speak to Donald Ward.'

'Mr Ward's busy,' the man said, more guarded now. 'He's just applying finishing touches.'

'We didn't ask you for his employment status,' Slater said. 'Where is he?'

Their footsteps ricocheted off the curved roof through the

expanse of empty space. There was a pleasing smell of wet paint, and everywhere that bright sense of something old being renewed or revived. Balconies stretched off to either side of the main space, wrought iron painted seaweed green, the dark red seats plush and refitted. Rainbow light splashed across the mosaic tiling from stained glass latticework windows; Lomond stepped into a bright red ray, as if to warm himself.

There were a number of working people inside the centre space, some of them standing at the bottom of the great rectangle itself. One of them laughed, the sound shrieking around in the air like a banshee. This sonic imp reminded Lomond of the sound of children at play in the swimming pool he'd gone to as a child. And here was in fact a swimming pool emptied of water, and freshly decorated.

The walls and the tiling of the pool itself had been decorated with images of the sea: impressionistic rather than cartoon-style, which Lomond liked. There was a pleasing liquescence in the way the figures and flora had been rendered, with fish, dolphins, whales, eels and a full colour palette of corals and kelp conjuring the creatures of the deep. A red squid's tentacles seemed to blur together, caught in the same current as undulating sea grass. At one corner was an alarmingly large and aggressive shark, with teeth like tent pegs and one eye visible; a perfect circle in an artwork with few regular shapes; a pure black disc with a thin corona of white.

'Some job they've made, right enough,' Lomond said to no one in particular.

'It'll win prizes,' the thin, dark-clad press officer replied, with quiet conviction. 'If you wait here a moment, I'll speak to Mr Ward.'

He left them waiting close to the doors leading to the changing booths, footsteps like whipcracks as he walked to the far end of the pool. There they could already make out the figure of Donald Ward, his straggly hair a close match to an anemone that bristled on the walls over his shoulder. Ward was talking to another man in front of the most striking image of the entire pool: a mermaid, her black hair threaded with gold, a carefree expression on her face and her blue–green tail set at a jaunty angle. This image was different from the marine smudges and scrapes that defined the other figures in the pool: more naturalistic, a real figure rendered as the fantasy creature. She was framed with shells, conchs, lobsters, cockles and mussels, rendered in very fine detail down to the oily sheen on their shells.

The press officer tried to keep his voice low, but the acoustics of the place were such that Lomond and Slater heard him say: 'Someone here for you, Don.'

'What, this early?' The tumbleweed thatch of his head turned. He took in the two detectives, then said, 'Oh.'

The man Ward had been speaking to – older, bigger and paunchier, with a pure white Santa beard, a red beret on his head and a paintbrush in his hand – gazed at the two newcomers with a comic expression of astonishment as Donald Ward made his excuses and came forward to intercept Lomond and Slater.

Ward was wearing old clothes, Lomond noticed, proudly bearing their scars of many colours, dabs and strokes with brushes. 'Hi,' he said, a friendly expression on his face. 'What can I do for you?'

Lomond showed his warrant card. 'I'm Detective Inspector Lomond, and this is Detective Sergeant Slater.'

'Oh yeah. You were at the launch.' Ward clicked his fingers, and a sly amusement crossed his otherwise kindly face. 'Didn't you get your shoes wet yesterday?'

'Shoes, trousers, good jacket, phone, you name it,' Lomond said drily. 'Mind if we ask you a couple of questions?'

Ward shrugged. He glanced at the older, white–haired man, who said, 'I'll hold the fort, Donnie. It's fine,' and swiftly returned to the painting of the mermaid.

Ward beckoned Lomond and Slater towards a quieter part of the empty poolside, their footsteps echoing.

'Who's Santa?' Slater asked him.

71

'I beg your pardon?'

'The older fella. White beard. You know.'

'You're serious? You don't know who that is?'

Slater shrugged. ''Fraid not.'

'Painter, isn't he?' Lomond said. 'Artist, I mean.'

'That's right.' Ward nodded. 'Sir Erskine Copper. Ringing any bells?'

'I'm awful sorry,' Slater said. 'That stuff's not my strong point. I can barely do stick men and cats with little ball faces and bodies, you know? You ask me to draw a car, I'll do one of those Stickle Brick blocky numbers.'

'He's famous,' Lomond said. 'Maybe a bit before your time. Ran an art show, late at night on BBC Two. Got quite a lot of attention, nationwide. I'm sure I remember watching him on the Russell Harty show or Wogan or something like that when I was a kid. I thought it was odd, someone with such a strong Scottish accent being interviewed on national telly who wasn't Billy Connolly.'

'That was before my time, too,' Ward admitted. 'But he's getting a bit of traction online, now, with those old shows on video sharing sites. The Bob Ross effect. There's talk of it getting a run on BBC Four or Sky Arts, maybe, but he's a bit shy about all that these days.'

Lomond glanced back at the older man as they reached the far end of the pool. Ward invited them to sit at a long fibreglass bench sculpted in the shape of an open clamshell, and anchored himself at the other end of it.

'You know, guys, this might be the first time arses have been placed on this bench outside of test conditions. This is a premiere, if you like.'

'I'm flattered.' Lomond sat down, and was surprised by how comfortably the moulded crenelations fit his buttocks. Slater perched uneasily beside him, looking less impressed. 'Some project, this.'

'Yep. All part of Torin's plan, really. Public–private drive to polish the city's gemstones. This pool's one of them. They've been neglected too long.'

'I thought it had been closed for good,' Lomond remarked. 'I remember a campaign to save it . . . God, we're talking fifteen, twenty years ago, maybe. Protests, the lot.'

'That's right – only thing using this pool was the rats when we bust in. You'd never think a building so grand and so . . . *useful* would go to seed, but it did. There were bushes growing in the guttering. Hell of a mess. Halfway to turning into a jungle.' Ward shook his head. 'But we've restored it. Mix of community grants, fundraising, corporate sponsorship. Torin spearheaded all that, you know.'

'What's your angle?' Slater asked.

'I'm sorry?'

'What's this got to do with you?' He corrected himself: 'What part do you have to play in it? What's your role?'

'Artistic director. Chief designer. So all this mess is technically . . . my mess.' Ward gestured around the space.

'It's very grand,' Lomond said. 'Colourful. I lived near a swimming pool, you know. As a kid. Talk about an oasis. I remember going when the rain was lashing down in summer, just to be in a place with blue water. They closed it down, said it was being refurbished. A whole year. We thought it was going to reopen with flumes and wave machines, all that kind of thing. Turned out they just wanted to strip out the asbestos.'

'Sounds like "refurbishment" was a euphemism, in that case.' Ward's demeanour was still agreeable, but he held up a hand. 'Umm . . . I don't mean to be rude, but we're on a schedule here. Finishing touches. What is it you want?'

Lomond said, 'We're here to talk about the body that was found in the Clyde two days ago. A twenty-year-old girl. You'll have seen the press reports.'

'Oh, God.' Ward squeezed his eyes shut. 'I saw the pictures on the news sites. Beautiful girl. Terrible shame. Was she killed?

I mean, bodies in the river . . . God knows, you know it goes on.'

'No. What goes on?' Slater asked, frowning.

'Suicides.'

'It wasn't a suicide,' Slater said. 'She was murdered. Off the record, her throat was cut.'

'My God.'

'Her name was Aylie Colquhoun. Her mother's only child. We talked to her yesterday,' Slater told him. 'She's all over the place.'

'It's a grim business, being a polis. I don't envy you one bit. Don't think I could do it. But why would you be asking me about that?'

'Two reasons,' Lomond said. 'First of all, the girl's connected to you.'

'What?'

'Your production company – Langoustine International. Funny name, really. Rolls off the tongue, but it isn't pretty.'

'So? What about it?' Now Ward was agitated.

'It has a subsidiary company called MyGirl. Is that right?'

'Sure,' Ward said.

'Aylie Colquhoun was working on MyGirl – she'd not long started, in fact. Doing quite well out of it. She had an act, her own style – burlesque. Nineteen-fifties. Vintage clothes. And taking vintage clothes off. You know about it?'

'I know about MyGirl, obviously. I helped put the company together. It was a way for models to make money outside traditional channels.'

'Models – you mean, art? Painting?' Slater asked.

'Or photography. Or sculpture. These were girls comfortable with taking their clothes off. It helps them make money between jobs. Good money.'

'Seems a bit sleazy to me,' Slater said. 'You being an artist, and all. Not the kind of thing I'd expect a portrait painter to be involved in, frankly.'

74

'Well, the entire history of art might prove you wrong. I've painted plenty of nudes in my time.'

'Big difference between nudes and pornography.'

'This is interesting. Tell me more about it,' Ward said, sitting forward. He had a toothy smile – a winning smile, Lomond thought. Part Kenny-Dalglish-right-after-a-goal, part Tom Cruise, part shark in *Jaws*. Ignoring the hair that was running scared of a comb, there was something of the movie star about Donald Ward. 'Fill me in on this theory of yours.'

'Well, just my opinion, this,' Slater said, considering his words carefully, 'but – there's art, and there's creeps ripping the head off it to young lassies on webcams.'

Ward shrugged. 'That's your opinion. Maybe ask another guy, you get a different opinion. But who are you to judge anyway? Sex is the first reality. It's how we all got here. And it's *interesting*. Eternally interesting. Even to two policemen. If you can't accept that, well . . . you're being a bit of a hypocrite. Just *my* opinion.'

'Did you know Aylie Colquhoun?' Lomond asked. He held up his phone, opening a screen grab of Aylie in one of her videos – hair up, forties Bletchley Park style, thick red lipstick, the crimson neck scarf. 'This is what she looked like about twelve days ago.'

Ward stared at her. He tutted and shook his head. 'Oh, man, that's wrong. Beautiful lassie. But I'm sorry, I don't know her. I am one of the owners of MyGirl, but I'm not hands-on. I don't vet the girls, I don't package the movies and I'm not in direct contact with the site. I have a production team who does that for me.'

'Do you make the movies or get involved with the decision-making at all? Even stuff to do with style, clothes, make-up, that kind of thing?' Slater asked.

'No – it's all user-generated and uploaded by them. The videos are moderated, of course. No sex on MyGirl, strictly speaking. To spell it out – no penetration, no ejaculation shots.

We're quite clear about that. We do permit some interaction between performers, some touching or kissing, but it's framed as a performance – like a dance or a scenario that's acted out. Absolutely nothing gratuitous. And to go back to your earlier point – what's your name, Slater? Slater. Right, Detective Slater – MyGirl's different. You said it yourself. It's a class apart from what you might see on the internet, when your girlfriend's not around the house, say. It's paid content, for a start, so it has to be polished. And there's no sexual activity. It's based on performance. It's art, in other words. Separately, it's not cheap. We're a premium website, with premium customers. And my God . . . I can see why this girl was with us. Great look. I'll look her up.'

'You've no history with Aylie at all?' Lomond asked. 'You don't recall her?'

'No.'

'Haven't met her? Did you know her outside a professional context?'

'Sorry, no.'

'Be sure. Take as long as you like to look at her face.'

Ward did so, a touch sorrowfully. Lomond was surprised to see the artist tearing up, just for a moment. Then he blinked. 'I don't know her, and I've never met her.'

'We'll need to take a look at your staffing lists, who's been involved, that kind of thing,' Lomond told him.

'Not a problem.' Ward waved a hand. 'If you think it'll help. And I'll see to it personally that you get every piece of interaction we ever had with . . . was it Aylie?'

'Yes.'

'Aylie. Nice name. How we spelling it, E–i–l?'

'No, it's a different take on the traditional spelling.' Lomond set the letters out for him. 'We'll send you along all the details, if you're on email.'

'Great. Now . . . was there anything else?'

'Yes,' Lomond said. 'I spoke to Torquod Rafferty about it yesterday. Perhaps he's mentioned it?'

Ward shrugged, which of course meant he had.

'It's to do with Daisy Lawlor. Is that name familiar to you?'

'Familiar . . . until the day I am put in my grave,' Ward said. He cleared his throat and folded his arms. 'I've nothing new to say to you about Daisy Lawlor. I've spoken about her a lot, to the police, and to other people. I think I made it all quite clear at the time. There's nothing to add.'

'You won't have a problem going over it again, then,' Slater said. 'Just for our records.'

'Actually, I do have a problem with it. Do either of you have a warrant?' He looked from Lomond to Slater, and back again. 'Am I under arrest?'

'You're not under arrest,' Lomond replied, 'but we'll take note of your responses. Did you know Daisy Lawlor?'

'As I've said . . . I'm not going to answer anything else about that matter. I've said all I want to say.'

'She didn't turn up at your rich pal's party? In his very big house in the country?' Slater asked.

'This is . . . guys . . .' He held up a placatory hand.

Slater's demeanour hardened. 'You had nothing to do with her death, is that correct? You didn't sleep with her, you didn't stab her and cut her throat?'

'No,' Ward said hoarsely. 'No, I didn't.'

Slater was relentless. 'You didn't dump her body in a big pond and leave it there in the summer? In the heat? You didn't blame travellers for it, then get your rich dad and your pal's rich dad to set up an injunction meaning your name wasn't ever released?'

'Hold on a minute . . . hold on, here . . .'

'Who was with you at the hunting lodge?' Lomond asked.

'What?'

'The day after the party, you and Torquod went to a hunting lodge with two lassies. What do you know about the two lassies?'

'Well . . . one was Lana Galbraith.'

A tiny flicker in Lomond's mind, but no more than that. 'That name's familiar.'

'She was on the telly,' Ward said, fidgeting with his hands. 'Presented a music show. Scottish. She was on MTV as well . . . you remember?'

Lomond looked at Slater, who shook his head.

'She died a few years ago.'

Lomond scribbled down some notes. 'I'll look into that. What about the other girl?'

'I can't remember. Rebecca something? I'm not sure. That's all I know. It was years ago.'

Ward was about to say something else – until someone did it for him. 'Don't say anything else, Donald. Not a word.'

The tall, broad man with the air of an American secret service agent who had accosted Lomond and Slater at the Clydeside event strode towards them. He wore the same suit as at the launch and his shoes looked plenty tough, although he had masked the sound of their approach well in that echoey space.

Ward looked relieved.

'Who are you when you're at home?' Slater asked, rising to confront the newcomer.

'Didn't I tell you yesterday? You can call me Gerry.' The tall man smiled. With his shades off, he appeared handsome, with sharp ridges and angles across his nose and chin which were almost mask-like, although his eyes were unsettlingly small. 'Gerry Finlay. I can give you a card, if you'd like?'

'Are we supposed to know who Gerry Finlay is?' Lomond asked.

'You do now. I'm Mr Ward's solicitor, and I will speak on his behalf. And I am here to tell you that he has no comment to make on the matter you've just mentioned. I'm also representing Mr MacAllister in this and other matters. If you do not wish to question my client formally, then the interview is terminated. As he's already stated, he's a busy man.'

'Aren't we all?' Slater said, taking a step forward.

Lomond sighed and got to his feet, worried for a second that his legs wouldn't support him after sitting at a funny angle in a clamshell. 'It's been an interesting conversation, Mr Ward. And . . . Gerry? What was your second name?'

'Finlay. No d.'

'Mr Finlay with no d, I will take your card,' Slater said, solemnly. 'Assuming you were serious.'

Finlay did indeed pass over a card, poised carefully between index and second finger. 'I'm always serious about business. Drop me a line, business hours or otherwise, gentlemen, if you require anything else.' He smiled, and indicated the door, where the receptionist was gazing through the window with a worried expression. She had called him, Lomond realised – not Ward.

'I'll be sure to,' Lomond said. 'Mr Ward, good luck with the pool, it looks amazing. And tell Sir Erskine Copper his mermaid is stunning.'

All four men glanced towards the man at the mural on the far side of the pool. He paid them no attention whatsoever, focusing on the tip of the mermaid's tail, drawing a brush beneath the greenish fronds at the very edge. He was placing the final curve on his signature.

10

Lomond arrived back home to the sound of shouts and cries from the dining room. He was more easily nettled when he was tired, and not particularly careful about concealing it, either. After he kicked his shoes off and hung up his coat on the hook, he entered the room without knocking and not making a sound.

Siobhan and Mint were huddled close to a laptop screen on the dining table, the place mats and candleholders swept aside in an untidy pile. Camera equipment plugged into the laptop was absurdly sized next to the viewing screen, and red lights blinked. The laptop screen was a mock representation of what Lomond presumed was a film studio, complete with blinking red and green lights and retro-style dials and knobs, notched with slimline white measurements. On the screen-within-a-screen was a good-looking if stern woman with grey or white hair cut short and swept into a mannish fringe – bizarrely, Lomond's first comparator was Lee Marvin, although this didn't fit the face at all. Round, thick-rimmed spectacles gave this woman a hard aspect, but it was offset by a pixie nose and a delicate, rounded chin.

Lomond's daughter and her friend seemed spellbound, occasionally snorting laughter or yelping with delight at her utterances. Mint wore a sleeveless black top that accentuated a long, muscular neck and lean shoulders. The musculature and her general style might have triggered Lomond's curiosity as to how Mint identified in terms of gender, had he not already checked her out and discovered that Mint's real name was Minette Carruthers, she had been born a genetic female and she self-identified as a woman. Mint had her finger on the mousepad of the laptop while the video of the white-haired woman played on-screen.

'. . . what you have to realise is, we're at war,' the woman was saying, in what Lomond recognised was a cultured Glaswegian accent, possibly second-hand. 'We don't like the idea of war – don't like the term used even as a cliché – don't want the weapons and everything associated with it . . . but what we also have, without a doubt, are the battlefields and the bodies. Bodies of women like you and me. Women who wanted to earn a wage, or have a good night out or go for a run, or try different sexual partners, or simply wanted to walk down the street minding their own business. These cases aren't isolated incidents, far from it – we're up to around one a week in terms of women who are unlawfully killed by men. It's a number that outstrips most war zones, over time. So how could I describe it as anything else but warfare?

'And make no mistake – we have to fight back, hard. The age of understanding is over. Women don't want to clean up men's messes any more, we're goddamn sick of it. This is what we get for an eternity of raising your children without you, sons who sometimes grow up to be man-babies who need looking after in their own right, and cleaning your houses, and cooking your food, and having to look presentable for you, and overlook your transgressions and lack of loyalty, and—'

'God almighty,' Lomond said, 'does she ever stop to breathe?'

The heads spun round, Siobhan's expression shocked, Mint's quite baleful. 'Didn't hear you knock,' Siobhan said, tartly, straightening up in her seat.

'Didn't know you both were going to be in my house,' Lomond rejoined, meeting Mint's gaze until she looked away. 'Anyway, I'm not back long – just changing clothes, grabbing a quick cup o' tea. Is your mum about?'

'She's gone back out.'

Lomond frowned. 'Didn't she have dinner?'

'Just said she wanted a sandwich.' Siobhan turned back to the screen. 'She's gone out to her art class.'

'Art class? I thought that was next month? Still life, something like that?'

'She's signed up to another one, I think. Live modelling.'

'Male models,' Mint said, with some relish. 'Fully nude.'

'Sounds awesome. You know, I think I'll stick on a hot dog,' Lomond said, completely straight-faced. 'I've just taken a notion for one. We got a jar of them in the other day, with some of the buns and relish. German numbers. Would either of you like one?'

When they shook their heads, Lomond approached to peer at the screen. He crouched down close enough to Mint to rest his chin on her shoulder, if he wanted to. 'Is that who I think it is?'

'It's Ursula Ulvaeus,' Siobhan said, stifling a yawn. 'I've no idea who you thought it was, though.'

'Yeah, that's the one. Lass you spoke about last night. This off the internet?'

'No,' Mint said, 'we shot this footage today. For our project.'

'Today?' Lomond frowned.

'Oh yeah,' Mint said, smirking. 'About an hour and a half ago, in fact.'

'She's here?'

Siobhan was a little thrown by the fact that Mint had so glibly revealed this. 'She's in town, yes.'

'So she's already planning a protest of some kind, I take it.' Lomond loosened his watch strap and rubbed at the tender skin under there.

Siobhan took a breath. 'I was going to let you know, but she's planned it for tomorrow afternoon. She's going to put out a press release, so I guess it's no big secret to tell you.'

Siobhan had hesitated a little; Mint had no such reluctance. 'Pitt Street,' she said. 'Tomorrow at eleven a.m. It won't be anything that'll close the streets, but it could cause you a problem.'

'What's she protesting about?' Lomond asked, genuinely hurt. He pointed to his own face. 'Be honest, this isn't the coupon of a well-rested man, I think you'll agree. I'm knackered. I'm not taking breaks or anything. Well . . . maybe the odd one at the kiosk.'

'I don't think it's purely about the police,' Siobhan said. 'It's about society in general. Patriarchal society.'

'Meaning men?'

'Meaning men. Sorry.'

Lomond grunted. 'I suppose we've had it coming. All the same, I'll need to call it in.' He caught Mint's eye and nodded at her. 'Thanks for the tip.'

'Don't mention it. We'll be there, too. A few of us are going down to get it on camera. Maybe you could talk to her?'

'Maybe I will.'

★

Chief Superintendent Sullivan's office had a perfect view of the crowd as it slowly proceeded down St Vincent Street. Lomond was years out of uniform, but he could still judge crowd numbers, and this was a big one. A banner sagged in the middle of the protesters like a tired old set of goalposts before strengthening again and pulling its message taut: *Why won't you save us?* Lomond actually covered his mouth when he saw this.

Annette Sullivan looked like a movie star, and countless fools had supposed that was why she'd got the job. She had God-given cheekbones and a strong jawline, and never looked less than immaculate, even with her long milk-chocolate hair crudely pinned back. She had a consistent air of mild amusement when it came to dealing with the rank and file which irritated the boors, excited the sleazebags and intimidated Lomond.

'It's like an Orange Walk,' Sullivan mused. 'The singing's a little bit better, though, wouldn't you agree?'

'The dancing, too, ma'am.' Lomond fidgeted in his seat.

Still they came, a broad phalanx blocking the road. Car horns shrieked and howled, but the demonstrators refused to yield.

Lomond's keen eyes picked out a lightning bolt of white hair in the middle of it. She had a loudspeaker, though the double glazing kept her voice out. TV cameras were positioned at either side of the road, mounted on shoulders. Lomond strained his eyes for Siobhan and Mint.

'This seems to have come out of nowhere,' Sullivan said. 'No signals on social media. Nothing until she put out the press release. Then this . . . Kind of encouraging, in a way, that she can get the message out there. So long as it's the right kind of mob.'

Lomond had a queasy feeling that she was probing for something, and he didn't want to open the door to it. 'Causing bother, all the same,' he offered finally.

'Nevertheless, they've got a point.' She got up and walked over to the window, a tall, imposing figure in black, with her back turned to him. 'Are we any closer?'

'No, ma'am. The burnt-out car turned up a blank – stolen by a very clever thief. There's some footage of the same car passing some bungalows in Ranaldstown. Cameras fitted on doors by nosy neighbours. It ties in with the timeline and one of the locations the body might have gone in the water – completely secluded, close to a side road. Simple matter to stop the car, dump the body, and drive off without anyone noticing. Which is probably what happened. But the car was utterly destroyed – forensics haven't been able to turn up a hair, literally.'

'No tips?'

Lomond shook his head. 'Nothing. Everyone who was in the area came up blank. All known weirdos rounded up, spoken to and eliminated. Anyone who seemed a bit dodgy from the lap-dancing club was actually inside the place on the Saturday night.'

'So what *have* you got?'

'Two things, linked to the camera work. We're examining traffic to MyGirl, tracing URLs and phones. There are a few snags. Lots of people were looking at Aylie's content on the site via VPNs, through Ukraine and Lebanon, six of them in Russia. Little chance of finding out who that was. But I think that's a strong line – I'm sure her killer was watching her, either online or in person at the club. Just a feeling.'

'I'm happy to go with your feelings, Lomie. I've heard all about them.'

Lomond was too embarrassed to speak.

'You mentioned two things?' Sullivan prompted.

'The other is a cold case.'

'Daisy Lawlor. I know. I was speaking to Torin MacAllister's lawyer about it, in fact.'

Lomond frowned. 'Gerry Finlay? He spoke to you?'

'He made a call. I wasn't busy,' Sullivan said, a touch defensively. 'Made his client's position clear. As politely as he could.'

'Lawyers are great at that,' Lomond said drily. 'He's also representing the artist, Donald Ward.'

'All the same, it's hard to argue with their position. They had alibis on the night Daisy Lawlor died.'

'Whether they had anything to do with it or not, there's a connection that's nagging at me. Woman with her throat cut, dumped in the water. There are some details that match up, some that don't. I think it's worth taking a fresh look.'

Sullivan turned and smiled. 'Yes. So I understand. Cara Smythe's too good an officer to be assigned to loose threads, I would have thought, inspector.'

'She's too good an officer to be taking down statements all day,' Lomond countered, irritated at the strong possibility that Cara had gone over his head about her assignment. 'I think it's an important line – that's why I gave it to her. Even if there's no link, it's another lassie who didn't come home, and I don't like unfinished business.'

'You worked on the Lawlor case, didn't you?'

He looked away as he said, 'I worked the scene. Didn't speak to any of the suspects.'

Sullivan nodded. 'I trust your instincts. But don't waste too much time on it. The Aylie Colquhoun case is about to get a much bigger profile, if it hasn't already.'

'Previous protests Ursula Ulvaeus has been involved with have caused bother,' Lomond said. 'She's good at stirring a nest. Broken shop windows, cars burned, a few polis put in the infirmary. Usual weirdos, troublemakers, rent-a-causes and the rest have attached themselves to it. One or two bad actors who want to close her mouth, too, I suppose.'

Sullivan smiled. 'Don't worry. They won't get through to the front gate.'

'I don't want anyone near the front gate. Well . . . maybe one person. With your permission.'

'Spell it out for me.'

'The main man. So to speak.' Lomond peered out of the window, where Ulvaeus was much more prominent now. The sound of the crowd was apparent through the double-glazing, chiefly the insectoid burr and rattle of her voice amplified through the loudspeaker. Ulvaeus shook her fist at the window, and the crowd roared. Somewhere cars beeped, though not quite in harmony.

'I'm not sure that's the world's best idea,' Sullivan said. 'Plus, it's the chief constable she wants.'

'It's important, ma'am. I want to speak to her. I think there's a way through to the public with this. At best, it might keep her off our backs for a couple of days.'

'And you think she can help us.'

Lomond nodded. 'That's what I'm hoping, ma'am. At the very least, let's not make her any more of an adversary than she already is. She's trouble, no question of it, no matter how much of a point she's got.'

'All right. But for God's sake, don't go down there alone. I'll get some of the heavy mob to go down with you. And don't let yourself get drawn into the crowd.'

'I also took the liberty of having some surveillance set up on the crowd. We'll get some eyes and ears on them, see what turns up. Keep an eye on the males, most of all. There's a chance our guy will be there.'

'You put that plan in operation about eight minutes before I did.' Sullivan grew serious. 'I was told you were crafty. A word I've heard about you more than once. It's a good plan. But in future, make sure you run an operation like that past me, first.'

'Trickett owed me a favour, ma'am.'

'I couldn't care less if he owed you his life. In future, it's done on the books, where I can see it. Understood?'

'Yes, ma'am.'

'OK. Your public awaits. Give me five minutes to make sure we've got a team down there to pull you out if necessary.'

Lomond glanced at the crowd – close enough now to focus on individual faces, close enough to hear the chant Ulvaeus led: *No more victims. No more killers. No more victims. No more killers.* He swallowed, fastened his coat, and headed for the door.

'Oh. Just before you go,' Sullivan said, as she sat back at her desk. 'Your bad lieutenant. Slater, is it?'

'Yes, ma'am.'

'Lock him in a cupboard. Don't let him speak to the crowd. Don't allow his face anywhere near the front doors. Got it?'

Lomond couldn't be bothered raising an argument. He sighed. 'I'll get a team down there to barricade him in the canteen. I'll distract him with something. Permission to break out the emergency shortbread?'

11

Lomond was no burly six-footer, but he was generally untroubled by his lack of height. However, he felt every missing inch of his five foot eight the moment he stepped outside the front door and was flanked by the two biggest, meanest officers that could be mustered at short notice.

The initial plan had been to put a few more of them on duty, but Lomond didn't want it to seem as if he was confronting the mob. Unfortunately, it felt as though he had been lifted up between the two hulks to be paraded in front of the crowd, rather than being protected from it. He had heard the marchers singing, but it was a shock to hear them in full cry, the sound directed right at him. And then, for the first time in his life – even after working at football matches – Lomond was booed. The crowd surged a little, but the two officers spread their hands and warded them off.

Standing not a dozen feet away from him, with a gap between her and the crowd, Ursula Ulvaeus bellowed into the loudspeaker. She had spotted Lomond and now looked him in the eye, without pausing or stuttering once. 'Here we see a prime example,' she yelled. 'The chief superintendent is in that building right now – and who do they send out? Another middle-aged white man!'

Lomond was booed again. He took a deep breath and squared his shoulders. Faces leapt out at him from the crowd – some of them he recognised. One was Mint, with a camera on her shoulder and a viewing screen angled towards her face; it lit up her grin in a sepulchral blue glow. Someone was with Mint, a tall, older man with spectacles, who was saying something in her ear. Another familiar face, a few feet over Ulvaeus's shoulder, was strikingly beautiful. It was the girl with the volunteer boat crew. The one who'd helped recover Aylie Colquhoun's body from the Clyde . . . Lottie?

Where's Siobhan?

'I want this policeman, whoever he is, to tell us what he's going to do about the death of Aylie Colquhoun,' Ulvaeus continued. 'Another day, another woman murdered by a man. And we're no nearer a solution. This city, the city that gave the world Ian Brady, Peter Tobin, Peter Manuel, Bible John and Mr Flick, spawns yet another sicko who provides an example for others to follow – who tells us that women are worthless, that we can be used and dumped as a man pleases, dumped in the river like trash!'

They weren't all women's faces, of course, but it was the women Lomond noticed most – angry, shouting, and one or two even spitting, though not with any expectation of hitting him. *Weird that I should focus on the women*, he thought, in a curiously detached way. *Maybe I'm a bit of a sexist?*

Ulvaeus continued: 'And I am going to make this pledge to you now: until this man is caught – and it is surely a man who did this – I am going to stay in your city. I am going to make a noise. I am going to make a fuss. And I am going to reach out to every woman here and make this request: join me. Stand with me. Accept nothing from men, accept nothing from society. Women don't rape and murder. Women don't poison the planet. Women don't rip up the trees and wipe out the animals. Women don't build concentration camps. Women don't start fucking *wars*.' This final statement generated a proper, last-minute-goal roar.

Lomond's feet seemed to move by themselves. He shrugged off the two policemen flanking him. He raised his hand, appealing for calm. For a moment, he thought Ulvaeus was going to react badly to his approach. *She could tell them to rip me to pieces*, he thought, *and they probably would*.

'Listen,' he shouted.

They didn't. Something sailed over Lomond's head; there was the crash and tinkle of a detonated bottle, close enough to cause the two officers to flinch, and draw closer. Ulvaeus looked delighted. Had she smacked her lips it wouldn't have surprised Lomond.

'Listen!' he shouted again, louder this time.

'Let's hear what he has to say,' Ulvaeus said into the loudspeaker. 'Give him a second or two. Let's show a bit of courtesy.' She did not hand him the loudspeaker, but perched it on her shoulder, like a hunter with a brace of rabbits.

In the sudden lull, he spoke from his gut, as he would in the briefing room, but painfully aware of a slight tremor in his voice. He was used to projecting to the back of a room or towards a TV camera, but this was something else. Only when he spotted Mint and her camera again and chose her as his target did his voice settle down.

'I understand why you're all here. I'm the senior investigating officer looking into Aylie Colquhoun's murder. I don't need to tell you that we're sickened by what happened to her, and I promise that we are doing everything we can to find the person who killed her.'

'The man,' Ulvaeus interjected, pistol-quick, as she brought the loudspeaker to her lips. 'Be real – it's a man.'

'We don't know that at this stage, and it isn't useful to make claims we can't prove. We are working on the basis that a man did this, but we have to keep an open mind. We ... no, wait,' he said, alarmed by the crowd's reaction. 'That's the truth. I am telling you the truth. First of all, by doing this today, you are diverting manpower ...' he cursed himself, 'you are diverting resources away from the inquiry. This event is counter-productive, no matter how well meant. But more than that ... I promise to keep doing everything I can to bring Aylie's killer to justice. We have hundreds of officers working thousands of hours, trying to bring the person responsible in. To say we don't care, or are complicit, is not true. There are women working on the case at senior levels, as well as knocking doors, taking statements, finding things out, using their expertise. As for the men, we have wives, sisters, mothers and daughters, colleagues, friends . . . we're going to bring this person in, I guarantee you. I'll work until I drop.'

'Looks like you don't want to drop hard enough,' Ursula said.

Lomond allowed this barb to glance off him, but he pointed to her. 'And I want to extend an offer to you, Ursula, now. If you call off the protest, I'd like you to come inside and talk to me, face to face, on camera if you must . . .'

'Absolutely not!' Ulvaeus cried. 'Not a chance!' She turned to the crowd. 'This is just another way of silencing us and marginalising our voices. This man – whoever he is, I didn't catch his name – is just another middle-management type who thinks he can tell strong, united women what to do. Well, I'll tell you, Detective Whatever—'

A shriek of static over his shoulder caught Lomond's attention – and everyone else's. There, in full uniform, was the chief superintendent. A lectern complete with a trailing microphone wire had been brought out of the front doors. If there had been camera flashes and red camera lights before, now there was an electrical storm of them, all directed at the force's most recognisable commander.

The PA system had been brought out and installed with the same brutal efficiency as the stand, and it carried Sullivan's voice over everyone's heads.

'I'd like to thank everyone for coming here today,' she said evenly. 'This has been a peaceful and effective demonstration of the public's feelings on a callous, sickening murder which has robbed a young woman of her life and devastated her mother.'

Sullivan paused, making sure she had silenced Ulvaeus as well as the crowd.

'I would like to take this opportunity to invite Ursula Ulvaeus inside the building to have a conversation with me, to bring her up to speed on the case, and also to ask if she has any particular insights she would be willing to bring to the table, or indeed to hear any offers she might make to help the inquiry. We value her campaigning and her intellect. Ursula?'

Ulvaeus weighed things up for a moment, then smiled. 'Finally, someone in authority I can respect! I will accept your offer. And I will also take up the earlier invitation to bring in a camera crew, so that people can be sure they will know what has really happened. Everyone else, feel free to disperse. We've made our point – our starting point – but know this. To everyone inside that building, and everyone watching at home or online, and especially the animal who killed Aylie Colquhoun: we aren't going away, and we won't stop. And once we've got the murderer, we'll get the next one. We are bigger than one single case, bigger than one man. Watch this space!'

She handed the loudspeaker to one of the women standing near her shoulder and beckoned to Mint, who came forward along with – at last, where had she been? – Siobhan. The two of them followed Ulvaeus as she walked past Lomond up the stairs towards the front door, where she was greeted with a handshake by Sullivan. Siobhan followed her, staring straight ahead, not meeting her father's eyes.

Quite forgotten by the crowd already and almost unnoticed by the two officers assigned to protect him, Lomond wandered in by the side door.

12

Lomond waited until the press conference was over. It was often said of him that he didn't get angry, but of course he did. Rather than simply being good at hiding it, he was better than many other people at transmuting that energy into something else – chiefly curiosity, helped along by a big dose of pragmatism. He also suffered from indigestion – again, not widely known.

He had clocked his daughter and Mint, front and centre, during the impromptu conference in the foyer of the police headquarters. This had done nothing to aid his dyspepsia. Mint controlled the camera, a delicate-looking digital device on a tripod with a viewing panel that emerged from the side – technology meaning she didn't have to put her eye to a lens. She grinned throughout, as if she was in front of the device rather than behind it; she had a piercing through her lower lip that Lomond hadn't noticed before. It caught the light, and it irritated him a little, as if she had something on her mouth that needed wiping.

Siobhan cut a less assured figure. In front of the camera like a TV reporter from the analogue age, she held forth a microphone and tried to shout a question over the top of the more seasoned members of the press who jostled each other at her shoulder. Lomond fought a very natural urge to intervene and came very close to doing so when Siobhan's darting eyes met his for a moment or two. He saw an edge of panic. He saw an appeal.

Sullivan didn't take many questions, so it was over quickly. Mainly a recap of what had been said outside when she confronted the crowd. Lomond had to admit, the chief superintendent looked and sounded the part. She knew when to allow Ulvaeus to speak, even to grandstand, but it was clear to any observer who was in charge. To describe someone as a politician was pejorative, but Sullivan was a politician, in the sense that whatever 'politics' meant on any given day, she was very good at it. A little bit of theatre went a long way, Lomond supposed. Or maybe 'showbiz' was the better word.

In the moment when the tension began to dissipate, the reporters beginning to file outside after their requests to speak to Ulvaeus were politely refused, the equipment being unplugged and packed away, Lomond took his chance, creeping up on Ulvaeus from the sidelines.

'About that chat I wanted to have,' he said, ignoring Siobhan's wide-eyed stare and Mint's maddening smirk. The latter raised her camera.

'I think we had our chat,' Ulvaeus said. She had a frank gaze, and leaned towards Lomond, a little too close. For an absurd moment he thought she was going to kiss him on the cheek. 'I spoke to your boss instead.'

'That's right, but *we* didn't have *our* chat. About the investigation. I thought you might be interested.'

'Ah. Maybe we could have a talk about that.' She didn't step away; Lomond supposed this was meant to be intimidating. Strange fishy, he thought. This close, the unpleasant thought occurred to Lomond that he wouldn't like to tangle with Ursula Ulvaeus. She wasn't particularly tall, but she looked powerful, as if she spent a lot of time in the gym. The flicked-up fringe and high crop at the back and sides, and above all the silver colouring, aged her prematurely. He could see in close-up that she wasn't much over forty, her face unlined, even radiant, when she wasn't snarling into a loudspeaker.

'Away from the cameras,' Lomond cautioned, staring towards Siobhan and Mint. They both frowned at him. 'Sorry. It isn't because I'm shy. Operational reasons.'

Ulvaeus smiled. 'Sure. We've got what we came for. I can spare you a couple of minutes.'

Lomond nodded towards the two girls. 'If you could leave us for a minute or two?'

'Fine pair of lassies, those two,' Ulvaeus said, as Siobhan helped Mint dismantle her camera and tripod. 'Keen as you like. Switched on. Absolutely fearless, too. How do you feel about the younger generation questioning you?'

'Those two frighten the life out of me,' Lomond admitted.

'So – what can I do for you, Inspector . . . ?'

'Lomond. I just wanted to be honest about where we are in the investigation.'

Ulvaeus smirked. 'I kind of gathered from your boss that you're nowhere.'

'Correct.' Lomond folded his arms. 'I won't waste your time here – I know you've got things to do. I know I have. But it goes without saying that we're dealing with a devious, dangerous person. Off the record, it doesn't look as if Aylie Colquhoun died at random or . . .'

Ulvaeus raised a hand. 'Please. There's no "died at random" in this case or any other. It's a power imbalance.'

He sighed. 'We've already heard the lecture.'

'It's no lecture – it's something you have to get into your head. It might help reframe your thinking. If Aylie was murdered by a maniac, then society created him. I know that sounds like something a sociologist might say. Or something you might hear in a podcast. But it's true – and it might help you find your man. Look at a power imbalance, somewhere – an impotent man, acting out his fantasies.' There was a trace of a Scandinavian accent, but it was distorted with Scottish speech patterns – Glasgow was her adopted city, he had read. Lomond was briefly, ludicrously reminded of a Danish footballer who'd played in Scotland so long that he had taken on the inflections and the slang of his adopted city, but in a beautiful Nordic tone and cadence.

'Profiling and psychology is kind of useful, sometimes,' he said. 'But it doesn't really help catch killers, whatever you might see on the television. It's interesting after the fact, but by that point my job's done. I'm more into who did it, how they did it, and the trail they leave. The "why" can wait. But off the record, this one worries me. He's very good at not leaving a trail. So what I wanted to say to you is be careful.'

'Worried he might come after me?' Here, for the first time, she sounded smug.

'You're high-profile, and you're making a lot of noise about this case.'

'And I will continue to do so.'

'So there is a risk he might come after you. Or maybe nothing so dramatic. He might contact you. There's a chance he was there today, among the crowd. So any unsolicited contact whatsoever from any male, I'd appreciate it if you let me know. I want to run checks, put names to faces, speak to more suspects.'

She nodded. 'I can do that for you. But I must warn you, I get a lot of weirdos. Garden variety sexists and boors, mostly. And then there're the kinky ones. The ones that I turn on. There's a link between both types of men – you know what it is?'

Lomond shrugged, grateful that Slater was somewhere else in the building, so there would be no comebacks.

'It's because I *speak*,' Ulvaeus said. 'It took me while to understand. They simply don't want me to speak. Or to be exact, they aren't used to being spoken to. The boors feel slighted and want to shut me up. The weirdos think it's perverse. A woman being assertive, like this. It turns them on because in their minds it's fundamentally wrong. They think I'm trying to dominate them. Just by speaking.'

'Takes all sorts,' Lomond said briefly. 'If you agree to help, I would like a list of names, or internet handles, if anyone contacts you with a detail out of the ordinary. Or volunteers any information about the case. It should go without saying, and you'll be well versed in all this, but I'll say it anyway: don't agree to meet anyone alone.'

'I'll be just fine,' Ulvaeus said. 'I've done this before. The case of the Ankara strangler – you know about that?'

'Read about it online somewhere.'

'There was a podcast. You listen to those?'

'Don't get time for anything like that.'

'Strange.' She seemed genuinely puzzled. 'I assumed police-men would be true crime buffs. Tricks of the trade, and all that. Anyway, I hung around in Ankara until they caught him. They didn't take kindly to me, either in the police or the media. But I think I helped. And I remember the women who were out on the streets with me. Just like here, just like in Los Angeles, just like in Leeds. Angry women. Women who've had enough. And I'm going to stay in Glasgow alongside them until you . . . or someone else . . . catches the man who killed Aylie.'

Lomond stared into her eyes. 'When people say "we're working round the clock", we actually mean it.'

'That's good. I look forward to seeing our man in court soon. I'll be there with Mrs Colquhoun. Have you met her?'

'Yes. The day Aylie's body was found. You take care now, Ms Ulvaeus.'

'And you take care too, Mr Lomond.'

'Please take my card – it's got my contact details on it.'

'I'll be glad to.' She slid the card into an inside pocket. 'But I thought there was an easy-to-remember number for calling the police?'

'Ah, if you dial 999, a strip-o-gram shows up.'

'That's exactly what the world needs now.'

'I'll see you out.'

Ulvaeus grinned, enjoying some private joke as she indulged him. 'Is this a police escort?'

'Absolutely. I can put on my blue lights if you like?'

She walked ahead of him at pace as they passed people in the corridor – quite deliberately, he supposed. Struggling to keep up, he directed her towards a side door. 'Smokers' entrance will let you get out quicker.'

Ulvaeus shook his hand. 'I'll be in touch. Don't be fooled by my bravado. I want the same thing as you, and if I thought I could help make it happen I would. So I won't hesitate to call you if I find something out.'

'We'll get him,' Lomond said. 'Promise.'

As they emerged into the damp, grey afternoon, Lomond was alerted to a scraping sound along the pitted, uneven concrete. Slouches and furtive apparitions were not uncommon at this corner of the building, unaffectionately and unimaginatively known as the Smokoe. Many of its patrons had the nerve to complain about how infrequently the place was cleaned, and any given day its containers were an unseemly scrum of fag-ends. Lomond despised smoking, but he had had more than a few useful conversations out here. But there was something about this sound of feet moving across the poorly finished concrete that put him on alert.

He had intercepted the man before Ulvaeus realised he was there. Forties, certainly, lantern-jawed, shaven-headed and with big grey watery eyes; wearing jogging trousers and a branded top that might have worked for him more than twenty years previously.

Ulvaeus took a step back, making room to strike. She had something in her hand.

'Want something, son?' Lomond asked.

The man ignored him. 'Here, you that woman that was on the telly?' He said it halfway through a snort, like a hippo surfacing.

'Never you mind who she is,' Lomond said. 'What are you doing round here?'

'Here to get my boy,' the man said, understanding Lomond's authority. 'Just out for a smoke, mate.'

'Well, you keep yourself over there by the smokers' shed and have your smoke, then on your way.'

'Awright. Only asking, mate,' the man said petulantly. 'Wanted an autograph, like.'

'Get in touch with my website,' Ulvaeus said. 'I'll have something sent to you.'

'I will,' the man vowed, with a touch of malice. 'I'll do that.'

Lomond nodded to Ulvaeus, and they walked past the shed towards the barrier at the bottom of the senior staff's car park. He was relieved to see some hi-vis stationed at the bottom. People milled past, but it was the usual traffic of ordinary business; earlier, this part of the street had been thronged with people who had come to hear Ulvaeus. The crowd had dispersed.

'What's that in your hand?' Lomond asked.

'You mean this?' Ulvaeus held up a compact mirror.

'No. I mean . . . what did you take out of it?'

'Nothing.' She shrugged.

'It's still in your hand.'

Her eyes narrowed in clear irritation. 'Nothing to do with you. It's broken. A bit of it fell out.'

She held up a shard of mirrored glass, silvery at the fresh edge, a crooked triangle with a nasty point. She flipped open the compact and placed the jagged piece in its space, like a jigsaw puzzle. She gave it a pat to secure it, then clicked the compact shut.

'Give you a nasty cut, that,' Lomond remarked.

'Don't patronise me, inspector.' Then, ignoring Lomond, and ignoring the uniformed officers who flinched so comically at her approach that they must surely have been interrupted in some gossip about her, she walked into the street and was gone.

Footsteps pounded the concrete behind Lomond at that moment. It was Slater, jogging, his suit jacket in his hands. His shirt collar was unbuttoned, his face pale.

Lomond was alarmed by this apparition; he fancied the detective sergeant might have intended to burst into action, utterly inappropriately. Maybe he'd have rugby-tackled Ulvaeus? 'It's fine, Malcolm,' he said. 'Jeezo. You're sweating. How far have you run?'

'Why did you have your phone switched off?' Slater breathed hard and leaned in close.

'I was talking to Leslie Nielsen there . . . Why?'

But he knew why. The moment he asked the question. An instant before Slater said it.

'Gaffer. There's been another one.'

Sheonaid

13

On the screen, the dead girl waved at Lomond and smiled. Bubbles escaped from the side of her mouth. The water cast her skin in delicate baby blue, and blades of sunlight dappled her skin in gold. Her bikini top was the same aquamarine as the water, jewelled with silver scales, catching the light in brief flashes in all the colours of the spectrum. It was the same material as her tail. This became apparent when she undulated and spun in a perfect circle, head tilted back, leading with a fine, grooved, perhaps masculine chin. She had the shoulders and musculature of a lifelong swimmer or gymnast. But more than that, Lomond thought, there was her hair.

To say it had a life of its own wasn't quite the cliché he wanted. It was as if it was sentient, maybe even in control. When she finished her arc, the dead girl faced the camera, black eyes open and staring before she remembered to smile. The hair never obscured her face, always framing it, even as it billowed overhead. She controlled her movements so perfectly, it was always tossed this way or that. Never once did her hands interfere with that natural black flow.

Lomond's heartbeat grew louder; he realised he was holding his breath in time with the dead girl. Finally, she waved, and bulleted towards the surface with a flick of her tail.

That hair was pulled back from her face when Lomond saw her on the slab, when Minchin cut her open, named the parts, pointed out the places where her rivers had been dammed for ever. All the while, Lomond focused mainly on the cut, ear to ear.

Minchin, to his credit, or his eternal damnation, still had a twinkle in his eye when he rested his backside against the table in the interview room. 'I bet you a fiver I can guess what your exact questions are.'

'Cut in the throat. The same?'

Minchin nodded. 'Something very sharp, Lomie. Something nasty. He does it quick.'

'What about the little kink, at the side?'

'Yep, I guessed you would say that, too. I'm on the money so far.' Minchin gestured with his pinkie, slightly above where his jaw merged with his neck. He flicked an indelicate accent in the air. 'Little jagged bit. Right here. A kink in the wire where he withdraws the knife. When I saw the cut on the previous lassie, I didn't think much of it. Now I think it's deliberate.'

'What's that about? Trying to make sure?'

'Good question, but nope. Your man here, he's all about the blood vessels. Vein and artery. Lot of ooze, lot of splatter. He cuts the carotid arteries, that's where he starts. Wants them out of the game quickly. There's no reason for that wee flick, if we're talking about murder – except for a private one.'

'He's skilled. Maybe medically trained?'

Minchin almost chuckled. 'I don't recall slitting people's throats in med school, Lomie. Maybe they do that these days, I don't know. It's been a while since basic training.'

'Now that you mention basic training – military?'

'Could be. Para reg, special forces, they get shown all the tricks. One hundred and one interesting things to do with a knife.'

Lomond made a note. 'I'll check that out.'

'But it's the old Jack the Ripper argument, really.'

'Come again?'

Minchin made an alarming stabbing motion in the air. Lomond, saturated with stress, could not altogether avoid flinching. 'Well, with Jack the Ripper, people think he was a medical man because of the wounds he caused and some of the body parts he removed. But you wouldn't need to be a surgeon or even a slaughterer to find someone's kidneys or liver. Bet if

104

I gave you a scalpel and a shot at the title, you could find my kidneys for me. You don't need training. You just have to be mad.'

'This guy's not mad. That's what has me worried. Lots of control, here. Very carefully prepared.' Lomond bit the side of his mouth. 'You know, I had a theory he was an abortionist.'

'Eh?' Minchin cried. 'Our guy?'

'No, Jack the Ripper. Anyway. The flick's the thing, isn't it?'

The pathologist grew serious. 'It's not Flick, Lomie.'

'No, that's not what I meant,' Lomond stammered. 'Bad choice of words. I know it's not Flick.'

'Not that daftie. Just a different daftie.'

'Yes. A prime daftie. Star prize. Not had one of these for a while. One in a million. That's two he's done in the space of a week. But I didn't mean Mr Flick. I meant . . . the flick. The wee cut, at the side of the throat there. That wee afterthought. It's telling us something, but I don't know what.'

'Hard to say. Could be a calling card. Might be a question of technique. Assuming he's right-handed, he grabs her from behind and cuts from left to right – no Adam's apple in the way, of course. Interesting – he doesn't cut the windpipe. Cut that savage, knife that sharp, but he's just after the blood vessels. Clean kill. She died in seconds. Hopefully before she knew what was happening to her.'

Lomond nodded. 'I'm assuming she died on Tuesday?'

Minchin frowned, as if carrying out a calculation. 'That's true. Been in the water less than twenty-four hours before two fishermen found her. Are we talking about an escalation?' He said this last part quietly.

'I hope not. Isn't looking good, though, is it?'

'We'll get him, Lomie. He'll have bought petrol. He'll be on CCTV somewhere. Someone will have seen him. He can't just vanish in and out of thin air.'

'This bugger's clever, Chick. Like I said, for a maniac, he does a lot of planning. Either that, or he's got the luck of the devil.'

As he said this, Lomond sat down, heavily. He didn't make a sound, but the lights had cut in somewhere stage left, blotting out reality; a sheer curtain shot through with diamonds that stole over his vision for a few seconds.

Minchin was over to him in a flash. 'Whoa there, space cadet. You looked like you were about to capsize there, Lomie. You OK? Look at me a second.'

'I'm fine,' Lomond said. 'I said I was off chocolate bars and biscuits until Christmas. Might check out what's happening with the vending machine in a minute.'

'You're not going type two on me, are you?'

'Nah, just no sleep. Lots of coffee. And I've got a daftie to lift. You know how it goes.'

'Just don't be fading out,' Minchin admonished him. 'Take it easy. Get your sidekick to take some of the load.'

★

But the thing was – as Lomond had gone on to explain to Minchin, in fairness – Slater also had that haunted look about him. He'd shaved badly, as if in a hurry or with a razor that needed stropping. He gulped down coffee as they viewed the video of the dead girl together.

'Some name,' Slater said. 'You know how it's all pronounced?'

Lomond did, and he said it, slowly. 'Sheonaid Aird Na Murchan.'

She also called herself the Black Selkie, as she explained on her personal blog, because she liked to swim. That was the galling part, the detail he really hoped Slater wouldn't joke about, not even to break the tension. She performed as a mermaid, and there was startling video footage on her professional-looking website. She wore the same tail each time; sometimes she was in a swimming pool, sometimes she was arcing her back and flopping her fluke on the surface of a slaty, freezing-looking sea – somewhere off the west coast, Lomond guessed. And sometimes the underwater footage was shot somewhere tropical, or maybe somewhere closer to home, in the unearthly blue of the Ionian.

In one incredible sequence that Lomond found almost too intense to watch, she undulated alongside an enormous shark with a face like that old dear in your close you never, ever messed with. Going by the whiplash striations along its back, Lomond guessed it was a tiger shark, but it didn't take an expert to know the fish was big enough to cause Sheonaid the Black Selkie a problem.

But she glided alongside it, utterly insouciant, even giving its tin-can-scar tail a wee tug as it arced away from her and escaped into the blue. She turned to the camera and grinned, giving a thumbs-up. Lomond, who knew that the worst had in fact happened to her, and that she had suffered an appalling end at the hands of a different predator, still felt a surge of relief as she undulated towards the surface and the source of the radials of light spearing through the scene.

'I don't know how you even pretend to be relaxed, doing a thing like that,' he muttered.

'Seen too many films, gaffer. Sharks are our friends now.'

'Yer bum.'

'Anyway, I thought you were an expert on the denizens of the deep these days?'

Lomond cleared his throat. 'Aye. Anyway. Her family's in Oban. Shot a lot of her videos there, out on the water.'

'Someone else must have shot the videos.'

Lomond nodded. 'Someone attached to a scuba-diving club, name's Matthew Ellinn, according to the credit line and metadata on some of them. Cara's checking him out. Though it seems he's based in Oban and has been there for the past few weeks.'

'Boyfriend?'

'Hard to say.'

Lomond clicked on the next item the team had sent him.

The thumbnail appeared to show Sheonaid topless, on dry land, although her hair covered her breasts. In the next shot she was posed like the statue of the Little Mermaid, wearing her costume, her back turned to the camera. Definitely a swimmer, Lomond noted, barely any fat on her at all, strong, sleek, the shoulders and upper arms well defined. Aylie Colquhoun had not quite been built the same way. He knew Sheonaid was taller, more athletic, though there were similarities, the chief one being the long hair. Sheonaid's jet black, Aylie's blonde.

On the next video, Sheonaid was definitely topless, though glimpsed from a distance and through bottle-green water with poor visibility. Lomond was taken out of the moment, entranced by the flexible grace of the images, the seemingly easy turns, the hands angled like a rudder, the way Sheonaid's entire body moved into the curves with poise and elegance. The hair seemed to caress her ribs, running its dark fingers down her spine.

And she had died, quickly and horribly. Probably, whoever had done it had gripped her under the chin from behind with the left hand. With the right, the blade punched in, just under her jaw, beneath the left ear. It cut from left to right, almost ear to ear, with that intriguing apostrophe at the right hand side. Same as the one on Aylie Colquhoun's throat. Carotids cut cleanly.

Then she had been pitched into the water. She had inhaled some of it, reflexively, but she had died before she had time to drown. That was the saving grace. Like someone bitten in half by a shark, the horror was slightly, only slightly, countered by the relative speed with which her life had been extinguished. The body was otherwise unmarked. No struggle. No fight. Nothing under the fingernails. 'She didn't even have a bruise I could find,' Minchin had commented. 'Might have been sculpted in marble. Except for her neck.'

Lomond imagined the pure, deadening shock of an arm locked around the throat, a hand, gloved, gripping the neck . . .

108

Animal husbandry? he wrote on his pad . . . and then, the final, obscene sting. Was there time for realisation? Was there time for any reaction at all before the literal last gasp? Lomond shivered and closed his eyes for a second.

'What is it then – a kink or something?' Slater asked.

Lomond jumped. 'What's that?'

'This stuff.' Slater pointed, with some distaste, Lomond noted, as another video ran a series of edited shots showing Sheonaid the Selkie getting ready. She wore her regular clothes, jeans and a white T-shirt with *Hug a Whale* stencilled on the front; then she spun around, there was a quick, clever cut, and she was wearing a white string bikini; then another spin, and she had on her mermaid outfit, her breasts bare.

'It's beyond me,' Lomond admitted. 'Maybe it is. Maybe it's totally innocent. Maybe she sees herself the way she saw mermaids when she was a wee lassie. Taking her top off would mean nothing, if you think of it that way.' He sighed. 'Could be that it's something we can't really comprehend. Maybe it isn't made to give men a thrill. We see a lassie taking her clothes off, dressed – or half-dressed – as a mermaid. We might have our own thoughts, but . . . we're men who like a lassie taking her clothes off. So we're blind. We look at it, but we see nothing. Or if we do, it's like tunnel vision. We only see what we want to. We're missing an important bit, and we'd never know. Cognitive bias, I think they call it. We're seeing a body, but we're not seeing the performance, the form, the setting, the clothes even. We could be looking at identity, how someone thinks of themselves, how they want to present themselves. Art, in other words. All we see is a lassie with her top off. We're looking at it, and we don't pick any of that up. We see something else.'

'We do.' Slater scratched his chin, then shook his head in some irritation. 'God, what a beauty she was. They both were. What an absolute crime.'

'Crime is the word,' Lomond said grimly.

'No sign of sexual assault?'

'None. None in Aylie Colquhoun, either. We're dealing with a very strange . . .' Lomond had been going to say 'fish', '. . . an absolute daftie,' he concluded. 'Worst one in years.'

'He must have seen her,' Slater said. 'On these videos, on the blog. Same way he saw Aylie Colquhoun.'

'She wasn't on MyGirl.'

'She doesn't have to be on MyGirl. She's all over the internet, for free. She has a Twitter handle, Facebook pages, Instagram.'

Lomond grunted assent. 'We'll see if there's a link. Some of the images on the blog look as if they were professionally done. There'll be something.'

Or maybe not, he thought. Technology fixed the blemishes and rough edges; people could edit and package videos from their own bedrooms these days − he hadn't long seen his daughter and Mint do the same thing at his dining room table. Perhaps that's all there was to it: a strange girl, and a strange hobby. Or perhaps not so strange. He thought of Siobhan − even the assonance linking their names caused him to flinch; he could barely stand even a coincidental proximity. His daughter had loved ponies as a girl, unicorns, Pegasus, anything of that nature. He recalled the delight on her face when he'd told her that no, it was the truth − Scotland's national animal was indeed the unicorn. 'Then they were real!' she'd declared. 'Unicorns were real!'

There was a comparison to be made between that pure, inviolate sense of wonder and joy on the face of Lomond's little girl and the smile on the mermaid as she waved at the camera.

'Two in a week,' Slater said. 'He's done, surely. Can't be that lucky again. No matter how well organised he thinks he is.'

'Let's hope so. He's very, very organised, though. He's thought it through. And he isn't angry. He's not normal.'

'When's the presser?'

Lomond checked his watch. 'I'm talking to them in twenty minutes.'

110

'It's going to kick off, gaffer. This Ulvaeus woman is all over social media. She's been on the telly already. National and satellite channels.'

'Aye, she's been giving me some hints and tips all morning. Very keen. I should be thankful.'

'There'll be another demo. She's talking about a torchlight march tonight.'

'I'm trying not to think about that. The boss was keen enough to deal with her last time, so she can do the talking from now on.'

There was a brief knock at the door, then a tall man in a new charcoal suit came in. Myles Tait was roughly the same age as Slater, perhaps a little taller, dark-haired and dark-eyed. He had an almost mocking nonchalance about him, and his accent marked him out for the Glasgow Academy former pupil he was. He merely nodded at Slater before turning to Lomond.

'Sir, trace came back on the CCTV. You busy at the moment?'

'Bring it over, Myles.'

Tait had a tablet computer in his hand; he tapped at the screen, fed in his pin code and presented it to Lomond.

'He picked Sheonaid up in Govan, Monday night. Time . . . nine thirty-four p.m. That's the day the first body was found by the rescue boat. We've got video, got a licence plate, got the car.'

Lomond leaned forward, staring at the CCTV footage that showed the tall, dark-haired girl standing at a bus stop. A white car stopped opposite, and the girl's head snapped up. The footage was not pristine, but it was possible to see Sheonaid Aird Na Murchan's expression change. She smiled – Lomond was well acquainted with that expression, and a chill darted up his spine – before she scrambled in.

The face of the driver was indistinct.

'No clearer view of him?'

'No, sir,' Tait said. 'We'll put out a call for dashcam.'

'Mobile phone signal?'

111

'It cuts out about five minutes after she gets in the car – switched off. Nothing after that – zip. No signal after that.'

Lomond frowned. 'Doesn't make sense . . . how's he managing that? If the phones are switched off, that suggests he's persuading them to do that, rather than just smashing them. Anyway . . . No matter. Car licence plate?'

Tait cleared his throat. 'This is where it gets tricky. Nothing came up on the plate. It's a dud.'

'You what?' Slater said.

'A dud,' Tait said, slowly. 'Knocked off. Fake licence plates.'

'What about the car? No trace on the make? Stolen, I suppose?'

'We're carrying out some checks, but nothing was reported, and there's nothing on the database either.'

'So the first car he steals,' Lomond said, writing notes as he spoke. 'The second one looks like it was knocked off, fake licence plates, and doesn't appear on the ANPR database.'

'Afraid not, sir,' Tait said.

Lomond put his finger to his lips and frowned. 'And he was known to this lassie somehow. That's how he does it, surely. He knows them. From online or something else.'

'Sneaky bastard,' Slater muttered.

Lomond looked at Tait. 'Did we turn anything up on links to webcams?'

'Nothing so far, sir. Just what we've seen on her website.'

'Thanks, Myles. Keep on it, see what you can get me. We need to know who Sheonaid knows, where she's been, who she's spent time with.'

'Sir.' Tait nodded to Lomond, shut down the tablet, and walked out without acknowledging Slater.

'I'm going to assume that tension wasn't sexual,' Lomond remarked once the door was closed.

'What? Tait? He's an arsehole,' Slater said, with unusual venom. 'Playing at being a polis. What's the score? Is he on our team now?'

'He's good at what he does,' Lomond said. 'All I'm interested in.'

'He's not a team player, gaffer. Never liked how he goes about his business. All about him. Like a fitba player that only cares about scoring all the goals.'

'Just try not to cause a problem, eh?' Lomond snapped. Then he sighed. 'Sorry. Long days. I'd better look in on my notes, and check in with the boss, before I faint at the press conference or something.'

He stared at a looped video of Sheonaid Aird Na Murchan doing the backstroke. Her tail trembling on the surface.

Then he banged his fist on the table.

It was Slater's turn to jump. A coffee cup beside the laptop followed suit, threatening to tip over.

'Christ's sake, gaffer!' Slater yelled. 'Outbursts from you, now? That's my job. This is all wrong. What's up?'

'We know her,' Lomond said. He tapped the mousepad, opened up one of the previous videos, and spooled back the video footage. 'Now. The position she's in now. Right at the beginning. Hang on, I'll start it again.'

Slater's eyes followed the progress of the shimmering, emerald-studded creature on the screen as Lomond triggered the start of the video, ran it back, played it again. It was a haunting *mise en scène*. Sheonaid hung in the water at the start of the video, the hair coiling and curling around her moon-bright face, suspended upright, barely even moving her hands to keep steady. Surrounded in blue, diamond streaks of light cast across the sequins and scales of her tail costume.

Slater got it on the third replay. 'The swimming pool. The mural.' He turned to Lomond. 'The artist.'

Lomond nodded, eyes bright. 'Sir Erskine Copper. Lift him. Right now.'

14

'I must say,' Sir Erskine Copper said, glancing around at the walls, 'this isn't quite what I'd imagined.'

'What did you imagine?' Lomond asked.

'Well, two-way mirrors, for one thing. The place where your superiors hide and make judgements. Those kinds of things.'

'That's just on the telly. Same with earpieces,' Lomond said. He tapped an earlobe, trying to reassure the older man, and failing.

'Perhaps in America?'

'Aye, maybe.'

The older man put Lomond in mind of a former teacher he'd bumped into on Sauchiehall Street one Friday lunchtime, a while ago – McArthur, History. A bit of a tosser was the common consensus, though Lomond had found the man pleasant enough, if you were pleasant to him. The latter-day picture was a departure from the one that had been fixed in Lomond's memory from childhood. Twenty-five years' difference was all too apparent on Mr McArthur's face. He retained the beard that had been the stuff of cruel caricatures scribbled on jotters and elsewhere, but now it was pure white, and ill-kempt. The kind of beard that might yield unspeakable debris were it to be thoroughly groomed. A simple portrait of ageing, the inevitable fraying round the edges. Sir Erskine was the same. His clothes were something out of *Viz*, or perhaps *Rupert Bear* – a red cardigan with an actual cravat and baggy beige trousers. No one on *What's My Line?* would have mistaken him for anything other than an artist.

But the face told a story of confusion, rising to consternation. The eyes tended to boggle when Sir Erskine considered his answers – a feature that would have been seized upon by any caricaturist. The contrast between him and his charcoal-suited, coal-haired young lawyer at his elbow was so stark it became wearying to the eye.

'Sir Erskine, we want to ask you about Sheonaid Aird Na Murchan,' Lomond said.

'The Selkie. Yes.'

'When did you first meet her?'

'She was a life model – she came to my classes, I'd say, about eight or nine months ago.'

'How do you get to be a life model?' Slater asked.

'An agency, sometimes. Or, as in Sheonaid's case, you are a fully responsible, mature adult and you make an inquiry.'

'She was nineteen,' Slater said. 'Seems right on the edge of "adult" to me.'

Sir Erskine took a deep, theatrical breath, and said, 'Nevertheless . . .'

'So which classes were these? Was it part of a taught course?'

'Oh no – this was just one of my little off-piste efforts. Something I like to do now and again. I take little tours, move around Scotland – community centres. It flies under the radar, but if you know, you know. Drumchapel, Toryglen, anywhere who will have me. I do it for free. A few times I've had kids throwing stones at the windows while inside, behind the curtains, everything they've ever wanted to see was on display.'

'Nude art classes, you mean?' Slater asked.

'Oh yes,' Sir Erskine said, nodding. 'Quite often, though not always. It was up to the model, really. When I teach art, I want to teach them about articulation. How the hands move, the elbows, the knees, the fingers. All the bits that start to complain once you get past a certain age. These are the bits that are hardest to draw. The angles. This is the part where art can go wrong . . . or delightfully right, if you want to get weird. I want them to focus on that, and not just the parts that you're thinking of, gentlemen. A variety of poses. Tasteful, you might say. I always find a mature attitude among the artists. Commendable. Beautiful, in its way. I teach pensioners. Men who worked with their hands their whole lives. Talented young people who can't or won't attend university. I teach prisoners, and ex-prisoners. They come together for art. In some ways . . . in some ways, I'd say it's my greatest triumph.' He actually teared up for a second or two.

'And was Sheonaid a nude model?' Slater asked.

'Not to begin with – she put a proposal to me based on the act she had. Cabaret.'

'Cabaret?' Lomond looked up from his notepad.

'Oh yes, she had a live act. Very elaborate.'

Lomond wrote something down and underlined it, then asked: 'Did you see it?'

'No. She sent me a video, though. I suppose you might say there was an erotic element to it, no denying it. She had the most beautiful body. I make that statement, as my friend beside me would say, without prejudice.'

'This was something that she did onstage?'

'Yes – she had a ten-minute spot at a club. A glass tank was dragged onto the stage – she told me it had been lying around in there for a donkey's age, requisitioned from one of the theatres, I gather. Apparently there used to be live sharks in it, in the olden days. You'd get a lassie in a bikini swimming with them, give the punters a thrill. Anyway, she filled it with water, decorated it, and did her mermaid act in front of an audience. Very clever, I have to say – like sleight of hand, you never noticed her taking a breath. Then again, there were distractions.'

'How's that?' Slater asked.

'How is what?' Sir Erskine said, blinking.

'What were the distractions?'

'Well, she was topless. Usually she performs on her website with something on, you know. For the club, she didn't.'

'What's the name?' Slater asked. 'Of the club.'

'Trapeze. Bottom of Garnethill. It's had a few name changes over the years.'

Slater shook his head. 'Never heard of it. Burlesque-type thing? People still do that?'

'Burlesque is as old as theatre, son,' Sir Erskine said. 'People will be doing it long after we're in our boxes. It's no fad. But yes – burlesque is correct.'

'You mentioned she sent you a video,' Lomond said. 'Was it a link or a file? Do you still have it?'

'I'm sure I do – even if I've deleted it, it'll still be around. I can pass it on, no problem.'

'How many girls would you say get in touch about being your models, sir?' Slater asked.

'Lots, over the years. Also lots of boys. I notice you didn't ask me about those.' Sir Erskine showed his teeth then: a gruesome parting of the brittle foliage bordering his mouth.

'The reason why we're asking you about the girls . . . or women . . . is kind of obvious,' Slater said evenly.

'Of course. I'm being mischievous. I suppose this is not the time or the setting.'

'You suppose? Me too,' Slater said.

'When was the first time Sheonaid posed for you?' Lomond asked quickly.

'She came to a class at Glasgow Caledonian University. Off-piste, as I say – amateurs. This time it was students. I remember they were quite a rowdy bunch, but they fell silent when she came in. Sheonaid was exceptional.'

'All in the eye of the beholder, I suppose,' Lomond said. 'What was it that you felt was exceptional?'

'The line of her, really. She's a swimmer, so there're those muscles, a dream for me to sketch and draw. I wish I had the skill with bronze; I'd have sculpted her, if so. Exquisite. But equally, she could have been on page three of a tabloid. Or painted on the side of a bomber during the war. Or the bomb itself, I imagine.'

117

'You always think of your models in these terms?' Slater asked.

'Son, don't let these trousers fool you. I look at women the same way you do. So in other words, yes, she was very attractive. But this informed the art. It wasn't grubby. She had that quality to her: she drew the eye, whatever she chose to do, whatever she chose to wear. She was aware of that.'

'Have you had relationships with many of your models?' Lomond asked.

'Ah, you've been reading some naughty books about me, inspector. I used to. When I was younger. I'm an old man now. A long way past that. Some of my models went on to become famous, you know. One's a newsreader. Another led a dance troupe you saw on kids' TV in the eighties. I won't deny my work allowed me privileges.'

'These days they call it harassment,' Slater said. 'Heard of #MeToo?'

'Oh, I didn't harass anyone, son. You can ask me more about it, if you like.'

'This isn't relevant to the inquiry, is it?' asked the lawyer.

'Did you have a relationship with Sheonaid Aird Na Murchan?' Lomond asked.

'No. As I said, purely professional. I've been married thirty years. Faithfully married. To one of my models, in fact. Hazel. The one that wouldn't let me go. So those days are over.'

Slater said, 'So Sheonaid posed for you more than once?'

'Three times. The other two times were at community centres. One in Rutherglen, the other, I think, in Battlefield. That was a library, in fact. I can get the dates to you.'

'And how about the mural?'

'Well, that's a thing. I asked her to pose in my studio for an oil painting, a nude.'

'And where's that?'

'A nude?' He stressed the word with something like contempt. 'No, your studio. *Obviously*.'

'Ah, I'm sorry. "How's that" . . . "where's that" . . . when grammar slips, I get confused. My studio is my house. I mean, I have a studio in my house, but the other rooms tend to turn into studios, too. Depending on the light. And my mood.'

Lomond, not liking the rising colour on the nape of Slater's neck, interjected: 'She was happy to pose at your house?'

'Oh yes, all too eager. She knew all about me. Charming girl, great subject. But I was not satisfied with the result. When I was asked to paint the mural at the swimming pool, I had a brainwave. I more or less worked from memory – just the odd reference point saved to my phone, really. I added the tail, the details on the costume, the shells . . . a flight of fancy. This is rare for me. It was all one. I felt it very strongly – I never oppose these forces, you know.'

'What forces?'

'Coincidence. Coincidence and chance grease the wheels of everything – art, history, politics, you name it. You're a fool to ignore them. And so I had a mermaid in my lap, you might say, and then I had a community art project at a public baths where I could set her free. Isn't that gorgeous? I mean, I'd have done the job anyway – it's a lovely thing to do, a truly public artwork. But the coincidence is one of the main reasons that drew me to the project. You know . . . it's a terrible shame.'

Then the old man's face crumpled. There was an awkward silence as he gulped in a breath. He took a glass of water from the table, but choked on it alarmingly. They saw for the first time how fragile he was, even frail.

Lomond pushed over a box of tissues. 'Everything all right? Take it easy.'

'Sorry, gents. The façade crumbles. Ha. I'll be fine.'

'Take your time, Sir Erskine,' Lomond said gently. 'We can take a break – head out for a cup of tea? There's no rush at all.'

'Let's take a break,' the lawyer said. But as he rose from his seat Sir Erskine laid a hand on his arm.

'No, let's have it out. Don't mind me. Delayed shock. That

119

something like that could happen to someone I know . . . someone I worked with so recently. It's no wonder you've brought me in, I'll say that for nothing.'

'I wouldn't say it at all,' his lawyer said. The overtone of cringe almost made the two policemen laugh.

'With this in mind, we need to ask you where you were on Saturday and Tuesday,' Lomond said after a moment. 'All movements, all day.'

'Well, I'd need to check my diary, to be sure, but . . . I've been on community art classes all week. This is my farewell tour, you could say. Bit like Bob Dylan's – it'll end when I do.'

'Both days?'

'Yes. I was in Kirkintilloch for one class – portraits. That was from six to ten p.m. Big success. Then Bishopbriggs. Same deal.'

'Where did you stay both nights?'

'Bed and breakfasts. I go rough 'n' ready when I can. It's been very worthwhile. Met some lovely people, absolutely charming.'

'Was your wife or anyone else with you?'

'I'm bound to say I was in the pub both nights and with people until closing time. Then I was off to bed. My wife wasn't with me. And, I should make clear, I was also alone.' He grinned again, pleased with his quip. 'I can get you the names of the places and tie up the dates.'

Lomond nodded. 'That would be a help. It's been good of you to talk to us, Sir Erskine. Before we finish here, there's another thing I'd like to clear up.'

'Oh yes?'

'Just a question about your relationship with Donald Ward and Torquod Rafferty.'

'Oh – those two! I can't get used to "Torin". He'll always be Torquod to me. I still think of them as a pair of scamps. Grown men now, of course. I was friends with Torquod's father, Cuthbert – the Earl of Strathdene. We were schoolmates. Glasgow Academy FPs. Thick as thieves, you might say. Torquod was always going to be a politician – and a good one, too. I've always been Labour, but he's changing the tide a little, isn't he? Strange times. Never thought I would see a Glasgow MP elected for the Tories on first past the post. But he has a brilliant chance.'

'So you knew Torquod's father, the old earl. And was Donald Ward a fixture, too?'

'Oh yes – he was always up around the hall. I took a particular interest in him, you might say – he idolised me when he was a child. I suppose I was flattered, helped him in his career. He was always more of a draughtsman than an artist – no surprise to me he's gone on to do so well on that side of things.'

'Did you stay at Rafferty Landing?' Lomond asked.

'Yes – I was a regular visitor. Still am. Me and Hazel stayed there maybe nine or ten months ago, in fact. Perhaps it was Burns Night? There was a piper there, I remember that much. Someone stabbed some meat, anyway.'

'So do you know anything about a girl called Daisy Lawlor?'

Sir Erskine's face was cleansed of any expression. His unsettlingly restless eyes finally fixed on Lomond, and he laid his immaculate hands flat on the table.

'The girl in the pond?' he said quietly.

'That's right. If you were close to the earl and stayed over at the hall a lot, you must know what went on there that summer.'

'I didn't know the girl at all,' Sir Erskine said. 'A bad business.'

'What do you think happened?' Slater asked.

'Oh, I don't know. Aliens landed, with sex on their mind. Jack the Ripper travelled forward in time and kept up his old hobbies. How should I know?'

'Were you at Rafferty Landing that weekend?'

'No. As it happens, I was staying on the campsite of the music festival. The one the dead girl was supposed to go to. All weekend. Me and Hazel and our two daughters.'

'Have you ever spoken to—'

'I haven't spoken to anyone about it. If you want my

opinion, you need to track down the crowd of travellers who were there at the time. The earl was a little slapdash about who he allowed to use his land. A sixties liberal is particularly prone to those mistakes. I'm sure I saw Hells Angels there, once, or the Scottish equivalent. It's a dangerous world. Not a playground. Naturally, the boys have never discussed it with me. Nor should they. It's a legal matter.'

Lomond nodded. 'It is indeed. Thank you so much for your time.'

15

Lomond scanned the press pack from the lectern for a moment. There were more video cameras nowadays, he mused. Even the print reporters had them; they had websites to fill, too. Not the bulky numbers perched on shoulders that he remembered from his days in uniform, but dainty things that stood on top of flimsy tripod stands. He had a strange anxiety for these devices when they were left unattended to record footage; it was like watching a child's expensive Christmas present subjected to rough treatment.

'What we can say for certain,' he began, 'is that both Aylie and Sheonaid were picked up by car in the city. It's most likely that they got a lift with the person who killed them. I'm about to show you a picture of the car that picked up Sheonaid on Tuesday night. We've already established that the licence plates were false, but I'd ask you to think back to what you were doing at that time, and on that night. Do you recognise the car? Do you think you saw the person at the wheel? Most importantly, did you see Sheonaid at any time on that day?'

Lomond clicked through the images on the big screen – images that had already been sent out to papers, broadcasters, wire services and websites. Ones he knew very well, ones that had smiled at him from his own phone and the front pages of the newspapers. Mostly, he was just relieved that the presentation software had worked.

'Both women were creatives – Aylie was enthusiastic about vintage clothes and late fifties and early sixties Americana. Sheonaid was an underwater performer and called herself the Selkie. We might say "mermaid", too – that was a term she used on her online content. They didn't know each other, so far as we can tell, but this is a very important link in both cases. If anyone out there knew Aylie or Sheonaid, or was familiar with them through their online content and the MyGirl site, then please let us know. Any information you can give us about their movements, people they knew, any suspicions you might have – nothing is too small or unimportant. Any information you can give us could be crucial.'

A hand went up. A thin, pale-looking young journalist with a haircut straight across his forehead that gave him a somewhat Frankensteinian aspect, asked: 'Isn't MyGirl a sex webcam site?'

Lomond had prepared for this. 'In actual fact, MyGirl has a range of content, so it wouldn't be fair to say that, no. There is no suggestion either victim was involved in MyGirl for anything other than artistic purposes and following their own creativity. That's why I want to reach out to the creative community, to fans and admirers, both in Scotland and around the world – did you know either of these women? Did you know of someone who was obsessed with them, worked with them or maybe talked about them in any way that made you suspicious? Any hunch or memory could be very important – please share it with us.

'Lastly, I want to make sure that everyone is aware that we have a very dangerous person out there who has killed two people in quick succession. I want to caution women and girls across this city and further afield as well – be careful who you get into a car with. Make sure people know where you're going. If you have to meet someone you don't know, meet them in a public place.'

'Are there any distinguishing features in the case that you can share with us, inspector?' one of the broadcast reporters asked, a famous face across the UK.

Lomond tried not to blink. He visualised those horrible trenches across otherwise beautiful throats, bloodless thanks to immersion, both featuring the little nicks at the right-hand side of the throat. 'Nothing that we can share, for operational reasons.

I'm sure you understand. I can only confirm that both girls met a violent death.'

'What about phone evidence?' another woman asked.

'Their phones are missing. Transmitter evidence has pointed to both girls being on the rural roads I mentioned earlier before their phones were abruptly switched off. We'll circulate images of the types of phone they used – if anyone is offered one of them for sale, please get in touch immediately.'

'What about the cars?' someone asked. 'Is it true that the car in the first case was stolen?'

Lomond kept a straight face, but tension radiated from his neck and jawline. Someone had leaked a confidence already. 'We're still examining all available evidence on the cars.'

A long arm with black nail varnish shot up, two rows from the front. Lomond acknowledged the question with a nod a split second before he recognised the speaker.

'Inspector, do you think your job is on the line if you don't make an arrest soon?' Mint asked, smirking. There was a wave of discontent in the room, from both the assembled reporters and the attendant police.

'That question's irrelevant,' Lomond replied as calmly as he could. 'All I'm focused on is catching a killer. We're going to put all available resources into finding this person and bringing them to court. There's a degenerate out there, someone very sick and very dangerous, and we're going to put him away.'

*

Lomond pulled the team into a separate briefing room. Some of them had coffees; one or two, he knew, had been on duty that morning. Tait was at the front, his back straight, taking notes in a pad.

'The cars are important,' Lomond said. 'Let's look at everything available, beyond any direct evidence that might come through. I'm talking about the petrol station where they were last filled up, when the tyres were last changed, anything. Damage, superficial or otherwise. Whatever station the radio might have been tuned into if it's possible to get that. Anything. And I would ask . . .' His voice broke for a second, and he coughed until his throat was clear. 'I would ask that none of you share any details with the press. We'll have another meeting tomorrow morning at nine a.m. Meanwhile, keep in touch on the WhatsApp groups, and let me or DS Slater know the minute you hear anything.'

He dismissed the team with a nod and stepped away from the whiteboard at the front. The chief superintendent stared at him, inscrutable, her arms folded over her uniform, until he approached.

'Ma'am?'

'Someone told me you're flying out of here first thing in the morning?'

'It's something I have to do, ma'am. I prefer to operate this way.'

She nodded. 'So who's in charge, now that Slater's out of the way for a bit?'

'Myles Tait is our point of contact in the city. I'm flying back tomorrow afternoon.'

'I hope you've looked out your expenses form online.'

'Oh, one rule for me, when it comes to expenses,' Lomond said, with half a smile. 'Never file them. Ever.'

16

Lomond closed his eyes and imagined what it would be like to go on a real holiday – cocktails, sand, the coconutty decadence of sun cream, hot tiles under his toes as he padded towards the edge of the pool and then dived into a cool cyan dream. Drip-drying on a sun lounger, stretched out in the heat like a house cat in a sunbeam, cracking the spine on a paperback book – not a murder mystery, of course – and then, then, maybe a beer. He might not even drink very much of it, at first. He might just stare at the bubbles rising up the golden flue, bursting into bloom on a perfect head.

The plane bounced, rumbled, and then they were down. Lomond opened his eyes, saw the beach scrolling past them, white sand under a grey sky. The sea was spread out beyond that, rolling back in with white frosted waves. They had made it to the island, a place that could be just as inviting as a holiday resort abroad when it came to the websites but looked unwelcomingly cold and dark beyond the plane's window.

The young woman beside him opened her eyes too, and then extricated her hand from his. 'That was . . . different,' she said.

'Suppose so,' Lomond said, clearing his throat.

'I didn't know you were afraid of flying, sir.'

'It's the weirdest thing . . . the older I get, the worse it gets. Someone suggested it was because I have more to lose now. Hard to say. My wife does this for me every time we go away . . . I guess I won't be telling her you had to do it too. Thank you. Please don't mention it to anyone else. Especially Slater.'

'My lips are sealed,' she said solemnly.

Lorraine Kemp was the specially trained officer Lomond had seconded on to this trip – the first available flight out, which happened to be a tourist service departing from the Clyde and landing on the beach at one of the islands. It was becoming a key step for island-hoppers and Munro-baggers, and an excited group of them, all aged about twenty-two at the most, had sat behind the two police officers for the duration of the flight. Lomond had been particularly struck by their manners, even as he clutched the armrest of the twelve-seater in stark terror. Good behaviour among young people wasn't the norm for him.

'Just wondering,' Kemp said, unbuckling her seatbelt as the propeller by the window outside her head ceased its revolutions, 'if you'd been on this flight with Slater . . . or Tait . . . what happens? You hold their hands, too?'

Lomond narrowed his eyes, suppressing a smile. 'That's confidential information.'

They had pre-booked a taxi to take them to the house, a winding route through a mountain pass where the dwellings were scarce, except for the bizarre sight of a field filled with wigwams. 'Some expenses claim, this,' Kemp said, staring at the grey smudge of the water beyond the windows. 'Hope you're signing it off for us, sir?'

'Ah, no. It's on me, actually.'

Kemp, who Lomond already knew had little in the way of reserve, even when it came to speaking to senior officers, gasped. 'You what? That can't be right. You're paying for this?'

'I learned something a long time ago, Lorraine,' Lomond said. 'Never claim expenses. Even when it's totally justified.'

'That doesn't make sense. This must have cost you hundreds.'

'Actually . . . the pilot owes me a favour,' Lomond said, a twinkle in his eyes.

'Is that from a case?'

'That's confidential,' Lomond said.

Their mood darkened when they saw the house – Victorian, twin garrets on either side, red sandstone carted over from

Dunbartonshire sometime in the 1800s (Lomond imagined dray horses straining in front of wagons), and strangely foreboding in the gloom of a November morning.

Kemp's mischievousness had entirely disappeared. She had checked her make-up in a compact mirror in the car. Lomond had wondered what might happen if she'd actually tried to reapply it while the car crept up the hill, but knew better than to make any remarks. She was a tall woman of about twenty-eight, with tight red curls tied at the back of her head. She had a pale complexion, and Lomond wondered if she concealed freckles under the make-up. A smile utterly transformed her face, but now her features only expressed calm neutrality.

'Does he have anyone with him?' Kemp asked, as Lomond pressed the bell.

'Not sure,' he said.

Mr Aird Na Murchan was shorter than his social media profiles had made him look. He was about five foot five, and one of the few people in Lomond's orbit over the past few days who made him feel taller than average. He was grey-haired, white-stubbled and brawny, with wide shoulders and big hands. He almost crushed Lomond's as he darted forward to shake them. 'Come in,' he said, in a thick voice. 'You'd better come in.'

Lomond, somewhat startled by the man's swift welcome, said, 'I'm Detective Inspector Lomond, and this is Detective Sergeant Kemp. Is it OK if we come in?'

'Well, no use standing out here, is there?'

'That'd be great,' Lomond said. He followed the man inside, with Kemp following. Knuckles throbbing, Lomond reflected that this was the second time that day he'd had cause to regret his hand being clasped in another's.

*

Barry Aird Na Murchan had worked on the boats, according to the local officers Lomond had already spoken to. When Sheonaid was twelve he had sold his boat and bought the guest house. Judging by the professionalism on show on the website and the block bookings lasting as far as Christmas week, the place was doing well.

Fish on the walls, fish on the banisters, fish on the windowsill as they climbed up three flights of stairs in the wake of the grieving man. It was less of a motif and more of an obsession: there were figurines of fish, some plastic, some ceramic, and many of them crystal, the last casting rainbow beams and shattered prisms of light against the floral print wallpaper. There were paintings of fish parting the water or lying in the brown shade of river hollows. On one occasion there was a photo of a grinning shark, lurking just underneath the surface of a cobalt ocean, its dorsal fin speckled by the sun.

Barry spoke to them as he led the way at some pace; Lomond had to strain to make out what he was saying.

'Excuse the fish. Mostly to do with Sheonaid. Her idea. Her thing, you know? Her and her mother. Funny, they didn't tie it in with me working on the boats, you know? It was like a totally different world. Sheonaid took it further. Always obsessed with mermaids, she was. Always wanting to go to the swimming baths. Her mother wouldn't have her swimming out in the sea. Too dangerous. Currents, riptides. But she did it; she was a great swimmer. The mermaid stuff was something she just picked up again after school. I never knew exactly what she was up to with that, but I left her to it. Best way when they're seventeen, eighteen, still in the hoose . . . You know the score. Keep too tight a leash on them, you get a problem.'

'When did she move out?' Lomond asked, a little out of breath as they reached the top floor, where a forbidding black door opened into a clear, bright kitchen space, with a fine view out into the bay.

'Never,' the little man said. 'She never really left. Came and went, you know? It didn't bother me. I never took a penny off her in dig money. Even when she was earning. She was that sort of spirit. Suppose she got it from me – when I was away on the boats. Her mum was the homemaker. Pushed me into selling the boat and buying this place. She'd got it up and running and turning over money when she died. But I kept on at it, you know? Kept on.' He gestured at a table and chairs. Lomond and Kemp sat down; they both felt extremely awkward when Barry didn't join them at the empty place, but stood against a wall unit and cupboard, arms folded.

'She spent a lot of time in Glasgow, is that right?' Lomond asked.

'She did. I always worried. But I didn't say so. I maybe should have. Maybe.' He scratched his head, twitched slightly, then charged forward.

On instinct, Lomond was already halfway out of his seat before the attack. It had been a long time since he'd had to fend someone off – he'd still been in uniform, in fact – but while he wasn't much use at doing the dancing, he still remembered the moves. The other man's face had morphed into a hateful mask, all twisted lips and acute eyebrows like a dropped anchor.

But it wasn't an attack. It wasn't a charge, either. The man moaned and sagged; Lomond, who had been prepared to bend his assailant's arm out of its socket, instead found himself struggling to hold the little barrel of a man up. Barry was still heavily muscled about the back and shoulders, and Lomond felt his own back sending out a distress signal right up until Kemp realised, well ahead of him, that what was happening was in fact a complete collapse.

'Mr Aird Na Murchan – please,' she said, 'we're going to get you over to this chair, over here. Can you get your balance? Can you?' Kemp's face was red with exertion, but finally they managed to edge the man over to the chair where he landed with a dull impact. His face twitched and trembled – Lomond feared he was having a stroke until Kemp fetched a glass, filled it with water, and put it to his lips.

There were as many words for grief in Lomond's world as

the Inuit had for snow, but there were far fewer words for shock, and this was what the two police officers were seeing now. *May I go my whole life*, Lomond thought, *and never know what this man knows*. 'We're here for you, Mr Aird Na Murchan,' he said. 'Just take your time. You don't have to say anything for now.'

'I maybe should have . . . maybe should have asked her to stay here. She would have done. She would have stayed eventually. The sea was in her blood. It was what she lived for. Lodge in Glasgow for twenty years, she would have found her way back here.'

For the second time that day, Kemp held the hand of a tremulous man, and they let him sob for a while. 'Tell us about her,' she said at last. 'Tell us about the mermaid thing.'

Barry wiped his eyes. 'Just something she always loved. She would draw them, over and over, when she was a kid. Loved the fish, loved the documentaries about them, David Attenborough, that kind of thing. Never happier than when she was in front of a TV screen, with that colour of blue everywhere. You know – colour of swimming pools.'

Lomond nodded. 'Cyan, I think they call it. Aquamarine.'

'Maybe turquoise?' Kemp offered.

'You get the picture.' He took up the glass, but his hand shook so badly that he put it down again before it reached his lips. 'She wanted to draw them, or paint them, but she was never an artist. That frustrated her. She wanted to create stories, so she wrote them. But it took too long. Her mother realised it. She always did. Quick on the uptake, her mother. So was she. Quicker than me, both of them. Doesn't take much, mind.' He laughed, then stopped himself.

At close quarters, Lomond could see, and smell, that the T-shirt he wore could have done with a wash, the same way the man himself could have done with a shave. He'd have to organise the funeral soon, alone. The death certificate. The final plot or spreading of the ashes. One positive, if anything was positive, was that he had a little more time than most grieving parents to sort things out. For now, Chick Minchin and the team had his daughter's body. They would literally strip it to the bone, leave nothing unchecked, look for every clue. Ashamed that this reflection had occurred to him, Lomond said, 'What was her thing, then? What did your wife realise?'

'Film,' Barry said. 'Making movies. They looked into it all. Video cameras at first, a second-hand one that still loaded up tapes. Then the digital stuff came in. Waterproof camera – cost us a bomb, that one. Then she made her own costume, and disappeared into her own wee world. Making her movies. She was a mermaid. A selkie, they call it here. You know what a selkie is?'

Lomond nodded. 'A water horse. Beautiful word, that.'

'It is a beautiful word – but it's no' a water horse. That's a kelpie. A selkie is like a seal person. But she was happy to be known as a mermaid.'

'Oh, right,' Lomond said, slightly embarrassed, and wondering how long he'd been mixing up selkies and kelpies in his life.

'Do you want to see her room? I've no' been in it much. That's for a bit later. Some of your people were already in there . . .'

'Do you mind?' Kemp asked.

'Naw. I want him caught. Take whatever you like. Pack the whole place up, if you like. Catch him.'

'We will. Before we go,' Lomond asked, 'how about boyfriends?'

'She had a couple. Guy called Fraser was the main one. Works on the boats, but never with me. Funny – his da', old Cowan, he runs a guest house at the other side o' the bay. Never put to sea in his life, as a working man. But his boy worked on the boats. Him and Sheonaid – childhood sweethearts. Knew each other since they were five. Partners at their holy communion. You believe that? But there was something in her . . . She wouldn't settle with him. He came here one night when she was in Glasgow doing her filming or studying.

133

I thought he was going to ask permission to propose. But he was lost. A lost soul. He asked what he could do to persuade her. I didn't know what to say. My Olive, she would have known what to say. All I could say to him was, one way or the other, son, you've got to let her go. She'll come back eventually. You're both young. She does love you. And she did, you know.'

'Fraser Cowan? Is that his name?' Lomond asked.

'That's him. Handsome big bugger, to be fair. Blond, you know? Tall, like six-five. Like those boys from the Highlands. There's a Norseman in there. Wouldn't like to wrestle him. Sheonaid was tall, mind.'

'We'll talk to him later.'

Barry shook his head. 'Forget it. He didn't do it. Couldn't have.'

'I talk to everyone I can on a case. Everyone can help.'

'Do you have someone?' Barry asked suddenly, leaning towards Kemp. 'Is there a suspect? You arrested anyone?'

'We've got good leads,' Lomond said. 'It won't be long. We'll get him. Promise.'

'Was there anyone else she mentioned in Glasgow?' Kemp asked.

'Nobody . . . that was a closed book to me. I saw a couple of videos . . . I thought it was weird. I never quite got it. I knew to stay away. Never stood in her way. Was it dance, was it synchronised swimming? I'll never know . . .'

'Did she ever mention anyone on the filming side?' Kemp asked again, very gently. 'Anyone at all?'

'Sorry. No one. I only ever asked how she was. Fine, she told me. Always fine. Two days before it happened, tae. Her last words to me: "I'm fine, Dad."'

'Do you mind if I have a look now?' Lomond got to his feet. 'I promise I won't take anything away. You can come with me, if you like.'

'You're fine,' Mr Aird Na Murchan said, somewhat impatiently. 'I'll stay here. Not ready to have a good look myself.

It's pretty much the way she left it when she went away, about six weeks ago. They've been in to look already, like I said.'

Lomond got to his feet. 'Is it . . . ?' He gestured towards the door at the far end of the kitchen.

'Through the hallway there. First on your right.'

Lomond expected Barry to come with him. But the broad, squat man stayed where he was, and turned away from Lomond to gaze out towards the bay. Lomond shared a glance with Kemp. She gave a tiny nod, barely noticeable as a gesture. Then he opened the door and went into the dead girl's room.

*

He was surprised to see it so tidy. He'd have to ask her father if he had rearranged things in any way. The bed was made up and its blankets were folded underneath the mattress to almost military standard. The quilt cover was a mahogany colour which Lomond quite liked; the pillowcases were starched white, bleached out. Barry had hinted that he was slapdash and been kept in check by his wife, but there must have been a clean and tidy element to him in order to succeed with a bed and breakfast. Certainly, the reviews Lomond had read on price comparison sites and elsewhere had been very high when it came to cleanliness, though some commentators were less than enamoured with all the fish.

The walls were decorated with prints of the sea – tropical waves in one case, and in another a frigid Arctic blue with an off-balance iceberg shot through with turquoise which actually elicited a shiver in Lomond. One framed print showed two grotesque fish, huddled together in a jewelled coral cave and cast in an unhealthy blue light, with their mouths agape in the manner of eels, their eyes hard little grapes. The word 'hagfish' was on the tip of Lomond's tongue, or maybe even 'wolf-fish', but he didn't know for sure. There was some text superimposed over the image at the bottom: *Just the two of us.*

135

Lomond flipped the picture over. A handwritten inscription was on the other side, in a tiny, diffident hand that Lomond had to stare hard at to make out. *To Shinnie. Love always. Fraser.* No kisses.

As he replaced the picture, Lomond noticed the tiny apertures pressed into the wallpaper, which wasn't new. Tack holes. She'd had posters, Lomond thought. He wondered at them – pop stars? Maybe not. Sheonaid had probably been one of those animal-crazy kids. Without closing his eyes he could visualise the rectangles of light showing other undersea scenes, their corners plotted out by the tack holes. In his own house, Siobhan's wall had been a barroom brawl of pictures of pop stars cut out of magazines, the staples eased out of the way but still somehow getting under Lomond's thumbs. First the teeny-pop idols, and then the boy bands of course, graduating to other boy bands who had the alternative selling points of long hair and guitars and piercings. Some of these pop stars remained on her wall; whether through some ironic nods towards the person she used to be, genuine lingering affection or laziness, Lomond was unsure.

But Sheonaid's room was clean and tidy. No clothes piled up on the chair. On the dressing table against the far wall were jewellery boxes picked clean, a horizontal mirror marked with what might have been Post-it note wounds, and bangles and other jewellery left on a pewter hook. Nice piece of work, that, Lomond thought of the latter, noting the scrollwork. Hand-made.

One concession to the girl who had called this place home, and had grown up here from the age of twelve – a hairbrush, left at the far corner of the dresser, spikes poking upward. It was threaded with fine black hairs. Lomond had the temerity to touch them. The girl's hair looked thick in the images he'd seen, but he barely felt it beneath his fingertips.

You made connections – you had to, really. There was no way to detach entirely, and Lomond wouldn't have wanted to.

In a way it helped him to remember days spent with his daughter, helping her through her difficult and volatile teenage years. It had pained him when she had become a stranger for a while, when his mere presence had been enough to offend her. If something happened to her, Lomond wondered, would it be the points of conflict that he would remember? Harsh words, his patience tested to its limits, the insults hurled at him in response? Or would he remember that for the most part he had been nothing less than loving, a man who hugged his wife and daughter easily? Would grief choke and kill him by slow degrees, as it almost surely would Sheonaid Aird Na Murchan's father?

He closed his eyes for a few moments in what seemed a deep, absolute silence, and allowed the image of his daughter to fade, as if sinking in a dark pool. He allowed the black-haired mermaid to return, her beautiful locks billowing in a gentle current, completely freed. Not the figure irretrievably changed under Minchin's blade, an obscene intimacy Lomond never got used to, but the girl from the videos and the JPEGs.

He opened her drawers and cupboards, systematically, looking through them. He sought the signs of secrets, the Xs that marked the spot, and soon found a pile of letters bundled up in an old shoebox. From Fraser, addressed to her. The same tight-packed lettering. A random one showed they'd been lovers, all right. Lomond's fingers were quicker and more subtle than many of the criminals' he had put away; he even replaced the elastic bands around the letters before slipping them back into the box.

In one cupboard – a fine oaken old-timer with an iron key in the outside lock – he found one of her costumes, bright turquoise sequins decorating a neoprene-style sleeve. It would have hugged her hips and legs tight. She would have had no option but to perform her weird undulations beneath the waves in that, he thought, pinching the edge. No chance for her to kick. All the while, every scale glistening. Perhaps the dazzling electrical-charge-blue rippling across her lower body would have drawn the eye of predators.

It did, he thought grimly. A great big nasty one.

He wasn't looking for anything in particular, but he got his moment. A justification for the trip out here: a vindication for his gut feelings.

In the back of the wardrobe was an old battle-scarred backpack, cicatriced with half a dozen examples of teenage graffiti. They had called these scrawls and tags menshies when Lomond was a kid, a corruption of mentions, though he supposed such names changed every few years. Bombs, he had heard them called not too long ago. The bag was quite a good size, bigger than a weekend holdall or something Sheonaid might have taken to college. The double zip around the front of the backpack had a padlock.

Lomond fiddled with his Swiss army knife, extending the pick. Within moments he had the bag open.

Inside, slotted into a clear plastic wallet, were A5-sized prints. Lomond slid on a pair of surgical gloves without looking at his hands, wincing slightly at the unpleasant pinch and contraction on his skin, took the wallet by the very edge and lifted it up. Inside was a series of images, the first one white, red and solid black. Lomond had no idea what he was looking at; it seemed abstract, a type of art he'd never cared for, whether before, during or after the gnomic explanation. But something in the composition bothered him. It looked like light stippling turbid waters, and below the surface was a spreading cloud of redness.

★

Lomond made sure he had tucked the gloves firmly into his inside pocket. He smiled at Barry, who looked up from the table, where he sat very close to Kemp. She also smiled kindly and nodded more decisively than she had before.

'Everything all right?' Barry said, his voice thick. Lomond noted his eyes were bright red.

'All good. But I'm afraid we're going to have to get a forensic unit in.'

'What . . . now?' The man had gone white. 'But I've got guests . . .'

'Guests – right now?'

'Aye. Work, you know. Have to keep on, don't I? Have to keep this place going. It's all I've got, inspector. What do you need forensics in for? Have you found something?'

Lomond didn't answer directly. 'You said Sheonaid wasn't artistic. Is that right? I mean, visual arts, that kind of thing?'

'Yep. Never drew seriously. Wee designs for her costumes, but they were just outlines. Sketches. She had pals to sort out the detail, then make them up for her.'

'No visual arts, paintings, that sort of thing?'

He shook his head. 'No. Nothing like that. Like I say – creative, just on the photography and video side o' things.'

'There're some things in there we'll need to check.' Lomond sighed, taking his phone out of his jacket. 'It's going to take a while. I'm so sorry.'

★

Lomond had barely begun to discuss it with Kemp before they noticed the young man detaching himself from the lamp post and approaching – a little too fast for the detective inspector's liking.

'Hold up,' Lomond said, but Kemp, her antennae far more fine-tuned than his, had already intercepted the newcomer, laying a hand on his arm.

He was as tall as Aird Na Murchan had said, blond, broad, not much past twenty, probably in his prime, and if he'd wanted to try anything unpleasant there wasn't much either of them could have done about it unless they were very lucky.

He didn't glare at them, exactly, but there was a horrible purpose somewhere in him.

'Help you, son?' Lomond asked quietly.

'You the polis?'

'We are. You must be Fraser.'

'I think . . . I wondered if you wanted to talk to me.'

'We do. Were just on our way to knock your door, in fact. Saves a bit of time. We're going to walk down to the seafront. Fancy coming with us?'

He hesitated. 'I thought you'd want to talk to me down at the station?'

'Is there a reason for us to talk to you down at the station?'

'Well . . . Just in case I'm a suspect.' The hardness melted into uncertainty, callow as it came. Lomond wanted to laugh. He did.

'If you were a suspect, my man, you'd be sitting in the cells right now, worrying about things. C'mon, you can show us a better way down to the beach, if there is one. We followed the direct route on our phones on the way up the street, and that will be murder on my arches.'

★

Fraser responded more willingly to Kemp's questioning, so Lomond left her to it. A cool breeze had come in from the water, and Lomond enjoyed it, cooling the sweat that prickled his brow. Their feet sank in the white sand so far and no more before they moved on. Lomond did not find the sensation unpleasant, as if the land itself had a tide. A hundred yards down the beach, the water rolled in, grey beneath clouds, fizzing over the rock formations, spitting out seaweed.

'I did love her,' Fraser said, faltering on those last two words. 'I thought she loved me. But she had things to do, places to go. She said she would be with me eventually, but first she wanted to build up her portfolio, her career. I never got into it, never

140

followed it, never understood what she wanted. I mean . . . mermaids?' Again, his voice began to fail him. Instinctively, Kemp laid a hand on his arm, and his face crumpled.

'This has been a terrible shock,' she told him. 'Not many people go through anything like this. It's too big a thing to think about, and it's too big a thing to go through on your own. You will need help. And I'm going to make sure you get it.'

'Take your time, son,' Lomond said. His instinct was to comfort the lad too, despite a few literal rough edges. Lomond noted a severely bent nose, and indentations along his jawline that looked like a kiss goodnight from a broken bottle. But he was no more than a boy, for all that. Lomond deferred to Kemp, but he studied Fraser closely, every flicker of the eyes, every twitch of the hands, the slope of the shoulders.

'She was always into it. I knew her at school. There were eight of us, the entire roll. Had the same teacher all the way through – Mrs Duncan. Me and Sheonaid were the same age. We were together all the time, from when we were seven or eight. Everyone acted as if we were married already. I loved her hair. Her black hair.' He fashioned a wave around about his own shoulders, miming the flow of her locks. Bizarrely, Lomond imagined Slater's ghost, mocking this gesture at his ear.

'When we were teenagers we were together, and I thought that would be it . . . Rest of our lives, y'know? But she wanted other things. Always mad about the swimming. I knew I'd work on the boats, but she loved the beach, the creatures on it, the crabs, even the mussels and barnacles. She woke me up in the middle of the night once because there was a rumour that there was a humpback whale out in the bay. We never saw it. I stayed all night with her, out there on the sands. Thermos flask and a blanket . . . When she was about sixteen, she saw a video online. A real mermaid. Down in Dorset or Cornwall or somewhere like that. And that was it. Like the missing piece, y'know? She was going to be the Selkie. Started making videos, going to Glasgow, contacting film-makers, meeting people . . . I'll be honest, I was jealous. It wasn't for me. My dad, he knew somebody who worked on the boats, got me started. I knew I'd stay here. Never wanted to go anywhere else. And I knew I'd lose her. But she said she would come back. Whatever she did, wherever she went . . . And she always did. It was . . . hard. I was jealous, I suppose. I don't think she ever . . . I can't be sure.' His eyes were red. He could hardly look at Lomond.

'Did you meet any of the people she knew through her videos?'

'Aye. Boy called Finn. Dunno if it was short for something, probably was. Plummy-voiced prick. Sorry,' he said to Kemp. 'We had a bit of a row one night . . . he chipped my tooth, the bastard. But he regretted it. A few times over.' Fraser smiled at this recollection – not a pleasant expression. 'Came back to make the film with her, right enough. I admired him for that. He was the camera guy. Knew scuba diving, and snorkelling. Took her out in the bay, filmed her underwater . . . Got her the gigs abroad. I think he went with her. I can't be sure. Something weird was happening. I got used to it. It was like whenever she was away, she turned into someone else. I didn't want to know. I could pull the shutters down on it. But she always came back.'

'We'll speak to this Finn,' Lomond said peremptorily. 'Was she into anything other than her performances? As the Selkie?'

'How d'you mean?'

'Was there photography. Or art?'

'Paintings and that?' Fraser almost barked this.

'Anything like that. Theatre or film maybe – apart from her online videos?'

'Well.' He hesitated. 'There was something she was into. One night, about three in the morning she sent me . . . well, I don't like to show you. Kind of private.'

Lomond, who knew more about Sheonaid Aird Na Murchan's body than Fraser ever would, nodded solemnly. 'If you would prefer to show it to Lorraine, that's no problem, son. Anything you can tell us will be a help.'

'Here,' Fraser said, clicking through his phone. 'You can see . . . There it is. That's what she sent.'

'Is that a painting?' Kemp asked, taking the phone from him. 'It's very lifelike.'

'Aye. She sent that, three in the morning. A Sunday morning. We were just bringing a catch in when I got it. Three a.m. She's naked. "What do you think? Amazing, eh?" That was the only thing she said. I never asked her, but I was . . . I was seething with it. What am I supposed to think? I mean, what was that in aid of? Was I meant to be pleased? Nude paintings? On top of the mermaid stuff, taking her clothes off on the internet for any old wank stain?

'I was starting to think she was a weirdo. She was winding me up. Maybe she thought I'd be pleased. I couldn't bring myself to speak about it. If I was angry, I'd spit at her. And that meant I'd lose. Maybe that was the idea. Maybe that's what she wanted . . . wind me up so I'd get angry. So she could make the break. So she could be free.' He was silent for a moment. Perhaps this was the first time it had occurred to him. 'But I was saving, you know. Saving for a ring. A good one. One anyone would be proud of. I was going to talk to her da . . . We got close after his wife died. He told me, again and again – you're going to be my son-in-law. But now I won't.'

No one looking at Lomond's face would have known his inner tumult. Perhaps a deliquescent quality to his dark eyes, in a certain light, might have tipped off someone who knew him well. Other than that, he was a study in calm, even benevolence. He cleared his throat, and said, 'Son, it's very important that I look at the picture. Do you believe me?'

'Will it catch him?'

'It'll help rule someone out. Or . . . it'll mean I get on the phone and have someone arrested in the next five minutes.'

Wordlessly, Fraser took back his phone and handed it to Lomond.

It was her, all right. Nude, lying back in the sand. The

texture of the brush – he assumed it must have been a painting, though it might have fooled the eye into thinking it was a photograph – had caught the golden grain very well. It shone, glossy, as though the tide had just retreated, leaving a perfectly flat, perfectly smooth surface. Sheonaid's hair was spread out behind her head in all directions, as if she was underwater. Her eyes were closed, her chin tilted back at an almost unnatural angle. There was something which might have been powerfully erotic about the image had the observer not seen Sheonaid Aird Na Murchan in the same pose with her throat slit.

'Well?' Fraser said, jaw muscles bunching.

'I'm not arresting anyone,' Lomond said, 'but it's a very good clue. We'll need the file. And anything else she might have sent you.'

★

Back on the plane, Lomond scribbled notes at incredible speed. He peeled back the pages as the engines began. A fine rain began to dot the windows, tiny droplets slanting upwards, like bubbles escaping.

'Penny for them?' Kemp asked.

'It's the art, isn't it?' Lomond said. 'It's the art.'

'Erskine Copper?'

Lomond hesitated. 'It's a different style, I think. Same face, but painted in a totally different way. This one's very realistic. Erskine Copper's more . . . expressionistic, is that the word?'

'Impressionistic, I think you mean.'

'Aye. Even without knowing it I could probably have told you that the swimming-pool mural was done by him – his faces look like they're carved out of granite, like blocks, all proper angles, like the Giant's Causeway, you know? Pentagonal, multi-faceted . . . what's the word?'

Kemp didn't know, but she couldn't interrupt her boss.

'Anyway, this face is different. Naturalistic, maybe. I'm no expert. But I'm going to talk to someone who is.'

144

He capped his pen, then placed it and the notebook in his inside coat pocket and rested his head against the seat. Kemp glanced at his hand, expecting it to reach instinctively for hers, as it had done back in Glasgow once the propellers cleared their throats and began to turn. But Lomond's hand was relaxed on the armrest. Kemp was astonished to see that he had fallen asleep in a matter of seconds.

17

Slater saw her running through the rain, a dark streak through the windscreen with a takeaway coffee in her hand. When she reached to open the passenger-side door, it was still locked. Flustered, Slater scanned the dashboard until he found the right button.

'I'm so, so sorry,' he said, when Smythe got in. 'I must have had the automatic lock on . . . Tell you the truth, I've not even looked at the manual. It locks itself.'

'It's absolutely fine,' she said, though Slater could see it wasn't. Her blonde hair was dripping wet, as were the shoulders of her long dark coat. 'My fault for grabbing a coffee and chancing the weather. At least it'll warm me up.'

Slater pulled into rush-hour traffic, the windscreen wipers fighting hard against the downpour. 'Now it's winter,' he remarked, as the queue of traffic stopped for a red light. Just ahead, he stared longingly at the bright portal marking the entrance to a café. Through the beaded driver's side window, Slater fancied he could see steam rising from a mug of tea on the counter inside. He pictured the grease on the paper bags containing the bacon rolls, the transparent promise of salted pork. His stomach grumbled.

'Take us a while to get out of here this morning,' Smythe said.

'Yeah.' Slater would normally have cracked a joke or two by now, but something about Smythe's poise set him on edge. Her reserve was something he couldn't have discussed logically or reasonably, like a joke or a nasty comment that got through his defences, or a buried memory of something unpleasant.

He had wondered if it might have been that he found her attractive; he had asked himself the question honestly. But he didn't think so. She had a coldness to her that discomfited him – a sense that he might ask her questions all day, and never get closer to the person she was. Perhaps that was the issue. Perhaps it was because he had to work hard to gain her attention, never mind her trust or affection, and he resented this. Like any other daftie. An old man at the pub, snarling at the barmaid for not smiling enough. Is that who he was? Deep down, was that how he dealt with a woman who might be cleverer than he was?

Park it, Malc, he thought. *Park it for now.*

'You want some of my coffee?' she asked.

Slater laughed. 'For real? Two's on your latte?'

'I'll have you know it's a mochaccino.'

'Even better! All right, you're on – I'll take a swig.'

'It's a bit hot,' she said, handing it over.

'Not a problem.' Slater took a careful sip, but he burned his tongue anyway, hiding the pain fairly well. 'So . . . we've got a decent run at it,' he said, handing the cup back as the lights changed. 'Shame about the weather. On a clear day it's beautiful up there.'

'It's a strange gig,' Smythe said. 'I must admit, I was hoping to be by the seaside with the gaffer today.'

'He always wants to have a talk with the family. The phone won't do, he says.'

'Does he always send you off on little side-missions like this one?'

'No. But I know he wouldn't take us off the board in Glasgow unless it was important.'

'Seems like a wild goose chase,' Smythe said. 'Level with me – you think Torin MacAllister is a murderer? The Tory messiah? Guy who's probably going to take a seat next month? *Here*?'

'Hard to say,' Slater said. 'We both know it – some guys, they kill people, they'll sit across the table from you and just lie and lie and lie. Even after you've told them what the truth is.

They're naturals. Rafferty – MacAllister – is also a politician, so he scores double points there. Only way it could be worse is if he was a journalist. But I have to say . . . I don't dislike the guy. But he's a Tory, so, y'know, he has that in the debit column.'

Smythe made no comment and betrayed no reaction to this last remark.

'His two mates are more interesting,' Slater said.

'Donald Ward? Gerry Finlay?'

'That's them. Now, the artist: Ward. Guy looks like he's on the wacky baccy. Did you ever meet guys like that, at school or just after, sort of permanently stoned rich kids? Ward made me think of that.'

'Can't say I remember anyone like that,' Smythe said, sipping her coffee.

'And the lawyer, that lump of a guy, Finlay. Without a d. Getting a "wrong 'un" vibe off him. Which I know isn't strictly scientific, before you jump down my throat.'

'So you think one of them was involved?'

'There's just something not right. If I didn't know about the dead girl in the pond all those years ago I would still feel uncomfortable. They seem . . . weirdly tight with each other. Even for a bunch of schoolmates. That stuff usually drops off by the time you're thirty. It's weird to see it continuing in three guys in middle age.'

'Stuff? What stuff?'

Slater shrugged. 'Fraternity. Looking out for your pals, having them look out for you. Like the Musketeers. It's usually burnt off by the time wives and mortgages come along, and maybe kids. These guys still have a close relationship. Makes you think.'

'I don't know if it's weird. They're friends. You've got friends, haven't you?'

'Course I have.' Actually, outside guys he knew in the police he might have a very rare beer with, Slater had hardly spent time with anyone he might have termed a 'friend' in years.

Even some of the people he'd known as a boy or a young man had drifted away from his locked-down social media channels, quietly unfollowing or unfriending him in the shady valleys online where old friendships came to die.

'Well, there you go,' Smythe said. 'They're just friends.'

Slater squinted into the rain as they got onto Great Western Road. 'Here's a thing, though. They're still really close mates, yes?'

Smythe shrugged. 'I guess.'

'So what's the glue that connects them, after all this time, and three separate careers? What keeps things fresh in the friendship? I'd say . . . guilt. Collective, mutual guilt.'

'Guilt over the girl in the pond?'

'For sure. It's dodgy as sin. Whether it's connected to our two girls, I don't know. But the gaffer's got a bee in his bonnet, that's clear.'

'We'll find out more today,' Smythe said. 'I'm certain of it.'

★

The rain let up as they went past Drumchapel and Clydebank, and finally onto the A82, where a blue sky began to peek through the clouds as the backgrounds got more rugged. The Sleeping Warrior came and went. Slater experienced an improvement in his mood. Partially it was the fugitive glee at getting out of school for a while – he had handed over to Tait that morning in a rare good humour – and partially it was memories of trips out to Loch Lomond in his father's car as a boy. Happy memories of being enclosed in greenery, as if fired through a lush tunnel out of the grey city. This atmosphere seemed to have infected Smythe as well – or perhaps it was the coffee she'd sunk.

'Lana Galbraith, then. That's why we're out here, aye?' Slater said.

'That's right.'

149

'Lassie who was on the telly? One of the two mystery girls who went to the hunting lodge with Rafferty and Ward?'

'That's her.'

'Let's do a quiz. What do you know about her?'

'You mean, you want me to fill you in on the bits of the brief you missed?'

'Aye, that as well,' Slater said, grinning.

'Society girl. Had stints on MTV Europe and one or two other arts shows in the mid-nineties. Scotland's answer to the It Girls – Victoria Hervey, Tara Palmer-Tomkinson, that kind of thing.'

'Always fancied Tara Palmer-Tomkinson, I have to admit.'

'Shame she died.'

'What?' Slater barked. 'You're kidding.'

'Nope. Died very young.'

'I did not know that.'

'Perforated ulcer, they say. Still in her forties.'

'God . . . that's so sad. When was this?'

'Dunno . . . about 2017, maybe?'

'I don't know how I missed that. Busy, I guess. Don't always see the news, unless I'm involved in it.' He scratched his chin. 'Shaken me up a bit, that.'

'Anyway . . . you get the idea. Lana was the Scottish It-Girl. Good-looking lassie.'

'I remember. Redhead, right?'

'Think she was blonde for a phase, too. Changed it after the Spice Girls came out. Too much like Geri, they said. She had one of those sort of Kelvinside accents, used to get on my mum's nerves when she appeared on that Scottish arts show. But she dropped off the scene quite quickly. A couple of stories in the tabloids. "What happened to Lana Galbraith?" kind of thing.'

'Drugs, wasn't it?'

'Yep. The big one. Heroin. She was in and out of various detox places, AA, that type of stuff, but they were no good for her. Parents are big landowners, grandfather owned a distillery:

mega money, mega conservative. So they paid for her to enter treatment. And this is where it gets interesting for us.'

'This is where we get the connection with Daisy Lawlor?'

'She was one of the two girls who apparently provided an alibi for Torin MacAllister, aka Torquod Rafferty, the Earl of Strathdene's son. Apparently, they'd all gone to a shooting lodge miles away on the night Daisy Lawlor was killed and dumped on Rafferty Landing. No mention if Lana was romantically involved with any of them.'

'Did you get back to the ex-copper who worked the Lawlor case? Whicklow, was it? One of the SIOs?'

'Yep. He didn't tell me to fuck off this time. Bit of a breakthrough. He told me without telling me that although the alibis were watertight, he thought Lana Galbraith was lying. He couldn't name the other lassie who was there. Neither could Ward or Rafferty. Strange.'

'Whicklow was told to back off that inquiry, wasn't he? Some funny handshakes business going on, if you ask me. I'm sure of it.'

'Well, you tell me,' Smythe said. 'Surely you're in the Masons?'

'What? Me? You must be kidding. Sooner cut my hand off than join any secret societies.'

'Pity. You could have found out what happened at Rafferty Landing.'

'Aye. And who Jack the Ripper was. Anyway. What's the deal with Lana Galbraith? Didn't she die young?'

Smythe nodded. 'Car crash. Out of her mind on drink. Decided to drive to an off-licence to get some more booze once she'd run out of Cristal. Didn't make it. Loch Lomond got in the way. June 2001, this was. She was twenty-five.'

'Wasn't there a horrible urban rumour she was decapitated?'

'She wasn't, but she must have died instantly. Out the window. Into a shale cutting. Then rebounded into the water. I saw the photos in the file.'

'Jesus,' Slater whispered. They drove in silence for a moment.

'So,' Smythe said finally, 'we're here to find out about the person Whicklow told us about. The person who sent him a letter – a personal letter – explaining that Lana Galbraith knew a bit more about what happened that night than she ever let on. A fellow resident at the place we're going to now.'

Slater glanced at the clock on the dashboard. 'They're not going to let us look at the files without a court order, are they?'

'Doubt it. But there's nothing stopping us talking to people. It's a private facility. And I have a trick or two up my sleeve.'

★

Slater wondered if the person who met them in the foyer of the grand hall had dressed up especially for the occasion. Marilyn Brownlie was somewhere in her forties and had a bleached, ascetic look that seemed to have stripped her of much of her humanity, as if she had been dipped in lye. It could be said that her hair and features were immaculate, but not attractive. Her eyes were piercing, stark black above very pale skin, a little bit like an impressionistic artwork of a hated teacher. Her hand was dry when Slater shook it, and he had a feeling that it might leave a powdery residue on his own when he inspected it. Had she revealed that she was wearing a mask, it wouldn't have been a huge shock.

Slater, who had been told many times that his first impressions of people were sometimes atrocious, and he should work on this aspect of his character, made a mental note not to mention any of these considerations to Smythe.

With the formalities done, Brownlie smiled and folded her hands. 'Welcome to Kirrin Hall. We can have tea in the cafeteria, if you like?'

'That'd be lovely,' Smythe said.

They followed the woman down a corridor into the main hall itself, as grand as the name implied. The room was oak-panelled, dominated by a heraldic shield over the fireplace showing a lion rampant, and a chandelier hanging from the ceiling. It was in want of a long table, soft furnishings in the corners having taken the place of one. A sullen-looking young man with long hair tied back sat reading a green cloth-bound book from one of the shelves. Slater thought it was slightly jarring that a room which had clearly seen some drunken revelry in its time should be dedicated to a lifestyle that was the polar opposite. Slater had imagined somewhere neat, clean and clinical, with white walls and white uniforms. Instead, Kirrin Hall had the look of an ennobled youth hostel. When they came in people had been coming and going in the grounds with no obvious signs of security, but when Brownlie led them outside again into a vast stone courtyard – Slater pictured medieval archery tournaments taking place here, with goblets dashed against flagstones – the ominously squat, functional buildings where the real business of residency was conducted came into view.

'Amazing place,' Smythe commented, as they headed towards the security door into the complex.

'Isn't it?' Brownlie said, grinning. Her accent was hard to trace – perhaps a touch of the Midlands, though she spoke at a gratingly slow pace, like a toy whose batteries were running flat. 'The Hall was bequeathed to the charity by Sir Alfred Kirrin in the sixties. He had well-known issues with alcohol but managed to conquer them, and he never forgot the help he received. It gave him a purpose, once the bottle was gone; he set up a trust. The rest of the buildings appeared in the eighties.'

'Seems expensive,' Slater said, and Brownlie frowned. A real expression, at last.

'We have provision for people from all walks of life to come here. Addiction's a disease that runs through society. Well – you're police officers; I don't need to tell you about the consequences of substance abuse. Maybe you even know some fellow officers with problems? Trauma must be a big part of the picture in your line of work. Addiction follows.'

'Everyone knows someone,' Smythe said. 'And if you don't, maybe it's you.'

'That is very true. Drugs, alcohol . . . even sex addiction.' Brownlie turned towards Slater as she said this last part. With considerable effort, he mustered calm, sobriety, even seriousness, when what he wanted to do was laugh in her face. 'We get them all here, all ages, all stages in life.'

'How long have you worked here?' Smythe asked.

'Since May 1989. Beautiful weather. One of the best springs and summers I can remember out here. Only one that came close to it was 1995.'

Slater studied Brownlie's face for any trace of irony or malice. There was none: just that peculiarly gruesome smile, a doll in a shop window that you didn't want to look at for too long. 'That was a very interesting year,' he said. 'That's the year we've come to talk about. You would have been well established here by then, is that right?'

'Oh, I'm in with the bricks. Kind of a personal mission for me now, as well as a job.'

'How's that?'

'As your colleague here just said, everyone knows someone. It's something of a crusade with me, now.'

The canteen was surprisingly lively. Slater wasn't sure what he was going to see – perhaps his mind had been unconsciously poisoned by *One Flew Over the Cuckoo's Nest* or any number of depictions of mental hospitals in films and television. He'd thought everyone would be in white. The odd Victorian-era hysteric might not have seemed too outlandish. But instead, it was just . . . lunchtime. A normal cafeteria, with perhaps a few too many cheese plants and other green things poking out of every corner. There were some spare tables, but there was normal conversation, the customers looked sensible enough, although one man had an unusual pallor on him, a terrible mustard yellow colour.

Slater spied a rocky road slice under glass on a cake stand,

and instantly wondered what might be more beneficial – buying the slice and saving it for Lomond or eating it himself and gloating about how good it had been.

Brownlie insisted upon buying the detectives coffee, and soon they were seated at a table in a corner, being eyed with some suspicion. Slater had always wondered if there was something about him that simply stated 'polis' wherever he went. A dodgy cousin had once said this to him, even before he had decided to join the force. 'It's like a video game, mate,' the cousin had said, 'a wee light blinking on the top o' your head. You're screaming "polis" at me. Going nee-naw.'

Smythe said, 'We know that you're very busy, so we won't take up too much of your time. We're here to talk about something you might have heard about in the news.'

'Oh yes?' Brownlie's expression was earnest. Slater noticed she hadn't touched her coffee since she had set it down on the table, with steam curling up from the cup.

'The two girls who were found dead in the water these past few days,' he said.

'The Ferryman?' Brownlie said, too loudly.

Slater ground his teeth. He had a name now. Like Bible John. Or Mr Flick. 'That's the tabloid name. Off the record, we believe there may be a connection between this case – a very, very tenuous connection – and Kirrin Hall.'

Now Brownlie frowned. 'I'm not sure I follow. Were the girls residents here?'

'Not that we're aware of,' Smythe said. Her tone was softer than it was in her dealings with colleagues, Slater noticed. Either she had the gift of appearing emotionally invested or she was better at putting on the mask. Either way, it was something Slater envied. 'This is more of a historical link, going back to 1995. We believe there is someone who was a resident here back then who could help us with our inquiries.'

'Our patient files are confidential,' Brownlie stated. She lifted her coffee, sniffed at it, blew on the surface, then placed it back on the table, undrunk. 'I'm sure you understand.'

'We do,' Slater said. 'And we'd rather not go to the time and trouble of getting a court order to have the books opened – either for you or for us. We're trying to catch a very dangerous man. Now, the link is tenuous, as I said, but we have to investigate every lead we get. We're here about someone who stayed here in 1995. Lana Galbraith.'

'I know exactly who Lana Galbraith was,' the administrator responded. 'I'm happy to talk about that since she's no longer with us. It was a horrible case, but we can't save everyone. It's the nature of the beast.'

Smythe said, 'Dreadful case. So young. So much to offer.'

'She was just twenty-five when she died. A star, even in here. She drew people to her. So much charisma and talent.'

So much money, Slater thought, sourly.

'She enjoyed the fast lane too much, in more than one way. It happens. Some stars burn out. She kept some bad company and any intervention that was staged just didn't work. Some people desperately want to change. They need help, they beg for help, they get the help . . . and they respond. She was in that mould. She tried her hardest. But out there, in the world of celebrities . . . it doesn't happen. She's a forgotten figure now. Young people have no idea who she is. If she was a singer or an actress there'd be a whole cult around her. She'd be worshipped, kept in their memories. Lana Galbraith is someone their fathers might remember being on the cover of *FHM*.'

'We want to know about the people Lana was in here with,' Slater said. 'There might have been someone she got close to – someone she confided in. That person might have information that could help us with the case we're investigating today. Any names you could give us, on or off the record, would be a help.'

'As I said, the files are confidential,' Brownlie said. 'People come here to be anonymous, fight their addictions, and move on. You know how many times the tabloid press have tried to infiltrate us? Twice this year, three times last year.'

'We totally understand,' Smythe said. 'Why don't you take us to your office, and perhaps talk a bit more about Lana Galbraith? If something was to come up, something you haven't thought of till now, then I'm sure you'd tell us if you could. It could help preserve Lana's memory, in a way.'

'This man . . . the Ferryman,' Brownlie asked. 'They say he cuts their throats. Is that right?'

'We're not allowed to say anything about the case,' Slater said. 'Confidentiality.'

'Then I don't see the link . . . I'm sorry,' Brownlie said. 'Lana Galbraith was here a long time ago. There are probably files and notes somewhere on the system – I think we'd become computerised by then, and we do keep our filing in good order. But I don't see how this could help you in any way.'

'Someone who knew Lana might have information from a connected case. One that took place the year Lana came to Kirrin Hall.'

'Oh – the girl at Rafferty Landing, you mean? The one they found in the pond? Why didn't you say?'

Slater and Smythe caught each other's eye, perplexed.

The smile was back again. Brownlie wiped her hands on a napkin. 'Once we finish our coffee, come on up to the office. I'll see what I can find.'

⋆

This was more like it, Slater mused – a dark corridor, a winding staircase up the turret of the main hall. 'This is my office,' Brownlie told them outside a heavy, black-painted door. 'It seems a bit gothic on the way up, but you'll see why I like it.'

The door had her name inscribed on a brass plate. It looked like a place not many people came to visit. Natural light was somewhat strained through ornate but tiny windows on the way up. It felt a bit like a janitor having his name printed on the cupboard where they kept the vacuum cleaners. Then she opened the door into a space so bright that it hurt the eyes for a moment or two. Windows on three sides of the turret; views across green space; patches of blue sky up above.

'I see what you mean,' Smythe said. 'I'd kill to have an office like this.'

'No pun intended, I hope,' Brownlie said – and was that a bit of a smirk? Slater wondered if he was starting to like her. She indicated two chairs in front of a stiff, black-lacquered desk, and booted up a very new, very expensive-looking desktop computer.

'I think you understand the need for confidentiality,' she told them. 'As I said before, whether we get royalty or people who've been found on the streets by their families and brought here, they deserve anonymity.'

'But you keep very detailed files?' Slater asked.

'Of course.' She seemed surprised by the question. 'This isn't a holiday camp. People die here.'

'I know. My first murder on the CID was a death at a care home, very like this place,' Slater said. 'Elderly man choked with a chicken bone . . . very nasty case. Proved it, too. Senior staff member had had herself written into his will. She made it look as if one of the carers had done it, a Polish girl. Horrible. The perpetrator's still in jail.'

'That would be Carruthers and Stott. About eleven years ago now . . . I remember it.' Brownlie did not look away from her screen as her fingers worked the keyboard. 'Here it is. Records of 1996, in fact, not 1995 . . . And here she is, Lana Galbraith. Just eighteen when she came here. Cocaine addiction, alcohol . . . she got clean and sober within three weeks.' She turned to Smythe, who had been taking notes. 'Anything I show you or tell you is strictly off the record. I am happy to comply, here. I'll answer your questions. But I can't let you print anything out or see the screen.'

'I understand,' Slater said. 'But I also need you to understand that if we need to, we'll have to see what you've got on your computer. It might end up in court.'

'I'm well aware of that. But there are rules – I don't just open up confidential files for anyone who asks.' She didn't say this unreasonably. 'You'll see the difficulty.'

Smythe said, 'Did Lana Galbraith have friends here? I'm not sure how detailed your files are.'

'Quite detailed. We take a very scientific approach to recovery – though it still sometimes looks like chaos. That's been the case since this place opened in the sixties. Our founder was a visionary, in his way. He understood that the human side has to be balanced up with data. Even if it's down to heights and weights. That's how we measure alcohol out, after all. But yes, going back to your question: she had a friend. We've got a picture.'

'I'd rather you gave us a name,' Slater said.

'It won't be necessary.' She turned her screen around.

Slater felt as though he'd been hit by a thunderbolt when he saw the face on the screen – a scanned picture from the nineties, already looking like ancient history. The woman was in her early twenties, with a lot of hair and bright red lipstick. He knew her name but restrained himself from saying it aloud. 'No,' is what he said. He shook his head.

'It *is*,' Smythe insisted. She was on the same wavelength. 'It's her.'

Slater blinked, his composure broken. 'There's a bit of a resemblance, but it's not enough. We need the name. Please help us – this is too important for rules.'

Smythe flipped over her notepad and wrote something in block capitals before presenting it to Brownlie. 'This name?' she said. 'All you have to do is nod or shake your head.'

Brownlie nodded. Then she turned the screen back. 'One of our success stories. I'm still proud of her. She was one of the first crystal meth addicts we'd ever had in here. She had spent a year studying in America on an exchange programme – Chicago. That's where she got into it. She was deported, and ended up here when she resumed her studies back in Glasgow.'

'I didn't know she studied in Glasgow,' Slater said.

'She comes to visit us occasionally. Never mentions it – I can see why she wouldn't, of course. She's made financial donations – a big one, in fact, after her books started to sell. Fascinating character. I'd say she was a warrior. She was a warrior then, in different ways. She said she'd make sure no one else suffered what she did. She had a controlling partner who got her into crystal meth . . . She came back. That's a success story.'

Smythe laid down her pad. 'What about Lana Galbraith?'

'Her initial treatment was a success. She came back twice – that happens a lot. Her friend never came back as a patient. They had a lot in common. Both young. Both liked a night out. Both exploited, in their way.'

'Exploited?' Slater asked.

'Yes. Lots of women come in here because they were put into horrible situations by men. They might have liked the glamour of it at first. But addiction can come out of bad situations, and so many of them end up in worse ones. Bad husbands, bad boyfriends, bad fathers. Like crime, it's one of the cornerstones of addiction, and one of our jobs is getting them to trust themselves and other people without being out of their minds on something.'

Brownlie looked tired when she stopped speaking. It was the closest she had come to a loss of composure. After a moment, she went on: 'Some of the girls who arrive here, I read about them later. In the newspapers, once they're gone. Lana Galbraith was one of them. I know every name. I could give them to you if you like. If it can catch this Ferryman, then I'll do everything I can to help you.'

'One other thing,' Smythe held up her pad again. 'Ursula Ulvaeus. When she was here, did she use a pseudonym?'

Brownlie peered at the notes. 'I think she did . . . Rebecca Stewart, it says here. That was the name she went by.'

18

Lomond laid a coffee down in front of Ulvaeus in the interview room. 'Black with one sugar, was that what you wanted?'

Ulvaeus grinned. 'Not too good on details, are you? That's not very reassuring in a policeman. Black with two sugars, I said.'

Lomond shrugged and unfolded a napkin on the table. Several sachets of sugar were nestled inside. He tossed two of them towards Ulvaeus, then laid a stirrer on the plastic rim of her cup before pushing it over to her.

After adding the sugar and stirring it in, she took a sip of the coffee, and said nothing. In the harsh lights, her eyes were downcast, but there was nothing insecure about this. She might have been reading a mildly amusing column in a newspaper resting on her knee. It was the studied indifference of a cat on a wall.

'We're here to talk about something that happened in the past,' Lomond said. 'When you were studying in Scotland. After you'd come back from your year in Chicago.'

'OK.'

'It was 1995, which I know was a long time ago. Do you know a house called Rafferty Landing?'

'I've heard of it.'

Slater sat forward suddenly. 'June the thirtieth, 1995. You like your details, so maybe you can remember what happened at Rafferty Landing on that date?'

'I'm not sure about Rafferty Landing. I think I spent that weekend at a festival, in fact,' Ulvaeus said, focusing on a far corner of the room. 'Yeah, I'm pretty sure that's right. Hot weekend, wasn't it? I got sunburned. You don't expect that in the west of Scotland. Britpop summer. That's what they call it, isn't it? Britpop. Indie bands. I saw Elastica, I think. I loved them. Supergrass, too.'

'You weren't ever at a house called Rafferty Landing?' Lomond asked. 'It's a very big place – a stately home. You'd remember it, I think. I've got a picture of it on my phone . . .' Lomond reached into his coat, but Ulvaeus raised a hand.

'I never went to a stately home back then. I'd have remembered that.'

Lomond took out his phone anyway. 'Never mind. I wonder if you could tell us about a friend of yours – or someone you knew, anyway. Her name was Lana Galbraith. This is her.'

Ulvaeus studied the phone. Then she sat back and sipped at her coffee. 'Yes, I remember Lana Galbraith.'

'How did you know her?' Slater asked.

'She was a friend. What else is there to say?'

'But how did you meet her? When was your first meeting?'

'Look, I went to a lot of parties back then. I was just a girl really. Still a teenager. And I had a great time. I guess what I'm saying is, I did a lot of partying. I can't recall everyone I met.'

'So you met Lana Galbraith at a party?'

'I didn't say that.'

'Where did you meet her, then?' Slater held her gaze.

Ulvaeus hesitated. 'When I was younger, I used to have unhealthy habits. I picked some of them up abroad, when I was travelling. I used to think I was invincible. That's part of being young, isn't it? And the culture of the time was to get as wasted as possible. Especially in this country. That was how you earned your stripes. That was how you made your bones, socially.'

'Lana Galbraith was quite a well-known person at the time,' Lomond said. 'Bonnie lassie.'

'What do her looks have to do with it?'

'They made her distinctive. As did her fame. You couldn't miss her. She would have been in the papers every other day, whatever she was doing, whoever she was doing it with. So if you lived in Scotland at the time, even for just a year, and you were about eighteen, say, you'd know exactly who she was, and you'd remember where you met her.'

'I was coming to that,' Ulvaeus said, recovering some of her poise. 'This isn't a story I like to tell just anyone, but I'll tell you. When I was in Chicago, studying, I kept company with the wrong man. He got me into a bad scene.'

'What kind of bad scene? Drugs?'

'You know all this, don't you?' she said. 'You know my story already.'

'I want to hear it from you.'

She smirked. 'Think you're being clever or something? Trying to catch me out? Well, let's find out if our stories tally up. I was, and this is a technical term, a tweaker. Methamphetamine. Meth, if you want to fit it into a headline. I used to party. Hard. I hooked up with this guy who got me into it . . . It had effects on the libido, you could say. It was euphoric. It was everything ecstasy was *supposed* to be. So I thought, anyway.'

'You were addicted to it?' Slater asked.

'I was never an addict, it was purely fun, but I could see it was becoming a problem, although I didn't have the sores, the black teeth, that some people get. I could stop if I wanted to. That's a familiar story, right? Really, the problem was supply. When I couldn't get access to it, it became a bigger problem. My family and friends here noticed the change when I came back. Something in my face, they said. Not just because I was thinner. I decided to head any escalation off at the pass. My daddy back in Sweden heard about a place called Kirrin Hall, and I went there for several weeks of treatment. That's where I met Lana Galbraith.'

'What was she in for?' Lomond asked.

'Heroin. I think she checked in later for other problems. Cocaine, I think . . . but I can't be sure. Shifted one addiction onto another. Lovely girl. You could see the changes there had been in her, compared to what you saw on the television. She fell in with another bad guy on the music scene. She loved him, but butter wouldn't melt in his mouth. You'll hear a lot of stories about bad guys in certain scenes or other. Good-looking, charming. Not much happening under the surface. Think only about themselves. Very old story.'

'And you obviously had no choice whatever in the matter,' Slater muttered.

'What was that?'

'I mean you had all your choices made for you? That's what you're saying?'

'That's a man's answer, all right.' Ulvaeus wasn't quite stirred to anger, but Lomond thought: *Danger.*

'Do you know this bad guy's name? Someone in the music industry, you said?' he asked.

'Oh yeah. He was in a band.' She told them the names of both. Neither Lomond nor Slater expressed any sign of recognition.

'And he was a singer?'

'Bass player. Still alive, I think. I sometimes think I'd like to track him down. No one remembers who he was. Lots of people now will have no idea who Lana Galbraith was, in fact. Younger generation won't have a clue. This was just about pre-internet, remember. Last gasp of the analogue age. Lived her career on the physical pages. She was so funny, you know? Really quick with her responses and retorts. Skin you alive with a single phrase. It happens with some beautiful women. They do all they can to avoid their gift. Turn away from it. Self-deprecation, they call it. Seems like a fetish to me. Being so dazzling, but trying hard to turn the lights down. It plays into the hands of some people. Makes you weak.'

'Do you think Lana Galbraith was taken advantage of?' Lomond asked.

'Sure she was. She had the society girl thing going, and an

unlimited supply of folding money, it seemed. But there're reptiles in that world, too. She wanted to break the connection and start again. When I met her, I was sure she was going to succeed. I never saw a junkie look so determined. I thought she meant it. Appalling, what happened to her. *Appalling.* I think there was a suggestion she might have deliberately driven the car into that cutting before she ended up in the water.'

'Did Lana Galbraith mention Rafferty Landing to you?'

'I don't know anything about that. I told you.'

'Did she mention a weekend with Torquod Rafferty, the Earl of Strathdene's son?'

Ulvaeus took a quick, sharp breath through her nose, then shook her head. 'No.'

Slater leaned forward. 'If we were to suggest that you were close to Lana Galbraith, and that you might know something about a murder case she was connected to, what would your reaction be?'

'That's a loaded question and I don't think I want to answer it without a lawyer.'

'Here's another one: do you want us to catch the Ferryman or not?'

Ulvaeus's brows knotted. 'The Ferryman? What does this have to do with the Ferryman?'

Lomond looked stern. 'You might not know this, but Lana Galbraith provided the alibi for two men who were suspected of killing a girl in the summer of 1995. This girl's body was found in a pond in the grounds of Rafferty Landing. There are certain similarities between her death and those of the two girls we found in the Clyde recently.'

'The same killer?'

'We can't be sure. I wouldn't bet on it, either. There are similarities, that's all. But we can't leave anything out in looking for this person. And we still want to know what happened to the girl who was killed all those years ago. Her name was Daisy. Here she is.' Lomond turned his phone round. Ulvaeus peered closely.

'Daisy Lawlor was having the time of her life,' Lomond went on. 'She had earned a lot of money working as a waitress in between studying. She budgeted well, saved up, and was having a big summer. Music was what she loved. She was travelling to a music festival in Scotland that weekend. Britpop bands. It was probably the same one you went to, in fact. Somehow, we're not sure how, she ended up in the grounds of Rafferty Landing. The Earl of Strathdene was a former hippie, and had a very liberal attitude to who he allowed on his estate. Some would say he was negligent. There is a suggestion Daisy Lawlor was killed by travellers, but that never quite stacked up. There is also a suggestion that the earl's son and his friend might have had something to do with it. On the day before Daisy died, there was a party at Rafferty Landing, while the earl was away. To this day, we're not sure exactly who was there that night. But we know that one of them was Lana Galbraith. She knew the earl's son, Torquod Rafferty. He was about nineteen at the time. Roughly the same age as you, I'd say. They mixed in the same circles. The theory is that Daisy was at the party on the Friday night, and at some point in the next twenty-four hours she was killed, and her body thrown into the pond on the estate.'

'So – maybe talk to the earl's son. Talk to the earl, in fact.'

'We've talked to him,' Lomond said. 'And we'll talk to him again. But I want to know about a letter we found in the Daisy Lawlor files. We can look at it here.' Lomond opened his laptop, and the letter appeared on the screen. It was torn from a student's notepad, A4, fine-lined, with binder perforations. The handwriting was heavily scored, deliberate, with the odd flourish and filigree. Someone had taken their time to make it look distinctive. It simply read: *To the senior officer, murder squad, Glasgow CID: in the case of Daisy Lawlor, Lana Galbraith knows who did it.*

'Did you write this letter, Ms Ulvaeus?'

She smiled. 'I've never seen it before.'

'You're sure? Look closely. Very distinctive handwriting,' Lomond mused. 'But it's weird with it, you know? I'm not an expert on – what do you call it? Calligraphy? – but I'd say it looks like someone's tried hard to disguise their real handwriting.'

Ulvaeus brightened. 'Can I ask why no one spoke to Lana Galbraith at the time? She died years later.'

'We did,' Slater said. 'And she gave Torquod Rafferty an alibi. Said that she went to a hunting lodge on the Saturday with him, one other man and one other woman. Everyone else at the party at the Landing was traced and eliminated. Most of them had been at the music festival that day. Daisy Lawlor died on the Saturday evening.'

Ulvaeus spoke calmly, looking Lomond and Slater right in the eye as she did so, her gaze moving from one face to the other. 'I knew Lana Galbraith at the clinic. She was a lovely girl. We spoke about a lot of things – mainly men. I don't know anything about how the girl they found at Rafferty Landing was killed. If I did, I would tell you. I could tell you about hundreds of other women and girls who've been killed, though, if that's your thing. Dozens of them in this city. And not all by creeps like your Ferryman. He's one in a billion. But those odds drop a bit when we look at the other cases. Women killed by their partners, husbands, family members, people they knew. I could talk about that subject all day, inspector. I can give you times, dates and names. I can even give you what street it happened on, everything. All up here.' She tapped her forehead. 'But Daisy Lawlor? Summer of 1995? I can't help you with that one.'

Slater said, 'Donald Ward said the other girl with them at the hunting lodge on the day Daisy was pulled out of the pond was called Rebecca. That name ring any bells?'

'Not particularly.' She smiled. 'I think we're done here.'

19

Lomond and Slater made their way down the stairs.

'Don't like her, don't trust her,' Slater said. 'I respect what she does and the points she makes . . . Don't look at me like that, gaffer!'

'I wasn't looking at you like anything,' Lomond said, with a smile that seemed to blend into the wallpaper . . . unless you knew him.

'It's true. She's a scrapper. I like that. And I agree with what she says. But she's one o' those folk, if she changed course . . . just a few degrees to the right . . . she'd be an absolute wrong 'un. Horseshoe theory, I think they call it.'

'Luckily for us, she's not a fascist,' Lomond said. 'She's trouble, though. She's been all over social media. Every cough and fart on this case, she puts it out there. When I checked the news after I got off the plane, I couldn't believe George Square. I thought it was a fake crowd. Someone good at computer graphics, a mock-up.'

'Nope. Full rally,' Slater said, sighing. 'Place was packed out worse than when they switch on the Christmas lights. Seemed to appear out of nowhere. They used to call it flash-mobbing. Sort something out online, and they just show up . . . from where? They not got jobs to go to?'

'I've not seen a crowd like that for a demo for a while,' Lomond said. 'Not outside the football or the last referendum anyway. Better hope we get a result soon. Ulvaeus did say she's sticking around for the duration.'

'She can't sustain that kind of exposure,' Slater said, frowning. 'Media will get bored of it, move on to the next story, and that's it. She'll still be rattling on about it, but no one will listen.

She'll be like one of those nutters you see on the street. Ranting about God. Or conspiracies. Or aliens. Or whatever.'

'Let's hope we get our man, and then she's out of the picture.'

'Reckon she's telling the truth? About Lana Galbraith?'

'I'm edging towards "no". No idea why, though: something in her manner. But you know what I think about gut feelings. I've got a couple of things I want to test out. If they don't fit, we're pulling her in.'

'You would think, gaffer, that with all the activism and stuff, if she knew something about a murdered lassie she wouldn't keep it to herself.'

'Aye. You would think.'

'Think she might be Brownlie's Rebecca? The one at the hunting lodge?'

'Good chance of it,' Lomond said. 'Why is Ward so vague about it? Is he protecting someone else or himself?'

'Probably himself. Could be that he just went to a party with somebody called Rebecca. It was years ago. They were young.' Slater shrugged.

'The weekend someone died at his friend's house?'

'Hmm.'

An officer in uniform stopped them as they reached the front door. Tall, well-built, but only twenty-one, and Lomond read the fear in his eyes as plainly as a set of traffic lights.

'Can't go out that way, sir,' he said, with a tremor in his voice.

'How many?' Lomond said.

'All of them. We've had to set up a cordon on the perimeter.'

'When you say perimeter, do you mean all the way round, or is the back way clear?'

The young officer stumbled over his words. 'Um, yes, the back way is clear for you to get out. I'll escort you down, sir.'

'Won't be necessary, son, but you can keep us company,' Lomond said. 'C'mon.'

As they made their way down the stairs, Slater said, 'There was no one in front of the office when we brought her in.

Street was empty.'

'News travels fast. And she's got a lot of fans out there. Usual rent-a-mob getting involved. Dafties who like causing bother on somebody else's behalf. As well as the dafties who just like causing bother.'

'If we bring her in again, we should probably get her out somewhere quiet. Or the unit at Govan.'

'Agreed.'

The junior officer escorted them out into the car park. It was brightly lit, but even so they didn't see the creeping figures until it was far too late.

'There they are! It's him!' someone screeched.

'Time we looked lively,' Slater said. He took off towards where Lomond had parked earlier; Lomond and the young policeman struggled to keep up.

Then the missiles flew. One detonated against a bonnet with a loud thud, not a metallic sound at all, indicating alarmingly good purchase. Another hit one of the overhead arc-sodium lights which illuminated the shadowy corners. Another whizzed past Lomond's ear and hit a squad car. There was a wet crunch; yolk dripped, slowly, from the shattered wing mirror as the three officers darted past.

'Get back inside,' Lomond told their escort. 'We're just about there.'

'No, sir – I've been told to keep an eye on you.' As he spoke, an egg struck his shoulder. Yellow rills coursed down his epaulet and crept over his arm.

A strong light blinked on ahead of them. Below the intense white beam – it hurt to focus on it for too long – was a smaller red light. A camera, coming closer, its wielder faceless. But not legless. Lomond clocked the slim black jeans, tapered to a painful point above a pair of scuffed Doc Martens. Other boots drummed into view. Then more missiles flew. Something glanced off Lomond's shoulder just as he triggered his key fob, his car's lights blinking in recognition.

Officers flooded in to tackle the intruders at last, but they were still alarmingly close, and alarmingly hostile. Egg yolk and shell fragments continued to appear on windscreens and bodywork all around Lomond and Slater.

'You have to say, gaffer,' Slater said, cheerful in spite of the ridiculous scene. 'It's a good one. Clever idea.'

'Clever how?' Lomond said, exasperated, as he fumbled for the door handle, a hail of off-white orbs crashing around them, the mob getting closer as it threaded its way through the cars, arms catapulting.

'I mean, a feminist mob. And they're throwing eggs. See?'

'You off your nut, Malcolm?'

'Feminists, man. Feminists. Eggs. Fertility 'n' that. You get it?'

That was when something hit Slater full on the forehead. It stuck in place, drooping in dead centre for a second or two, a ludicrous stubby appendage, before he clawed it off his skin with a cry of pure disgust. A smudged red stain showed where it had struck him, dead centre.

Lomond stared at the used tampon by Slater's feet for a full two seconds before he started to laugh.

★

Lomond took a mouthful of coffee. Not as cool as he'd have liked, but he let it burn.

The team had relocated to Cranhill station while the protest continued. On a TV screen, Lomond had caught sight of Ursula Ulvaeus ranting into a microphone on the rolling news coverage of the fresh protest. He recognised a grinning face over her shoulder, a camera pressed to one eye, filming the scene. Lomond made a note in his pad, underlined it several times, and gritted his teeth. The image on the television switched to a police car, turned over and on fire.

'Switch that off, please,' Lomond said to one of the detective sergeants. The man hurriedly complied.

Lomond stood up and addressed the team, staying away from the lectern at the front of the briefing room. 'I know there's utter chaos out there. We've got to contend with that, as well as catching this guy. The one they're calling the Ferryman.'

He paused, and surveyed the faces among the Major Incident Team, more than twenty officers in plain clothes, and several in uniform. Individually they might have passed muster; collectively, the exhaustion was clear. Bags under the eyes, unshaven faces, unwashed hair pinned back. More than that, it was a question of demeanour. Not quite the faces of people about to fall asleep: more the faces of people who had been brutally awoken. It was clear in the behaviour, too. Signs of confusion, signs of irritability, the nerves ragged like the torn edges of the notepads. But at the mention of the tabloid nickname – the first time Lomond had used it, in any context – they sat up a little straighter. Pens paused at pads, fingers halted on laptops.

'You can call him the Ferryman if you like,' Lomond continued. 'You can even say it to my face. But there'll come a time when he won't just be the Ferryman. We'll have his name, we'll have his face, and he'll be inside, for ever. The Ferryman won't even be a bad joke. And we'll have him soon. That's a guarantee. He's clever, no doubt about it. He's careful. He's organised. But any intelligence he has stops dead at whatever perversion is driving him. He'll slip up, if he hasn't already. And we're on to him.'

Lomond's voice seemed to suck up the oxygen in the room. His steady gaze shifted from face to face – Smythe, Slater, officers in uniform, plainclothes officers in disarray. There was that curious magnifying effect on his unassuming figure whenever Lomond spoke to the team, something that was absent when he addressed the public. Silence was absolute for a second. Then he turned to Tait: 'We've an update now from Myles. It's a significant breakthrough. Myles, it's all yours.'

Tait took a sip of water at the lectern before starting his presentation. He carried no notebook; everything was controlled by the click of a button, doubtless rehearsed, almost tiresomely professional. 'OK – thanks for attending, everyone,' he said. 'I'll keep this brief, and I'll email it out to everyone after we're done. It concerns a second burnt-out car, which we think might be connected with Sheonaid Aird Na Murchan's abduction. We started by checking car sales records through second-hand companies, and got one match which seemed to fit the bill.'

He turned to the main screen, where a black car with a dent in it was presented in a single frame. Bright lights shone on its contours, etching the bodywork in silvery slashes like moonlight on dark water. A code of some kind was superimposed on the side of the image.

'This picture is several years old. What you can see is a production shot of the car. And here . . . we can see the car as it was used in a movie six months previously.'

Another image appeared: a well-known movie star, possibly a decade or more past his prime, dressed in a long dark coat and brandishing an oversized handgun, scowling at someone off-camera. The car was in the background, with a dent in its front door panel and bullet holes pock-marking the bodywork.

'You'll recognise the actor here – he was shooting a movie which hasn't long dropped onto the streaming services, *Reckless Intent*. You might recall it from media coverage at the time – he was a big star in his day, and he came to Scotland to shoot the movie, which was produced by a company called Claymore Films. Claymore started out as a very low-key outfit which has gone on to make a lot of money with low-budget films. Some of them are, uh, highly acclaimed, and some of their TV shows have been . . . ratings hits.' Tait looked unusually uncomfortable at this point, and one or two of the men in the room sniggered, until Lomond shot them a look.

'The car was used for production stills, as well as featuring in the actual movie. The car was purposely damaged in such a way that it could still be driven, and then used in one shoot-out scene before it was swapped for shells which then got burnt.

'This is where it gets more interesting. The car was sold by Claymore Films to a second-hand car company but failed to sell on, and although it wasn't a write-off, it was eventually passed on to a scrap merchant, Grange's, based near Tradeston. It was sold at auction to an unknown buyer, cash in hand.'

Slater said, 'An unknown buyer? But what about ID? He must have shown some identification to the scrappie to complete the registration, surely.'

Tait almost relished the question. 'I'm afraid the auctioneer was a naughty boy. He agreed to be paid in cash, with a drop made at a certain location where he would leave the keys to the car, which would be parked nearby. It's in a CCTV blind spot. That's where the fake plates must have been fitted, and the car didn't appear on the road again until it was picked up Sheonaid Aird Na Murchan.'

'Any idea of the figures involved?' someone asked.

'Our man at the scrappie says he is having trouble with his records on that point,' Tait said dryly. 'Obviously, he must have sold it off the books for a large sum, to make the risk worth his while. We've no idea where the fake plates came from – could be any number of places. The car was burnt out, as I said, but there is evidence that work had been carried out to replace the door panels which were damaged during the movie shoot.'

'Was there much left of the tyres?' Slater asked.

'At least three of the tyres on the car were brand new,' Tait said. 'So – we need to put this car out there, link it to the movie shoot, and ask people if they've ever seen it since, and if so where and when. And there's one more thing that we should bear in mind.' He switched the image again, revealing a flow-chart of companies spreading out of Claymore Films. 'We should note that one of the companies affiliated with Claymore Films is Langoustine Productions, which is in turn affiliated with MyGirl.'

20

Lomond cleared the room except for Slater, Tait, Smythe, and three other detective sergeants. He leaned against the whiteboard, arms folded. Images of the dead girls flanked him: images in life, and post-mortem shots when they'd been dredged straight from the water. A stream of telephone numbers propped up these printouts, scrawled in bright red. The central space surrounding Lomond was clean, however, like the outline created by a school of tiny fish edging away from a predator.

'First, the car,' Lomond said. 'How's he doing it?'

'He knows them, gaffer,' Slater said. 'No way they're getting into a car with him at random.'

'Close friend?' Lomond uncapped a pen, wrote the word 'car' on the whiteboard, circled it, then added 'knows them'.

'Think we'd have made the connection by now if they were really close. Plus . . . these lassies seemed like outsiders, to me.'

'How's that, Malcolm?'

'Well, they're good-looking, that's obvious. But they didn't seem to have any special mates. No big circle of pals. No besties, you know? They didn't seem really tight with anyone. They were into things, they had close contacts here and there, but no friends.'

'I agree,' Smythe said slowly. 'I hadn't considered it in that way before. They were sociable, they got involved with things in their scene, they didn't seem to be shut-ins, and they weren't shy, you can say that for sure. But they were definitely their own person. I was going to call them "loners", but that isn't the word, exactly.'

'Weirdos probably isn't the word either, but it's what we're all thinking,' Slater offered.

Tait tutted.

Lomond wrote the word 'misfits' and circled it. 'So work colleague? University lecturer?'

'Good chance of that,' Tait said. 'I'm more interested in the art and performance side to it. Only one of them was on MyGirl, but both of them are well known on the internet. At least, they've got thousands of likes on their videos – hundreds of thousands, when it comes to Sheonaid doing her, eh, topless swims. Aylie had a good number of followers on MyGirl. I know that the material means that any old Herbert with an internet connection might have clicked on it, though.'

Smythe said, 'The thing that makes me pause is . . . their material isn't what I would call sleazy. It's in the eye of the beholder, and both of them have been naked on the internet, or at least topless, in the case of Sheonaid. So that'll get a reaction. We know that. But there's an art to it – it isn't just a case of taking their clothes off.' She held up a hand towards Slater to cut off his protest. 'I know your opinion on this – that it makes no difference. But it's a link between the two girls. With both of them, it's not quite just your average, well . . . porn.'

'I'm not saying what they did with themselves doesn't matter,' Slater protested. 'It does. Or it did to them. I get what you mean. It was their art. I understand that. I'm thinking in terms of a typical straight male. I'm thinking in terms of the guy who killed them.'

'So you think the guy who killed them wasn't paying attention to their videos? I'd say it's a cert that he was,' Tait said.

'No, listen again – carefully,' Slater said tetchily. 'He might well have been into the artistic side of it. Did it feed into his motives when he killed them? Really? When we get right down to it? I doubt it. This guy's a creep.'

'No sign of sexual assault,' Smythe pointed out.

'That we know of,' Slater said. 'Bodies were dumped in

the water. They might not have been penetrated; doesn't mean he wasn't a sleazebag. Clothes are missing, and there'll be a reason for that. You can't rule out a sexual motive. End of the day, it's all these guys are interested in.'

'We're assuming it's not a woman,' Lomond said. He paused with the marker pen on the board.

'What were you about to write, gaffer – Ursula Ulvaeus?' Slater smiled. 'I would laugh if it was her. But I can't see it.'

'Can't see it either, but we're not ruling her out. She was in Glasgow ahead of the killings. She's not really told us why that was. You're more likely to get into a car late at night if a woman is driving it. And there's her funny wee vanity mirror. With the surprise inside for anyone who gets wide with her.'

'That can't have been used to cut Aylie or Sheonaid's throats, though,' Tait remarked.

'No,' Lomond said. 'But it does prove she's prepared to use violence. And with her, we've got someone attached to Rafferty Landing, no matter how obliquely. She had links to the campus where Aylie studied before dropping out – she was NUS president in her final year, ran for rector a couple of years back . . . narrowly lost. And it would explain why Aylie and Sheonaid got into the car.' Lomond linked the word 'car' to the empty bubble he had just drawn, which he filled with the word 'woman?', alongside 'work colleague?' and 'lecturer?'.

'Any other reason she might have got into the car?' he asked.

'Someone she didn't know, but trusted,' said one of the other detectives. 'A serving police officer?'

No one said anything, but Lomond felt the discomfort spread through the little group: a joint flinch or maybe a sudden change in the current. Lomond felt it run through him in turn.

'It's happened,' the detective said, somewhat less assertively. 'Warrant card. Uniform. There's precedent. We'd be daft to ignore it.'

'You're right,' Lomond said, and drew a 'police?' bubble.

'How about the two trust fund boys?' Slater asked. 'Rafferty and Ward?'

'They have alibis,' Lomond said.

'They have alibis for Daisy Lawlor, as well. Doesn't exonerate them totally. And with them, we've got more than one link to what happened to that lassie.'

'We do,' Lomond said. 'But nothing concrete, yet.'

'And there's every chance Ursula Ulvaeus lied about writing the letter you showed her,' Smythe said. 'So it looks like someone knows what happened there. And someone buried it.'

'A police officer,' Lomond said. He drew a line between the 'police' bubble and 'Daisy Lawlor', which he also linked to 'Ulvaeus'.

'What about Langoustine and MyGirl?' Tate asked. 'That's a clear link to the Rafferty Landing murder, isn't it?'

Lomond nodded. 'Donald Ward. Absolutely.'

'How about the crazy artist?' Slater asked. 'Sir Hubert de Banknote?'

'Sir Erskine Copper's diary completely checks out. There's no chance he killed either of those girls. But he is linked to the Rafferty Landing boys, and he is linked to Sheonaid Aird Na Murchan. The mural at the pool, for a start.' Lomond made the additions to his flowchart. A sweat had broken out on his brow; he wiped it away, hurriedly, frowning at the smeared moisture on the edge of his finger, glittering in the harsh lighting. 'What about the cars?'

'One stolen, one linked to Langoustine,' Tait said. 'The fact it's linked to Langoustine feels like a mistake. By the killer. That's my gut feeling.'

'It could be a coincidence. But I agree, the cars are crucial. I think we might get him through the cars. It's close; we'll probably kick ourselves when we find it.'

'It shows he's careful,' Tait said, tapping his pen on his notepad in a steady metronomic rhythm. 'It shows he's brilliant at covering his tracks.'

'The other thing,' Lomond said, eyes flaring wide. 'The

phones. He switches the phones off in transit. How is he managing to do that?'

'Threatening them,' Slater said. 'Might be that simple. Country road. Pitch black. Late at night. He pulls a knife, maybe a gun. "*Hand over your phone*". That situation, most folk would give him the phone.'

'Both cars had the child locks engaged,' Tait said.

'Captive audience,' Slater agreed. 'That's the simplest explanation.'

'Maybe,' Lomond replied, 'but even so . . . I wonder if he's more subtle than that. I wonder if we're missing something there.'

Slater shook his head. 'I dunno, gaffer. Think about it. How do you convince someone to give you their phone? If he didn't force them to hand it over, and he isn't a master pickpocket – which I'm not ruling out – then how did he do it?'

Lomond tutted, and underlined a new bubble, 'phones?'. 'Again . . . we might never find out. But if we can find out, it could be crucial. We'll come back to it. Nice work on the car, by the way, Myles.' Lomond capped his pen and stepped back. 'So how's it looking? What are we thinking?'

There was silence for a few seconds as they considered the jumble of bubbles, terms, lines, arrows and question marks arrayed on the white surface like a child's lettered blocks.

'It looks,' Slater said, 'as if we've got fuck all.'

They all laughed – an explosion of nervous tension. Even Smythe let herself go – perhaps dangerously so, fighting for breath, tears spilling down her cheeks.

'Maybe we have,' Lomond said, finally. 'Tomorrow we're going to pull the Rafferty Landing boys in again. Speak to them.'

'What about the art?' Smythe asked. 'The artwork from Sheonaid's bedroom up north? The stuff you couldn't identify?'

'I'm seeing to that personally,' Lomond said. 'Tonight. I'm taking the rest of the night off. Malcolm, you're in charge until tomorrow morning. Myles, I want you to coordinate a search of everyone who ever taught Aylie Colquhoun when she was at university – lecturers, tutors, supervisors, freshers' buddies, anything of that nature. Cara, I want you to get me a full rundown of what our three amigos from Rafferty Landing are doing tomorrow. We'll check back in at 9 a.m.'

'Begging your pardon, sir – can I ask what angle you're looking at? Just so we don't cross-contaminate.' Tait looked uncomfortable with asking.

'The artistic angle,' Lomond said, with a smile. 'Have a rest if you can, folks, when your shift's done. We've got a long few days ahead.'

21

Lomond's driveway wasn't big, but it was wavy, slaloming through lots of trees. This was quite deliberate, and meant it was difficult for people to spot anything parked at the house – or not parked there. Lomond knew the clues, however, and so he clocked the Volkswagen through the branches in good time as he slowed to make the final turn.

It was unmarked, and probably didn't belong to any of the few handymen he knew and trusted in the area. It had taken up his own bay – the less convenient one, with his wife's car taking its usual spot in front of the door – so he had to park a little way behind the interloper. He'd already put a name to the licence plate by the time his key turned in the latch.

Lomond lived in a quiet house, he liked it that way. Siobhan was his only child, so it was somewhat discomfiting to return home to activity, noise, even hilarity ongoing in the front room. The absurd sense of invasion was difficult to shift. Lomond cleared his throat, and the three people huddled together at the long table looked up.

Mint was still laughing at something frozen on-screen, covering her mouth when she caught sight of Lomond. His daughter was sitting to her right, her eyes puffy and tear-blown in a sign of mirth, not distress, that the inspector knew better than his own face, while Martin Granger, their course supervisor, was seated on Mint's left. He was amused rather than hysterical. At the far side of the table were three drained mugs, forming a protective cordon around one of his wife's good dishes, dotted and blobbed with the remains of a chocolate cake.

Lomond coughed, not to grab their attention, but to provide some off-the-ball running for his growling stomach.

'Sorry, Dad,' Siobhan said, recovering her composure. 'We were just reviewing some footage, and . . .'

She turned the laptop screen towards him. There, with the tampon stuck to his forehead, his face a picture of confusion and consternation, was Slater.

'It's a good look,' Mint said, when she could draw breath. 'Who's that guy off *Doctor Who*? Davros?'

'Davros didn't have an eye stalk,' Lomond said. 'Dalek, you mean, surely?'

'Davros is funnier,' Mint muttered.

Granger got to his feet. His glasses were large but they suited him. He was roughly the same age as Lomond, certainly into his forties, but less noticeably so than the inspector. 'Mr Lomond – hi. How's it going?'

'Not bad,' Lomond said, accepting the handshake. 'I thought I recognised you at the protest today.'

'It was funny,' Mint said, bursting into fresh laughter. 'I mean, whoever made the shot with your sidekick, it was a hell of a throw . . .'

'We're sorry about that,' Granger said. 'Mint, maybe we should . . . ?'

'Oh, yeah.' Her hands moved over the mousepad, and the image collapsed into a kaleidoscope of video thumbnails, static images superimposed with white 'play' symbols. She clicked on one of these, and a crowd scene opened up, too brash, too noisy. Lomond thought the footage was impressively clear. The camera panned across the people standing at the front. A familiar face appeared.

'That guy . . . isn't he Torin MacAllister?' Mint said.

'He is,' Lomond said. 'That is interesting. Wonder what he's doing there?'

'He's gone all woke,' Mint said. 'Trying to be in with the cool kids. Or something.'

'I don't know if woke's the term,' Granger said. 'Maybe more like clever. He's the law and order candidate for the by-election, he says. But he also thinks the police should be reformed.'

'I know all about reform from guys like that,' Lomond said soberly. 'Been through it a couple of times. Reform meaning cuts. Reform you all the way to the brew.'

'You said you wanted to know about any males we might see at the demo,' Siobhan said. 'I thought him being there was interesting.'

'It is. I'll ask him about it next time I see him.'

'Is he a suspect?' Mint asked. 'In the Ferryman case, like?'

'No,' Lomond said. He glanced at his elderly desktop computer, perched on a table in the far corner of the room like a grand-mother relegated to a rocker. Switched off, he noticed. 'Listen, folks, I don't mean to leave you in the lurch here, but I'm going to. I'm going to take your mother to her class tonight. Have you guys had tea?'

'We were just getting stocked up,' Mint said. 'Lovely cake, we've had. That's another dinner I owe your wife.'

'Carry on. I won't be too long, here.' All the same, he paused and scanned the screen in front of him. He took in the shot of Rafferty with the camera zoomed in on him, even as Ursula Ulvaeus ranted into a loudspeaker somewhere in the background. The man's features were set, his face pale, chin pointed low in the sharp breeze. He didn't look as if he wanted to be there, Lomond thought, although he clearly had to be present.

'I hope you don't mind us using your Wi-Fi,' Granger said. 'We had to upload somewhere and it's difficult to get a signal outside . . . It's a lot quicker than heading back to the editing suite.'

'Blame me,' Mint said, waving a hand as she bent closer to the screen. 'All my idea. I'll pay you back for it. Once I, eh, get a degree. And a job.'

'It's fine,' Lomond said. 'Tell you what – I'll do you a

wee trade. You can use my Wi-Fi tonight, so long as you upload every bit of film you've taken today.'

That dealt with any jocularity in the room. 'Um . . . we shot a lot of footage,' Siobhan said.

'No problem,' her father said affably. 'I can be dead patient. Just make sure you send it to my email address. The official one. I'll want to take a close look at your footage. Specially the stuff you shot in the car park. Where Malcolm had his wee accident. I'm not really happy about that, to be honest. No one should have been in there. I'm talking about you in particular, love.'

Mint shrugged. 'Guilty as charged. But it's a public place.'

'I especially want to see any footage showing who did that.' Lomond pointed to another frozen image at the corner of the screen: the squad car upside down and burning. 'There's protesting, and there's being a bloody nuisance. I'm going to have whoever did that.'

He felt a hand on his shoulder. It was Maureen. 'Thought you'd be back earlier,' she said. 'There's some tea in the kitchen, if you want some.'

'I'll maybe grab a bite before we head out,' Lomond replied. He led the way into the kitchen.

'We?' Maureen said. She was ready for her own night out, it was true: casual in jeans and a black and starburst-gold blouse that she'd probably outworn but couldn't bear to part with. If they ever decided to walk around the corner to the Key, their local, on a rare Sunday night, or to get lunch on an idle afternoon, it was usually what she put on.

'Yeah. To the painting thing. With Sir Thingummy.'

'It isn't your thing,' she said peremptorily.

'Oh, it definitely is.'

'You're coming to a painting class? You?'

'That's right.' Lomond grinned.

'To paint?'

'What else?'

'*You?* Painting?'

'I was all right doing the ceiling that time, was I no'?'

'You'd best get changed,' she said. 'And don't keep me waiting.'

'I won't, don't worry,' Lomond said deferentially, as Maureen headed out of the room.

'You've spoiled Mum's night,' Siobhan said gleefully. 'That's as furious as I've seen her in ages.'

'Ah, she'll be fine,' Lomond said, shrugging. 'Anyway. You guys all loaded up or whatever?'

'Sure, just about finished,' Mint said.

'Great. So maybe stop chewing up my data, then?' Lomond said, a little tetchily.

'I do apologise,' Granger said. 'I was against using your Wi-Fi, for the record.'

'Well, you're in charge, aren't you? You're the . . . what is it, lecturer?'

'In a way. Editor is how I term it.'

'Editor. Right. Well, that means you've got responsibility, doesn't it?'

'Sure.'

'So make sure that footage of my detective sergeant being assaulted doesn't make it to the internet. I know you shot it, and I know what the footage looks like. If I see it on any funny video channels or whatever, I'll . . . actually I dunno what I can do, legally. I'll find something, though. I'll crack open the books.'

'Now it feels as if you're checking up on us,' Granger said wryly.

'Already done that, pal. The day I first saw you. When you were with Mint at the protest, showing her where to point her camera.' Lomond smiled. 'Name, address, licence plate, phone, the lot. Polis prerogative. Anyway – Mint, you decided to use my Wi-Fi to upload videos, did you?'

Granger looked dumbfounded for a second, then he laughed.

'I was showing initiative,' Mint sniffed.

'Well, you'd better apply the same initiative to finishing up. Quick as you like, love. Ideally before I come back in here with my dancing shoes on. And next time, do it back at your college.'

22

The polished corridors, drab walls and chaotic noticeboards at the community centre reminded Lomond of school, for good and bad reasons. 'Hopefully without the asbestos,' he muttered to Maureen.

Two young people, a boy and a girl only just in their twenties, if that, waited by a desk to take the registration details. The girl was tall and lithe in a shapeless jersey worn at an angle that showed off a milk-pale shoulder. Her hair was long and dyed an outrageous shade of red Lomond would have struggled to define; all he knew was that it complemented the green eyes peering through her fringe perfectly. The boy was wiry and blond and looked as if he might surf for recreation, maybe in California. He wore a skinny-rib T-shirt with what seemed to Lomond like impossible self-possession.

'Hi there,' the surfer boy said, grinning at Maureen, then looked questioningly at Lomond.

Lomond handed over his warrant card. 'I'm sorry, I don't have a slot. But I do want to speak to Sir Erskine.'

The boy peered at the card, and his assuredness seemed to shatter. 'Um . . . I don't think . . . umm . . .'

'It's quite important,' Lomond said. 'Also . . . I fancy having a crack.'

'A crack?' The lad was baffled, and half out of his seat.

'At the painting. Daffodils, and that. You know. Easels.'

The boy arched an eyebrow. 'I'd better go and get him,' he explained to the girl.

'What?' Lomond said, in response to his wife's look. 'I'm serious. Gimme a bowl of fruit, and I'll draw you a bowl of fruit. I used to be all right at that, back at school. I'll draw the fruit. Not like I'm eating it.' He chuckled. No one else did.

'It's a *life* class, sir,' the girl said, at half-speed.

Lomond shrugged. 'Even better.'

★

Erskine Copper rested his hands on his hips and surveyed the room just as Lomond entered. Most of the seats were already filled. Low chatter gave the room an atmosphere of expectation, even excitement, similar to an auditorium before a classical concert. As many as two dozen easels and paint boxes were set up in a semi-circle arrayed before a low stage decorated with burgundy drapes flowing over a stool. The older man at the centre of all this wore beige or possibly camel-coloured chinos, set almost comically high on his waist, topped off with a blue tank top over a white and green pinstriped shirt. There were some men who could carry off the shabby genteel look, Lomond reflected; he wasn't one of them, but Copper was.

The older man's eyes narrowed when he spotted Lomond. Instantly, he darted off the stage, the movement at his knees and hips surprisingly supple as his boat shoes squeaked across the polished linoleum floor.

'You're a familiar face,' he drawled, his brows lowered in mock suspicion. 'Quite welcome, of course. Is there something I can help you with, inspector?'

'I was hoping to pick your brains about something, Sir Erskine. Sorry to spring it on you like this. Also,' he said, cutting off the artist's reply, 'I fancied having a go.'

'Having . . . a go.' Copper crossed his arms and leaned back, lip curling. He was enjoying this, Lomond thought. Enjoying the speculation, the gossip, the riveted attention from his students. He was a very different person in his element from the person Lomond had spoken to in the interview room. 'Have you ever . . . had a go . . . at art before, inspector?'

'I was quite good at line drawing when I was fifteen. But it was only line drawing. And I was fifteen.'

Copper snorted. 'Well. This requires a little more finesse. But I confess I'm intrigued to see what you produce. Like a spider spinning its web, no? We'll find you a space. And it's a bit more messy than line drawing with the old HB. I'm assuming I'm not looking at your best clothes?'

'Not quite,' Lomond chuckled, resisting with all his strength the urge to say *I'm assuming I* am *looking at yours.* 'I've got something I'd like you to take a look at. A shot in the dark.'

Erskine tutted as Lomond handed over a manila folder. 'Shot in the dark? That's rather dark humour, isn't it.'

'Just a figure of speech. I'd like to get your professional opinion.'

'Shop talk? You could have left a message on my website. It would have reached me. My assistant is very thorough.'

'It's important, and I don't want to set up meetings and waste time unnecessarily. Yours *or* mine.'

'I quite understand.' Copper took a deep breath and peered at the folder in his hand, as if he could discern something from it.

'Um, the piece I want you to look at is inside.'

Copper's gaze – slowly, very slowly – rose and met Lomond's. It was a look of such stunning insolence that Lomond was reminded of some of the cheek he'd faced during his days in uniform. It kindled a latent sense of . . . what was it? Vengeance? Justice? Retribution? Bullying? He very badly wanted to lift Sir Erskine Copper. It was a look that cut across all boundaries of class, race, religion . . . anything. A Presbyterian minister could draw him that look, or a shuffle-shouldered, twitchy teenager collared outside a crashed car.

The artist flipped open the folder and slid out the scanned page. And the expression altered.

'It's her,' he said simply. 'Sheonaid the mermaid. My God.'

Lomond suppressed his rising hopes and said nothing, his own expression mild.

For a few moments there was only the artist's breathing, whistling through gill-slit nostrils. 'Well, it's very interesting,' Copper said at last. 'Quite an unusual composition. The central figure is very well detailed . . . but the sand is what I'm most interested in, inspector.' He chewed his lip. 'Yes. That's what springs out at me here. That and the hair.'

Sheonaid Aird Na Murchan lay face up on the sands in the scanned picture of the painting Fraser Cowan had shown him back on the island. Closing his eyes for a second, Lomond had an intense visualisation of the dead girl as she'd been pulled from the water. He knew the term 'flashback' in all its contexts, but he wasn't quite sure what one was, subjectively experienced. Was it a takeover of the senses by a memory – something akin to the power of a religious vision, a spiritual ecstasy? He saw Sheonaid Aird Na Murchan's true face, as he'd witnessed it, after she'd apparently tried for one last embrace of a fisherman: smudged and grey, the textures ruined, the colours run out, her last beauty spots a domino effect of grime and dead leaves across the skin. Lomond's hands twitched.

And now, there was her face on the wet sand in the painting, black hair spread out behind her, pale shoulders, fine-bladed eyebrows. The lovely throat intact. Ignoring the perspective, this would have been the exact angle of her chin just before the crude invasion of the knife.

The person who painted this killed her, Lomond thought. *Or the person who killed her saw this painting. I know it.*

Copper turned the picture of the painting on its side. 'Yes, that detail on the sand is incredible, I'm bound to say. Look how he's captured that glaze effect, a second or two after the tide makes a retreat. That smooth, organic sheen. It would be quite hard-packed, you know. That kind of sand. I'm not sure about the nude; in this instance, it seems like an indulgence. The face is quite enough. I might have been tempted to cut it off round about the shoulders. It's an unsettling image, all the same.' Copper's expression was different now. 'Is this a piece of evidence of some kind?'

'I've no idea. This is why I need your help. I think it was produced in Scotland. If I put "greatest living Scottish artist" into a search engine, your name comes up. You live here, you're generous with your time, you have an emeritus position at the School of Art. Anyone in Scotland who's achieved anything in painting in the past forty years has probably had some connection with you. I need you to look very closely at the painting. Do you recognise any part of it?'

'I'll have to take it away with me,' he said abruptly. 'Do you have the original? Is there a signature on it?'

'We don't have the original. This is a scanned copy of a photo that was taken of it. There's no signature that we can see. We've carried out all kinds of searches and checks to see if there was one there – changing colour gradients, flipping the image, putting it in negative . . . there's nothing.'

'I will have to have a look. It's very interesting . . .'

'First impressions – does it remind you of anything?'

'Inspector, you were very kind about me, just there, and it was flattering. And you are correct to say that a lot of work passes under my nose. Thousands and thousands of paintings. I'm sad to say I can't recall every brushstroke by every artist any more. But this painting . . . it's extremely interesting, that's what I can tell you. If it doesn't trigger my memory banks, it'll trigger someone else's. I'll have to make some inquiries. I will take this away, and I will get back to you.'

'That would be good. I'll give you my card. It's very important, Sir Erskine, that you let me know the minute you have any ideas about who might have painted this. It's someone I want to talk to.'

'These will be the dead girls, yes? Fished out of the Clyde? The Ferryman?'

Every one of those sentences was a whiplash to Lomond. He tightened his smile. 'Yes, it's related to that case.'

'Some mess out on the streets. People are *fuming*, aren't they?

Police cars burned – now there's an image. I do believe this is the angriest I've seen people in this city since the days of good old Mrs T.'

'I understand why they're angry. I'm angry.'

'You don't look it, inspector. You look like one of those men who never loses his temper. I'm sure it's in there, of course. Everyone's burning up inside. Aren't they?'

'I don't know. Are they?'

'Of course! Right now, I bet you're aching to arrest me for something!' Copper gave a bark of laughter. 'I sometimes have that effect on people. Yes, you're stewing in there, I can tell. But you don't have an outlet. It all just smokes and hisses . . . then just fizzles out.'

'That's partly why I'm here, Sir Erskine. My wife believes I should have a creative outlet.'

'Well, you've come to the right place!' He barked again, presumably for the people at the back. And now that he had everyone's attention, he turned towards the artists. 'Now, every-one, let's get started.' He replaced the scan in the manila folder and put it into a battered leather satchel by the side of the stage before buckling it shut. Then he gestured to somewhere off stage. 'Remember, let's take as long as we can. Roya is going to be on stage for quite a while, and it's a little chilly, so we're going to drape her in these sheets . . . Roya, if you would?' There was some hesitant applause. Copper grinned. 'Yes, abso-lutely, applaud, go mad! Here she is!'

The girl from the front desk appeared, smiling brightly. Her comic-book-red hair was loose around her shoulders. She wore a silver dressing gown with an unidentifiable floral print, etched in a fine black line, and nothing else – a fact which became clear when she untied the robe and let it fall to the floor.

Lomond looked away at first, astonished and embarrassed. He caught the eye of his wife, who was staring right at him and laughing behind her hand.

The applause had been polite at first, but grew louder,

drowning out any discomfort that might have been felt. One bold soul called out, 'Whahey!' causing an undercurrent of laughter which crested on the face of the model herself.

'Whahey is right!' Erskine Copper said. 'This is the body beautiful. The summit of all creation. Every artist in history knows it. All the greats . . . and the not-so-greats . . . know what you're feeling right now. They know that your heart has started to kick. They know your joy, your surprise, your discomfort, even your lust. Take that feeling. Harness it. Now unleash it onto that canvas. I'm going to just . . . if I may . . .'

Copper lifted the red tide of sheeting draped on the stool – it looked like a curtain, perhaps from the stage itself, but was far too velvety and new to have been hung up above, surely. The artist gazed at Roya, who had sat down on the stool, arms at ease. For a moment her eyes locked on Lomond's. He felt utterly at a loss and didn't know what to do with his hands. They were halfway towards his pockets before he realised that that might represent the worst optics of all.

'Yes . . .' Copper said, meditatively. After considering a moment, he put his hands on the model, posing her impersonally, the way a child might twist and manipulate a doll – a raised leg here, the neck dipped, an elbow articulated just this way or that. Then he brushed Roya's hair off her neck and chest, fully exposing her breasts. He smoothed the red hair back with a sinuous, even sensuous motion that made Lomond uncomfortable on the girl's behalf. To him it was something of an affront. The model's calm, self-possessed expression never changed, however, even when Copper parted her legs slightly. But then someone in the class wolf-whistled, and for a moment she did seem to flinch. Lomond wanted to intervene.

Then Copper draped the covering over one shoulder and across her legs, granting her a modicum of decency, though leaving one breast bare. 'Pay attention not just to the body, but to the material,' Copper said. 'How we articulate the body on canvas can often be a matter of how we articulate the clothing, too . . . which is a difficult thing to do. One of the most difficult in art, in fact. That, and the hands.' He clapped his own together as he stepped back. 'Well. Let us try what we can.'

The expressions of the artists became as one from that moment: deep, detailed, even detached scrutiny. Pencils moved across canvas in calm susurrations. Water tinkled in pots. Copper pressed Play on a digital machine connected to some speakers, and delicate ambient music was heard, with a muffled drum track that sounded like the heartbeat of a lover against the ear.

Copper approached Lomond. 'Ready to creatively outlet yourself?' he asked.

Lomond scanned the desks and easels; every place was filled. 'I don't think there's a space for me, after all.'

'Oh, there is. You're going next door. Come with me.'

Copper tugged Lomond by the sleeve. The inspector pulled – rather than wrenched – himself away from the artist and followed him out of the room and into a smaller one adjoining it where soft classical music was the theme.

'This is the other life drawing class – we do two rooms, at random. There's been a late call-off or two, there always is, so you can use that easel over in the corner.'

'I don't have any paint,' Lomond said. 'Or brushes or . . .'

'Not to worry.' Copper rummaged in a pocket. 'Here. Line drawing, you said? Here's a charcoal pencil. Best you can get. Feel free to keep it.' He bade Lomond sit before an empty easel, right in front of another short stage, raised only a foot off the floor.

Lomond sat down, ignoring the stares of the other artists, wondering if he should simply leave when the opportunity presented itself.

He was still considering this when the young man who had been beside Roya at the front desk appeared in his own dressing gown, dropped it, then stood not less than two feet away from where Lomond sat.

23

Lomond took a sip of coffee and grimaced. 'It was like a bloody paddle,' he whispered. 'It wasn't as if I could look away anywhere. It would still have been in my line of sight . . . it was hanging there like a windsock on a calm day. If I'd shut my eyes, I might still have been able to see it . . . a shadow on the blinds. I can see it now. My God.'

'Art! Art my *arse*!' Slater laughed aloud. He seemed to explode: it was a sound born of hysteria, and maybe one step beyond that, into despair. Tears rolled down his cheeks, and he struggled to wipe them off. That kind of laughter was almost like grief, Lomond supposed, past a certain level. 'No way,' Slater said at last, when he could get a breath. 'That's brilliant. He's stitched you right up, gaffer. An absolute bam-up. "Just you sit here and sketch something for me." Talk about a masterpiece!'

'Then I had to *draw* it,' Lomond said, staring into space. 'I mean . . . I couldn't give it that much detail, you know? I didn't want to *overstate* the case. Like something out of Frankenstein. And you can't exactly take an inch or two off, either.'

'For good behaviour?' Slater collapsed into high, alarming shrieks, his head in his hands.

They were in the briefing room, alone. They had arrived in a state of some tension. The reason for this became apparent as footsteps grew louder in the corridor outside. There was a slight pause – Lomond supposed it was for dramatic effect – and then Chief Constable Drummond came in.

If there was an identikit image of what a CC should look like, it wouldn't be too far away from the picture Drummond presented. Mercilessly thin – in the common parlance, 'if he turned sideways, he'd disappear' – with a deeply lined, fleshless face and two deep-set eyes bleached of colour, he had built a reputation everywhere in the force from his earliest days in uniform. He was younger than Lomond, and not much older than Slater; his face and manner added at least ten years to his actual age. It was often said that Drummond was respected, and generally acknowledged that he was feared. His was a difficult character to decide whether you actually liked it or not, because it was so deeply hidden behind the uniform and the prestige that came with his job. He might have been born to be someone's boss.

Drummond stopped short a few paces inside the door. 'If there's a joke, let me in on it please, boys. I could do with a laugh.'

Lomond said nothing, his face composed. Slater said, 'It'll have to wait till we go for drinks after we lift our man, sir. It's that good.'

'I'll take your word for it.' Drummond laid his phone down, pulled up a chair and sat down. He didn't exactly relax; his posture was still rigid, even with one ankle crossed over the other. 'The good news is people went home and stopped setting fire to our motors. There was a rally in George Square, but nothing too disruptive. Usual queue at Greggs. The bad news is . . . well. You tell me the bad news.'

This startled Slater, who wasn't sure what the Chief was driving at. Lomond, however, was. 'There're a couple of leads we're working on,' he said. 'In particular a painting of Sheonaid that we can't trace. A photo of it was given to her not long before she died. I've asked Sir Erskine Copper to see if he knows anything about it.'

'Sir Erskine Copper?'

'The artist. If I ask who's an authority in the art world, that's the name I hear. He's a collector, works in the community, unofficial mentor for just about everyone who graduates from the School of Art. Interested in the next generation . . . and the one after that. He also painted Sheonaid, for the mural at the baths.'

'That's all ye've got? A painting?'

'The thing that's bothering me is that we can't source the original. We've found every video she recorded online, every piece of film she put on YouTube, and even the ones that were rejected. Same with Aylie Colquhoun. Every portfolio she put together, every video she loaded up to MyGirl, every fan who got a bit lairy or over-familiar on message boards . . . the painting is the only piece that doesn't quite fit.'

'I don't understand,' Drummond said. 'You'll have to explain. Art wasn't my strong point at school.'

'I was all right at it,' Lomond said, colouring slightly. He opened his phone and found the picture Sheonaid Aird Na Murchan had sent to her boyfriend – the one he'd copied for Erskine Copper. 'Take a close look at it.'

'Nude woman. Lot of that in art, I suppose.' Drummond shrugged.

'It's her – it's Sheonaid. But look at the posing. Look at the neck, the eyes. The throat particularly bothers me. The way the head's thrown back. You've seen the images of her post-mortem. There's no indication of who painted this – no inscription, no identifying marks. All we have is a copy – a scan of a photograph; we haven't found the original. But I think this is a lead we should be chasing, hard.'

'It's a wee question mark,' Drummond agreed. 'I kind of see what you're saying. But aren't you taking a bit of a leap? It's a theory – not evidence.'

'That's thin on the ground. Whoever it is has covered their tracks well. No details on CCTV or doorbell cameras or dash-cams, nothing we can use. The only other piece of evidence is the cars used. And so far that's turned a blank.'

'Actually, it hasn't,' Drummond said. 'Myles Tait has found out that the second car had new tyres. Probably bought whole-

197

sale, probably bought in advance. That's where we should be looking. Surely?'

'We are. There's nothing but dead ends. The broker who sold the car in the Sheonaid case – the one used in the film – told Myles he had no records of the sale: he's not the type to talk too much about what business he does, apparently. Seems it was sold a couple of years ago. But,' Lomond went on, leaning forward, 'there's something in that that makes me think the killer's been planning it, maybe for years.'

Drummond sighed. He relaxed his shoulders. 'I trust you, Lomie. You get results. No doubt about it. Everyone knows what you can do. Everyone knows what you've got in the locker. Problem is, we're not seeing any results. And that's giving me a pain in the arse.'

Lomond squared himself up.

'You maybe didn't see what happened on *Newsnight Scotland* last night?' Drummond asked.

'I've heard about it. Ursula Ulvaeus versus Sullivan. Great box office.'

'To be fair to the gaffer, she gave as good as she got, and put Ulvaeus on the back foot a little,' Drummond said, with a crafty smile. 'Suggested that her past might not be lily-white.'

'Bad move,' Lomond said. 'We need Ulvaeus onside.'

'I wouldn't have done it,' Drummond conceded, 'but there we are. That's why she's chief super. But I have to tell you, Lomie – your name was mentioned, a lot. It gets mentioned a lot online, anyway.'

Lomond paused. 'In what way?' he said at last.

'Between your Greg Louganis incident in the Clyde, then being pelted with eggs and coming off badly with Sullivan at the press conference . . . it's not good.'

'Guessing you'll have told the public the work we put in? The dafties we've put away?' Slater said quickly – too quick by half. 'I'm guessing you said something like that?'

'We've played it with a straight bat,' Drummond said,

glaring at Slater. 'Well, as straight as we can when one of our own is being called 'Davros' on Twitter across the planet.'

Slater bit his lip, and said, 'As I've said several times, Davros was the leader of the Daleks, he did not have an eye stalk, and—'

'Save it, son,' Drummond said, waving him aside. 'When the public's making jokes about you, something has to be done.'

'Like what?' Lomond said sharply.

'Nothing for now. But whatever it is you're doing, step it up. There's a lead somewhere, Lomie. Ex-boyfriends, course colleagues, deranged fans . . . there's a grubby wee link waiting to be made here. You know the score. You need to give me some good news. I can't remember an investigation coming under anything like as much pressure. Usually, we get these guys. It's a husband or a boyfriend. Even when it's a maniac, we can stick a pin in the guy who did it, no problem at all. Phone records. Number plate recognition. Nosy neighbours recording everything that happens in their street. But here . . . we've got nothing.'

'You see my problem,' Lomond said. 'These lassies . . . if there's a link between them, it's that they might have been beautiful, they might have been all over the internet, but they were shy kids at heart. They were known to be wallflowers at school – some of their old schoolmates didn't recognise them when we showed the pictures of their modelling shoots. They didn't get on well at school, didn't have close friends, didn't stand out academically. They found another life once they left and went to college or uni. They reinvented themselves. And someone out there took advantage of that – took advantage of the art. It's someone from that world. Someone very clever. That's why we have to find out who painted that picture of Sheonaid.'

'I'll leave you to it, Lomie. I think I've been clear.' Drummond nodded, got up, and left.

When the coast was clear, Slater said, 'So that's it, then. Myles Tait in charge of the investigation? Place your bets.'

'We go on doing what we're doing until someone tells us not to,' Lomond said. 'This was a friendly warning. I expected Drummond to be roaring at us. That was him a good mood. I'd say we've probably got about a week. At least the Ulvaeus carry-on's dying off a bit.'

'I wouldn't be too sure about that, gaffer.'

Lomond's phone rang. It was Telfer, a detective constable. 'What's up, Joe?'

'Our man's on the move,' Telfer said. 'Van arrived, just now. Transit. He's moving some stuff packed into crates.'

'No, he's not,' Lomond said. 'Stop him, now. Put cuffs on everyone if you need to. I'm on my way. He asks about a warrant, tell him I've got one.'

'Understood, sir.'

Lomond hung up.

'Who was that?' Slater asked.

'Telfer. I assigned him to keep an eye on Erskine Copper. He's trying to move some stuff out his house.'

'I like the sound of this.' Slater smiled, grimly. 'We'll take my car. It's my turn.'

18

'Long driveway,' Slater said. 'I'm expecting a fanfare here. Guys in uniform with trumpets. Hey . . . I think I can see a house. Over there, on the horizon. Tell you what, gaffer, it looks like painting pays off. My da always said painting and decorating was a great career.'

'Think we're looking at old money here. Like, hundreds of years old,' Lomond said, inspecting the grounds of Sir Erskine Copper's home as they scrolled past. Everything about it was handsome, well ordered – the sort of place that might hold weddings, booked up years in advance. The building was rendered in stone – imposing but mottled over long exposure to the elements. There was a gravel drive, and a stilled fountain, and no lawn. In such surroundings the greenery knew its place.

Two squad cars were parked at the end of the driveway, before a broad, squat mansion with tall windows. A white transit van was parked in front of the house, the driver in the front with a phone at his ear, glancing at the approaching car nervously.

They spotted Sir Erskine well before they parked – literally waving his arms, with two officers either side of him, their hands clasped before them, ready to strike out should Sir Erskine be foolish enough to get shirty.

Lomond marvelled that the little man should actually dress like an artist while he was at home: in a pinstripe shirt and trousers, with navy blue braces over the shoulder, all that was missing was the wee beret. He saw Lomond, and jogged towards the car as it stopped at the bottom of the driveway, shoving aside the police officers and one or two extremely good-looking young men, and one doughty, short woman of about fifty.

'The meaning of this? What's the meaning of this? What are you playing at?' he shrieked.

'I'll explain, Sir Erskine,' Lomond said amiably. 'Just as soon as you explain what's going on with the van.'

'Absolutely none of your business.' Copper pushed his sleeves up his wrists. Had this florid little Zebedee put his dukes up and employed some fancy footwork on the gravel, it would not have been a stunning surprise. As it was, he merely shook a fist at Lomond and Slater. 'This is not a police state. I will not have this intrusion on my own property – my own home! This is a private matter, and you have absolutely no right—'

'I have a warrant, Sir Erskine. Why don't you calm down and talk to us for a minute or two?'

'It's irrelevant, utterly irrelevant. Why do my movements have anything to do with you? How did you know what I was doing?'

'You're a person of interest, Sir Erskine. You have a close connection to a dead girl through your art. I think the person who killed her also had a connection to her through her art. I want to explore that.'

'I won't be a party to your games. I simply won't. I'll stop you physically if necessary.'

'You won't,' Slater scoffed. 'What you'll do is stand there and watch, if you're lucky.'

Sir Erskine Copper set his white-whiskered chin to an absurdly high angle and half-turned on his heels, arms folded. 'Will I indeed,' he muttered.

Lomond's demeanour was conciliatory. 'We'd appreciate your cooperation, Sir Erskine. But with or without it, we'll get what we need.'

'We'll see what my lawyer says about that.'

'He can say whatever he bloody well likes,' Slater snarled. 'Get the van open. Now. What have you got in there?'

Paintings, as it turned out. Painstakingly packed into pine cases of several different sizes with '*Fragile*' stencilled on the front.

'Open them,' Lomond told the two blue-overalled curators who emerged from the back of the transit. 'Please and thank you.'

'This is delicate, precious artwork,' Sir Erskine Copper implored. His flesh had gone pink above the white whiskers; his eyes – watery, if not exactly tearful – were unsettlingly like painted marbles. 'I have to ask you, in the strongest terms . . .'

'They'll be gentle with it,' Slater said, nodding to the workmen as they began to dismantle the boxes. 'Experts, aren't they?'

'Sir Erskine,' the first man said, 'I'm not sure about the situation with insurance . . . I mean, if we have to do this out here . . .'

'Yes, we have to do this out here, right now,' Lomond said. 'Do it.'

The first painting was uncovered – a seascape, maybe four feet by two, with a black and white helter-skelter of a lighthouse before a troubled sea with high, white-flecked waves. The effect of the sky was weird, and remarkably true to reality – the dense grey of a cloud perhaps seconds away from unburdening itself. Although it wasn't desperately cold outside, Lomond shivered at the vision. Evocative – that was the word. 'Who painted this?' he asked.

'Me, since you're asking,' Copper replied petulantly. 'These are all originals by me. Out of the ordinary because there're no figures in them. And that makes them value-able.' He expressed these last syllables with an excruciating, juvenile sloth. 'I'm moving them to a warehouse just outside Stirling. They're going on exhibition there in the new year.' He nodded to the two workmen, who began to cover up the glass-fronted painting with plastic sheeting.

'Just a minute,' Lomond told them. 'I didn't say we were finished with those.'

'You've seen one,' Sir Erskine said. 'What's next – your expert opinion?'

'Maybe,' Lomond answered. 'Actually, I'm just looking at the size of the package. Seems like a lot of depth, there, for just that one painting. Let me see the frame, if you would, lads.'

'For goodness' sake!' Copper snapped.

'Just a minute,' Slater said, striding towards the workmen. 'I can see something else in that case.'

'That's what I was thinking,' Lomond said. 'Open it all out, lads. Let's see.'

The policemen watched as the first painting was edged out of the packing again, the curators straining to stop the gilt-edged frame coming into contact with the gravel driveway, and Lomond pointed towards a second square package, mummified in bubble-wrap, previously hidden behind the seascape in the same packing case. 'And describe this second one for us, Sir Erskine. What is it?'

'Not sure,' Copper said, blinking. 'Could be cornfields in Anstruther. I can't be sure.'

'By you?'

'By me, yes. For the same exhibition.'

Slater pulled at the bubble-wrap. 'For God's sake,' Copper said in a reedy voice – a tired old man's voice. 'Take care, will you? Be careful with these. They're worth a fortune.'

'What did you say this one was?' Slater asked, nodding towards the canvas he had exposed. 'Cornfields in Anstruther, was that it? It doesn't look like cornfields in Anstruther to me. Been a while since I've been out that way, mind you. And didn't you say there were no figures?'

It was the silhouette of a woman, posed like a ballerina, balanced *en pointe* above a dark sea. The head was tucked into the chest, the arms crossed over the breasts. The figure was etched in red, with thin red lines trickling towards an impression of black water with the choppy red waves rendered in darker crimson. The woman's hair streamed out behind her.

She was nude, but the figure had the quality of a silhouette, the colour close to neon but without the glare. It had very few distinguishing features – certainly not her face or even skin tone. The body seemed to be suspended above the waves in a black background which looked to have been trowelled on thickly, as if shellacked or even tarred, such was the dense, noxious texture of the night sky as it blended with the surging water. Lomond had a strange inkling that he'd seen something like this before, and realised he was thinking of *Christ of St John of the Cross* in Kelvingrove Art Gallery.

Slater burst out laughing. 'Oh, mate. You're lifted,' he spat gleefully. '*Lifted.*'

'This painting is also one of yours, Sir Erskine?' Lomond asked.

The old man's arms were still folded defiantly, though his chin was thrust almost into his chest now. 'I'm saying nothing until my lawyer arrives.'

'And I believe he just has,' Lomond said agreeably, as a car raced up the driveway. An Audi: black and shiny as oil. Gerald Finlay got out of the driving seat and slammed the door behind him imperiously.

'Stop whatever you're doing,' he ordered. 'Gentlemen, this is private property. I presume you've got a—'

Slater strode towards him, waving the paperwork in his face. 'Right here, my learned friend. Have a good look at it. Take your time. Fancy a trip to the station with us while we talk to your boy here?'

25

Lomond switched to fizzy water, but it made him embarrassingly bilious. He coughed to suppress open revolt in his oesophagus, not altogether successfully, before facing Copper across the interview table.

'I'm now showing Sir Erskine the printout of the painting sent by Sheonaid Aird Na Murchan to her boyfriend.'

'You showed it to me before,' Sir Erskine said tersely.

'This painting was sent to a girl who was killed recently. Her body ended up in the Clyde. This girl modelled for you – her name was Sheonaid Aird Na Murchan. She is the face of the mermaid painted on your mural at the community baths. Would you agree with that statement?'

'That's correct.'

'Sir Erskine – did you paint this picture.'

'Absolutely not.'

'Do you know who painted this picture?'

'No.'

'Not even an idea? A suspicion?'

'No. I do not know who painted this picture.'

Lomond frowned. 'If I ask anyone connected with the art world – and I've spoken to several over the past few days – who the foremost authority is in modern Scottish painting, whether portraits or landscapes or more avant garde stuff – anything created with a brush that wasn't decorating someone's living room, basically – they mention one name: yours. Take your time and study it carefully. Are you absolutely sure you don't know who painted this picture?'

Gerald Finlay, a stolid, glowering presence whose gaze never moved from Lomond as he questioned Copper, interrupted before the inspector had finished speaking. 'My client's already answered your question. Several times. The answer was the same each time.' He turned to Copper and said, 'Don't answer it again.'

Copper looked as if he wanted to say something; Lomond's arm hairs bristled. He was sure there was some admission or other to come. But then Copper apparently thought better of it; his shoulders relaxed, he sighed, and he closed his mouth.

'I spoke to you last night,' Lomond said, 'at one of your community art classes, and I gave you a printout of this picture. Would you agree that's the case?'

'I think so, yes.'

'You think so, or you know so?'

'Yes, you passed me a printout. I folded it and put in my jacket pocket. It's still there, I think.'

'You took a good look at the painting while I spoke to you, is that correct?'

'Yes, I studied the picture. I study lots of pictures. Several of them last night . . . including yours, inspector.' A slight arch of one goosefeather eyebrow as he said this.

Lomond continued: 'This morning, you moved several paintings from your property, Greymark. That's the name of the house?'

'It is. And yes, I was moving paintings from my house to a storage facility in Stirling. There's going to be an exhibition of my work there next year, a career retrospective. I've already explained this, and I hope the company in charge of the removals did so too.'

'Strange one, that,' Slater said, scratching his chin. 'First of all, aren't your paintings privately owned? Most of them, anyway?'

Copper sighed and closed his eyes. 'These paintings were on loan to various galleries around the UK – I had them sent to me first because I couldn't be sure when the exhibition was going to be put on. We got confirmation of the date three weeks ago – there were some articles in the press if you wish to check – and I arranged to have the paintings transported to Stirling this week. This is all easily verifiable.'

'It is,' Slater said, nodding. 'Though I don't get what the other pictures were doing there. The ones we found doubled up in the crates.'

'Detective Sergeant Slater is referring to three paintings which were packed in among Sir Erskine's own works,' Lomond said, again for the benefit of the camera. 'These are illustrated on the screen now.'

He tapped at his laptop. One after the other, colour pictures of the concealed artworks shuffled past each other on the big screen. There was the one that Lomond privately called The Ballerina – the red thread, the turbulent, crimson-shaded waters, the strangely vulnerable figure, seeming to curl into a ball despite the balletic positioning of her legs. The background of the second painting was an eye-searing green forest – too bright, perhaps, and too yellow: the green of sunlight through fresh shoots. The textures laid on the canvas were suggestive of trees without showing any bark or timber. In the centre of this lush riot was the figure of a naked woman, her arms held aloft and her hands and feet splayed out, the toes and fingers spread as wide as they could be. She was being a tree, Lomond supposed. Her eyes were focused away from the viewer's gaze, but they were dull and black. Lomond had a flashback to another face just like this – someone he had found lying on the floor of her flat following a tip-off from a neighbour, head propped up against a cat-shredded armchair. An overdose. Her expression had been the same as that of the figure here – fixed at a slight downward angle: shy, even in death. Almost beatific.

The third painting was somehow more disturbing – a starfield in a night sky with straight lines traced out as a join-the-dots, using bright, flaring, pointed stars. These lines crisscrossed and formed an intricate, detailed picture of a woman's face. She was obviously upset, and weeping. Stars spilled from her eyes and mouth. Lomond supposed it was an approximation of the kind of star chart the ancient Greeks had consulted when they named the constellations – Andromeda, Perseus, all the gang. For some reason, the stars and their flicked tails made Lomond think of vermin coming from the mouth and eyes of a corpse, as they might in real life. He shivered with disgust, amid an eruption of other unwelcome memories.

'Did you paint these?' Slater asked.

'Again, as I've already informed you – no.'

'Are these going to your exhibition?'

'No.'

'Then what are they doing packed in among your other paintings? The ones you're sending to Stirling?'

'I have been in the process of moving out some of my own collection. I'm a hoarder, you see. Collect lots of art. Lots of it's wretched. But I can't stop. The way some people are with books. There's a beautiful Japanese expression which covers this. *Tsundoku*. The practice of buying more books than you read. Well, I'm the same with art. I need to have it. I need to plunge my hands into it. I keep every single crayon stroke my grandchildren provide me with. I would frame the drawings they stick to my fridge door. My wife used to joke that I would store the puddles outside if I could, and she's right. Occasionally, she nudges me, and I sell some. Or give some away. Having access to a storage facility was a good way of moving out some of the material I've been hoarding for years. Most of it's useless. And most of it's worthless. In monetary terms, that is.'

'You don't reckon much to these paintings, then?' Slater asked. 'The ones you're sending to Stirling?'

'I happen to like them – or I must have done, at some point. I wouldn't have bought them if I didn't. But you have to make hard decisions, especially when your collection is out of control.'

209

'So . . . we going to hit the ball around all day, then?' Slater asked irritably.

'I'm sorry?'

'Give us the name. Who painted them?'

'Well, this is the difficulty. These images were painted by someone called . . . you'll never believe this . . . John Smith.'

'John Smith,' Slater said, nodding. 'Uh huh. How did you find out about them or come to buy them?'

'Well, John Smith was an artist . . . but not in the professional sense. A good twenty-five years ago . . . maybe more, in fact, maybe early nineties . . . John Smith started a correspondence with me. That was still a thing people did, back then. Sending letters, I mean. He sent letters to Kelvingrove; eventually they came to me. Said he wanted to work outside the mainstream. Had no time for art schools or organised education in any respect. A juvenile letter, a young man's letter. Well, I've been around when it comes to angry young men, inspector. I took it with the required pinch of salt.'

'When you say angry, what do you mean?' Lomond said. 'Aggressive?'

'No – it's just an expression. You know what young men are like. Surely you know that term? The angry young men? I'm sure we were all one of those ourselves.' He nodded towards Slater and cleared his throat. Before the detective sergeant could comment, Copper went on: 'It's more a term of exuberance. Drive. Heightened motivation and the strength to execute it. The expression our American friends would use . . . well, you may smile, but I'll use it . . . is spunk.'

Lomond knew if he made any sort of eye contact with Slater, the latter would laugh. Before a silence could develop, he said, 'What else did the letter say?'

'He said he was an artist but had no inclination to share his work with the world through any of the usual channels. Said he knew that that was a route to failure. He sent me a painting. I thought it had promise, but then every student I ever speak to

210

has promise. Every child struggling to hold a paintbrush between their fingers in primary school. What struck me more than anything else were the words he used, the maturity. He said he wanted to go through an authority, someone who knew what it was all about, someone he could trust, rather than a faceless examiner. I'll be honest, and this is the embarrassing part – he wanted a mentor. He told me I was that mentor. He said he wanted to work off the grid. Leave no trace. He told me he was seventeen at the time. I was intrigued. I confess, I was also flattered. And I wrote back.'

'Do you still have those letters? Or a note of the address?'

'I do vaguely recall the forwarding address. They were to go to a youth club and hangout spot, somewhere in what is now called the Merchant City. Still just about known as Candleriggs to the old timers, back then. Not quite so gentrified. Place connected to Strathclyde University: a gallery, modern art events, what they might call pop-up exhibitions and club nights and other things of that kind. DJ sets. It had an exclusive vinyl record shop. Had quite a reputation, I gather. For excellence, I mean. I think it only closed in the past ten years or so.'

'Not Sloane's, is it?' Slater asked. 'A bit like the Virginia Galleries, had a lot of units rented out. Second-hand clothes, bong shops, vinyl records, that kind of thing.'

'You may be correct. Sloane's.'

Slater wrote the name in block capitals. Lomond fought a rising excitement. *Blood*, he thought, unbidden, somewhat ashamedly. *I smell blood. His blood.* A trail of it. A definite trace. It was closer, now. The elements of identity. A fingerprint, a single strand of hair whose width couldn't even be measured in millimetres, a fingerprint, a coil of DNA, a name, and, finally, a face in front of Lomond in a room just like this.

'Anyway, allied to the work, which was really rather good, I thought the letter was interesting. Even if I hadn't been a fan, in my experience this creation, this genesis . . .' For a moment he struggled to express himself properly, in a kind of ecstasy.

'This was where the interesting things are born, really. The kind that breed whole movements, new schools. That letter came from the kind of place where life and creativity happen. The kind of place where life began. Rockpools.'

'Rockpools?' Slater said.

The older man shrugged. 'Again, just a figure of speech. You boys are so bloody *literal*.' Finlay chuckled at this, a sound like loose scree tumbling down a cliff face. 'No, what I'm talking about is where the interesting things happen. In art, as well as in life. The point of mutation. So I indulged this John Smith. I wrote to him. He wrote back. He sent me more art.'

'What did he look like?'

Copper sighed. 'I am sorry to say I never met him. But our correspondence continued. His forwarding address changed – first another art outpost, then, I think, a squat – somewhere young people living off grid got together. They don't exist any more.'

'You're saying you never met him face to face?'

'I'm sorry to say I didn't. It was something of a flirtation, a dangerous game to play, and – you'll forgive me for saying – I never could resist a chance to flirt. He would send me the odd piece, including the three you've seen.'

'You don't like them? John Smith's paintings?' Lomond asked.

'I like them very much. But I'm going to have to find some-where to store them or sell them. Wife's rules, as I said.'

'My client is in the process of moving various objects of art to various storage units around the country,' Finlay explained. 'A clearout, as he stated.'

'What for?' Slater asked.

Finlay hesitated, but Copper responded for him. 'Oh, it's not too great a secret. I'm looking to have a permanent gallery set up. Probably in the dear green place, but we'll have to see. Some of my later works. The ones I'm fond of. I've had a renaissance in the past few years, you see. I think those honorary doctorates and BBC Four documentaries, and the painting show went to my head. Gave me a new lease of life. The mural at the swimming pool, you know – that felt like a culmination.' His face fell. 'That poor girl,' he said quietly.

'When was the last time you spoke to or heard from Smith?' Lomond asked.

Copper sighed. 'I would say as much as eight or nine years ago, possibly more – ten, twelve, fourteen. You know how the years roll away from you. Hard to say. And that was one sheet of paper, talking about the weather, asking me how I was. I'm afraid I didn't respond to him. Before that . . . God. We could be talking about just before the Twin Towers came down, as long ago as that. That was to sell me the last painting. The star girl.'

'How many of his paintings did he sell you?'

'Just those three. Plus other pieces of folderol which I didn't keep.'

'How about the letters? Did you keep those?'

'I'm afraid not.'

Slater glared at the older man. 'You just told us you were a hoarder.'

'Of art, son. Not of folderol.'

Slater frowned. 'You sure? You told us your wife said you would have stored the puddles if you could. Seems to me a man of art who collects and archives everything might be the sort of guy who keeps all his correspondence. Might think of seeing it all together in a book one day.'

Copper shook his head. 'No. My other half draws the line at scrap paper. She indulges me with the finished artworks, the canvases and frames, and spots of paint on her walls now and again. But not anything *untidy*. I'll have a look, of course. There might be something lying in a trunk somewhere or buried among some dusty box files.'

'Do that, Sir Erskine,' Lomond told him. 'As I said earlier, it's easier if you cooperate. The more time we have to take applying for warrants for people who dither and stonewall us, the longer it takes to catch the killers. And you want to see this killer caught, don't you?'

'Of course.'

'Good,' Lomond said. 'As a point of interest – did John Smith donate these paintings to you?'

'No, I bought them – they came as three of a kind.'

'How much for?'

Copper scratched the side of his nose and sniffed. It was the closest Lomond had seen to diffidence in his responses. 'Ten thousand pounds, I think it was.'

Slater sat forward and ran his hands over his stubbled scalp in some exasperation. 'Can I just take a wee moment here, gaffer? I want to be sure . . . Sir Erskine, are you telling us that you paid ten grand for a bunch of paintings you're not even sure you like to someone you've never met who called himself *John Smith*?'

Copper cackled. 'Not ten grand for the bunch. Ten grand *each*, son.'

'Holy shit. Excuse my expression.'

'It was a long time ago. I was sillier and I had money to burn. If you had lots of money I'm sure you'd do the odd silly thing too, detective.'

'There's silly, and there's insane,' Slater said.

'Nonetheless. I did like the paintings. And I liked the artist – or the idea of the artist.'

'One last thing, Sir Erskine,' Lomond said. 'Take a look at this image, again.' The inspector's hands flickered over the keys of the laptop. The screen to Copper's right brightened, revealing the image of Sheonaid Aird Na Murchan, laid back on the glistening sand. 'Did John Smith paint this?'

'I have no idea,' Copper said.

'Have you ever seen this painting before? Before I showed you the copy of it?'

'No,' Copper said.

'That'll be all,' Lomond said brightly. 'Thank you for coming to the station. We'll be sure to contact you soon if we require anything else.'

Copper's expression darkened, and he folded his arms again. 'What about my paintings?'

'Your paintings are evidence, Sir Erskine.'

'What's going to happen to them?'

'They're going to be examined very closely.'

'Have you got a warrant for that?'

'Oh aye,' Slater said. 'And for the rest, back at your house.'

26

He was like any other grandad, pushing the swings, whirling the roundabout, hitching his trousers up before sitting down on the bench, and, on more than one occasion, lifting the little poppet in the bright pink anorak high over his head, joyous.

Taller than every other adult in the fenced-off playpark – indeed, in the entire garden area, a grassy spot jammed between tall, handsome ex-tenement flats – and gunslinger-slim, legs honed to toothpicks by long afternoons on bowling greens rather than pounding the streets, he still had a great head of hair, though it was pure white now.

The face was gaunt, and the smile, augmented by floodlit dentures, was somewhat grotesque. But there was no masking the old man's pleasure in interacting with the giggling three-year-old on that bright October morning. He was clearly in the regal phase of grandpaternalistic pride, yet with the child in his arms he was also comfortingly gentle.

Lomond closed the knee-high, red-painted steel gate behind him with a deliberate clang.

The old man didn't turn round, but he began to speak, in a markedly different tone from the one he used with the little girl. 'You know, if somebody'd put ten grand in my hand and asked me to bet on which one of the squirts in uniform would make it right to the top, I would never have put it on you.' He watched the little girl scamper over to the babies' slide and climbing frame before turning on his heel to face Lomond. 'But here you are.'

'You know me, Eddie?' Lomond said.

'Never forget a face or a name,' Whicklow said. 'PC Lomond,

as I recall. Green about the gills. Keen, mind. There was a brain in there. Never a guarantee that a polis will make it into plain clothes, though.'

'I'm flattered.'

'Have you grown since the last time we spoke?'

'Just oot the way, instead of up and down,' Lomond said, smiling. 'How you doing?'

'Better than you,' Eddie Whicklow sneered. He studied Lomond, his eyes quick, taking in every detail. The face was a cold, hard mask, every point of human expression contracted and reduced. He might have been an entirely different person from the whooping playmate of a few moments ago. 'Saw you on one of those online videos the other night. Taking a dip in the Clyde. My son pointed it out. Nearly spat out my falsers. "Didn't know they did synchronised swimming in the polis these days," my boy says. "Changed times, eh?" Should have seen his face when I told him that I knew your name. That I used to boot your erse for ye. So let me guess what brings you here, then.'

'I want to talk about a case you worked on a few years ago.'

'Yes,' the older man said, in a bored voice, 'go on.'

'Girl who was found in a pond at Rafferty Landing. Big stately home. You know the place. You know the case, as well. You were one of the SIOs.'

'Yes, yes.' Whicklow folded his arms and patted his lip. 'I already told one of your team to fuck off. C'mon, I promised I'd take the wean for a pineapple cake at the baker's in ten minutes. Time's wasting, Lomie.'

'Daisy Lawlor. You remember her?'

'Yep. I'm old, but I'm not wandered. Names and faces. Live and dead.'

'There's a name and a face I don't know. Someone wrote you a letter. We found it buried in the files. It was about the lassie who was at the party at Rafferty Landing that night. Lana Galbraith.'

'So? We get lots of letters when a lassie turns up deid. You're getting a few yourself, I bet.'

'Thing is, I've seen a photocopy of the letter. And I don't think anyone wrote you a letter at all. In fact, I reckon you wrote it. I think you left it in the files for us to find. I think you're annoyed about that case, Eddie.'

'I don't know a thing about that,' Whicklow said, with a perfectly straight face.

'I think you do, Eddie.'

'That's Detective Inspector Whicklow to you!' the old man suddenly boomed, mock-serious. 'Come on, straighten up, son! You're no' at the Scouts now!'

The effect was startling to the two mothers who were attending their children nearby, as well as the little girl on the climbing apparatus, who looked uncertainly at her grandfather for the first time, but not to Lomond. He smiled, and then Whicklow broke character.

'Ah, it's as if it was only yesterday,' the older man said, chuckling. 'That's the exact same words I used to you. And that's the exact same reaction, tae. You just stood there like a cat. You know – when they sit in the middle of the road, with a car coming towards them. Not giving a monkey's. It just bounced off you. It's as well you didn't give me that smile back then, though. I'd have slapped it off you. I remember saying to myself: "I thought Lomie would scare easier than that."'

'Maybe you're not very scary?' Lomond ventured.

'And you've got cheeky, with it.' Whicklow said, sighing. 'You'll be good in the interview room, I bet. Wee feint. A wee shuffle. Then wallop.' He smacked his fist in the palm of his hand.

'I think there was no letter to you, Eddie,' Lomond said. 'At least, not one you received. As I say, I think you wrote it. Toner was your senior officer on the Daisy Lawlor case. There was a wee plainclothes team attached to it – surprisingly wee, I'd say. You're the only one left alive out of it. That includes

McKinlay, the pathologist. It was all wrapped up very quickly. Death by misadventure. But there're still the knife wounds, post–mortem. I'm interested in the knife wounds.'

'You think they're connected to your wee problem dripping away in the background just now? The Ferryman?'

'Yes. And so do you. That's why you finally agreed to speak to us. You didn't really try to cover your tracks – if I didn't know better, I'd say you did it because you *need* to tell me what you know about that case. Because you know more than anyone connected to that case ever let on, Eddie. From the boys in uniform to the forensics team, the papers . . . the lot. I got shuffled off that one straight away. It struck me as a bit weird at the time. Never sat right with me, that case. So why don't you save me a lot of time and bother? One polis to another, if that means anything to you. Tell me what you know. Who carved up Daisy Lawlor?'

'If I knew that, I'd have had him lifted at the time.'

'Who was it? Torquod Rafferty? Donald Ward? Someone else who was at the party?'

'I don't know. I don't think it was Rafferty or Ward.'

'There was a party at Rafferty Landing the night before Daisy Lawlor died. We think she attended it. According to you, according to the fatal accident inquiry, she died from overheating after taking ecstasy.'

'She did.'

'Then what about the wounds?'

'Pathologist's opinion, they were administered post-mortem. That's true. That's all we know about it.'

'So now I'll ask you the big question. Why the cover-up?'

The older man burst out laughing and moved away. He stopped at some waist-high railings, painted a jolly red. 'You have to ask? Seriously?'

Lomond stood beside him at the railings. 'What was it – funny handshakes? Bowling club blazer and tie? Spit it out.'

'It was all to do with the young master of Rafferty Landing,' the older man said, spreading his hands. 'Lad o' pairts. Master of the universe. Going places. Daddy's special boy. He had to be protected. Old money and connections. Funny handshakes, if you must. But it was more likely straight-up-and-down favours between friends, rather than anything on the square. It was covered up. Torquod Rafferty was not to be hindered in any way. Even back then, before he gave up the earldom, they were saying he could make prime minister, all the way to the top at Westminster – he's that good, they tell me. He was an innocent party to all this. Daisy Lawlor fell in with a crowd of travellers who sometimes squatted on the earl's land. He was very liberal, until his son got into trouble. Then he was all business. That's the size of it. It was shut down.'

'I'll need a statement,' Lomond said.

'I might give it to you. We'll see.'

'Eddie, if you don't give me what I need, I'm going to lift you. Here and now.'

'Could you, though?' Again, that narrow-eyed appraisal, both amused and menacing. 'Could you really?'

'We're about to find out.'

'Know what I think I'm going to do here?' Whicklow said. His pupils had engulfed his eyeballs.

Lomond cocked his head. Whicklow darted forward.

There was a clanking sound. Whicklow stopped short and gaped at the handcuffs linking his wrist to the red playpark fence. Stupefied, he tried to advance, snarling, as if dismissing the cuffs. They stopped him. Whicklow tugged twice at them, swearing, then noticed the children and parents staring at him. He recovered some poise and moved back to the fence. 'Fuck is this?' he spat.

'It's my party piece. I was never any use at caird tricks, but I'm no' bad at that. Everybody needs one good trick, eh?'

'Get these fucking cuffs off, or I'll strangle you with them,' Whicklow said, with an expression so feral that drool appeared at the corner of his mouth.

'Never mind the threats, Eddie,' Lomond said, laughing. 'You asked if I could lift you; there's your answer.'

Whicklow glared for a second, then he smiled and nodded. 'Very good. Very good.'

The little girl in pink returned to Whicklow's side, discomfited by his display of temper, and tugged at his trouser leg. 'Can I go on the castle again, Granda?'

'That's a good idea, tootsie,' the old man said, grinning. 'See if you can climb to the top!' Lomond waved at her, but she paid him no attention, her wellies squeaking as she trotted off towards an elevated structure designed for little leggies to run up and down without falling off.

Whicklow turned back to Lomond. 'Instead of doing the wrestling at a weans' playpark, we could have a wee seat on the bench.'

Lomond shrugged. 'Have it your way, Eddie. Let me get my keys.' He looked stunned for a moment, checking his pockets frantically. Then he grinned, and pulled out a set of keys.

'Very funny,' Whicklow muttered.

Whicklow didn't assault Lomond after the younger man unlocked the cuffs – something of a surprise. They sat on a bench and watched the little girl and boy about the same age playing well together, utterly lost in a fantasy of castles and knights and unicorns. 'Makes everything worthwhile, dunnit?' Whicklow said. 'Just watching the weans having a laugh.'

'First grandchild, Eddie?'

'Naw. Christ, got seven of them now, would you believe. First daughter got a taste for it – she had four, pop-pop-pop-pop. Second daughter had two. This is the youngest – my boy's first. I look after her every Thursday.'

'She's going to be tall, I think.'

'Aye. Beanpole genes winning out, there.' Whicklow stretched his own legs out. 'So what is it you want to know really, Lomie?'

'Why the secrecy about Daisy Lawlor? Why the letter? If

she was a drugs victim, and you're sure the wounds were made post-mortem, and you reckon it wasn't done by Torquod Rafferty or Donald Ward, why not say so?'

'Well, it wasn't just covered up for the young squire's benefit. It was to do with a third party.'

'Who?'

'I'll come to that. In a roundabout way.'

'I didn't really come here to shoot the breeze, Eddie.'

'Don't get excited.' Whicklow coughed. 'We'll get there. Let's think back to Rafferty Landing. Weekend Daisy died, the Friday night, yes, there was a party. But what people don't realise is that it was wrapped up early. Because the old man returned home unannounced. We've all been there, eh? Think you've got an empty house . . . think you're going to get someone's knickers off . . . think you're going to be taking wee pills and potions, you know the score.'

'So what happened?'

'It all spilled out into the grounds. Old man Rafferty was a soft touch. Or had radical views, I can't remember which. Wanted the young team to have a good time; he was all for that. He just didn't want to catch anyone shagging on the Chippendale, you know? Spewing on the unicorn rug, and so forth. Drawing on the Canalettos. So he turfs them all outside.'

'How many people are we talking about here?'

'Party at a stately home?' Whicklow snorted. 'Dozens. You can imagine. All the waifs and strays, as well as the junior jet set. They spilled out into the grounds. Usual teenage stuff. Dramas, couple of fights, bit of scandal. Daisy Lawlor appears, along with a couple of bums she had been moving around with. You still get the type. Not long out of nappies, copy of *On the Road* in the backpack. Nice-looking lassie, comes from a nice home, thinks the whole world's a playground. But the reality's different. Anyway, the two bums get chased off the premises – literally, with dogs. Daisy Lawlor stays where she is. We were never sure if that was by design or not. Somehow, the lassie takes too much ecstasy. She's outside, she has a tent, she pitches it, and then, we think, she dies in the tent. Overheats. Kind of thing that happened now and again.'

'Still does,' Lomond mused.

'So far so good. Now, we head into the next day. As they've already planned, Torquod Rafferty and Donald Ward are off the premises. They've booked a weekend at a hunting lodge in the middle of a forest, off the A82, somewhere in Argyll and Bute. Long drive, but not an all-day effort. Sort of place where you find the keys in a combination lock, let yourself in . . . everything's prepared for you. It seems the bold laddies had female company on their hunting weekend.'

'How much female company?'

'Oh, just one each. Lana Galbraith, and . . .' That unsettlingly stark grin again. 'Well. This might be your first surprise.'

'Ursula Ulvaeus.'

Whicklow rolled his eyes. 'Gads, you must be a laugh when they read out the Christmas cracker jokes in your hoose. Leave me one trick, at least? How did you know that?'

'We did some digging.'

'Yep. Well. Lana Galbraith and Ursula Ulvaeus head to the hunting lodge with the likely lads. Not long after, someone finds something nasty in the pond at Rafferty Landing. It's only our Daisy.' Whicklow spread his hands. 'Now – thoughts?'

'Sorry, Eddie – *you* were telling *me* what *you* knew.'

'And that's it. That's all. Dead girl shows up in the pond, full of drugs. Nobody's fault. The whole thing is hushed up. Torquod Rafferty carried on with his career.'

'Then what about the wounds on the body?'

'Post-mortem, as you say, though the body was in some state.'

'I know, Eddie. I saw it.'

'Well, you know how it works, then. They did their tests, worked out how she died. She'd taken a lot of pills, Lomie – nine, they reckoned, and it was strong stuff back then. There was enough to go on to come to a conclusion. The cause of death wasn't the wound in the throat or the wounds in the back. No signs of the body having been bound. What the theory was, was that the girl died after she took the eccies, then someone carved her up – maybe to make sure she was dead. Maybe to make it look like she didn't die 'cause she was full of drugs. We don't know.'

'The cutter – didn't you wonder who *that* was?'

Whicklow drummed his fingers on the bench and whistled. 'Of course I did. But Toner shut it down. Someone committed a crime, Lomie, that's for sure. The person who supplied the eccies, for a start. And the person who dumped Daisy Lawlor's body. And – bear in mind we could be talking about three separate people here – the person who cut her throat and stabbed her in the back. But she wasn't murdered. I can tell you that. No jury would see it that way, either.'

'C'mon, Eddie,' Lomond said, in a low voice. 'Suspects, mate. House party full of people? You surely traced them and talked to them all.'

'Yep. None of them knew anything about drugs, yes sir, no sir. I'd be interested in finding out what they've done with their lives since then. Lawyers, politicians . . . actors . . . some of them were on the telly already. Like the Galbraith lassie. And Ursula Ulvaeus, she's an interesting one.'

'And it was all shut down and hushed up, just like that?'

'Just like that. With an interdict taken out, so no one could talk about it in the press, either.'

Lomond shook his head. 'Sorry. There's got to be more. You haven't told me anything more than I didn't already guess. I didn't even need your letter to understand that. I'll never prove who gave Daisy Lawlor the drugs. But I could prove who cut her throat. And that's the person I'm interested in. Tell me now. A name.'

'It wasn't anyone who was at that party. At least, I don't think so. We carried out all the checks. There's every chance, you know, that it was exactly the way it was framed at the time – that she came to grief thanks to someone . . . whit's that word again? I don't like it. Hard to spell, hard to say . . . *itinerant*.' The glowing false teeth bit down with every hard consonant. 'We'll never know. It's been forgotten about. A drugs death in the nineties. A lassie living off the grid. No real family around to make a fuss about her, that was key. She was an orphan. Inherited mummy and daddy's property and savings and decided to bugger off on her travels with it. Maybe that was good luck for us, I don't know. Whenever I asked about it, I was advised it was one I should let go. And you probably should, as well. But you're not going to, are you, Lomie?'

'You'll have to make a statement. And whatever else you're keeping back, you might as well tell me now and save a lot of hassle.'

'I'd look forward to you trying to get anything out of me,' Whicklow said evenly. 'Something tells me you're itching for it.'

'Eddie, the day's wasting. I need to catch this guy. I'll be polite about it, but only up to a point.'

'Don't worry, I'll tell you all I know. There *is* something you're not seeing, something you don't suspect. Something no one knows.'

'You're playing games with me, and I don't like it. You'll have to come down to the station. You can bring a lawyer if you like. I need a statement.'

Whicklow sighed. 'If I must. But if you're expecting me to speak in court . . . I've got another wee shock for you. Here . . . I've kept it on me, look.' He reached into his inside pocket, removed a battered tan wallet which could have belonged to his father, and pulled out a folded-up letter. Lomond spotted the NHS letterhead immediately. 'Six months tops, Lomie. Big C. Spreading fast.'

Lomond sighed. He relaxed a little in his seat. 'I'm sorry, Eddie.'

The older man shrugged. 'You never know how you'll feel till you get here, but . . . in a funny way, it's set me free a bit. I'm taking notice of life, looking after the wee one. I don't look too bad for it, eh? Every bugger says so. Asks me if I've been working out, losing weight, getting lean. But if you saw the nick of me under this jaiket . . . Can barely pinch any skin to get needles in. A lot of chemo – and what a laugh that is, Lomie, I tell ye. The best. Then after all that, they finally tell you you're on a timer. Next week is the last time I'm allowed to take the wee lassie out on my own, you know that? In case I hit fast-forward and drop dead. It could be just weeks away, Lomie. It straightens you out a bit, knowing it's coming. Scary, don't get me wrong. But there's the odd silver lining. Every day matters. It counts.'

'Make this one count, Eddie. For Daisy Lawlor. Even if it's just for her, and it's nothing to do with the guy we're looking for today. Help me. Make it right. Give me everything you know. What's the thing nobody knows?'

'The second bit of the cover-up. It wasn't all hushed up for the sake of Torquod Rafferty. It was to do with the hunting lodge ladies.'

'Ulvaeus? You think Ursula Ulvaeus cut Daisy Lawlor's throat?'

Whicklow chuckled. 'No. Goodness me, you're in a mess, son. You're all over the place. No, you need to dig a wee bit deeper than that. You get me? *Cherchez la femme*, Lomie.'

27

'An exhumation?'

Chief Constable Drummond looked somehow more officious without his hat on. With his industrial grey hair flecked with black and a very high forehead, he seemed like a painting of a military figure, utterly unable to stand at ease.

'Lomie,' he went on, 'we don't have the time or the resources to waste on this. Daisy Lawlor died more than a quarter of a century ago. We've got two dead lassies and a maniac to catch in the here and now.'

'It's important, sir.' Lomond leaned back in his seat in Drummond's office. Something cracked, either in the plastic chair backing or in his spine. 'I think there's a clear link between what happened to Daisy Lawlor and the person we're looking for.'

'What's your *evidence*?'

'There's a connection that's too obvious to ignore.'

'I said, what's your *evidence*?' Drummond showed his teeth on the last syllable.

'There is a similarity between the wound in Daisy Lawlor's throat and the wounds in the two lassies.' Lomond gestured to the right-hand side of his throat. 'A slight nick. I'm tempted to say a finishing touch. I spotted it on Aylie Colquhoun, then on Sheonaid. There's something . . .'

'What – grab the chin from behind, then cut across? It's literally in the textbook for cut throats. Page fucking one! Plus, the Daisy Lawlor cut was post-mortem, isn't that right?'

'Whicklow basically admitted that the investigation had the curtains pulled shut on it. He gave me a tip – and nothing else.

He as good as told me to check Lana Galbraith's grave.' Lomond looked Drummond in the eye. 'He's out of the game. Cancer. Six months is the most optimistic prognosis. I checked – it's true. He's got nothing to lose. I want that grave opened. Sir.'

Drummond sighed. 'And what are you expecting to find in there? Treasure chest? A map? Cryptic clues?'

'If this isn't showing up on your radar, then you're not really a polis. Sir.'

'Don't speak to me like that,' Drummond growled, half-stunned at what the inspector had said. 'I've sent pricks like you down the infirmary for less than that.'

Lomond paused, listening to his heartbeat. 'I want a basic ID check. I want records compared. Are you going to authorise it or not?'

Drummond stabbed a finger towards Lomond. 'I'll authorise it. But I'm looking for results soon, Lomie. Not mad hunches. Not gut feelings. And I don't want you literally digging up cold cases.'

'Whicklow's refusing to give a statement,' Lomond said. 'But he will.'

'Suppose he does, Lomie? Suppose he does give a statement. About a case from twenty-five years ago . . . what about our case, in the here and now? What's the link?'

'I'm going to uncover it. I'm sure there is one. I'm waiting on results coming back.'

'Don't play games with me! Spell it out – what are you looking for here?'

'I'm having some paintings analysed. They might provide a link between the Daisy Lawlor case and, at least, the Sheonaid Aird Na Murchan case.'

'And the exhumation?'

'I'm checking the only proper new lead I have. It's important, sir.'

Drummond's face twisted in disgust. 'Well, as soon as you find it, I want to know about it. And I'd be quick about it,

Lomie. I'll get you your exhumation. But it'd better be worth something.'

Lomond nodded and left the office.

Slater was waiting in the corridor outside, face ashen. 'You look calm, gaffer,' he said, 'and I don't like it. Why are you calm? Didn't sack you, did he?'

'No, he went for it.'

'Raised his voice while he was at it.'

'He likes to bark. He's good at it.' Lomond grinned.

'Mind telling me what you want Lana Galbraith exhumed for? I mean, what's it got to do with our case?'

'Tell you the truth, it's just a hunch,' Lomond said. 'Gut feeling.'

★

Back in the briefing room, Tait and Smythe sat side by side, sipping at coffees. Lomond nodded at them. 'Thanks for coming. Cara – you first.'

'It's a blank, sir,' she said, without getting out of her chair. 'I've passed the images of the paintings Erskine Copper was trying to sneak out of his house on to every art department I could – no one's heard of anyone called John Smith, and no one recognises the paintings. I'm waiting for a lot more departments to come back to me, but so far John Smith's a blank.'

'Is there something automated you can do?' Slater said. 'Maybe some online thing . . . ways of checking for art fraud, maybe? The guy squeezed thirty grand out of Erskine Copper; he's got a bit of game to him.'

'It's possible,' Smythe said, with a touch of weariness. 'I've been onto auction sites, too. I'm waiting for news. Something might turn up there.'

'We're assuming the guy's domestic,' Lomond said. 'John Smith, if he or she is a real person, might be international. It'll make it harder to find a link. I'm sorry, Cara, you need to keep trying on that one. The international houses – New York, Paris, Florence – try them all. There's bound to be a link somewhere.'

Smythe nodded. She was drawn, fidgety; her jacket was badly creased down one side. Lomond wondered if she'd bunched it up somewhere and used it as a pillow for ten or fifteen blessed minutes.

'Any news on the X-rays?' he asked.

'In process by tomorrow morning,' Smythe said, more hopefully. 'Forensics are dusting the canvases down as we speak.'

'Excellent,' Lomond said. 'Between the art and what you've dug up on Rafferty Landing, you've pretty much cracked this one open on your own. Take the rest of the night off, Cara. I'll see you back here tomorrow morning. Careful on the road home, now.'

'Sir.' She allowed herself to look relieved, settling back into her chair.

'Myles?' Lomond said, turning to Tait.

'Again, sir, a blank. There's nothing new on the cars; CCTV or doorbell camera images just aren't distinctive enough. The car used to pick up Aylie Colquhoun was driven down some back streets. No witnesses. In the images we've got it looks like a white male . . . but we can't be sure. Could be a female. Looks like they're wearing a beanie hat and gloves.'

Lomond felt a chill at these words. 'OK. How about tracing the phone signal?'

'The same thing. The signal completely goes at a certain point on the map . . . well out of town in both cases. It's distinct up to a distance of maybe five hundred yards. I'll show you, if I could . . . ?' Tait crossed over to the lectern and signed in to one of the computers. In the flickering glow of the laptop at his fingers, Tait's face with its chiselled jaw and downturned mouth put Lomond in mind of an ocean liner pulling into dock. 'Here,' Tait said, indicating a map on the big screen behind him. 'This is where the signal cuts off on Aylie Colquhoun's phone.'

'Middle of nowhere,' Slater grumbled. 'That's south-east, miles outside Glesga. What's the nearest town?'

'Ten miles down the road. We're talking farms, a shooting lodge . . .'

'Shooting lodge?' Slater said. 'Which one?'

'Can't remember the name,' Tait said tetchily. 'I'll get it to you. There's not much else around. Signal disappears around about here.'

'It's on a hairpin bend,' Smythe remarked.

'I checked – there are no unmarked roads or dirt tracks round there. Nowhere a car could have turned off, basically. Now, here's the interesting bit. There is a similarity to the place where Sheonaid Aird Na Murchan's phone also drops off the network.'

The map changed. Again, greenery on either side of a twisty A-road, with a dog-leg turn.

'Another hairpin bend,' Slater said.

'Whereabouts is this one?' Lomond asked.

'Heading north-east, Campsies. Same – no obvious break in the road, no sign a car had been there.'

Lomond stared at the graphic, the circled section, the dog-leg turn. 'Carried out any searches?'

'There's no sign of a phone. We only checked a one-mile radius. No sign that a car had come off the road or disturbed the undergrowth.'

'Check it again,' Lomond said.

'Sir?' Tait's voice creaked a little. 'We've already carried out a search in a one-mile radius. There's no sign of a phone or anything.'

'Check it again,' Lomond insisted. 'A five-mile radius. Get the bodies out. Search for anything. Any sort of wreckage. Till receipts . . . chewing gum . . . anything round about those curves in the road. Do it soon.' Lomond chewed the inside of his mouth. 'This does tell us something – whatever he's doing to neutralise the phones, he's planned that out, too. He's very, very careful, this boy. Very, very clever. But he's not a ghost. He's not superhuman. He'll spill something. He'll leave a trace some-where. He'll make a mistake. Probably he's already made it.'

Tait looked flustered as he shut down the computer.

'Thanks for that, Myles,' Lomond said. 'It was good work. Gives us plenty to work on – short of a witness, it's a break-through. Supervise the new search – don't take any crap from any of the team, upstairs or downstairs. It's important. I want that whole area scoured. Dogs out, volunteers, sticks, metal detectors, the lot – I strongly doubt it, but the phones might be out there. Once you've actioned that, get some sleep yourself.'

Tait nodded. He closed the computer down and strode off the lectern, studiously avoiding Slater's gaze. Smythe drained her coffee and followed him out.

'The mighty Tait missed the boat,' Slater whispered. 'That's no' like him.'

Lomond shook his head. 'He's given us another clue. There's absolutely no doubt that the map locations for where the signals went out are important. Same with Copper's paint-ings. We're that wee bit closer.'

Slater's jaw cracked in a yawn. 'I spent the day looking at CCTV footage and phoning garages, gaffer . . . I think I might go home and pass out for an hour.'

'Not a bad idea,' Lomond said. 'I'd best head home too, and speak to my family. If they haven't left me already.'

28

Lomond patted down the last sods on the garlic bulbs then took a step back to survey his garden. Everything had been prepared for winter; he'd arranged the pots so that the winter pansies would thread their unruly colours in view of the patio door. Maureen preferred the hyacinths, a regal crown cushion of purple that arrived around about Christmas time. 'I don't like the expression on the pansies,' she'd declared one evening, sparking delighted laughter from Siobhan. 'They look like they're pulling a face. Wee meanies.'

The patio door opened fully, and footsteps thudded towards him.

He knew who they belonged to without looking; he knew what mood she was in and indeed what face she was wearing.

'What do you think you're doing?' his daughter shouted.

Lomond took his time to straighten up before dropping the spade into loose soil with a grating slap. He turned to face her. 'Darling . . .'

Siobhan's eyes were bloodshot: tears of rage. She folded her arms and glared at him. 'Never mind "darling". You showed up at my work . . .'

'It's not your work, pet. They're not paying you.'

'Let me finish what I was saying! And as far as I'm concerned, it's work! You showed up, you embarrassed me in front of the course leader, and my project mate . . . Then you basically warn me off! In front of a team of journalists! What were you thinking?'

'I wasn't thinking anything,' Lomond said. But the words were sour in his mouth. 'Maybe I was thinking that I'd check the place out. Given that they're selling dodgy videos of me and Malcolm to the highest bloody bidder!'

'It's news, Dad. It's nothing personal. Everyone wants the Ferryman caught. Everyone's saying that you're not up to catching him. I've just been following events. *Are* you up to catching him?'

Anger surged through the sinews in his neck, white hot and casting sparks. 'How dare you say that to me? In my own house?'

Siobhan said nothing, but she didn't back off, and she stared fit to burn holes in him.

Lomond swallowed it down. 'I've got hundreds of officers chasing this guy . . . I've got to know every single piece of information, down to those lassies' faces when they were pulled out of the water. I'm throwing everything at this case, everything. And you come here and speak to me like that? And yeah . . . I went to your "work". I was concerned. You know how I felt seeing you in among the crowd during those moments? You and that Mint character?'

'Mint is a brilliant journalist. She's going places. Maybe I'll be her producer.'

'She's dodgy as sin, and I didn't like the look on her face when bother broke out at the station. I don't want to see her back at this house. Not while I'm on this case, anyway.'

'It's about you, isn't it?' Siobhan asked, a curious tone in her voice. 'It's about how *you* look.'

'It's about the case. Can you no' see that? If I make a mistake or slip up somewhere . . . that can be the thing that lets this guy get away with it. The sort of thing a lawyer can jump on, a legal technicality . . .'

'You're just worried you'll get into bother.'

'Of course I'm worried I'll get into bother! I'm the senior officer on this case, and someone in the press is wandering around my house unsupervised. "Get into bother" is on a whole different level than handing in your bloody assignments a couple of days late!' He sighed and pinched his nose. 'I'm sorry.'

'Oh, don't worry. I won't be back. Will we, Mint?'

That glowing white face swam into view at the patio door. Although the lamplight reflecting off the window partially obscured the newcomer, Lomond could read her expression. 'Nope,' Mint said, waving. 'Cross our heart and hope to die. By the way, "dodgy as sin" . . . I really like that. Can I stick it on a CV?'

'You can stick it anywhere you like, love,' Lomond said tersely. 'I meant exactly what I said. You – out of my house.'

'And how about me?' Siobhan said.

'You're disturbing me here,' Lomond said simply. 'I was in the middle of something. I had some time, for once. A spare half an hour, and thought I'd do the garden. And here you are.'

'I won't keep you away from it. I'll be staying over at Mint's tonight, I think.'

Before Lomond could come up with a reply, or even a look, she was gone.

Maureen was the next to appear in the garden. It was a clearer night than they'd been used to lately, and the stars were out, scattered by the first chill intimations of the winter. Her expression matched that of her daughter a few moments before.

'Doesn't sound like you handled that well.'

'Och, not you as well,' Lomond sighed. 'How was I supposed to handle it?'

'Seems like you made an exhibition of yourself at the college. She's worried her marks will go down.'

'Her *marks*? She's sticking her neb in where she shouldn't – I couldn't care less if she gets five per cent lopped off an essay! And how should I have handled it?'

'The way you did before. Calmer. Cannier . . . nosier.'

'Yeah. I suppose I've got things on my mind.' They shared a smile, in the semi-darkness.

'Think you could manage a night in front of the telly?' she asked. 'Me and you?'

'Why not?' He stripped off his gardening gloves. Then the phone buzzed in his jacket pocket.

Slater. Out of breath.

'Gaffer.'

That one word. That one delivery. It cold-cocked him. Lomond actually sank to one knee. 'Aw naw. You're kidding. You must be kidding.'

Roya

29

Callum Baird took the boat west along the river, going with the tide. It was a challenging journey in the dark, and for that reason an absorbing, even exciting one. Even in the knowledge that something bad lay at the end of it.

His spotlight picked out ricocheting insects that hadn't taken to the earth yet for the winter, way beyond their time: comets in miniature, sparks and flares in the dark. It was getting late for them, he reflected. Within days they'd be either dead or asleep until the sun returned.

They passed a block of flats just before the trees closed in on either side of the bank. In one stark tableau, a man was washing the dishes, while a woman and two teenage children scooped up the last of their ice cream. In a cosier cell, two women were having dinner by candlelight, a raised glass of red wine turned suddenly scarlet as it passed in front of the flickering illumination.

The boat moved on. It got so dark that Callum and Lottie, his co-pilot for the evening, couldn't even see the trees in the gloom – not even an outline, the jagged etchings completely swallowed in the dark, until the beam pierced them. They were getting close. Callum knew this for a poorly lit spot – somewhere he was sure he'd never have haunted even in his scrubbier teenage days.

The helicopter passed overhead. Its searchlight formed a latticework of half-naked tree branches and startled the winter grass into colour on the ground, bluish under the brutal beam. Then the light picked out the roof of the car in the water, and the stricken faces on the bank, leaping up and down in the darkness.

'How many we looking for?' Lottie Carlsen asked.

'Three,' Callum answered. 'Students. Sitting out with a coupla cans. Got a fire going. They found it.'

'There,' Lottie Carlsen said.

'I see 'em.' Callum cut the engines and let the boat's momentum carry them towards the car, the water disturbed by the downdraught of the chopper. This, and the boat's momentum, created a breakwater of sorts, white crests in the dark as water spilled over the roof. The car had gone into the water but wasn't yet fully submerged. It might have been the carapace of a turtle, quiescent between the banks.

'They're just kids,' Lottie said.

'Aye.' Callum raised the loudspeaker, taking care to keep his tone neutral. 'Hey there. The police are on the way. We're volunteers. We're here to help you out. Please step back from the edge, and stay away from the car.'

One of the three, a girl in her late teens, her face laser-bright in the glare, cupped her hands and called: 'There's a body in it!'

'We'll handle it,' Callum said, his voice gentler. 'Have you touched the car at all?'

The three shook their heads. One lad, a rangy boy wearing a jumper and jogging bottoms despite the hour and the falling temperatures, had his arm around the girl's shoulder. Standing a little way back was a thick-set young man, perhaps a couple of years older, with a straggly beard that might have been snagged on his chin in the breeze.

Callum brought the boat about, perpendicular to the windshield, several inches of which were protruding above the surface of the water. He could tell the car was a beast going by the breadth. Certainly no 1.2 litre number or sporty hatchback.

'Big light,' he said to Lottie, who nodded and raised a bulky torch with a diameter bigger than her head.

The bluish beam hurt to focus on at first, a football flood-light concentrated in one circular frame. The car and the water lapping around it appeared as if caught in a flash of lightning. Water was visible inside the windscreen, the line of demarcation visible as the level outside dipped and rose; it was dirty yellow in the light, silty and brackish. Except for one thing.

Callum sucked in his breath, watching the light cling on to the car even as the boat drifted past. 'Blood,' he said tersely. 'Car is full of blood. You see that? I think I saw a hand, as well.'

Lottie shook her head. 'Not blood. Bring us about again.'

He did so, the turbid water swallowing the car for a moment as the boat's engine returned to life. Callum turned hard to starboard. Working against the tide, they had a little longer to scrutinise the windscreen.

'Not blood, see?' Lottie said. 'It's hair. Red hair.'

'That's definitely an arm . . . look.'

'Do you think it's another one?'

'God knows,' Callum said. 'God only knows.'

Blue lights penetrated the treeline somewhere back along the trail, cobalt fireflies flickering through the darkness. Callum saw the relief in the faces of the teenagers even as the new lights strafed them. The tall, skinny lad hugged the girl. They were both crying. The bigger lad was calm, worryingly so. *He's in shock.* Callum wondered if he had been the first to take a close look at the body in the front seat of the car.

★

'Nobody touch anything,' Lomond said to the officers on the bank. 'I want the car left in place, I want every footprint out here down to the squirrels photographed and plastered.'

'Minchin's on his way,' Slater said.

'I don't want him to touch anything either. Leave it all in place.' He peered towards the whale's-hump obstruction in the water. His brain was fogging over. 'We need . . . Christ, what do you call it? Logistics?'

'How do you mean, gaffer?' Slater asked. 'If it's forensic stuff, it's the SOCOs we want to talk to. They'll handle it. What's the problem with the car?'

'There's no problem. For us, anyway. He's blown it,' Lomond said. 'This is his mistake. He meant that car to sink. He didn't want her found for a few days.'

'Are we sure it's a woman inside?'

Lomond signalled Callum and Lottie; they came forward.

'Callum, did you say you managed to get a picture of the face?'

'There was one decent one,' Callum said. He scrolled through his mobile phone. 'This one. Here you go.'

Lomond and Slater peered at the screen. The side of Lomond's face twitched, and he looked away. Slater wasn't sure if he had spat or if he'd said something.

'What's up, gaffer?'

'I couldn't swear to it,' Lomond said. He gritted his teeth. 'I can't be sure, but . . . I've seen that shade of red somewhere, just recently. It'd be an amazing coincidence. Or maybe it's not a coincidence . . .' His voice drifted off.

Slater and Callum made eye contact for a second or two. Slater took the phone from the man on the boat and zoomed in on the image on the screen.

It was just an impression of a face, as if peeking through dirty curtains, framed by that putrid water: a beautiful face, with high, prominent cheekbones and fine black eyebrows. The eyes were closed. But it was the hair that grabbed you, streaming out behind her, bright, brash red, like the freshest strawberries or a glistening new fire engine – a death ray in comparison to anything else on the spectrum. Her arms and shoulders were naked, though she remained in place, possibly still buckled in her seat.

Lomond walked across to the teenagers. Slater's brows cinched tight in concern, as he handed back the phone.

'Think it's another one?' Callum asked.

'Can't be sure till we see the neck,' Slater said. 'But I know what my gut's telling me.'

Callum said nothing for a few seconds. His jaw tensed. 'Place is going to erupt, man,' he said finally. 'Every lassie, granny, mother, auntie . . . They'll be on the streets.'

'They're going to be angry,' Slater said. 'And I don't blame them.'

'I hope to God you bring this guy in,' Callum said. 'Like, today.'

★

Minchin's terrier-like features were the stuff of comedy, stuffed into the white hazmat suit, though shaving off his moustache had removed the outright hilarity. His team moved quickly, setting up the tents and the searing arc lights. Lomond took a moment to admire the efficiency – he'd once seen a team of squaddies erect a marquee at an event in a public park, and the planning, logistics and sheer graft involved in putting up these temporary structures had impressed him a lot. But once you stepped back to view the entire scene, there was a sense of violation. The white curtains and the stanchions and rails and wiring seemed to slice through the weird angles and sharp edges of the trees and bushes, a pitiless intrusion by right angles, whitewashed edges and human hands. It had the same jarring effect as seeing plastic bottles and crisp packets poking through the bushes. Nothing about it belonged.

Minchin thrust out his chin. 'Not like you to be telling me my business, Lomie.'

'I'm making sure we're on the same page,' Lomond said. 'I want the inside of the car drained and collected before the car gets removed. And I want the water examined.'

'It'll take a while, but . . . sure. We'll do it. Make sure you get some officers out here, though, Lomie. This is going to turn into a circus once the papers and the telly get a sniff of it, if they haven't already. I don't want anybody getting in my road.'

'Nobody's getting in your road.'

'Good. It's my crime scene now.'

'You don't need to front up to me, Chick.'

'This isn't fronting up to you, Lomie. Just one professional to another. Having a discussion.'

'It's not a problem.'

'Smashing. Then we're all good here, aren't we? Nothing to worry about. You leave it in the hands of the experts.'

'Wouldn't dream of doing anything else, Chick. One other thing,' Lomond said. 'I want to see her face as soon as I can. As soon as the water is removed and stored.'

Minchin relaxed a little. 'Sure. Won't be for a while, mind.'

'I'll be right here. Any thoughts?'

Minchin sighed. 'I've taken a look, using the drone.'

'And?'

'Throat's cut.'

'Did you see any blood in the water?'

'Y'know, we just got here Lomie. Plus, blood diffuses in water. And water moves in and out of the car. Whatever it is you're looking for here, bear that in mind.'

'Any link. That's all I'm after. Any link at all. Any loose threads.'

'You'll get no more than I can find.'

Soon the evidence tent was set up around the bank. Inside, day-bright lights cast quick-morphing shadows on the stark white canvas as the SOCOs carried out their work. Lomond wasn't sure exactly what they used to drain the water from the car, but they got it done quickly. The machine's industrial drone reminded him of the day he'd had the pond drained at the house, for fear of Siobhan's tottering into it when she was old enough to walk.

Daylight had already begun to break – a sickly yellow glow, chopped and strewn across the uneasy waters – when the body was brought out, and Lomond finally saw her face. The odd slant of the cheekbones, the long limbs, the angled slashes of the tight-closed eyes. The arms, oddly graceful even as she was lifted out, elbows sharp as rigor mortis began to tighten its grip. The dainty toes pointed upwards. Milk-white shin, slick in the light. She would have green eyes, he knew, when they were prised open.

'I can ID her,' Lomond said. His voice was muted, but every head snapped round. 'She's a life model. She works for Sir Erskine Copper. She was with him a couple of days ago.'

He saw her again, being moved and manipulated like a marionette under Copper's hands; the sheer indifference of her face, until that one guy wolf-whistled at her. Lomond's shame, his anxiety, over her nakedness in the flesh. Close enough to touch, he'd thought, even with his wife lurking somewhere over his shoulder. Now here she was again.

Slater returned, grim-faced, from a round of phone calls. He glanced up at the sky, where a helicopter hovered over the scene.

'That's not one of ours,' he said. 'One of the satellite news channels . . . Smile, gaffer. I think we're on the telly. Probably live.'

'They want to get out of here,' Lomond growled, nodding towards the evidence tent where the red-headed girl was being worked on. 'Someone get in touch and tell them to go. Get Sullivan to do it. Or Drummond.'

'Pains in the arse, man. They're here as well. On foot, I mean. Edge of the cordon. Asking questions. We're in for a long one today, gaffer.'

'Did you get anything, Malcolm?'

Slater shook his head. 'Every exit . . . nothing. We're scouring the CCTV. Got a call out, anyone with dashcams . . . He picked his spot well. Again. No houses nearby, a single-track road but well paved . . . and no witnesses.'

'We'll get his footprints, but not much else. Could be anybody.' Lomond shook his head. 'There can't be nothing. There can't be. Not again.'

'We did get something on the car,' Slater said. 'And you're going to like it.'

'Oh aye?' Surely not. A surge of hope. Some kind of breakthrough, at last?

'It's an Alfa Romeo. Registered to your second-favourite artist in the whole wide world.'

30

Donald Ward looked as if he hadn't long washed his hair – as if he'd been surprised just out of the shower, perhaps in the act of plugging in the hair drier. It maddened Lomond that the artist's straggly locks didn't seem to get any less moist. Must have combed something into it, Lomond reasoned. Maybe the translucent gloopy stuff that was all the rage when he was a child, pink and pale blue and laser-beam green. That pale barroom light, streaked with frozen bubbles. Or perhaps he just gave himself a dose of olive oil. Drizzled, that's how they described it on the Saturday morning cooking shows. Just a slosh.

Lomond spoke loudly and clearly for the benefit of his lawyer, and for the interview-room camera. 'Mr Ward, recently we pulled a car out of the river Clyde. It entered the water several hours ago. Didn't quite go in as far as the person who shoved it intended. There was a breeze block sunk into the bottom, would you believe. Stopped it moving into the deeper water. Dented the front. The car might be salvageable, they say. Built to last, apparently.'

Ward frowned. 'No disrespect, but is there a point to this?'

'Yes,' Lomond said brightly. 'It belongs to you. It's an Alfa Romeo . . . actually it's seventeen years old, but it was fully restored by you. Intending to be sold, we suspect. Like the other cars in your sideline. Classic Autos? Wee garage you've got? About a mile and a half up from the scrappie where another classic car was bought – you know the one I mean. The one that's connected to the last dead girl we pulled out the Clyde.'

'Dead girl . . . sorry?' If it was a bluff, it was a good one. Genuine alarm showed on his features.

'Yes, the one we think was used to dump Sheonaid Aird Na Murchan. That name familiar to you?'

Ward said nothing.

'She was found in the Clyde with her throat cut,' Lomond went on. 'Bonnie lassie. Wanted to be a mermaid. Or pretended to be a mermaid. A selkie, I'm told. You know her. Your pal, Sir Erskine Copper, painted her on a mural at the baths you're helping restore. We found a burnt-out car, a classic car, that was used on a movie set for Claymore Films. Action movie, you know, one where the cops are doing a car chase and jumping off bridges and firing guns and that. Claymore Films, which is part-owned by you.'

'Sorry, you mentioned an Alfa Romeo? I've restored a few Alfa Romeos. Lovely cars. What's this got to do with . . . dead lassies? Sorry?' He sat back. Lomond noticed his lip trembling.

'Aye, dead lassies,' Slater said, with the slow, unblinking stare of a drunk whose attention was perhaps fatally arrested in a kebab shop. 'We found another one in the Alfa Romeo that we dragged out the Clyde last night. The one you own.'

'Another one?' Ward stared at his lawyer.

'Yes,' Slater said. 'Too early to say if it's connected to the other two dead lassies we pulled out the water. But I think the papers might have their own ideas. And the websites, and the national news. You'll definitely read about it in the *Glasgow Times*, Mr Ward.'

'Sorry . . . you found a dead lassie . . . explain this to me . . . in a car, one of mine? From Classic Autos?'

'Yep,' Slater said. 'Fully registered to you. I'll refresh your memory here . . .' Slater rattled the keyboard, then clicked the mouse. On screen were the licensing details, and the name and address attached. Ward's name and address.

The artist shook his head. 'I don't know anything about it. I don't even know . . . I can't place it. What year, what model?'

'It's right there on screen,' Lomond said. 'Take your time. Take in the details.'

The dented car still looked wringing wet in the picture. Flecked with slime. A leaf, dead but curiously green, looked as if it had been slapped hard against the headlights. 'I do recognise it,' Ward said. 'I had it at Classic Autos . . . I think I bought it at an auction at Grange's – the scrappie . . .'

'You bought it at the scrappie six weeks ago,' Slater interjected. He stabbed at the keyboard, and the image showed a receipt. 'Taken you about that long to fix it up. One of your sidelines, Donald, isn't it? Fixing up the motors? Classic cars, and that? Got some collection at your garage, I bet. Funny, it reminded me of being a wean when I looked at your catalogue. Cortinas, Sierras, Orions, Fiestas . . . They still make Fiestas, mind.'

Ward raised a hand. 'Listen, whatever you're trying to insinuate here . . .'

'We haven't insinuated anything,' Slater said.

'Whatever you're trying to imply, then – I'll say it for the record, here and now: I don't know anything about it. I don't know anything about these lassies. What . . . you're saying you found a lassie in the car? Inside it? In the river? My car?'

'Can't confirm or deny anything at this stage,' Lomond said shortly.

A change had come over Ward. He still had the self-possession, the maddening surety which seemed to bore so deep into him that Lomond suspected the artist, rather than being cool, might simply be dense. Now he was twitchy, agitated. It was dawning on him, Lomond thought. He was beginning to understand where the trail led, that the tyre tracks turned in at his driveway. In a manner of speaking.

'I had nothing to do with any of it,' Ward declared.

'Tell me again where you got the motor?' Slater said.

'I told you. An auction—'

'At the scrappie's?' Slater wrote some notes.

249

'And it's connected to the Ferryman?'

'That's right. Sometimes things come up there . . . well, not exactly off the books, you have to get the paperwork right, it's all legal . . . but away from the regular auctions. You get bargains. It takes a bit of time and effort to get them shipshape, but it's worth it. I love cars as much as I love art.'

'There's a connection between the scrapyard where you bought the Alfa Romeo we pulled out of the Clyde and two dead lassies,' Slater said. 'You sure you don't have anything to do with it?'

'My client has already answered that question.' His lawyer was just in her thirties but acted a fair bit younger. 'He's already told you – no.'

'Worth asking again – it's an amazing coincidence. Is it a coincidence?' Slater's expression was baleful. His eyes were bloodshot, as if he'd been drinking.

'No . . . Well, yes,' Ward said, blinking rapidly.

'No, yes, what? A coincidence? Yes? No?'

'The car must've been stolen. The Alfa Romeo. It's a coincidence,' Ward said.

Slater drew a deep breath, his nostrils pinched tight. 'Bit of a big one.'

'That's you saying that.'

Lomond interjected: 'What do you know about the previous owner?'

'Bugger all. You know more than me. You've got the paperwork, have you not?'

'That's right. I'm just asking. Did you have a buyer lined up?'

'No, I was going to . . . It was going to be farmed out for sale.'

'But not at a scrappie,' Slater said. 'Somewhere a bit more upmarket. Somewhere you might make a bit more money.'

'If you say so. I love doing the cars up. The risk is mine. If the profit's mine too, that's a bonus.'

'So what we want to know is, if the car got nicked from your fancy garage, how do you not know about it?'

'I've had a lot on . . . it's news to me, honest.'

'But you don't have security, cameras, alarms, that kind of stuff?' Slater looked down at his notes. 'You've got all sorts at that garage. An Aston Martin . . . Lamborghini Countach. You know, when I was about twelve, I had a poster of one of those on my wall. I'd have stolen it in a heartbeat. So how does someone steal an Alfa Romeo from under your nose, then use it in one of the most famous murder cases on the planet right now?'

'I don't know.' Ward stared at a spot on the wall, far from the unblinking eyes of Lomond and Slater.

'Inconvenient for you,' Slater remarked.

'The lassie was a model,' Lomond said. 'The lassie who was found in your car, I mean. Do you know her name? Roya Van Ahle. Dutch name. Second generation, in fact. Glasgow as they come, though. Her family's from Shawlands. She was living with her mum and three sisters. Making money as a model. Again, there's a link with Sir Erskine Copper.'

'Then maybe you should talk to Sir Erskine Copper.'

'Don't worry about him,' Lomond said. 'This is about you. Did you know her?'

'Name isn't familiar.'

'How about a face?' Lomond nodded to Slater, who moved the presentation on to the next slide. 'And a body? This familiar to you?'

On screen, that cascade of red hair. It mostly obscured her face, only allowing through the long, flat nose and the rounded chin, with one half of a smirk breaking through in between. A single green eye flared. She was extraordinary, even allowing for some trickery in the camera shot. She was naked, sitting on a stool in an empty barroom, her hair covering her breasts. She looked . . . the word was fleshier, Lomond mused, in this photo, compared to how he'd seen her the other night. When she was alive and well. Close enough to reach out and touch.

'I don't know her,' Ward said.

'You sure? We've found out she had sent videos to a site you have a stake in – we've talked about it before. MyGirl. Not sure if she'd been accepted yet.'

The picture on the screen changed to an image of Roya in her underwear. Her face was different, a change owing to her make-up – thicker mascara and eyeshadow. She was scowling, the expression too harsh for comfort. Red underwear matched her hair, which was styled differently – set in crazed bunches, like Catherine wheels.

'No, I don't know her. I am not hands-on with MyGirl. I never was.'

'Nah, you're just the owner. You just make money off it, then,' Slater said. 'Bit like with the cars. If some profit comes in, it's all a bonus, eh? Nothing to do with business. Just art.'

'What are you trying to say?'

Slater smiled and said nothing.

Lomond linked his hands on the table. 'If I told you that we'd made some progress on a case from twenty-five years ago . . . one that you're also involved in . . . how would you react to that?'

'I'll react the way I'm reacting now. With confusion. What progress have you made, exactly? I'm assuming you're talking about Daisy Lawlor?'

'My client's said all he has to say on that matter,' the lawyer said.

'That's right,' Ward said. 'But I do want to hear what these two have to say about it.' He jabbed a finger at Lomond and Slater.

'We may have a breakthrough on someone who was at the hunting lodge with you guys,' Lomond said. 'By you guys I mean you, Torquod Rafferty and Lana Galbraith.'

'Put it in writing and I'll get you a response.'

'Yeah,' Slater sneered. 'Maybe you should get it cleared with your boss.'

'I don't have a boss.'

'You do, though.' Slater slouched for a moment and spoke through a yawn. 'You've got a boss – Torquod. Or Torin. That's the relationship, isn't it? He's your boss. I mean there has to be something transactional about it. Folk don't really have friendships that last that long, do they? Not any more, I mean.'

'Speak for yourself,' Ward said.

'He's got some kind of hold on you, would you agree? I mean you're a smart guy, clever, talented even . . . and there you are, clinging on to this old-money Tory like a sticky willie. What's the deal? Is it influence? Funny handshake mob? Is it protection?'

'You're talking rot. Are you going to charge me with anything?'

But Slater had found a weak point. 'Does he know a secret? Or is he paying for your silence? Does he have a hold on you, or do you have a hold on him?'

'I told you, I don't know anything!' Ward roared this last, at scarcely believable volume. He had bitten his bottom lip hard enough to draw blood, and Lomond wanted to flinch away as he spluttered: 'I don't know anything about what happened at Rafferty Landing. Whatever happened to Daisy Lawlor, I wasn't there. I didn't know about the stolen car until you told me. And it must have been stolen. What happened to the girl on the mural was . . . horrifying. If you're asking me, realistically, if it's all a coincidence, all these things, then yes, it is. I was with my wife last night. Every record you can check will prove that's true.'

'If you're hiding something, son,' Lomond said, 'we'll find out. You'll be in trouble. You'll be an accessory. You'll be charged, along with whoever's responsible.'

'I don't know anything.' His face changed, the lip trembling, and then a barrier broke. For a few seconds he was weeping, as openly and bitterly as a child. Even his lawyer broke character for a moment, laying her hand on his forearm as he cried, 'I don't know anything. I don't know. I told you, I don't know!'

31

The wind tore the car door out of Lomond's hands and slammed it hard against the frame, giving him a fright. On the other side of the car, Slater had the opposite problem, having to close his door into the wind. He leaned into it, bracing his shoulder, like a man losing a fight with a recalcitrant umbrella.

'Where'd this come from, gaffer?' he said breathlessly. 'Force ten hurricane stuff, here.'

Lomond looked towards the high flats, huge, functional rectangles on a science fiction scale, grey and stolid in the face of the wind. 'Just as well we're not on the roof.'

'Near enough. What is it, twenty-fifth floor?'

'Aye.' Lomond fastened the upper buttons of his coat, wincing. 'Shall we take the stairs for a laugh?'

'Wait for the wind to pick up. We could fly up, Mary Poppins style, and knock on the window.'

Lomond locked the car. 'Could've done with one of the trained officers. No time, though.'

'I'll put on my sympathetic face.' Slater gazed up at the blocks as they made their way to the front doors. It seemed even colder in the shade. The area in front was a former children's playpark where the frames of the swings, slides and roundabouts had been cut off at the ankles. Two shaped metal benches remained, splattered with incomprehensible graffiti. Faces appeared at some of the windows as the two policemen angled themselves against the high wind.

'Pal o' mine used to live here,' Slater said, arching his thumb towards a row of wholemeal-coloured tenements. 'Did a paper round. Said he saw someone come off one of these. From the top. Said he saw him bounce. Like he was made of rubber, he said. Never sure if the guy fell or jumped. I'd guess he jumped.'

'Tip for you, Malcolm – don't mention any of this to these people.'

'Gaffer . . .' Slater muttered.

The lift was clean and reeked of lemon cleaning fluid. By the time it made off with a sullen shrug, the smell was unbearable. 'Wonder what they were trying to cover up?' Lomond asked.

'What, you mean murders?'

'No.' Lomond had to chuckle. 'I mean, what were they covering up in here? The lift. That smell. Mouldy lemons. Whatever it is.'

'Like I said. Murders, probably.'

The lift took a while to reach the twenty-fifth floor. The lights made their steady hopscotch progress up an ancient seventies-style console with numbered buttons. No one attempted to get in and hinder their rise, for which Lomond was grateful.

They heard the wailing the moment the lift disgorged them into a long corridor with red-tiled walls and patterned lino-leum on the floor that reminded Lomond of smoke. Both men hesitated for a second.

'Coming from flat five, I'm guessing,' Slater said. 'They know we're coming?'

'They know we're coming.'

Flat five was a closed door, a reassuring shade of dark blue without windows, unless you counted the single spyhole. Inside, someone was crying.

The wailing stopped as Lomond rapped the door twice.

The inspector was momentarily staggered by the face that greeted them – the double of the dead girl's. Those angled cheekbones and jawline, suggestive of the prow of a fine ship. But the hair was straw blonde, wild and wavy rather than silky-straight and red, and the green eyes, rather than smoky or sullen, were puffy and bloodshot.

'Inspector Lomond,' he said, displaying his warrant card. 'This is DS Slater.'

Her face crumpled, her hands to her mouth. Lomond acted instinctively, putting his arm around her shoulder. 'They've just been,' she said. 'They've just been to collect her stuff . . .'

'I'm so sorry,' Lomond said. 'You'll be Roya's twin? Maisie?'

'Aye,' was all she could say. Then her legs buckled, her strength almost gone, and Lomond held her up, with Slater at her side.

'There you go,' Lomond said, supporting her. Her legs might have been made of straw, collapsing beneath her weight. 'You poor lassie. You poor, poor lassie.'

'Let's get you in, eh?' Slater said. Like Lomond, he had spotted heads appearing round the other doors in the corridor. 'We'll talk inside. That's for the best.'

Before they closed the door, a woman marched up the corridor from one of the neighbouring flats. 'What do you think you're doing? Bloody waste of time! Get out there and catch the bastard!'

Lomond shut the door on her.

The hallway inside was narrow but clean. Family photos adorned the walls. Flashes of red identified the dead girl, impossible to miss, match-head flares that would only cause sharp pain in future, an absence fading to grey in their lives.

Two more faces appeared in the hallway then, young faces – one girl no older than twelve, still in her pyjamas and dressing gown, very like her twin sisters, and another maybe a couple of years into her teens. She had a school shirt on, minus a tie, and a short skirt over black tights. She was extremely tall, like Roya and Maisie, and her face showed signs of the same sharp angles.

'Let's get a wee chair for you, Maisie,' Lomond said. 'A glass of water as well. Where's the kitchen – through here?'

The teenager folded her arms. 'The polis have already been here,' she said. 'What is it you want now?'

'To help,' Lomond said. 'Please, I know this is hard . . .'

'You lot know nothing,' she screamed. The younger girl hid her face in her hands and began to cry.

'Where's your mum?' Slater asked.

'Where d'you think?' the teenager said through her teeth. 'In her bed! She's ruined!'

'In here a minute,' Lomond said. He steered Maisie into the kitchen, sitting her down at a wood-effect Formica-topped table blackened and pitted with cigarette burns at one corner. Slater found a glass in the dish rack and poured some water for her. She took the glass, trying to keep it steady. Her teeth chattered. Lomond crouched down beside her, and she struggled to focus on him, or on anything. For a moment he wondered if she'd taken something.

Through the net curtains in the window behind her, and the city beyond spread out before them. The wind was still fierce, and Lomond was aware of the whole structure moving beneath his feet. Nausea, now, to contend with, on top of everything else. He blinked, trying to find a horizon among the scattered buildings rearing into the gloomy skies.

'We need to ask,' he said, 'when did you last see Roya?'

'Two nights ago . . . was it three? Not long,' Maisie said. 'Came to give back twenty-five quid she borrowed off me . . . I told her not to bother, it was pay day for me.'

'Did you see her much?'

'Not since she moved out . . . She had money coming, she said. She'd just been paid for doing the cams . . . She told me not to tell our maw.' Her voice took on a plaintive tone, high and shrill, rather than the whisper it should have been. 'Please don't tell my maw!'

'We'll not tell your maw anything,' Lomond said. 'We need to hear this from you. Did Roya have a boyfriend?'

'Aye, Cesar. That's what she called him. I didn't meet him. She was staying with him – she'd moved out of her flat in Shawlands a while ago. She couldn't keep up with the rent.

So she moved in with Cesar. She said he was nice, didn't give her hassle.'

'Cesar . . .' Lomond's notepad was out, his pen a blur. 'Was that a nickname?'

'I asked her that – she said naw. That was his name.' Maisie attempted a mouthful of water; she almost managed it, but choked halfway, a rill spilling from the corner of her mouth. 'Sorry. I said to her – I called him the Roman. She said he had a Roman nose. It ran in the family, she said. She telt me his brother's name was actually Roman.'

'That's good,' Lomond said, nodding. 'Excellent. Did she talk about the work she was doing?'

'Modelling, for a painter. I didn't believe her, but she showed me some pictures, said she'd posed for a famous guy. Was it him?' She began to sob. 'Did the famous guy kill her?'

'We don't know who killed her yet,' Lomond said. 'But we're going to get him.'

'You're getting nobody,' said the belligerent teenager from the doorway. 'You've done nothing, and now this fucking maniac's killed her!' She lurched forward, followed by the young girl in the pyjamas. Their older sister flinched, dropping the glass. The water spilled over her lap before Lomond caught the tumbler just in time.

Slater folded his arms, shoulders tense, leaning against the sink. He looked to Lomond for guidance.

'We're doing loads,' Lomond said. 'We're closing in on him. Please believe me.'

'I believe nothing. What are you two, the Keystone Cops? We've heard nothing, just been told she's dead. A trained officer is going to come in later, they say. What does that make you, then? You the trained officer?'

'Please,' said the younger girl. 'Please, Kirsten. Please leave them alone. We need them to help . . .'

'Anything you can tell us about Roya's important,' Lomond said gently. 'We need to know everything she said to you in the past week or so. Did she talk about modelling jobs?'

'Aye – she took her clothes off for fucking perverts,' Kirsten snarled. 'Old men like you. That's why she's deid, isn't it? That's why she got killed. Doing the pervy camera stuff!'

'Did she do MyGirl?' Lomond asked.

'You tell me!' shrieked the teenager. 'You're the bloody detectives! Holmes and Watson there. Pair of crackers! You've no' got a clue! My cousin, when he gets here . . . he's told me, he's getting a few boys together. We'll have your fucking Ferryman on a lamppost by the weekend. We'll . . .' Suddenly, she collapsed, and Maisie caught her, sweeping her into her arms. The teenager sobbed, her long dark hair falling over her older sister's shoulder.

'She didn't do MyGirl,' Maisie said in a low voice. 'She was on another account, based in Holland. She was talking about doing MyGirl, though. Said it was a step up for her, more money.'

'But had she signed up to it?' Lomond asked.

'You tell me.'

Lomond refilled the glass of water and put it down on the table. 'I need to speak to your mum,' he said.

'Stay out o' there,' Kirsten growled, without removing her face from her older sister's shoulder. 'You've done enough. No more. No more of it.'

'I need to speak to her. It's important.' He was past the two older girls in a second. The younger girl was already running towards the room at the top of the hall, her pink fleecy pyjamas darting inside before the door slammed shut.

Lomond knocked on the door. There was no response, so he opened it and poked his head inside.

'Mrs Van Ahle? Are you there?'

The bedroom had yellow curtains; any light that made it through was rotten, and double-filtered through bluish smoke from the lit cigarette slowly disintegrating in an ashtray by the dresser. More pictures, more frames filled with the dead

259

girl's face. Blonde to start with, like her twin, but it seemed she'd gone for bright red at secondary school. Never quite naturally smiling, but posing, and beautiful from the word go, it seemed. *Her eyes mocked you*, Lomond thought. *God forgive me, they mock you.*

The younger girl had leapt into bed with her mother and was clinging to her. The mother could have been a corpse; the impression staggered Lomond for a moment, sensory overload, his eyes stinging, exhaustion and dread overwhelming him.

'What are you doing here?' the woman asked. The same cheekbones, of course, but the face gaunt, unhealthy. The eyes were dark, bigger than the girls' and more unsettling. There was no suggestion of how tall she was or what her body shape might have been – just a head encircled by her youngest child's arms. But you could see she was thin. *Is she even forty yet?* Lomond wondered.

'What do you want?'

'Mrs Van Ahle, I want to say I'm so sorry . . .'

'I never knew anything,' she interrupted. 'About my Roya. Never knew anything. Came and went. Organised her own life. Could have done anything: clever, but didn't stick in at school. "Here's my qualifications, mum," she'd say,' and Roya Van Ahle's mother framed her face with her hands, then fell back, exhausted. 'You've already taken away her stuff . . . her folders and stuff. You'll find out more about her from those than you will from me.' Her head turned on the pillow; her eyes closed.

'She's had enough!' whispered the little girl. 'Leave us alone! We can't handle this!'

32

'There was a lot I wanted to say there,' Lomond said, buckling his seatbelt, while the wind rocked the car. 'I wanted to say to tell the wee lassie about how these are terrible days, but we will help them all we can. And one day the days won't be quite so terrible. That kind of stuff, you know? I didn't get a chance to say any of that.'

'If you had said it, you might have been lying. Maybe all their days will be terrible now. Maybe they always were.'

Lomond turned out of the crescent, where the two concrete giants loomed. 'What did we learn in there?'

'We didn't know about the cam stuff. Cesar, was it?'

'We should get the twin in on her own. Maisie. She seemed a bit more switched on about Roya. The mum's . . . the mum won't be good for much for a while.'

'Maisie knew about MyGirl as well.'

Lomond nodded. 'Definite link.'

'We've pulled out nothing so far from MyGirl's staff. The footage is all self-shot. The editors who put the packages together and add in the music are based in London. None of them were in town when the other two were killed. So . . . what's next?'

'The boyfriend.'

'Cesar . . . If that's not his name, it's not much to go on. She mentioned a brother, though – Roman. That could narrow it down.'

'I've got him,' Lomond said.

'What d'you mean?'

'Sent it through to Smythe while we were in the lift coming

down. The sister was right enough, even about the brother called Roman. That's his actual first name. Cesar Kline. As in Cesar Romero: C-E-S-A-R.'

'Or Billy McNeill.'

'Yep. Got an address in Crowley Street. That's next.'

'Good work, Batman.'

★

'Nice flat he's got,' Slater said, peering up at the blond sandstone tenements, slick in the recent rain. 'I'd live here in a minute. Buying or renting?'

'Bought.'

Slater whistled. 'What's he work as?'

'Interesting one. Works in PR. Clubs, restaurants, tourism, bus and boat trips. At night he's a DJ.'

Lomond pressed a buzzer on the front door, next to a printed card under glass that simply read *Cesar*. The answer came quite soon.

'Hello?'

'Hi, Cesar. Police Scotland here. We need to speak to you about something very important.'

He hung up without replying. Both detectives braced for the buzzing sound that would herald their entry to the flat. It didn't arrive.

'He got a record?' Slater asked, stepping back to peer up at the tall windows.

'Nope, all clean.'

'What's he driving?'

Lomond gestured towards a silver Mercedes, its metallic sheen blistered with water droplets like an aluminium can plucked from the fridge.

'Hmm. Rich dad?'

'Rich-ish.'

'Hmm.'

Lomond pressed the buzzer again.

'Sorry,' came the reply, 'I was just getting myself ready.'

'Don't keep us waiting,' Lomond said, not too unkindly.

Soon they were buzzed up; the flat was at the top, the only one on the floor at the end of the spiral staircase. The close itself was beautifully kept, with immaculate white and royal blue tiling, gilded newel caps and bright green potted plants on the sills of the broad stairhead windows.

The storm doors opened before they could knock. In the background, a toilet bowl was still in the process of flushing.

A slim man of about twenty-six appeared, all sharp angles in his hair, his shirt collar, his eyebrows, and his jawline. He had tiny shades on, with octagonal lenses the colour of old brass. 'Gents,' he said. 'Some ID, please.'

Lomond and Slater produced their warrant cards.

'Mind?' Cesar asked, taking the card from Lomond. He studied it for an absurdly long time, turning it over.

'You expecting many in tonight?' Slater asked.

One of the eyebrows arched. 'What?'

'You expecting many in – you know, in here? This is a nightclub, isn't it? That must be why you're doing this. Checking our ID.'

Cesar appraised Slater coolly. 'I want to know who wants to come in my front door, pal. That's all.'

'Well, now you know. This is important business. We can talk about it inside, or your neighbours can listen to it all out here.'

Cesar sniffed and handed Lomond his warrant card without looking at him. He stepped back, and the two policemen went in.

The living room was untidier than might have been supposed from the pristine exterior and the stairwell: a traveller's flat or an old hippie's. Lots of art from around the world – Hindu gods, Thai figures, South American stone faces with tongues protruding. Moorish-style lamps hung low enough for even Lomond to bump his head on; ceramics and textiles decorated every surface, fighting for elbow room with smiling Buddhas, while sagging candles clung on to life in a frozen white cascade in every corner. Any surface not covered with carvings or masks or figurines of gods and animals and demons bore witness to Cesar; he had lots of photos, all of them showing him, some with other people, many just on his own.

Barefoot, still wearing his shades, in a pristine white T-shirt and pale blue jeans, he sat down on an armchair and crossed one leg over the other. 'Shoot, guys,' he said. 'I'm busy today.'

Lomond got to the point quickly. 'Roya's dead.'

Cesar quickly uncrossed his legs and sat forward. He removed his shades. He had tiny eyes, heavily lidded. They showed confusion and shock. 'Dead? She was here two nights ago.'

'I'm afraid it's true. She was found dead last night.'

'Hang on . . . hang on.' He stood up and began to pace, his head in his hands. One floorboard creaked in time to his steps. He had his back turned to them.

Slater met Lomond's gaze with a sardonic look.

'You need a cuppa tea or something, son?' Lomond asked.

'No . . . just gimme a minute. Gimme a minute.' He sat down again. 'Dead how?'

'We'll get to that,' Slater said. 'Just take your time.'

'It's . . . it's a lot to take in.'

'I understand she was staying here,' Lomond said. 'Is that right?'

'She crashed on the couch. She moved around quite a lot. She was here two, maybe three times a week. I don't know where else she went. My God. I can't believe this.'

'I'm sorry,' Lomond said. 'Do you want to take a wee minute and get a glass of water? It might help.'

Cesar rubbed his face. 'Dead how?'

'We believe she was murdered.'

Now there was no disguising his shock and agitation. 'Oh Christ, don't tell me she's the one I read about . . . the one in

264

the Clyde . . . don't tell me he got her!'

'Who?' Lomond asked.

'The Ferryman! Fuck's sake, who do you think? It's every-where! Are you daft?'

'Take a minute,' Lomond said.

'I don't need a minute.' Cesar got up and gazed out of the window, bracing one hand on the wall, his back to the policemen. 'I was here. Last night. When did it happen?'

'We'll come to that,' Lomond said. 'How did you know Roya?'

'Modelling,' Cesar said. 'I was doing a launch down at the Clydeside . . . It was for the boxing: Scottie Dalmally, when he fought that boy from Senegal. When they announced the fight, had the face-off, a bit of trash talk. You know the deal. I was in the PR team, played a set at the dinner and party after it. Roya was working – ring girl, you know? I think she'd worked at the boxing before. Holds up the cards that tell you what round it is. That hair, you know? Couldn't miss her. We got talking. She gave me her card. I used it.' Cesar lowered his voice. 'I love red hair. Always have. I got talking to her, got her on to some other events, hostess type stuff, at private clubs.'

'Private clubs how? What kind of stuff?' Slater asked.

Cesar held up his hands. 'Nothing dodgy. Hostess work. Private members' clubs. On Royal Exchange Square. There're some up on Bath Street now. Just a pretty face, you know. Serving. Sometimes they're just paid to be seen. With a private members' club, you need to encourage anyone under the age of thirty-five. Especially if they're female. Under-thirty-fives can't afford the membership, so otherwise it's just the place where old ravers go to die. No offence.'

Wondering for a moment who Cesar had just insulted, and why, Lomond asked: 'How long ago was this?'

'About a year, maybe eighteen months ago. She had come from nowhere, really. Think she came from the high flats in Drumchapel, but it took you ages to get that out of her. You wouldn't guess it. Well spoken. Educated-sounding, but she didn't go to uni. Don't think she worked, either. I mean, a regular job – she worked hard at what she did. Fair amount of modelling, right from school. Really looked and sounded the part, you know?'

'How was she supposed to sound?' Slater asked.

'Well . . . she came across very well, is what I'm saying.'

Lomond said, 'You said she worked an event at the Clyde-side . . . what's your PR company?'

'I work for Tyrone and MacArthur. But I've just started my own firm, Kline and Co. Branching out, you know.'

'Have you been involved in any political events recently?'

'Yeah, sure. Torin MacAllister, you know him? Guy standing for election? Tory? Sound guy, actually. Quite liked him. I did a launch for him. That was at the Clyde as well.'

'Did Roya work at that event?' Lomond tried to remember a fleck of bright red among the people at the waterside on that day.

'She did,' Cesar said. 'Torin was quite taken with her. And I think he introduced her to a guy, Donald Ward? The artist? Does a lot of conceptual work. He's doing that refit up at the old baths, you know? He took her card, too. Said he wanted her as a model. She did some life modelling, for cash, like. When she was quite young, up at the art school. Went into actual schools, too. Can't be an artist in this city who hasn't seen her arse, she's fond of saying.'

It struck Cesar, then. For real. He sat down. A tremor ran along the hard line of his shoulders, and his lips trembled. Lomond wondered when was the last time this man had cried. Perhaps he'd hidden his piggy little eyes behind his shades since he was a teenager, presenting that cool, insectoid countenance with its hard angles, never knowing a shiver like this, the clutch of horror and dread. He was a man who'd had doors opened for him wherever he went and might keep going that way. But this was a moment he would remember all his life.

266

'Sorry,' Cesar said, his voice hoarse. 'She was here . . . two nights ago, Jesus Christ. She stayed with me the night before – she slept on that couch! God. This makes me a suspect, doesn't it?'

'Let's talk about your relationship,' Lomond asked. 'Did she live here?'

'Nah. Like I said, she stayed all over. Some nights she would stay here, sure. She moved around a bit. It could depend on what job she was doing. She worked for me, she worked at the art school, she did modelling at night classes . . . sometimes it was the real deal as well, fashion shoots. I had a couple of contacts . . . underwear, that kind of stuff.'

'I'll need names, times and addresses,' Lomond said. 'Every bit of contact.'

'And you say she stayed over,' Slater said, frowning. 'On the couch? This couch?'

'Yeah.' Cesar swallowed. 'Sometimes not on the couch. You know.'

'You were seeing each other?' Lomond asked.

'You could put it like that,' Cesar said, in a quiet voice. 'Not a boyfriend and girlfriend thing. Casual. We've got busy lives. We hustle. We chase it. That's how it goes. You know?'

'I'm sorry, I don't know,' Slater said. 'So you slept together casually? But she crashed on the couch, sometimes? Not in your bed?'

'Sometimes in my bed. Aye. That's the way it was. Some people don't get it. We don't live our lives like other people – two point four kids, a house. It's different for our generation. You've got to chase it. Life's like that.'

'Sure, I can see life must be like that, in a flat this big, with a Mercedes the size of a cement lorry outside. Hustle. Drive. Chasing it,' Slater sneered.

'What do you mean by that?' Cesar said indignantly.

'You were using her . . . or maybe she was using you,' Slater said. 'That's what I reckon. I can't quite get a handle on you,

267

that's the thing. Not sure I get the vibe of an exploiter, really. You're not a tough guy or anything. I'm interested in your work history, pal. Worked for your dad to begin with, I take it?'

'Yeah. Worked hard. So did my dad,' Cesar said.

'I've heard that a few times the past coupla weeks,' Slater said.

'So,' Lomond interjected, 'Roya slept here sometimes . . . What, once a week? Once a month? A few days a week? All the time? Give me a picture here.'

'Like I said, she stayed in other places. I don't think she actually lived anywhere. She had places to crash. I didn't ask too many questions. She said she flat-shared, but never told me with who. I think she said it was in Shawlands, but she'd moved out.'

'She wasn't officially known to be living anywhere in particular when she died,' Lomond said. 'All her details were still registered to her mum's flat, but she rarely stayed there either.'

'Couch surfer type,' Cesar said. 'You run into them.'

'I suppose,' Lomond said. 'Now tell me about the last time you saw her.'

'I said, this week. Two nights ago. She didn't have any work on, and came over. She said she'd been fine-art modelling – a class at a community college. Nude stuff. Said she had a bunch of old men perving at her. She quite enjoyed that. You can't be shy in the modelling game, eh?'

Lomond said quickly: 'So what happened? She crashed on the couch? Or in your bed?'

'On my couch,' Cesar said evenly.

'Not in the mood, then?' Slater asked.

'Mood's got nothing to do with it. She's a pal. Sometimes more than a pal. The other night she was just a pal. She slept on the couch; she was knackered. Didn't want any food, didn't want any drink.'

'What else did she have set up?' Lomond asked. 'Did she say anything about it?'

'She said she had a modelling gig coming up, but she didn't say what. I had something set up with her next weekend. She was helping to compere at some awards – brewers' association, quite a big gig, at the SEC. Like I said, she spoke well. She had it all. People coming from all over the world. Paid well, too. She was looking forward to it. She was looking at what she was going to wear. I was going to buy it for her. I'll have to cancel . . .'

His voice fell away.

'When did she leave?' Lomond asked.

'Early morning yesterday. Got a taxi.'

'Private hire?'

'Yes.'

'Do you know the firm?'

'Aye, it was the one I use – got an account. She called it. Not sure where she was going, though. It'll be on their database.'

Lomond took down the details. 'And where were you last night?'

'In here.' Cesar swallowed. 'I'd had a long day. Yesterday I was playing a set, down at the Beau Regarde. Near Bath Street.'

'I think I know where you are,' Lomond said. 'Get finished late?'

'Someone was on after me, so I was packed up about ten. It takes it out of you, doing it on top of the day job . . . But I love it, I suppose.'

'And you came back here, about ten? Were you driving?'

'I was.'

'Alone?' Slater asked.

Cesar shook his head. He swallowed.

There was a creak somewhere in the hallway. A tiny sound. Slater was out of his seat, a springing whippet. He tore open the door, and there was another young woman with red comet-tail hair, her hand poised on the front door handle.

'Hello there,' Slater said brightly. 'Come and join the party.'

'I'd rather not.' She was tall, and her red hair looked mostly natural, with an auburn or hazel tint to some highlights. It was wet, and neither towelled nor blow-dried – she was leaving in a hurry.

'I'm DS Slater, and this is DI Lomond, and I'm going to insist,' Slater said.

If there had been a bit of an atmosphere before, now it was thick enough to draw tears. She was dressed in a white minidress decorated with what appeared to be knife wounds. Her breasts bulged over the top of the neckline. She had long legs, though not quite as long as Roya Van Ahle's, and took great care in crossing these as she sat down on an armchair opposite Cesar's, her handbag clutched in her lap.

'Can I ask, did you stay here last night?' Lomond asked, once he'd taken her name, address and phone number.

She nodded. 'I stayed over. Not on the couch.' She glared at Cesar.

'And was Mr Kline here with you the whole night?'

'Aye. But he was asleep for just about all of it.'

'Did you know Roya Van Ahle?'

'Never heard of her.'

Lomond tapped on his phone, finding an image of Roya in life. An unforced, unposed image, found on a digital camera she'd left at her mother's: her head turned, at a party somewhere, laughing at something.

The woman frowned. 'Actually, she is sort of familiar . . . Did she do camera work?'

Lomond and Slater sat up straight. 'Do you . . . do camera work?' Slater asked.

'Depends who's asking,' she said, and sniffed.

'We are,' Slater said. 'You can answer us here or down at the station.'

'I think I know her from CamJack.'

Lomond blinked. 'What's CamJack?'

33

The wind had dropped a little by the time Lomond was driving back to Govan, and the rain seemed to be slackening. 'All we need is that one wee thing,' he said. 'Just that one link. It's right there.'

'The tip might have come in already,' Slater said. 'Knocking doors, talking to folk . . . ex-boyfriends, people who knew Roya at the other camera service, the dodgy one . . . what's it called? CamJack?'

'That was it. Never heard of it,' Lomond said. 'I'd heard of OnlyFans, and MyGirl obviously . . . Do I want to search for it on my computer?'

'You absolutely don't want it on your computer. Maureen'd sniff it out in seconds. She's probably sniffed MyGirl out already, in fact. Wee alarm would've gone off in her head when you said the name.'

'Dodgy stuff?'

'Well dodgy. Makes MyGirl look like the art galleries.'

'We'll be checking that. Sharpish.' They considered this a moment. Finally Lomond said, 'Feels so much better out talking to folk. Even if they're throwing things at you.'

'There's a couple of updates on our Ferryman,' Slater said, scrolling through his phone. 'Got some facts 'n' figures that we didn't have before from the latest crime scene. You ready?'

'Spit it out, Malcolm.'

Slater took a deep breath. 'You want to guess the shoe size they got from the river bank?'

'I'll go for size nine.'

'Spot on! So we are looking for an absolutely average gadgie.'

271

'What about the wounds, the knife used? Same as before?'

'Can't tell. Could be a regular bread knife. We'll be talking to Minchin about whether or not it might be the one used on the other girls. After he's taken us through the post-mortem.'

Lomond glanced at the digital time display. 'We're just about on time. I don't really want to be late, especially for Minchin. He was a bit shirty with me this morning. Not like him.'

'Everybody's a bit shirty this weather. Doesn't help when you've got a full fitba crowd's worth of folk calling for you to resign. What do people want? We're no' psychic.'

'Anything else? No sightings?'

'An Alfa Romeo picked her up, Great Western Road, bus stop on the main road. Exactly like the other two. There's some CCTV, but guess what?'

'Nothing clear on his face?'

'Got it in one, gaffer.'

'How about where it came from?'

'Seems to have come in from the south side. This is different from Aylie Colquhoun – that car came in from the north, Blackhill way.'

'Totally the opposite direction. He's messing with us. He knows that we're on to him. Knows the tricks.' Lomond grimaced. 'What about her mobile phone?'

'Same deal as the other two.' Slater scrolled his phone again and frowned. 'Yeah . . . car took the A-road out past Bearsden. Mobile connection cuts out in a funny wee remote place.'

'This is crucial,' Lomond said, tapping the steering wheel impatiently as they waited at some lights. 'How he's doing it. He threatening them? Does he have a gun?'

'Could be. We're assuming there's just one person in the car, as well.'

'Still on your "a lassie is involved" theory?'

'Just a theory. One worth thinking about. I mean, even if this guy's not a stranger to them . . . we did put out the warning about getting lifts. Clear as day. Our consciences are clear there.

272

We did it after the first case. You stood there, you said it. We warned people to be wary about getting into cars. We got a slagging for it – one of the national papers, in fact. "Who do these coppers think they are? Next they'll be telling us not to talk to strangers." But that's exactly what it boils down to. So I reckon you've got two things that could be happening. First: he's someone they know and trust. So he's connected to either the art, or the cams, or both. Second: it could be a lassie. Size nine shoes is all we've got. Could easily be a lassie, as well. Think about Ursula Ulvaeus, someone like that. Christ, think about DI Henderson, before she was raptured into Gartcosh.'

'That's a bit unkind,' Lomond said.

'I'm just going by the size and the body shape involved. Henderson could have played rugby, and she could have skittled the pair of us if we were on the park with her. I'm just saying, if there's a lassie involved somewhere, they would have let their guard down. Everyone thinks it's a him, so nobody's thinking it's a her. The whole world is talking about this case now. CNN, Fox News, even Russia Today. Roya Van Ahle must have heard about it. But she still accepts a lift, or gets picked up by appointment, the day after she was doing the modelling thing with Erskine Copper at the community centre. Our guy takes her away. That night, he dumps her in the car. Really quiet spot. But it turns out to be a mistake: some teens arrive, light a fire, drink cans. Plus – there's a breeze block just off the bank which stops the car from sinking. He couldn't have known about that.'

'Our guy was unlucky with that, for once,' Lomond agreed. 'But what's interesting is, he changed how he operated. First – the car. Owned by Donald Ward. That's not a mistake.'

'You think he's setting Donald Ward up?'

'Gut feeling: aye. But I've been wrong with those.'

'Some way to go to set the guy up. Oh – apparently Classic Autos had a CCTV failure just before the place was broken into. One key is nicked, and one car is half-inched. The Alfa

273

Romeo. Ward's well known in the classic car fraternity. Alfa Romeos are his speciality. Refits them himself. It's his thing.'

'Man of many talents.'

'I don't think it's him,' Slater said.

'I don't either. He doesn't strike me as a maniac, and we are dealing with a maniac here. The only thing on his record is the big one, when he was a teenager.'

'You still reckon it ties in with the Daisy Lawlor case?'

'There are too many links now to ignore it. But I'm worried about getting too hung up on Rafferty Landing. Going with the theory, I reckon we're looking for a guy in his mid to late forties. That's my thinking. Christ, it's busy here.'

Lomond peered through the windscreen at two columns of people on either side of the main road. It dawned on him why they were there; and at that precise moment, Slater's phone buzzed.

The DS's eyes widened. 'Gaffer, get off this road. Quick as you can. We can't do Govan.'

'What?'

'Turn off. Now.'

Lomond did as he was bid, making a left at some lights.

'Christ, it's worse.' The road was thronged with people, completely blocking the road. Lomond cracked the window. He could hear a voice on loudspeaker. It was Ursula Ulvaeus.

'It's a protest,' he said. He put on the hazards and reversed. Angry horns tooted, and he braked suddenly, with nowhere to go.

'That's three points on your licence right away,' Slater said. 'Gaffer, this is a bit on the hairy side for you, no?'

'Where's everyone on the team gone? Guarding Govan?'

'Aye, looks like it,' Slater said. 'Gaffer, watch out . . .'

One thing Lomond noticed was that the crowd seemed more of an even split between men and women than before. One of the men turned to look at their car, turned back, then spun around sharply. He was about thirty, with a dark blue raincoat. 'Here!' he said, pointing. 'There's a polis there. He was on the telly!'

'Need to go,' Slater said, jaw tensed.

'It's one-way,' Lomond said. 'We can't go anywhere.'

'Just try to get through, gaffer.'

Bodies blocked the way, obscuring the road ahead, changing the light. Someone ran forward.

'I'd turn round, gaffer. Emergency manoeuvre.'

'Seriously?'

'Seriously!'

Before Lomond could get into gear, something rose through the air, cutting through the light rain. Lomond was reminded of a bird in flight, soaring and dipping, before the object arrowed right through the windscreen and hit him in the face.

34

'You want to get that looked at, in casualty,' Minchin said, after applying the final suture in Lomond's face. 'Head injury, Lomie. You know the score.'

'*Facial* injury,' Lomond said. 'Only my face. No big loss.'

'And your scalp. Near the temple. Bled a fair bit, judging by your suit. If your dry cleaner gets that stain out, gimme their phone number.'

'It was a bit of scaffolding,' Lomond said, wincing as Minchin snipped the thread in his face. 'Somebody slung it like a bloody javelin. Great shot, to be fair.'

'You did well to drive out of there, with a bastard spear sticking out the front of the motor.'

'I had to borrow another pool car to get here. Finance department will love me.'

Minchin leaned closer. He frowned, in extreme close-up. 'Hmmm . . .'

'What is it?' Lomond asked, drawing back instinctively.

'What day is it?'

'Eh . . . Tuesday.'

'Right. How many fingers am I holding up?'

'Two. Funny man.'

Minchin grinned and lowered the V-sign. 'OK . . . Now drag your eyes to the left . . . following my finger . . . now to the right . . .' Suddenly Minchin slapped Lomond – not hard enough to make a sound: a tap with the tips of his fingers.

'Hey!' Lomond drew back. 'What was that for?'

'Nothing. Just felt like doing it.' Minchin chuckled, along with everyone else in the pathology anteroom. 'Right, ladies and gentlemen. We're just about ready. I'll get scrubbed up.'

★

Later, back in the briefing room, Lomond and his team watched the video of the post-mortem. Minchin's voice came through on the speakers; it had a curious delay, which added to the unreality of the event. Lomond was present in the room on the video, and at the same time, he was among the team in the briefing room in Govan, watching himself watching Minchin cut the dead girl open.

In the examination room on the video lay Roya Van Ahle, stretched out on the table, whiter than white, the face cleaned, the hair brushed back. Someone had taken time to lay out the body. Lomond always felt a sense of comfort by proxy, here. Toes pointing upward, hands by the sides. Passive, even calm. No one would mistake her for the living, though. The colour of the flesh, the set of the face . . . knowing the face in life, knowing that sly smile through the straggled fringe . . . *Death makes a stranger of us.*

'*You see here,*' Minchin said, indicating Roya Van Ahle's neck, where the wound cut across in a horribly clean, clinical and antiseptic line, '*the same wound. Same perpetrator, little doubt about it.*'

'*How about the right hand side?*' Lomond asked.

The figure in scrubs nodded. '*Yep, I was coming to that. The little kink at the end. He's turned the blade – just like the previous two.*'

Lomond turned to the others in the briefing room – Slater, Smythe, Tait, and several more. They all had the same expression, even Slater – stolid, grim acceptance of what they were about to see. The utter, and entirely necessary, final destruction of that beautiful body.

'This is what I'm interested in,' Lomond said. He paused the video as Minchin pointed out the wound on Roya's throat. He zoomed in on the flick at the end, the comma in the flesh. 'Study this.'

'What are we looking at, sir?' Tait asked. 'Meaning – what are you seeing?'

'This is a signature,' Lomond said. 'Staring us right in the face. The killer is an artist – almost certainly the man Sir Erskine Copper knows as John Smith. He might have been sitting with me the other night at Erskine Copper's art class. This is a signature. He's a clinical killer – in other circumstances I might say humane. He kills them quickly. This little flick at the end is a personal touch. It's not cruelty. He's signing his work. He turns the knife at the end. It has no other purpose that we can see. It's not necessary for the killing stroke. It doesn't end their lives any faster – and it doesn't prolong their suffering either, for that matter. It's a personal touch. It's something he's thought about. Something he's done before.'

'Shouldn't we see it somewhere else, then?' Tait asked. 'On the paintings we seized?'

'It's there. We couldn't see it at first – but it is there. We X-rayed the paintings Erskine Copper was trying to hide. We're still examining them, and we'll see if we can extract a DNA profile, though the pictures have been in several different locations and passed through so many hands, it'll be difficult to lift anything. But the X-rays showed up something that's been done on each canvas during the painting process. We discovered the same thing on all of them.'

Lomond opened a new window on the screen to display one of the paintings – the star-face. The colours shifted, and a new dimension presented itself, a jarring clash to the blacks and reds of the images they were familiar with from Erskine Copper's collection. A whorl of bright blue and black, changing current from left to right, with the ghostly outline of a pencil sketch of the stars. Lomond pointed to the bottom left corner of the picture.

'Right there,' he said. 'See it?'

They did.

Lomond changed the image again: a new painting from the

seized artworks, seen as an X–ray.

'Here, again. See it? And once more . . . here. Same spot. He painted over it on the later canvasses, but not at first. Same signature. On the canvas, in the paint' – on the screen the image changed – 'and there, in the flesh. There is Roya.' Lomond changed the image again. 'Now Sheonaid Aird Na Murchan. See it? Now Aylie Colquhoun.'

Different girls, similar poses, and, at the right-hand side of each throat, that same sliced segment at the very end of the wound. A comma, an apostrophe. Punctuation.

'You can see it – the same little kink, by the same person – the man who painted the pictures. There's no doubt about it. We have to trace John Smith. He must have painted other things – he's been active in the field for more than twenty-five years, so he'll be in his forties now, maybe his fifties. He must have other paintings somewhere. We need to hit every art gallery, at home and abroad, until we find that signature. Find a name. That's the killer. This can't be a coincidence. The forensic evidence will follow, but the trail ends with John Smith. Bet your life on it.

'One other thing that came out from an examination of the tissue of the lungs,' he went on. 'It was even more apparent in the car; there wasn't much sign of Roya having bled out anywhere near it. And there was a similar result with the other two girls – the water taken from their lungs, the substance they aspirated when they died, had chlorine in it.'

Smythe said, 'They didn't die on the river bank. They died in a swimming pool.'

'That's right,' Lomond said. 'Our man didn't kill them outside. He killed them indoors. And after he cut their throats, he immersed them immediately.'

'Why?' asked Slater.

'He wanted to watch them bleed.'

35

'He executes them,' Slater said. 'Grabs them round the neck from behind, right hander, across the throat, then dumps them into a swimming pool.' Perhaps unconsciously, Slater demonstrated the cutting action across his own throat as he spoke. He finished with a savage, horizontal wrench.

'That's it,' Lomond answered. 'That's the how of it. The why of it – that's for the psychiatrists once we've got him inside. But that's what he's doing.'

Slater nodded. 'So – swimming pool. I'm just going to throw this out here – Strangbank Baths?'

'Already got it sealed off. We're going out there first thing tomorrow morning. On top of that, we'll get another chance to talk to Torquod Rafferty.'

'He's involved, somewhere,' Slater said. 'Alibi or no alibi, it ties in with him.'

'There's no chance he killed the first two girls,' Tait said.

'I didn't say he killed them,' Slater replied, colouring. 'It does tie in with him, though. That, *and* Daisy Lawlor. How far have we got with Lana Galbraith, by the way? Forensic anthropology people still involved in that one, aye?'

Smythe linked her fingers on her lap but said nothing.

'We're still looking at it,' Lomond said. 'The big problem was getting some DNA to match. An auntie turned up with a hairbrush in the end. I think things will move quickly there, soon as we run some tests.'

'Going to let us in on your thinking?' Tait asked.

Lomond shook his head. 'This one's just for a very small circle of people for now. There've been a couple of leaks to the press. You know how it goes: friends of friends, family members, down to the level of the uniform – someone talks. The papers still pay folk for tip-offs, and they'll be desperate to know more about this case.'

Tait frowned. 'Sounds like you don't trust us.'

'We need to keep some stuff to ourselves,' Lomond said. 'That's the way it is. You and Smythe will be on the Daisy Lawlor team from now on. There have been developments. I'll brief you on that later.'

Tait folded his arms, distinctly unappeased.

'As for the Rafferty Landing party boys, there's another link,' Lomond said. 'The Alfa Romeo ties Roya to Donald Ward, Torquod's best mate. He was at Rafferty Landing the weekend Daisy Lawlor died, but I don't think he's the Ferryman . . . that's just what the killer wants us to think. Which makes me think that the killer knows about Rafferty Landing. I suspect that whoever killed Aylie, Sheonaid and Roya killed Daisy Lawlor back in the nineties, but we can't yet know for sure, and we don't want to get sidetracked. They call it confirmation bias – it's let us down so many times, in so many different forces. You're convinced you know who you're after, and why you're after them, but until you can prove it it's only a theory. Let's bear in mind this could be two totally separate cases, two totally different killers. So after this afternoon, Smythe and Tait can sort out Daisy Lawlor, and the rest of us focus on the here and now, and our man John Smith.' Noting Tait's disgusted look, he said, 'Myles, I believe you've got something for us from the cars. This might be the biggest development yet.'

Lomond ceded his place at the platform and Tait stood up instead, his mouth set in a grim line despite Lomond's conciliatory conclusion. It was clear that his natural confidence – usually to the point of arrogance – was missing, and not just because he had been pushed onto the cold case.

He opened up some files on the big screen, and pictures of a bend in the road, flanked by trees and marked out by chevron signs, appeared.

'First of all, we reappraised the tyre evidence,' Tait said. 'And there was something we'd overlooked.' He raised his head and met their eyes. 'In the case of Sheonaid Aird Na Murchan and the American muscle car that was used in the Claymore action movie, we missed the fact that the tyres were mismatched.'

The image changed to the mangled, burnt-out wreck; there were only melted remnants of the tyres, but some of the tread had survived, the surfaces turned against the ground: four separate images, duplicated from a variety of angles, with a tape measure provided for scale.

'On this car, the front right tyre and both rear tyres were all a similar make and tread. But the front left tyre was different. It was older – but with a newer tread.'

'Replacement?' Smythe asked.

Tait nodded. 'We overlooked this at the time. That's down to me; it was my team investigating it. What we're looking at on the front left is a spare.'

'Who noticed this?' Slater asked.

'Carry on, Myles,' Lomond said, with an admonitory look at Slater.

Tait changed the image on the screen and went on: 'Re-examining the scene where Sheonaid Aird Na Murchan's signal disappeared off the A-road, we expanded our search and focused on this bend. Soon after it, there's a single-track road that leads, literally, to nowhere. There used to be some cottages, but they burned down more than twenty years ago. There's nothing on the site to indicate that our man was there, or the dead girl. We did find something though – just past the turn from the A-road, some shredded tyre material. Parts of the tread matched what we were able to find on the tyres on the car. We also found an old rake head – rusted, but still enough to puncture the tyre. That was discarded by the side of the road.'

'So he had a tyre blowout?' Slater asked. 'Surely the turn is significant. Any bodies of water there? Ponds, wee lochs or burns?'

'No, remember the chlorinated water found in the lungs,' Lomond said. 'They were killed indoors, I'm sure of it.'

The image on the screen changed again, and Tait went on, 'When we went back to where Aylie Colquhoun's mobile signal was lost, we found a similar area on the opposite side of the city, heading south, towards Lanarkshire. There's a layby just *here*' − he pointed − 'and another single-track road that leads out to a disused camp site. There is evidence that people have set a fire there at some time − wild campers maybe − but it looks as though it was well before Aylie was killed, possibly last summer. Our theory is that John Smith would have checked the place in advance, knowing how careful he is; we can look into that, maybe put the word out. Someone might have seen him. And we found something similar to Sheonaid's case on this road, just past the turn: a segment of an old iron railing, thrown into the trees. It was bent at an angle, and it had scraps of tyre on it.'

'Two dodgy wee roads . . . two blowouts,' Slater said.

'Today, we've managed to locate the last spot Roya Van Ahle's mobile phone was used. She suspected something. Her last message was to her twin sister. *Might run something past you*, she wrote. That was at 11.13 p.m. on Sunday night. She was killed maybe an hour later. The signal cuts off not long after the message was sent. Neither of the other girls refer to modelling assignments, cam work or anything of the kind in their messages or emails, so we can't rule out that they were abducted totally at random, for all the circumstantial stuff that points elsewhere. But going back to how Roya's signal cut-off relates to the cars − the closest thing we have to a match with the other two cases is a side road that leads into a farm track, and there's not much evidence that a car passed there. The zone where the signal cuts off is bigger, so it's harder to pinpoint than the first two cases. But we've found out that on the car in the river that held Roya's body, three of the tyres are of the same type and tread – front right, and the back two. The front left tyre was of a different tread. Probably a spare. Just like Sheonaid's.'

'Thanks, Myles,' Lomond said. He returned to the lectern. 'So here's what I think happened. For my money, he's staging a tyre blowout. Maybe he makes it a bit Hollywood – spinning the wheel, sudden stop, that kind of thing. In the confusion, maybe during the crash, when the girls have their phones in their hands, or maybe while he's asking for help to change the tyre, he manages to get hold of the phones and breaks them, switches them off or puts them out of order. Just a theory, but it holds with what we know so far. That explains how the signals vanish.

'From there, once the phone problem is dealt with, he takes them to the killing place. Probably somewhere remote, most likely nowhere near the pick-up zone. Check out this map: well spread out, these quiet wee spots. Might be worth seeing where the paths intersect . . . see if we can triangulate a possible location.' Lomond clicked through to a map, with virtual pinpoints fringing the outer edges of the city proper. 'It's a house somewhere, I think. Somewhere with its own pool.'

'Rafferty Landing got one?' Slater asked.

'It does,' Lomond said. 'We'll be checking that later on. But to recap – this is what we can extract from what we've found out so far. The killer has a signature move – the flick at the end of each cut. The same flick he left on the paintings that were sold to Sir Erskine Copper. He goes by the name John Smith – probably a pseudonym, but then again maybe not. We'll check out all the John Smiths and Jonathan Smiths who might be connected, but the key thing is the flick on the paintings. We need to scape up every bit of data on that – from the art world, from colleges, universities, auction houses . . . I'll assign a team to it. Meanwhile, this is what we need to put out there, to everyone: don't talk to strangers. Don't get into cars with strange men. Don't take a taxi unless it's from a rank or phoned in or booked through an app. Anyone involved with MyGirl, Claymore Films or CamJack, the one that we know Roya used – the less tasteful stuff – needs to be aware that they could be targets. We have to speak to everyone who ever worked on them. It's going to take a while, but we'll get there. The final pieces are falling into place. Let's get back to it.'

With a nod, Lomond cut off the computer screen, and walked out of the room without waiting for any response.

Tait straightened his cuffs and held up his hand to get the attention of the others as they began to disperse. 'I want to apologise,' he said. 'I made an arse of it. I didn't spot the odd one out in the tyres. The forensics people spotted it, and so did the gaffer, though he was too polite to say so here. I didn't examine the tyres individually and I didn't make the connection. It might have set us back. I'm sorry.'

'Forget it,' Slater said. 'You got that evidence – the rake and the spike. It fits for me. You made the connection. That's how he's doing it. You brought us closer to nailing him. That's what matters.' He clapped Tait on the shoulder. 'We'll get him. We'll bring him in. It's going to be brilliant. We can have a party. So forget about it. You're still a dick – I mean, you'll always be a dick, but you're one of the best polis in the building.'

'That's awful nice of you to say,' Tait said, almost smiling.

36

Lomond peered at the girl in the bikini until it felt as if the light of the computer screen had bleached his eyes. Hunched before the desktop in his alcove, moving his head one way or the other seemed to pull after-images like curtains, shadows chasing colours into the corners of his vision.

Roya Van Ahle's swimsuit was a style which he had discovered was called a triangle bikini, and it was a colour he had further discovered was called gold metallic – this latter throwing him somewhat, as he had assumed it was a strange type of green. He mistrusted the words first, then his eyes; he leaned nearer to the screen, and looked more closely at the girl in the bikini.

Yes, there were gold highlights in the material, similar to how a stony beach might shimmer in the morning as the tide crept over it. Not green at all. The girl's red hair cascaded . . . drenched . . . drizzled . . . dominated the off-gold colour. It set the entire surroundings aflame; everything was in contrast with it. Her eyes, her pale skin, the colour of her lips, the material; even the white wall she used for a background. It was bright enough to hurt, that hair. *There's redheads, and there's* 'redheads', he thought. *Hooker red*, he added, somewhat ashamedly.

True, though.

'I'm getting tired,' he said, under his breath, though there was no one in the front room to hear him. 'I'm getting old.'

He drummed his fingers on the table. The picture had ceased to mean anything in the way a woman in a bikini would normally have stuck him, secretly or otherwise. The curves, the hand on her hip, the bold stance. This was down to simple repetition. It wasn't one image; it was hundreds of them, literally – 217 separate frames. They had all been found on a memory card on Roya Van Ahle's digital camera. The photographs had been taken six days previously. These, and thousands of others on the memory card, were something of a portfolio – a tasteful one, in Lomond's judgment, with the emphasis on the clothes. But this final burst of bikini shots was an outlier. They looked nearly identical. They had been taken in the same location – Roya's bedroom, in her mother's flat – and the camera had been mounted on a tripod. That, and the camera itself, were an expensive gift from an absent father. But why the hundreds of images? They were all marked differently in the metadata, in sequence, one after the other. Was it an accident? Had she shot herself on burst mode? Had the camera simply duplicated the same image? A mistake or a glitch?

Every photo of a beautiful woman is a secret shared. The thought was a bubble, straining at the surface of his mind. *Sexist crap*, he shot back. *Don't think that stuff. If you can't deal with it without spitting at her, leave the inquiry. Half of the gaffers want that, anyway. Takes a decision off their hands.*

'What am I missing?' he muttered. 'What is it? There's something here.'

The living-room door creaked. Lomond flinched.

It was Siobhan. Tired-looking, and a little drunk. She threw her keys on top of the sideboard, then stood with her hand on her hips.

'Jesus,' Lomond said. 'Didn't hear you there.'

'Picture the scene. A daughter comes into the house, and it's late at night, and mum's in bed, and dad's on the computer, and he's looking at a lassie in a bikini . . .' she tutted.

'Help me,' Lomond said. 'C'mon over. Show me what I'm missing.'

She joined him, standing at his shoulder, her hand on the back of the seat. *Definitely been drinking*, Lomond thought. Something sweet. White bloody wine. 'That's the dead girl.

Roya,' she said.

'You're doing it too.'

'Doing what?'

'"Dead *girl*",' you said. Dead *woman*, you mean. She was older than you.'

'OK, dead woman. Score one for the patriarchy. What is it you don't get?'

'Look.' Lomond clicked the arrows by the side of the picture. Chevrons here: chevrons on the roads. He veered left after sharp turns, Lomond had realised. Used the chevrons as his marker. Headlights picking them out in the dark. Slid off road, just enough to spear the tyre on the pre-positioned spikes. Anyone behind him on the main road would just drive past. Front left. Bastard.

On screen, the images of Roya went through the motions as Lomond clicked through them again. It was like an old stop-motion animation; as the images ran together, there was only a slight change of articulation here and there, sometimes subtle, sometimes jarring. Occasionally the expression altered; you could see this happen in real time, if you spooled it fast enough. Smile to a blank look. No change in the light, just in the position, over time. An angle of the head, the elbow, the hip. A hidden hand manipulating the anatomy with each click. It was utterly obsessive, he thought. Who was this for? Her? A designer? A creep?

'Yeah, I see what she's doing,' Siobhan said.

'What?'

'Keep clicking through it. Let me see to the end.'

The numbers went through to the 200s, and finally the sequence ended. Lomond clicked on to shot 217; like the previous one, it was an extreme close-up, just her eyes. That faintly mocking smile. Her face would never smile again. *But her bones would.*

Lomond rubbed his eyes. 'I'll need to put a wee lamp on.'

'You should. Very lonely scene, that. A man sitting on his own, with that flickering blue light.'

'I'm depressed enough as it is.' It had just slipped out. 'I don't mean "depressed".'

'Yeah, you do. You're not yourself.' She put her hand on his shoulder. 'I'm sorry I was mean. The other day.'

'You weren't mean. I was being protective. It's kind of my job.'

'It's literally your job.'

'So you going to tell me what I'm meant to be looking at here?'

'Go back to the start again . . .' He did so. 'OK, click through once more . . . look at the wee details.'

'I can't see anything. Well . . . there's a necklace disappeared, for a start.'

'So you are seeing something. Keep looking.'

'I don't have time for this.' Impatience, rare for Lomond. 'Sorry.'

'Keep clicking . . . look, there's the nail varnish. Different shade of purple.'

'You what?' Lomond spooled back, zoomed in. 'It can't be. Hey . . . it is. You're right. That's lilac. Now it's a darker shade. Plum? I should have noticed that.'

'You weren't looking. Or you were looking, but you weren't seeing.'

'It'd take a close eye to spot that.'

'Ha ha!' she jeered, much too loudly. 'You're actually annoyed that I spotted something and you didn't! No, you don't need a close eye, you just need to not be a lumpy, middle of the road gadgie. Keep going . . . there. The mascara's slightly different. And there, she's toned it down a bit . . . Beautiful girl,' she said, after a pause. 'Natural skin tone's gorgeous. Pale. Was she a real redhead?'

'Suits her. What a shame. And, hey, can I have another look at the last couple of shots?'

Lomond clicked through to 216 and 217 again. Here were the close-ups. Just her eyes, open and then closed. Lomond

289

shivered. He remembered when he'd seen them closed in the flesh. He'd seen her in both states. Living and dead.

You never got used to it, never. Utter obscenity, the worst thing in life. Families had to remember the rest, the life before, or go mad. What made this case twisted was that he'd been privileged enough to know what Roya Van Ahle had looked like in life, but couldn't remember the rest; the final outcome meant he couldn't hang on to her, how she'd been represented in art, the way she'd want to be remembered. Loud in life, sullen in death.

Lomond felt very fearful, very vulnerable. He wanted to hug Siobhan close.

There was something else, he realised. Something in those close-ups . . . the eyebrows, heavier than usual.

'What am I meant to see here, Siobhan? Spell it out.'

'She's had them threaded. The eyebrows. Gives them that definition. Like someone in a cartoon or a comic. See? Look at mine.' She bent low, pointing to her lighter eyebrows. 'Bit of a mess. Need doing. Now look at hers.'

'Looks a bit like they've been painted on.'

'Exactly. That's threading. Or microblading. I'd do something about that bit in the middle, though. Strange she didn't smooth that off. It's like she's showing it off. Maybe it made her distinctive. There are models who don't shave their pits these days. That's the reason.'

Lomond leapt to his feet, startling his daughter. 'Hang on,' he said. 'Hang on there.' He clicked off-screen and found a folder. 'Shut your eyes.'

'What for?'

'Please, don't look.'

'Oh. Gory stuff.'

'Gory's the wrong word. But yes. Please don't look. I'm a policeman. And I'm your dad. Don't look.'

She did as she was told, sighing, turning round, hands on hips. 'You tell someone a bad thing is there, and that they shouldn't look at it, and they'll always kind of want to look at it.'

'That's the internet, defined. Here. Turn round. Don't worry, I'm not going to show you a body.'

Siobhan turned and frowned. She was bathed in a lush green light, the colour of plants at the bottom of a tropical lagoon. 'Hell is that? Another photo?'

'It's a painting.'

'Oh. It's quite good.'

Lomond wanted to bite back. *It is not good. Nothing about it is good, or could be good, in any decent mind, now or in a thousand years.* It was the painting of Sheonaid the Selkie, her head back on the sand.

'What am I supposed to be looking at?'

'Same eyebrows?'

'Definitely, yeah. Same model, is it?'

'No.'

'No . . .' She peered at the image. 'You're right – different model. Different hair, obviously. Rounder chin. Different mouth. And obviously, bigger up top.'

'Up top?'

'Don't tell me you didn't notice that. You're kidding me on, now. Creepy painting, though. The Ferryman didn't paint it, did he?'

'Going to have to ask you to turn round again.' He went to another file. It was Aylie Colquhoun, in burlesque mode, grinning. 'How about this picture? Look like she's had the same thing done?'

'Oh. She's beautiful.' A sadness came over her. It was the same face she'd shown to Lomond when she was a little girl and he'd told her off. He clicked on a new thumbnail. Here was Aylie again, out for a meal with her boyfriend, face lit by a candle. 'Yeah . . . looks like she might have. What is it you're driving at? We looking for a psychotic beautician? The nail bar killer?'

'No, it's . . .' He sighed. 'You're right. It's nothing. Probably nothing. Eyebrow threading is common, then?'

'Yep. Fairly common. Bonnie lassies, the three of them.'

'Yeah. I'm looking for similarities or differences . . . And I want to know why a lassie like Roya would take two hundred pictures of herself in the same pose, with only wee slight tweaks here and there. I mean, she must have been standing on the same spot on the floor after she'd changed her nail varnish or her necklace or whatever. She's hardly even moving her hands. Same pose – hand on hip. Same sort of . . . look at the position of the legs. What's it for?'

'She wants to look good.' Siobhan shrugged. 'She's picking her best side, her best angle.'

'Two hundred and seventeen photos! That seems a bit much. She could just use a mirror. It's like I'm missing something. It's driving me mental.'

'Maybe you're not missing anything. No big key or secret. It's all there in front of you; there's nothing hidden. That's because it's for her, probably. Meaning for her eyes only. She wants to pick her best photo. Think of it as art. How she looks is an art. How she presents herself is an art. How a photographer captures her is an art. You wouldn't turn in something that was just half decent. You'd want your best photo. What's this for, a portfolio?'

'Nobody knows,' Lomond said. 'It was on her digital camera.'

'Both the lassies you showed me have lovely necks – the one in the painting, too.'

Lomond shivered. 'That's right. I had noticed that much. Guess it was obvious.'

'If the killer painted that picture, he's showing it off to us. Showing what he's going to do.'

'You might be right. Off the record.'

'The other thing's the hair.'

'What about it? It's all different.'

'It's different colours – but there's a pattern, too.'

'How come?'

'They're all so bright. Roya – red, right? Like, super-red. Like something out of a comic, a superhero red. The fair girl – she was blonder than blonde. Marilyn Monroe blonde. And then the mermaid. Her hair was coal black. They're all pretty extreme. If he targeted them, that could be a reason. A sequence, maybe.'

'Maybe.' Lomond scribbled a note. 'There might be something in that. What does he move on to next?'

'Hopefully not mousy brunettes.' She drew some loose strands of hair over her ear.

'Don't even joke about it.'

She cleared her throat. 'Listen . . . I'm sorry. What I said the other day. It was a bit much.'

Lomond gestured irritably. 'Already forgotten about it.'

'And I thought about what you said about Mint.'

'Oh aye?'

'Yeah . . . I might take a wee step back there.'

'How come?'

'Something about her . . . I don't know. I get the impression that once the big documentary project's done I'll get dumped. Well. Dumped's the wrong word. She'll move on to another project, and I doubt I'll get much credit for the work I put in on the film. She's all front and centre. I've been editing it, too, along with Martin and a couple of others. She's not been involved in that side, but she wanted final approval on the cut. I think we should go closer on Ursula Ulvaeus, maybe focus on her. More interesting character. But Mint's started calling the shots. She's more into what's happening on the streets.'

Lomond chose his words carefully. 'What's happening on the streets relates to me. And what I do.' He tapped his scabby cheek. 'Up close and personal.'

'That's the thing, though – there's a lot of stuff happening, not just your case. The economy, politics, the independence thing, poverty . . . the usual stuff in this city: the blue men and the orange men and the green men. And now you get a killer. It's a catalyst, I think. Or society's the catalyst. That's the problem. That's what I'm into. It's all kinds of things; it's the times we live in . . . Mint just wants to focus on the police. She's got a thing about doing true crime.'

'Darling . . . I'm the SIO on this case. You can't get more connected to the inquiry. You stick my name into social media, some of the stuff you'll see . . . it's like they blame me. They do blame me.'

'Nobody blames you. You're doing your best. And you'll catch him,' she said matter-of-factly. 'You always catch them.'

'And as for the catalyst stuff . . . this guy's a sicko. Doesn't matter what state society or the economy's in, or if his team got hammered at the weekend. It starts and ends with him.'

'He's a special case, all right.'

Lomond shook his head. The outlines of his face were reflected in the glass cabinet on the wall unit opposite. 'Never had one like this before. Not since I've been out of a uniform, anyway.'

'When was the last one you had as bad as this, then?'

'Mr Flick.'

'Who was he?'

'Who *is* he, you mean. He's still out there. You know Bible John? Mr Flick was worse. More like Jack the Ripper. I saw one of his victims at the scene . . . I was nineteen. First time I saw a murdered woman. The fact we've not caught him is a disgrace.'

'I've heard about Bible John. Why did you never mention Mr Flick?'

'I try to keep that stuff away from you. He's still out there. I'm sure of it. We had a lot of them, across Scotland and England, seventies and eighties. Mostly before my time. I don't go in for the psychology stuff – you know: "This happened to him when he was a wean. That happened to him when he was a teenager. So that made him do this and that" – but I do wonder. Maybe it was because of the war. They were born during the war, a lot of those old guys, your Mr Flicks and Bible Johns. Their das and their uncles and maybe their cousins or brothers or grandas were wrecked by the war, and it had a knock-on effect. It made them monsters, one way or another. I suppose there's the telly and cinema and all that, too . . . Ach, I don't know.' Lomond rubbed his eyes. 'Maybe necks is something we should focus on. I just . . . I dunno what he's doing, but he's picking them out somehow. Modelling. Art. Even porn – I dunno. He's seen loads of these photos, I'm sure of it. We've trawled all the modelling sites, agencies, you name it, but I'm no closer. And he's out of control now. Escalating. He'll kill again if we can't stop him. Who's at risk? Why are they at risk? I can't have officers trying to protect anyone who has a *lovely neck*. I can't believe I'm still at this stage. I should have him in a cell by now. But he's lucky. Unbelievably lucky. He's left us nothing. No loose threads, no physical evidence . . . maybe I should step down.'

Siobhan placed her hand on his shoulder. 'No chance. You'll catch him. You'll see it; you'll make the connection. You're the guy.'

'Thanks, love.' He patted her hand, and sighed. 'It's nice to have you here. I like having you home.'

She ruffled his hair. 'Daft Dad. You were always worse for that than Mum. Waiting up till all hours. Driving out to pick me up whatever the time.'

'Well, y'know. Polis. I keep weird hours.' Lomond stretched and yawned, then shut down the computer. 'Speaking of which, it's time I went for my three-hour beauty sleep.' He turned to her. 'By the way. Something I meant to say to you . . .'

*

Maureen was awake when he slipped into bed, though you wouldn't have known it. Her breath whistled slightly through her nostrils. But she said, clear and fully alert: 'She all right?'

'She's fine. Staying here tonight.'

'Ah, that's good. I've got stuff in. Can have a nice breakfast maybe. Rolls 'n' bacon.'

'I'll be up 'n' away by then. Maybe save me one?'

'I'll get up with you and make you one before you go.'

He hugged her close, and they stayed like that for a while, her breath light. Siobhan was safe and home with them, which was the way he liked it, twenty-one years old or not. And he had precious moments here, cuddled in with Maureen in the dark, with only the faint glow of their ancient analogue clock to light the scene.

'Would be nice to take a wee holiday,' he said.

'Book the time. Once you've lifted this eejit we'll go away.'

'We can take the wean.'

She chuckled. 'Think she'd be seen dead with us?'

'Oh, I dunno. We could build sandcastles. Go for a wee paddle. Never gets old, that stuff, does it? Think of it. The sun. It'd be warm. Away from here.'

'Nope, it never gets old at all. That'd be nice, I think. The three of us again. Even just for a weekend.' His hand tightened in hers, or hers tightened in his. Six of one, half a dozen of the other.

'You know what would be good?' Lomond said. 'We could make a big spaghetti bolognese. Mind she used to like that? That'd be fun. She always scoffed it, any time I made it for her. With a load of oregano. Might still blitz a couple of carrots into it, disguise the veg. Wee garlic bread on the side, as well . . . I bet she'd be into that. As a one-off.'

'My God, I wouldn't want her to wear white,' Maureen said, mock-horrified. 'Remember? The state of her clothes! I swear she used to do it on purpose. That's why I asked you not to make it for a good while.'

'What a mess she would make. Stains on the walls and everything. A mini crime scene.' Maureen giggled at that, but he didn't.

Eventually she said, 'It isn't just you, you know.'

'Eh? What's that supposed to mean?'

'Looking for him. Everybody's looking for him. The whole

country wants to catch him. Someone will call in. I'm surprised they haven't already. Somebody will be looking at a husband, a boyfriend, and wondering . . .'

'They'd have done it by now, love.'

'Wait and see.'

They settled for a while. Her breathing deepened, though her nostrils continued to make that light keening sound. He could not get to sleep, and he knew why: he'd begun to dread it. The phone call. Someone would ring. He checked his phone was plugged in and charging: a brief burst of unnatural light, stinging him. Bleaching his eyes again. It was a while before he slept.

37

It came while he dreamed of being somewhere nice; you could tell by the blue sky and the odd lazy smudge of cloud. He was sitting down somewhere with a nice breeze. Maybe he had shorts on. Maybe he'd eaten a little too much. Maybe he had a beer in his hand. Then the irritation, an insect buzzing in his ears. No, not an insect – the phone.

Groping for it, not even fully awake yet. Not the alarm, although he'd assumed it was in his semi-conscious state. It was a call from Slater.

Slater sounded like Lomond felt.

'What's happening, Malcolm?'

'Somebody's come in, gaffer. We've got a tip.'

Lomond swung his feet out of bed. Still dark. Still quiet outside. He clicked on the bedside lamp and snatched up a pen and paper.

'A tip? In the middle of the night?'

'No' quite – about five minutes ago. I was in the office, in case you were wondering. Couldn't sleep.'

'Spit it out, then. Who?'

'Sir Erskine Copper's wife.'

'Oh aye?'

'Wants to talk to you. Just you, she says.'

'The address. Her phone number as well. Hit me.'

★

Lomond felt a curious foreboding as the car crept along the driveway. The long, low house was etched against the grey

298

horizon, squat and moody. Mews style, he supposed. Designed to make an impression.

She came out to meet him before he'd even got out of the car. A short woman, perhaps still in her forties but only just, dressed in jeans and a thick jumper, with vivid black streaks in her white hair. He'd seen her at Erskine Copper's country pile before, but only in the distance, not having had the chance to speak to her.

She had prominent cheekbones and a firm jawline that created their own shadows, their own sense of light and shade. Equally arresting were her husky-blue eyes, and, as he got closer, her seeming lack of wrinkles or lines. Lomond had heard it said that the skin was the thing that set models and actresses and pop stars apart from mere mortals: a quality that was just as important over time as looks, definition or bone structure. He wasn't sure about that, but there was no doubt Clarissa Ingram was a striking beauty. Type of person you'd want to paint, Lomond thought. Just for that face.

She greeted him warmly. 'Inspector. You were at the house the other day.'

He nodded. 'What can I do for you, Ms Ingram?'

'Come inside. Would you like a cup of tea?'

'Maybe later. Is Sir Erskine here?'

She shook her head. 'No, not for this. Shall we go in?'

The hallways and corridors were narrower than Lomond expected, even somewhat threatening. He surprised himself with the first thing out of his mouth. 'Quick question – do you have a swimming pool here?'

'No. Too much hassle with planning,' Clarissa said. 'I'm not much of a swimmer, either. Why do you ask?'

'I was thinking, I could see a swimming pool in a place like this – maybe round the back or in the basement. This house reminds of somewhere I stayed.'

'For a while it was a B&B – before I bought it,' she said, leading him into the front room. 'Terrible waste of a property.

It deserved to be a *home*. I was going to renovate it . . . I hated the red on the walls. But after a while you get used to it. One thing about red – it's warm. You don't get a cold red.'

'That's true.'

'But no – no swimming pool, no plans for one. I've got a deep bath, though.'

She led him into a bright, well-lit front room, with a pristine polished dining table like flat calm on a lake in one corner and an ancient leather sofa in the other, scuffed like an old school satchel but surely comfortable. Then something arrested his attention, and riveted his train of thought. It was not on a hook, rather laid against the far wall, a good two feet square, in a plain wooden frame that was more about function than ostentation.

Lomond was thunderstruck: fixed in place, staring. 'Where did this come from?' he said finally.

'That's what I'd like to know,' Clarissa replied. 'I came home one day, and he was here.'

'Sir Erskine?'

'Yeah. It's not unusual that we're in each other's houses – we are married, after all.' She grinned mirthlessly. 'But I wasn't expecting him to be here, and usually if he's coming over he'll tell me. He never actually explained why he'd come – he took me out to lunch, flattered me, wanted to see the horses in the yard. But he never said why, and I knew something was up. So I began to search around. I found it in the summer house – on the upper floor, hidden in a cabinet – and when I asked him about it he told me that he'd put it there last summer and forgotten about it. But I'm sure that's not true. I was in the summer house a few weeks ago, and I'm sure I was in that cupboard. It's where we keep candles and candelabras in case we want to eat dinner out there in the good weather.'

In that frame, there it was: the painting of Sheonaid Aird Na Murchan. Head back, hair shimmering and liquorice black, seeming to weave and wave and undulate, spread out on the wet sand. The neck beautifully detailed and muscled, the skin marbled and queasily lifelike. And there, at the bottom left-hand corner, was the detail that was missing from the scanned image sent to Sheonaid and passed on to her seething boyfriend: the cut that would soon be drawn across her throat, with a nick in the bottom right-hand corner. Maybe an M, maybe an N, maybe an R, maybe a U, maybe nothing.

'I saw this on the news,' Clarissa said. 'On the websites. On the police website. At your press conference, asking if anyone had seen it. I called you first. I wanted you to see it. And I don't want anyone to touch it.'

'Where is Sir Erskine?'

'On the road. Off on his merry tour of the art clubs. Think he's touring with still life, now. He didn't want to cancel the dates, even after what happened to the red-headed girl. He didn't want anyone to think he had something to hide.'

'Does he have something to hide?'

'Apart from this painting? You tell me. He didn't paint this, incidentally. I can tell right away; anyone could. It's not his style. Keeping it hidden isn't his style, either. He likes it but doesn't want me or anyone else to know he likes it. He's not jealous of art. He loves art, the way he loves women. He doesn't keep it to himself and isn't bothered about what anyone else thinks about it. He's devastated about Roya, you know. I'm not sure if they were sleeping together. He does that a lot less these days. Certainly since he got married to me.'

'Had he ever slept with Roya?'

'I don't think so. She was more of a muse. The sort of thing you read about in poetry. He liked the boy he took along with him to the classes, too. Very talented young man, you could say. Think Erskine used him for shock value, really. He's got a funny sense of humour.'

Lomond cleared his throat. 'Were you jealous of Roya?'

Clarissa smiled. There was a weariness in it. 'I accepted Roya. I accept them all. There are trade-offs to this life. He was up front about it. "I serve strange masters," he used to say. He's definitely got strange habits. Maybe that's how you define an artist. But I have a husband. He's one in a million. Maybe one in a billion. I support him, he supports me. It's just that I don't love him any more. I see how wrong it all is. Far too late. It wasn't so long ago that I was Roya's age. Twenty years, maybe twenty-five – it doesn't feel like that long. What a life we had.'

Her eyes brimmed with tears. Lomond said nothing. He gave her a moment. His heart was pounding.

'I saw the paintings you seized from the house,' she went on. 'I made the connection. They're the same artist, aren't they? The one who painted this one.' She pointed at the image of Sheonaid.

'I couldn't say for sure. I'm no art critic.'

'I am. They came from the same hand. He's very, very good. Or she. I can see why Erskine likes it. It chilled me. So did the others. Even before I knew what had happened. The man who painted these is your killer, isn't he? The Ferryman?'

'What do you know about him?'

'Nothing. Just the fact that Erskine has been hiding these paintings. And he hides nothing from me – nothing. It isn't worth it. We may live in different houses, but I'm still his wife. He moves, I know it. He dodges, I know it. He lies, I know it. Erskine's a fan of this artist – that's all I know.'

'Does the name John Smith mean anything to you?'

She laughed, a rough sound, the kind that might devolve into a coughing fit. 'Does the name John Smith mean anything to anyone?'

Lomond sent a message on his phone. 'I'm sorry. This house is going to be very busy soon.'

'I understand.'

'Maybe we'll get that cuppa tea now?'

She nodded, and led him into the kitchen – a bright, clear place, with a view out into a paddock where a handsome black horse stood and watched them back, its breath steaming in the air.

'I genuinely think it's only because he likes the paintings,' Clarissa said, over the rising squall of the kettle. 'That's a big reason why I married him. The conviction in what he was doing. The dedication. The belief. He never hid that. But he hid *this*. That's why it makes me feel so . . . sick. He was unusual like that. The honesty. I wouldn't say he's eccentric, just unguarded. That's a rare quality.'

'Big age gap between you.'

She shrugged. 'It didn't matter to me. I wanted out of modelling and acting. Grubby, at heart.'

'You've got a good life out here.'

'I didn't need the money, if that's what you're implying. Plenty of it in my family. Everything you see here? My money bought it. I made plenty from modelling. I was never a household name, but I was on the catwalks. Paris, Milan, London. That's where he saw me, I think. He painted me loads of times before he made his move. There are a lot of nudes of me out there.'

'You said he had other lovers?'

'Without a doubt. He was unguarded about those, too. It came with the territory. I accepted it. It was a different time. I think he would have been happy for me to take lovers, too, but I never did. Well . . . rarely. Not for long. And not for a long time. Do you think he knows him? The killer? Do you think he's visited him, been in his house?'

'He says not,' Lomond said. 'But we're going to find out for sure. Today.'

38

'Don't mess us about,' Slater snarled, stabbing a finger at the old man across the interview room table. 'You had a key piece of evidence in a murder case. You *knew* you had a key piece of evidence in a murder case. The lassie in that painting – the same lassie you painted in the mural at the baths – had her throat cut from ear to ear. You bought that painting from the guy who did it – assuming it wasn't you. John Smith? Ten grand a painting? For an unknown? Someone whose face and real name you don't even *know*? I don't believe a guy as rich as you can be that naïve, or you wouldn't have a ha'penny left.'

'I didn't buy it. It was a gift,' the old man whispered.

'Really? We've already got you for withholding evidence,' Slater went on. 'If you don't tell us everything you know, you're going to be charged with assisting an offender. And you will be going to jail for that, mate. I guarantee it. Your next art class will be at the Bar-L.'

The old man gasped like a landed fish. He stared at his lawyer, who said, 'My client has already answered these questions.'

'He better start answering them in more detail,' Slater snapped. 'When did he get this painting? He couldn't have had it long – it's only a few weeks old. Sheonaid Aird Na Murchan was painted by the guy who killed her. He sent her a photo of this painting. Sir Erskine – did you send Sheonaid Aird Na Murchan a picture of this painting?'

'No,' Sir Erskine Copper said, in a choked voice.

'Where did you find Sheonaid Aird Na Murchan? The truth, now.' Slater sat back, his face red, eyes smarting.

'I told you. I saw her videos on the internet – she's well

304

known, in certain circles. She's the Black Selkie. I was looking for something of that type as a model for the baths.'

'Some*thing*?' Slater asked, head cocked.

'Some*one*. You know what I meant!'

'And, what, she just happened to show up on an internet search?'

'Exactly right,' Sir Erskine said resolutely, arms folded. 'Go on, you can prove me right. Do it, now. Search for "selkie", "mermaid", "Scotland". She's at the top. She was at the top when I looked. You can check that too. I was captivated. She was lovely.'

'What about the painting?' Lomond said. 'That just shows up at your door, does it? Surely that's too much of a coincidence for anyone to believe?'

'It's what happened. It was addressed to me. It arrived in packaging. Not long after I was commissioned to do the mural at the baths. I talked about that a lot – I put out a call for models, to see if there was one that suited me. Maybe that gave him the idea. I don't know.'

'Where did you put out your call for models?' Lomond asked.

'I put an open casting call on MyGirl,' Sir Erskine said. 'But that isn't where I found Sheonaid. I saw her videos. I told you.'

Slater snapped his fingers. 'And what, just like that, a delivery driver just showed up with the painting?'

'That's exactly what happened. A courier in a van. I can't remember the company – one of the bigger ones. Well-known name, but I'd be guessing.'

'What about the packaging?' Lomond asked. 'Were you told by anyone it was going to arrive?'

'It was unmarked. No note, no letter. I knew who had painted it, though. I knew it was John Smith.'

'And you say no money changed hands?'

'No. As far as I am aware, it's a gift.'

'And now for the sixty-four-squillion-pound art question,' Slater said. 'You hid it. Why?'

'I . . .' He glanced at his lawyer.

'You don't have to answer,' the lawyer said.

There was a tension in the room, then, the kind you felt on the nape of your neck or caressing the hairs of your arms.

'I didn't want to part with it,' Sir Erskine said, finally. 'John Smith's paintings were extraordinary. I knew they were going to be valuable, in time. I knew they would be torn to pieces or taken away from me.'

'You're bang on the money,' Slater said. 'Spot on. We'll be seeing you in court.'

'There's something . . .' The old man's jaw worked.

'What?' Lomond asked.

'There's something else. Something I should probably tell you.'

'We're listening,' Lomond said.

'There's another set of paintings I was given. Just the other day. They were posted to a holiday cottage I have.'

'By who?'

'I . . . I don't know. They were anonymous. Unsigned.' He swallowed. 'They're still there now. No one's touched them. I think you'll want to see them.'

*

Lomond had everything on a computer screen, for once. The video perspective of the door being bashed in; the hi-vis-clad figures barging into a compact, chocolate-box cottage. The almost frantic changes in angle as the police officer with the connected body camera followed his fellow officers into the house.

No one was home, but it didn't take long for the paintings to be found.

There was silence for a second. The body camera image was static, focused on the first painting, leaning against a far wall in the front room. Then the camera moved on to the second painting, then the third.

'You getting this, sir?' said the female officer in uniform. She sounded out of breath.

'Aye,' Lomond said. He rubbed his eyes. 'Seal off the cottage. Get out of there, get the SOCOs in. Wait a wee second, though. Keep the camera trained on the paintings, just for a minute. Maybe get a wee bit closer . . . That'll do.'

There they were. The three dead girls. Bodies suspended in water, more like marionettes than people, their skin and the tremulous waters hued in the primary colours. Blood gushing from their necks, a thick cloud of it, taking on a strange consistency, like cotton wool or candy floss. Yellow for Aylie. Blue for Sheonaid. And red, of course, for Roya.

★

Lomond stared at yet another cup of coffee. His stomach shivered while the cup made its journey towards his lips; his very blood revolted. Nausea came in a swift wave. Too many coffees: no more for now. Maybe no more today. His nerves were taut, but he knew it wasn't just the caffeine. *We're closer.* He laid the cup down on the canteen table.

And yet, Slater said, 'Nothing.' He rested his elbows on the table opposite the detective inspector, kneading his temples. 'We've got nothing so far. No prints on any of Sir Erskine's pictures. Nothing turning up on art websites, no helpful auctioneers, no art tutors, no models even. Nothing but crank calls and false trails. Can we tear the painting apart? Is there something in there, a hair maybe? Skin?'

'We'll tear it apart,' Lomond said. 'We'll tear them all apart. It'll tell us something. The wound, the signature on the canvas – you see it now. He's making his mark. That's what a lot of this is about.'

'He wants to be caught, surely,' Slater said. 'They say that about these guys . . . a lot of it's a game they want to lose. They need to be identified, in a way. Get the limelight. He wants it.

The notoriety. He doesn't want to be an unknown artist.'

Lomond nodded. 'All of that's probably true. We just need to put a name and a face to him. Then I don't care what the art world thinks of his work – four walls and a flat roof, bars on his windows: that's his room with a view. That's his canvas. That's him finished, and that's us finished with him.'

It was a strange way of putting it, and Lomond was about to correct it when his phone rang. He flipped the button on the touch screen and pressed it to his ear.

'Model's got in touch,' said Smythe.

'Model? What do you mean?'

'The boy who modelled alongside Roya Van Ahle. The one who went out on Sir Erskine Copper's roadshow.'

'Go on.'

'He said he made a video with Roya. Hardcore.'

'We traced that,' Lomond said.

'He said she made it because she needed the money – she was being blackmailed.'

39

It was obvious the boy had been drinking, even before Lomond spotted the half-full tumbler on the bookshelf. Vodka, and lots of it, judging by the smell in the air, and emitted by the boy on the couch. He might have spent the night there, going by the state of his hair, the swollen red eyes and the slope of his shoulders. The stubble was as Lomond remembered it, when he had first spotted him taking tickets at the art class, or indeed when he'd seen him bollock naked a few minutes later. He still looked like a Californian surfer from maybe twenty years ago, but there were some stark differences. His name was Walter – or Watt - McTominay, and he came from Shettleston rather than Big Sur.

'Take your time,' Lomond said.

'Right.' Watt sat forward. 'Thing is . . . Roya was being blackmailed.'

Lomond said nothing.

'I guess you want to know what for.'

'In your own time,' Lomond said mildly.

'She was being blackmailed for a video she did.'

'What kind of video?'

'You know. Sex. Porn.'

Lomond nodded. 'Was it a personal video or something else? For public consumption?'

'A bit of both,' Watt said. He glanced out of the uncurtained window at the rush-hour traffic.

'You'll have to explain as much as you know.'

'It was a personal video, but . . . kind of posed, as well. It was uploaded to a site, a kind of semi-pro one.'

'Semi-pro?' Slater asked. 'Not sure what you mean.'

309

'It's like a typical upload site, but it's more . . . I guess you would say classy, if that's the right word. Quality. That's not right, either.'

'You mean like MyGirl?' Lomond asked.

'No, it's a bit more hardcore than MyGirl. Roya had sent in a demo tape there. This one's called Cesar and Romeo's. Clever, I thought.'

'Cesar?' Lomond wrote this down in his notebook.

'Yeah, Cesar and Romeo's. Like Cesar Romero. "Cesar" is spelled that way – only one a. Not like Julius Caesar, like the guy who played the Joker in *Batman*.'

'Heath Ledger?' Slater asked.

The boy laughed. 'No.' Then his eyes flew open. Lomond saw, in real time, sweat appearing on his brow in tiny blisters. He said nothing more, but flew for the toilet, hand clamped to his mouth.

'Charming,' Slater said. 'The sharp end of the glamour world all right.'

'He's taking it hard,' Lomond said. 'Just as well he's totally clear for that night. And hey . . . Cesar, he said.'

'Yep, I was paying attention, gaffer. I get the link. The silver Mercedes kid. Don't you worry. I've got my Highers, you know.'

When he came back in, the boy seemed faint. He stank as he passed, as if he hadn't changed his clothes in days. With the stick-thin arms and legs, Lomond thought he could have passed for someone who lived under a bridge, and not the marble-statue seraph of a few nights before.

'You all right?' he asked. 'Can I get a wee glass of water for you?'

'Be fine. I was daft. I'm not a big drinker. Didn't even go out.' He shook his head.

'OK,' Slater said. 'You were saying . . . ?'

'Right . . . see, she had this idea for a video and told the guy she was seeing, who runs Cesar and Romeo's.'

'Did you meet him?'

'Once. She called him Cesar, but I'm not sure that's his real name. Flash git. Let everyone know that Roya was his girlfriend, but I think it was a kind of casual thing. He'd got her a lot of work, a few jobs here and there. Hostess stuff, a bit of modelling. Anyway, he got her into it. The site. And from there . . . she got blackmailed.'

'Blackmailed how?'

'Someone got in touch with her after the video was uploaded. Had copies, threatened to send it to her family.'

'I'm not sure I follow this,' Lomond said. 'They threatened to expose a video of her – but she was a life model. She'd modelled underwear. She sent stuff in to a site called CamJack – another model confirmed this for us. So you don't have to look too hard to find images of her naked on the internet. Her family knew a lot of this. Her sister knew she had applied for MyGirl. I'm not sure how you go from that common knowledge to something you could blackmail someone for. What sort of video was it? Pornography, is that what you mean?'

He nodded. 'Hardcore stuff. Penetration. Sex. I don't have to draw a picture, do I?'

'No, but you have to show us,' Slater said. 'You know about this video. Have you seen it?'

'I've seen it.' Watt looked Lomond in the eye. 'And I'm in it.'

'You?' Lomond said. 'You and Roya are together, in the video?'

The boy nodded.

'And this video was uploaded to a website run by the guy she was seeing – Cesar? It's his website?'

Watt nodded.

'Bit odd,' Slater said. 'I mean, no judgment; Christ knows we hear everything in this job. But you uploaded a video with you and Roya – let's be clear – having sex?'

Watt nodded again.

'And this was uploaded to a website run by . . . her boy-friend?' Slater tried not to seem incredulous.

'They weren't a couple,' Watt said. 'It was a casual thing. I sat there at the meeting when he drew up the contract. It's a new venture, he said. The future. Pay-per-view is the future – people do want to pay for good quality porn, it seems. His words, not mine. They want personalised content. They want to know the models, the performers, whatever you call them. They've got favourites. They want a closer connection . . . they love them, I suppose. In their way.'

'And you signed a deal to make the video?' Lomond asked.

Watt nodded.

'Why you?'

'I was told that I had the right attributes for the job,' Watt deadpanned.

Lomond coughed. 'And how did you know Roya?'

'You know how I knew Roya.' He smiled. 'I knew her from the modelling. Life classes. We both answered the same advert online. Open casting call. Go on tour, it said. Seemed a laugh. Sir Erskine chose us. Looked at us. Our faces. We went on his roadshow with him, together.'

'You know Sir Erskine well?' Lomond asked.

'Oh aye. Lovely man. Like your mad granda. He's into it, you know – the craft.'

'Was he into Roya?' Slater asked.

Watt's face showed irritation, even anger, for the first time. 'No. I said – it wasn't like that. Sir Erskine's into the art. He said he loved our bodies, our shapes, our faces. He said we were perfect models. I believed it. There's nobody like him.'

'And that's how you got to know Roya,' Lomond said.

Watt nodded.

'How well did you know each other? I mean before the video.'

'We had slept together, if that's what you're asking.'

'How many times?'

'Enough. Half a dozen.'

Lomond's tone was solemn. 'Did you love her?'

312

'I'm not sure.' The boy's voice cracked. 'It's done something to me, hasn't it? Maybe I did. If it's done this to me.'

'Whose idea was the video? Cesar's?'

'Roya's.'

Lomond wrote this down. 'Did Cesar know you had already slept together? When she put the idea to him?'

'I'm pretty sure he did. He didn't care. He thought there was cash to be made. That was as bothered as he got.'

'And did you make cash?'

'We were due to get a royalty – on top of a small fee up front. A certain percentage after so many subscriptions. We posted a clip.'

'Do you have the video?'

'No – Roya had it; she sent it to Cesar. He uploaded the clip.'

'Can you find it for us?' Lomond asked.

Without hesitation, Watt snatched up his phone, tapped at it, and handed it over. 'It's here. The clip's not too long. Just a taster, not more than a few seconds. For obvious reasons.'

Lomond and Slater peered at the screen. It was undoubtedly Roya. She was being taken from behind. She moaned; even compressed into a phone speaker, the sound seemed far too loud in the echoey tenement front room. Over her shoulder loomed Watt's stubbled face. His hands, gripping her breasts, then rising over the black choker around her neck to smooth her livid hair away from her face and shoulders. Then he took her hair in one hand, made a ponytail, and yanked it. Head tilted back, neck muscles prominent, Roya cried out in genuine pain. Lomond felt a curious sense of shock in his own scalp.

The video stopped. 'It was . . . part of the brief,' Watt said, embarrassed for the first time. 'It was what she wanted, not me.'

Lomond took note of the site, the name of the video, then handed back the phone. 'What about the blackmail – when did you first hear about it?'

'She phoned me. Told me someone was threatening to leak it. She always knew it was a risk, but she couldn't face telling

313

her family about it just yet. Her mum had warned her not to sell herself too cheaply, not to go the whole way . . . she was in bits. It took it out of her control.'

'Were you part of it?' Slater asked. 'I mean – did anyone blackmail you or contact you?'

'No. It was all on Roya.'

'What did she do about it? Were there any details?'

'She didn't know a name or anything. Said she was called on a burner phone. No names. She said it was a woman – a female. Said she wanted two grand to make the video go away.'

'Did she pay it?' Lomond asked.

'No. She was thinking about it. I told her not to – said we should pull the video anyway, hand the advance back, and forget about it. I told her to call the . . . well, to call you guys. If she paid it, then they'd only come back – and then they'd probably try it on someone else. She said she'd been stupid. Knew it had been a bad idea. Or . . . what was it? A good idea for the wrong reason. Something she needed to do for easy money. Said she knew it would haunt us. And she said it ruined us. It did. Maybe we ruined ourselves. I regret it, in a way.'

'Regret what?' Lomond said.

'Being with her in the first place. Maybe I should have kept her as she was. Adored her the way Erskine adored her. As a work of art. She was a work of art. I loved her. I loved her, I think. I think I loved her.'

*

Slater was ebullient. 'Lifting dafties, that's what it's all about! I love this job!' He drummed the glove compartment on the new pool car with his fingers.

'We're getting there,' Lomond agreed.

'You don't think it's this Cesar character, though,' Slater said.

'Nah. He's not a suspect – we checked. The site must be

linked to his new company – though he said he was in PR, not production. Kline and Co., that was the company.'

'Well, Cesar's Romeos or whatever will be linked to it, I guarantee it. PR, videos, web content – it's all one these days. Cuts out all the middle men. Do it yourself, take all the profit. Probably a case of fitting stuff into the right template, then putting a pay wall over it, and what do you know? All's said and done, he's a dodgy git. PR, company livery, flashy motors, hostesses, high-end clubs . . . at the end of it all, he's a pervert. He deals in sleaze. A sewer rat, preying on young people. That's what it boils down to. I hated his guts, gaffer, I admit it. I can't wait.'

'I doubt it's him,' Lomond said. 'And we know it isn't Watt.'

'Imagine calling yourself Watt when your name's Walter. It should be Wattie. As in two Ts. That's how you do it. Not "Watt" as in "what". What's the world coming to, gaffer?'

Lomond tried to tune out the noise. 'What about the blackmailer?'

'What? Being a woman?'

'Could be a beard. If you're a coercive person, you can get a woman to make a phone call for you. Be no big deal. Pay someone else to take the risk. That's how these clowns work.'

'Sure . . . But I've had a wee suspicion. You know that.' There was no note of triumph; Slater's face was grim. 'That's what I've been saying all along, gaffer. I think there's a woman involved somewhere. I think that's how he gets them to go where they're going. I think that's how they end up in the car – people read the websites, they know the news, like anyone else. They wouldn't hop into a car with some guy, knowing what they know, and who we're looking for. I think that's the lure.'

*

Cesar's upper arms and thighs made for a comic picture – squeezed by clothes that appeared too small for him. A polo shirt with a famous logo, and powder-blue jeans that looked delicate enough to dissolve in water. Lomond guessed that was the style. He surely couldn't have dressed like that by accident.

'What I will say to you,' Cesar said, glancing at his lawyer upon every pause, 'is that I am a businessman. That's the beginning and end of it.'

'Sure,' Lomond said. 'So you'll explain why the video of Roya and Watt – and the sample – have disappeared from your website in the forty minutes or so since we spoke on the phone.'

'I deleted the video as a mark of respect.'

'Respect!' Slater spluttered. 'Are you serious? Why did you remove it today? Why not yesterday?'

'I took action as soon as I could. I'm not a robot. Neither are my staff. I've done the decent thing. Whether it's a coincidence or not, I don't care.'

'The decent thing,' Slater sneered. 'You treated her like you were her pimp or something.'

'Look, I . . .' Again, Cesar glanced at his lawyer, who said nothing. 'I told you before – we had a casual relationship. It was non–exclusive. I said as much. It's not uncommon.'

'It is uncommon,' Slater said.

'Whatever. Look – I approved the video, I signed off on it, I knew about it, I cut the deal, I sat there and shook that boy's hand. No jealousy, no messing, nothing like that. We're all mature adults. It's hard for squares to get their head around, but there it is. I knew Roya had talent. Always knew it. I could detach myself. I saw the bigger picture. When she was on CamJack. Saw where she could go. We are talking millions. She could have been a star. I was going to make her the face of Cesar and Romeo's.'

'Name needs work,' Slater remarked. 'Sounds like a male lap-dancing club.'

'I wouldn't know about that,' Cesar returned. 'You might.'

'Were you aware of the blackmailing?' Slater shot back.

Cesar shook his head. 'No. On my mother's life.'

'Did Roya talk to you about it?' Lomond asked.

'No. This is the first I'm hearing about it.'

'She talked to Watt about it,' Slater said. 'Funny she should go to him and not you.'

'I'm not a mind reader, mate. I don't know why she spoke to Watt. Maybe he was being blackmailed too. It was a good video.'

'That's why you'll find it and give it to us.'

'I think it's irretrievable. I made sure it was totally deleted, completely trashed.'

'Nothing's irretrievable,' Lomond said. 'We'll find it. Strange you should want it obliterated. What have you got to hide?'

'Nothing. I . . . I didn't want the video to get out. She was murdered. It didn't seem right.'

'What – you're ashamed of yourself? In this line of work?' Slater asked.

'No. It's not that simple, though. I don't know Roya's mother, but I know she had sisters, she talked about them. Showed me their pictures on her phone. I was thinking of them.'

'You didn't think of them when you signed her up to make a sleazy video,' Slater said.

'I'm a businessman,' Cesar said again. 'Roya made money from modelling. She knew the score. I made her a good offer, and she took it. A better one would have come along soon. I had plans.'

'You can show us the plans. Every piece of correspondence: emails, texts, the lot.' Lomond's gaze was fixed, and difficult to hold for long. 'Withhold nothing.'

'I won't keep anything back.'

'Good. Can I ask – were you involved in MyGirl?'

'No, though I'll admit MyGirl was my business model. That's what I was aiming for. They're making a fortune.'

'Did you have any dealings with Torin MacAllister or Donald Ward, other than the ones you've told us about?'

'No . . . just the press launch MacAllister had at the Clyde. That's it.'

'Have you been involved with Claymore Films?'

'No, never.'

'Who deals with the videos?' Lomond asked. 'Do you have your own team?'

'We do have an editorial board . . . which is mostly me. I outsource the videos for editing and packaging.'

'Where to?'

'Company called . . . I think it's Redway, something like that.'

'"Something like that"?' Slater sat forward. 'You'd trust someone to upload content like that, and you're not sure who you're dealing with? I think that's something I'd want to know.'

'They're an independent company.' Cesar lowered his eyes. 'I can get you the details. I can't remember them off the top of my head.'

'You do that,' Lomond said. 'Quick as you like. Where are they based?'

'Here. Glasgow.'

Lomond nodded. 'Why did you choose them?'

'I told you. I'm a businessman. I'm just starting out. I was looking for people to work with Kline and Co. full time. But it was easier to outsource it. Same with all my IT. Off the peg, you know? You could do it yourself with various online tools. I prefer to pay a few quid to someone I know, get it done right. But not too much. They were cheap, is what I'm trying to say.'

'Name, please,' Lomond said, patiently.

40

Back in the turret room at Kirrin Hall, Marilyn Brownlie glided over the black and white flagstoned floor bearing two cups of tea. Smythe was grateful; although Tait's car had been warm and comfortable, the weather outside had been brutal, and she craved the spreading warmth of a good cuppa.

'It's kind of you to see us at such short notice,' Tait said, setting his cup down on a coaster. 'We won't take up a lot of your time.'

Brownlie removed her cardigan, revealing a blouse that was a little too tight for her. She had a good figure – not quite so stout as Cara had supposed on their previous meeting. Her long, silver-streaked hair was pinned back, ending in a ponytail. Her cheeks were a little heavy, with the added putty underneath the jaw that would make you wince if you saw it in a photo. But there was a beautiful woman under there, Smythe thought.

'You said you had something for me to look at?' Brownlie said.

'Something you might help us to clear up,' Tait replied.

'We talked to you a while back about Lana Galbraith,' Smythe continued. 'We've had a breakthrough in the case.'

Brownlie clasped her hands in front of her. 'That's very interesting. I've been thinking about her a lot since the last time you visited.'

'I think we all have,' Smythe said. Opening her bag, she pulled out a glossy printed sheet she had liberated from a filing cabinet deep in the bowels of the Police Scotland archives. It was a black and white picture of a beautiful young girl with dark eyes and light hair that your brain wanted to colour in chestnut brown or light red. The picture was obviously the work of a professional – so clear and crisp that you could make out the freckles dusted across her high cheekbones. The light danced in those black eyes, waltzed with them, became dizzy in their depths. The girl was sitting on a set of stone steps beside wrought-iron railings, one elbow on her knee, her chin set on the hand above. The expression was a little sad. She wore a delicate fairy princess dress, and her arms were bare. 'Do you know this girl?'

Brownlie took up the picture. 'She's very striking. I'm not sure I recall.'

'You had a head for details, I remember,' Smythe said. 'Take your time. When did you say you first came here – 1989?'

Brownlie nodded, her eyes not moving from the glossy shot.

'So you must have been here when Emer Ross was a guest at Kirrin Hall?'

Brownlie looked up. 'I'm not familiar with the name. Was she famous?' She held up the photograph. 'This looks as though it's part of a modelling portfolio.'

Tait cleared his throat and said, 'Emer Ross was at Kirrin Hall in 1995.'

Brownlie laid the picture on the desk. 'Her face doesn't jog my memory. The details might.'

'Not long after the picture in your hand was taken, she got into drugs. She was a heroin addict for many years, and came to Kirrin Hall several times during that period.'

'Someone who came in here so many times . . . I should really remember her.'

'We thought so, too,' Tait continued. 'It's a very sad story. Sometime after her last stint in here – and long after her last modelling job – she went missing.'

'Really?'

'Yes. Vanished without trace. One of those horrible cases you get. Still lots of them out there – less common these days, but before the internet and mobile phones and CCTV people could slip through the net. And she did.'

'That's awful,' Brownlie said.

'Thing is, it's hard to find details about Emer Ross,' Tait went on. 'Hardly any files. No police record. Not much in her modelling contracts. She didn't have any family, either – dad died before she was born; mother died when she was eight. In and out of foster care – not much to quibble about in her records, there. Good kid, decent grades, just a bit unlucky. She got a place at a good school through long-term foster-carers, though the relationship with them was strained, for some unspecified reason. She was talent-spotted when she was walking home from school, in fact. Age fifteen, stood outside a newsagent while her friend went in to buy her cigarettes. Tiny bit dodgy, if you ask me, but that's how it happened. Not unusual for a model's first impression to be made when she's in a school uniform, I'm told. Some people in the trade remember her as being a bit rough round the edges, but she was well liked. She mingled with some dodgy types, got into drugs . . . you'll know this story well.'

'Quite well,' Brownlie agreed.

'Thing is,' Tait continued, 'all of a sudden, she's turned up.'

The dark eyes widened slightly. 'Really?'

'Yes,' Tait went on. 'Caught us all off guard.'

'Whatever do you mean?'

Smythe said, 'She's dead. We found her body.'

'Murdered?' Brownlie looked from one detective to the other.

Smythe shook her head. 'No, Emer Ross died in a car crash. There's no doubt about that. The condition of her remains leaves us in no doubt. What's odd about it is that she was in a regular grave, in a regular cemetery, with a headstone above it. But it wasn't her headstone. It was Lana Galbraith's.'

'Lana Galbraith's?' Brownlie showed no emotion, no sense of shock. 'This is quite a lot to take in.'

'It will be. It's extremely strange,' Smythe said. 'You know all about Lana Galbraith. We don't understand how Emer Ross

321

got into her grave – remember, Lana had a full funeral, in the papers, pictures on the telly, actors, actresses and pop stars present, the lot. We don't understand how it was that Emer Ross crashed into a slate wall in a cutting, miles away from anywhere, in Lana Galbraith's car, went into Loch Lomond, and ended up being identified as Lana Galbraith. She was badly disfigured; she had a very similar body shape to Lana. And she was packed full of drugs when she died. But it beggars belief how she could have been misidentified. And it leads us to another, obvious question.'

'How did you find this out?' Brownlie said.

'We've exhumed her body, carried out all the tests, and got a direct hit on Emer Ross from the old missing persons case.'

'And . . . why did you exhume the body?'

'We were given a tip about Lana Galbraith's grave in relation to another matter.'

Brownlie nodded. She seemed to be focused on something not physically present in the room, a horizon far beyond the ancient stone walls around her.

'And it presents us with a new problem,' Smythe went on. 'We don't know where Lana Galbraith is – dead or alive. It gives us a new mystery to solve.'

'You can help us,' Tait said. 'We've taken a look at the dates, and Lana Galbraith's time in Kirrin Hall tallies with Emer Ross's, as well as Ursula Ulvaeus's. We just want to know – were they friends? They were all young, glamorous women, party girls – you saw them in glossy magazines, they sometimes got in the papers. Lana got on the telly, of course. It seems obvious to me that they would have at least known each other in here, had something in common. Maybe they'd have been friendly.'

'They were,' Brownlie said. 'I remember.'

Tait sat forward, clicked his pen, and found a fresh sheet in his notebook. 'That's brilliant. Anything at all you can give us would help – it's a very complicated matter.'

'It is,' Brownlie said. 'You know, I had a feeling that it was too complicated to be resolved. I didn't expect any of those loose ends to get tied up.'

And here she unpinned her hair, and let it fall about her shoulders. With a pout – jarring on such an austere, prim face, almost an insult – she settled back in her seat.

'No?' she asked, smiling.

Tait frowned over at Smythe, unsure of how to continue.

'I wanted this to happen, really,' Brownlie said. 'They reckon some people who've done wrong want to get caught on some level. It's true. I've got on with my life. I've carried on, but . . . there's always something wrong. That background noise. I wonder if it's like that for the real baddies in life? Killers. Like this Ferryman they're looking for now.'

Smythe sat bolt upright. She didn't hesitate. 'Marilyn Brownlie, I'm arresting you on suspicion of murder. You have the right to remain silent, but I have to advise you that anything you do say to us can be used as evidence against you in a court of law.'

Brownlie grinned. 'Doesn't that statement work better if you use the right name?'

'What's going on?' Tait thundered.

'Which name do you want me to use?' Smythe asked.

'My real one.'

Smythe swallowed. 'Lana Galbraith – you have the right to remain silent . . .'

41

Scaffolding had been erected around the front door of Strangbank Baths, but not to paint, spruce, prune or scrub the sandstone exterior. The new signage was obscured behind antiseptic whites.

The man who made it all happen slammed his car door and strode towards Lomond and Slater. 'Think this is funny?' Torin MacAllister snapped. 'Think this is a joke?'

Slater said, 'You know, I think the prospective candidate looks angry here, gaffer. Looks mad enough to swing for someone.' He swivelled and eyeballed the looming figure. 'If he's stupid enough to do that, he's in for a really uncomfortable evening.'

'I've been out of the country . . . and I come back to this? What's the score here?'

'There's no need to be alarmed,' Lomond said. 'I promise you that the pool will be reopened as quickly as possible – hopefully as soon as planned. So long as we don't find anything.'

'What exactly do you think you're going to find?'

Lomond's face lost its kindly look. 'Torin MacAllister, I'm arresting you on suspicion of the murders of Sheonaid Aird Na Murchan and Daisy Lawlor. You do not have to say anything, but anything you do say . . .'

'You what? Daisy Lawlor? Who the fuck's Sheonaid Aird Na . . .' Then his face went slack. 'The Ferryman. You think I'm the Ferryman.'

'. . . can be used against you as evidence in a court of law. Is that clear?'

'You think I killed them? Seriously? You think they were killed here?'

Slater came forward and gripped MacAllister by the wrist. MacAllister tried to flinch away; Slater was insistent, bending his arm, and snapping on the cuffs.

There was a slight tussle – nothing more than a shift in balance, but it went very much in Slater's favour. 'That's it,' the DS said, in a friendly tone. 'No nonsense now, Mr MacAllister. Or Mr Rafferty. What's your name really?'

'The Earl of Strathdene, if you want to get technical.'

'Thought you'd given that up. To get into Westminster. Is a title something you can take to the pawnbrokers? Get it back later?' Slater grinned. 'Maybe I'll just call you Ernie. Into the car, please.'

'I'll want . . .'

'Aye, we know, a lawyer. You can call him when you get to the police station.'

★

'Let's take Daisy Lawlor first,' Lomond said.

MacAllister had on an immaculate royal blue suit, and the cuffs protruded, clean and sharp in the strip lighting. 'No comment.'

'Daisy Lawlor, found dead in the pond at your father's house – now your house – after she went missing after a party there on June the thirtieth, 1995.'

'I have no comment to make on anything regarding that case.'

MacAllister's lawyer, Gerald Finlay, sat impassively by his side.

'Daisy Lawlor was at your party,' Lomond continued, 'and some of the people who were there remember her. She was last seen in the grounds of the house. She was off her head, some folk said. On drugs when she arrived. She was an outsider. No one knew how she got there, no one knew her from school or university . . . she wasn't part of your set. At some point in the next twelve hours, she died. It was a really hot summer, you'll recall. When you're eighteen – and you were eighteen; so was Daisy Lawlor – these kinds of details lodge in your mind. A long, hot summer. Your whole life ahead of you – you were going into first year of university in the autumn, weren't you, Torquod?'

'No comment,' he said, from the back of his throat.

'And you would have remembered a girl like Daisy Lawlor. Bright girl, but some daft ideas. Probably read Jack Kerouac – she thought hitchhiking was a good idea. *On The Road*. You know that book?'

'I read it,' MacAllister said, 'and I can't remember a single detail about it. I was a child at the time.'

'You were eighteen,' Lomond mused. 'Good age. A good time to be young, as well. Even if you sort the wheat from the chaff, the culture felt alive. Britpop was just a wee part of it. It was probably the last big youth movement before the internet swallowed everything.'

Slater glanced up at Lomond, somewhat startled.

'Maybe a wee change was in the air,' Lomond went on. 'The country was ready to throw the Tories out. Sorry . . . I forget. It's your party I'm talking about, Torquod. That's just a statement of fact, for the record.'

'It's going on the record,' MacAllister said in a dull tone, nodding towards the camera. 'Of course I remember that summer. It was great. Were you in the police then, inspector?'

'Aye. Baby polis. In uniform.'

'Did you have to get your hands dirty?'

'Very much so. I'd say I got my hands dirty at Rafferty Landing. I was there, Torquod. I saw that girl's body. It had been extremely hot that weekend . . . well. You can imagine.'

Lomond allowed a silence to descend before continuing: 'Daisy Lawlor. She had been planning a big adventure over the summer. She had meant to do a part work, part study thing at a summer camp in the States. But something fell through, and

326

she dropped out. But she decided to travel anyway. Quit her job. Lived on the lam. The kindness of others, you might say. She had photos developed up and down the country, all the way from her house in the Home Counties. We didn't see the prints, alas, just receipts. We never found her bag, her purse, anything. No mobile phones, of course. Some people had them at the time, but they weren't everywhere; we were still two or three years away from that. Even you didn't have one, Torquod.'

MacAllister sat up suddenly. 'Listen. I've said it before – I didn't intend to say it now, but I will.'

At his client's side, Finlay raised a hand: 'No, hang on. You don't have to.'

MacAllister ignored him. 'I did not kill Daisy Lawlor. Jesus Christ, the number of times I've felt the chill at that house . . . walked along those corridors, been alone in those rooms, walked the dogs around at night . . . looked at the place where that fucking pond used to be . . .'

'Filled it in quick enough, didn't you?' Slater said.

'It had been drained and dug up and sifted through and God knows what – there wasn't a boating pond left once you'd finished with it,' MacAllister replied, with some bitterness. 'And there was an even more obvious reason for filling it in. Something terrible had happened there. My dad wanted it obliterated, removed from his sight.'

'Surprised you didn't just move,' Slater said.

'That supposed to be a joke, son?' MacAllister snarled.

'No, dad.'

MacAllister took a breath. 'I didn't kill her.' He looked Lomond and Slater in the eye. 'Did. Not. Kill. Her. I'm not sure I can even remember her being there. Blonde girl? Good-looking? Bit hippie-ish? There were a lot of good-looking hippie-ish blonde girls there. It was a big party – you know that. You should ask everyone else who was there.'

'We have,' Lomond said. 'For years. But there's been no evidence in the case. No breaks. Until just recently.'

MacAllister said nothing.

Lomond continued: 'She was absolutely full of drugs . . . she'd taken eight or nine ecstasy tablets, as well as hash, and she had plenty of alcohol in her system when she died, too. I'd be surprised if she could stand, let alone walk. We're sure that's what killed her, but it doesn't explain the stab wounds on her body.'

Slater said, 'We wonder if that was done post-mortem to make it look like she was murdered. To throw us off the scent with the drugs. Because it was the drugs that killed her. Maybe someone young did the stabbing, not knowing much about forensics.'

'I don't know anything about that. Why aren't you chasing the travellers? Gypsies? Whatever you want to call them?'

'Again, we are,' Lomond told him. 'Still. To this day. We've tracked a few down. They say they picked up Daisy Lawlor while she was on her way to the pop festival. She rode with them as far as Rafferty Landing, then disappeared into the grounds. Later that night, she was seen at the party hosted by you and your best friend, Donald Ward. That night, probably in the early hours – midsummer eve, when the sun hardly sets – she dies. Next day the house party is disbanded, all the guests disappear in taxis. You hire a professional cleaning crew to clear the wreckage, debris and empties before you leave for the hunting lodge. You and Donald Ward. By Saturday night you're at the lodge with two female guests, both of whom were at the party the night before. Ursula Ulvaeus and Lana Galbraith.'

'Who went with who?' Slater asked.

MacAllister bristled. 'What's that got to do with you or the case?'

'I'm just curious, mate. And we need to know every detail.'

'It was a . . .' MacAllister leaned back in his seat and folded his arms. 'It was a trip away. We had it booked. Me and Don. We invited them, and they came with us.'

'Aye, we know. Inspector Lomond just said so.' Slater leaned forward. 'I asked, who went with who? As in, were you all sleeping together, was it casual, was it boyfriend and girlfriend . . . what was the deal?'

'Donald and Ursula were together. Since the night before,' MacAllister said. 'But I don't want to speak for him.'

'Don't worry about that,' Lomond said. 'I'm interested in you. Tell us. Were you sleeping with Lana Galbraith?'

'No,' MacAllister said. 'I didn't sleep with her.'

'Not for lack of trying, eh?' Slater grinned.

MacAllister's face flushed. 'No comment.'

'Lovely girl, Lana Galbraith,' Slater continued. 'I remember her on the telly. What was that show she used to do? It was basically a top ten of some kind, music, films, whatever, but she was really good. Never out the papers. Went to MTV Europe after that. She was going places.'

'Terrible shame,' MacAllister said.

'Did you love her?' Lomond asked.

'Bit Barbara Cartland, inspector, if you don't mind me saying so,' MacAllister spluttered.

'I could see anyone falling in love with her. And she was in your league, that was the thing. Certainly in your class. Her dad was loaded, a very well-to-do solicitor. Mother came from money, too. Same kind of money you're from, old money, but different circles. I think she partied harder, though. From what I can gather, you dabbled in that sort of lifestyle, but nothing like the kind of stuff Lana Galbraith and Ursula Ulvaeus were into. Hard drugs. As hard as they got. That wasn't your thing, really.'

'No comment,' MacAllister said.

'What was your connection? How did you meet?'

'I'd seen Lana around a lot. We mixed in the same circles, went to the same clubs . . .'

'That's young for clubs,' Lomond remarked.

'What – seventeen, eighteen, nineteen? You kidding? Been a while since you had a night out, inspector?'

Lomond motioned for him to continue.

'She had just signed up for her show. I met her . . . God knows.

There was a place called *Bogota*, off St Vincent Street . . . it's changed its name so many times. That was a place to go and be seen if you were young, you know. The right kind of place.'

'Rich kids' hangout, you mean,' Slater said.

'It was what it was. I met her there.'

'Just you?'

'We were part of a crowd. Me, Don, a few others.'

'You don't hang out together so much any more, then? Apart from Don, obviously,' said Slater.

'Not really.' MacAllister shrugged. 'I was still a teenager. Now I'm heading for fifty. Do you still hang around with the people you knew when you were eighteen?'

Slater shrugged. 'The old stag do. Sure'

'That's how I met her. I gave her the invite. She came to the party. Next day, the four of us went to the hunting lodge.'

'How did you feel when she died?' Lomond asked.

'Sad. We weren't ever an item or anything, but . . . it was only a few years later. I was gutted when I found out. Broken up. It was so sad what happened to her.'

'What about the day at the hunting lodge?' Lomond asked.

'Details are hazy, I'm sure you can appreciate that. I couldn't swear to much.'

'I'm assuming you were hungover. Maybe on a comedown?' Lomond asked.

'On a hangover,' MacAllister said, firmly. 'There was a lot of champagne drunk that night.'

'That was always happening at teenage parties where I grew up,' Slater said, a glint in his eye. 'Everybody would chip in, buy a magnum of champagne and a couple o' jeroboams of vintage claret. Sometimes we could barely clear a space for the dancing for all the empties. Then—'

'What happened the day after the party?' Lomond interrupted. 'Rough outline. You don't have to give us full details. Just as much as you can recall.'

'Well, we were driven over by someone my dad hired,'

MacAllister said. 'His name was Pencaitland, ex-army, my dad knew him from National Service, gave him a job. Dead now. He drove us to the lodge, left us there.'

'Where'd he go after that?'

'Home, I would guess. I've no idea.'

'And this was when?'

'Mid to late afternoon. Two, three?'

'And after that?'

'We opened some more champagne, walked around the grounds . . . I think we watched telly. We had satellite. Was a big deal then.'

'No other people there?' Lomond asked.

'No. Just us. We had food. I tried to cook, I think it was tagliatelle with parmesan and truffle oil; I'd read the recipe, but it was a disaster. Ordered a pizza in, eventually. We weren't up for eating much. We weren't up for drinking much either. The girls slept a lot of the time; Don and I watched the telly. Later on, Don and Ursula disappeared. Into the bedroom, you know. Lana and I sat up and talked. Nothing happened. I guessed she wasn't really into me. She came along for a laugh. Said she'd never stayed in a hunting lodge before.'

'Where did she sleep?'

'We slept . . . not together, if you know what I mean. But in the same bed.'

'Seems awkward,' Slater commented.

'It's hard to explain. Nothing happened. She said she liked me, and that was it.'

'You couldn't have needed a torch,' Slater said. 'On the grounds, like.'

'Come again?'

'With balls that blue, you'd have been a one-man lighthouse.'

Lomond interrupted quickly. 'If I was to speak to Lana Galbraith today, Mr MacAllister, would she corroborate all this?'

'Yes, to the letter. I'm sure of it. It's the honest truth.'

'Because I'm going to talk to her in the next few minutes. I just wanted to be sure of your side of it.'

'Say that again?' MacAllister said, much too loudly. He shared a look with Finlay.

'I said, I'm going to speak to Lana Galbraith in the next few minutes. In person,' Lomond said.

'No comment,' MacAllister said, finally.

42

Lomond sat down. Same seat, same side of the same desk, same room. He had come to despise the sameness of it.

'Do you mind if I call you Lana?' he asked the woman seated opposite.

She smiled. 'I don't even call myself that in my head, now.'

'I'll call you Lana. It's what I've been calling you in *my* head for twenty-five years.'

'You've been working on my case that long?'

Lomond sighed. 'Not exactly. I was there to begin with. Picked it up again recently. Since bodies started turning up in the Clyde. You could say a wee light blinked on in my head. It put me in mind of your case.'

'Am I being charged with anything?' She still wore her work clothes, and looked more like the lawyer than the defendant, compared with the young man sitting next to her. She had a poise to her; this was someone who had been used to being treated with deference over a long period of time.

'You're being charged with several things,' Lomond said. 'But we've got lots to talk about before we do that. First: how did you come by the new identity?'

Galbraith smiled ruefully. 'People were pulling strings for me. I don't want to name them. You can probably guess. Official people. High-up people.'

'Polis?' Slater asked.

'Some were serving members of the police, yes. I don't know their names. My dad did. He's been dead eleven years now.'

'So, technically, you predeceased him,' Lomond said.

'Quite.'

'What happened to Emer Ross – the girl who ended up swapping places with you?'

'She was a junkie,' Galbraith said. 'One of the bad ones. Not like me. One of the ones who you just know isn't coming back, once she went down that road. Shame. She had style. She had talent. But flawed as you can get.'

'Was Emer a friend of yours from before? Or did you know her from rehab?'

'A bit of both. She tried out for the TV chart show. That's where I first met her. I beat her – I beat everybody – but she was nice about it. No one remembers what the show was called, you know that? People sometimes remember me being on it, interviewing Blur and Oasis and all the rest, but they don't remember the name of the show. Can either of you remember it?'

Lomond shook his head.

'Before my time,' Slater said casually.

'*Pop 'n' Popcorn*. It's been an answer on *Pointless*. I can't decide if it was terrible or awesome. A bit of both. Maybe that's your youth in a nutshell.'

'Most people's youths don't involve faking their own death and swapping places with a drug addict,' Lomond said severely.

She shrugged. 'Emer was on the road out. They get a look. A kind of pre-death. She'd already tried to take her own life a couple of times.'

'And, what, you helped her on her way?'

'Not exactly. She had herself a big weekend at someone else's expense. I was with her for part of the time. She borrowed my car. To get a wee message, she said. That's when she crashed, and ended up in the loch. She was identified as being me by dear old Daddy. The whole thing was very cleverly done.'

'We noticed that there weren't many photographs or reports on what happened in our files,' Slater said. 'Paper files and computer files. Sometimes they can go missing, but on top of the files from Rafferty Landing going missing . . . Very odd, that.'

'That's something you'll have to take up with your superiors. Or the superiors who were around back then. I understand there aren't too many of them left.'

'There is one, actually,' Lomond said. 'You're going to end up in trouble. I would suggest you tell us as much as you know. It's not just about you – it's about Daisy Lawlor and Emer Ross and their families. Please tell us as much as you know.'

She cocked her head at him. 'Are you offering me a deal, inspector?'

'No promises. But first tell us why you swapped identities.'

'I had to get out of the way. There was more than one reason for that. Even after rehab, I was still finding myself in among the wrong people . . . my career was starting to go south as a result. No one wants a junkie, really, do they? Word soon gets about. The people who are giving the gear to you like a dog biscuit one week are slamming doors on you the next. Someone like me loses their utility when it gets obvious.'

'You're telling us that you faked your own death to get away from drugs?' Lomond asked. 'Was this a decision that was made on the spot, when the car was found, after Emer Ross took it? I find that hard to believe.'

'I believe it had been planned,' Galbraith said. 'To the letter.'

'By who?' Slater asked.

'By *whom*,' she corrected him. 'I don't know. The same people who arranged it all for me. My daddy would be able to tell you. If he was still here.'

'Very convenient for you,' Slater said.

'It got me this far,' she said, smirking.

'Did someone put her in the car?' Lomond asked.

'Again . . . I wasn't involved in that. It's all very hazy. Or maybe I should say fishy. She took my car. Said she was going to a party. Next thing I know, she gets hauled out of Loch Lomond. Things started moving after that. I was told to stay quiet, I was given a house out of the way, I was given a new passport and told to cut my hair. After a while I was even given

335

a job at a wee gift shop where lots of people told me I looked like that poor lassie who was on that daft chart show. It blew over. I had a couple of boyfriends, but no one worth settling down with, and obviously I had to stay well away from Glasgow. I got bored, got a degree under my new name, and ended up here, after a few more doors were mysteriously opened, you might say. And that's the story of Lana Galbraith. Her life and afterlife.'

'And what about your other reasons for faking your own death?' Lomond asked. 'You said there was more than one.'

'The other one was . . . I was scared.'

She turned to her lawyer briefly. 'You don't have to answer,' he whispered, from somewhere beneath his fringe.

'I was involved,' she said, 'at Rafferty Landing.'

'In what?'

'You know as well as I do that something dodgy happened there. The dead girl. Stab wounds? I'm not daft. That's what happened to the girls they found in the Clyde. Do you think the guy who killed Daisy Lawlor killed them too?'

Lomond was thunderstruck. 'No one here said anyone stabbed Daisy Lawlor.'

She composed herself, then said, 'It's a very well-known case.'

'Tell us,' Lomond said. 'Please. We need the breakthrough.'

'I knew Torquod Rafferty,' she said. 'Could have told you he'd be a politician. Had that aura about him. Carried himself well. And plenty of money. He was shy with women – wanted to be a player, but he was a few years off that, if he ever got there. I thought he was quite cute, but I didn't really fancy him. I met him at a club in Glasgow. Rich kids' cop-off shop, long gone now. He invited me to stay at the hunting lodge – he and his friend were going.'

'That was his first invitation to you?' Lomond asked. 'To stay at the hunting lodge? Not to come to his party at Rafferty Landing?'

'Definitely. The party idea didn't come until a bit later. I met him at a place . . . what was it called? *Bogota*. That was it. I met him in *Bogota*. His friend was there. Artist. Had very long hair at the time. Donald something. I was more into him, to be honest. He had the confidence Torquod craved. But then Torquod suggested a house party. Invited half the club there, too. All part of the same scene. Rich kids. Unbearable, really.'

'So you went to the party on the Friday, then stayed at the hunting lodge on the Saturday?' Lomond asked.

'That's right.'

'What do you remember about the party?'

'Surprisingly chaste. They were trying to impress. They'd got some caterers in at short notice. Lobster, if you can believe that. Smoked salmon. Someone chased me around the room with a crab claw. Loads of champagne, but not a lot of gear about, until . . . my friend arrived.'

'Your friend?'

'Yes. You know her as Ursula Ulvaeus. I met her in rehab – more than once. She was Scandinavian but a lot of people took her for American. She sounded it and looked it. Beautiful teeth, the blonde hair, the attitude. And she also had the best contacts for the gear, whether she landed in rehab or not.'

'She didn't care much about getting clean?' Slater asked.

'She thought rehab was a game. I'd say I'm astonished how she turned out, but then . . .' She pointed to her own face, and grinned.

'What do you remember about Daisy Lawlor?'

'Quite a lot, earlier on in the evening. They called her "the tramp" and "the gypo", and worse, behind her back. She wasn't one of us. I thought she looked great, actually. Very boho. But she was also off her face when she showed up, on God knows what. Ecstasy maybe. It's hard to be sure. And necking champagne on top. Then at some point she hit the deck. I was busy trying to seduce Don, but he was more interested in Ursula. You know how it goes.'

337

Lomond was nonplussed. 'So you stayed the night at Rafferty Landing?'

She laughed. 'It was a party, not a sleepover. We were up most of the night. We were young, you know. Hardly anyone over twenty. There was a fight between a couple of guys, some people left, people copped off left and right . . . it was kids' stuff, though. Kind of thing you'd expect among fifteen-year-olds.'

'How about you and his lordship?' Slater asked.

'What? Torquod? I kissed him, for a little bit. I was trying to make Donald jealous, but I got that one wrong. I found it hard to believe he wanted Ursula more than he might want me. I was affronted, what can I tell you? With Torquod, it was like . . . he hadn't been with many girls before.'

'So you didn't see Daisy Lawlor again that night?'

'No. Next I heard of Daisy Lawlor, she was being pulled out of the pond two days later.'

Lomond frowned. 'When did the party break up?'

'I think Torquod's driver showed up late Saturday morning. I'm not sure if that was by design or if his dad had sent him along – I can't say. But that changed things. He was a hard little man, ex-forces, I think. He sent everyone packing and they didn't argue much. Then he arranged for the mess to get cleared . . . and then he drove the four of us to the hunting lodge. There I had the most boring day and a half of my life. I thought we were going shooting, you know? But we hardly left the building. We watched MTV, ate crisps, had a pizza delivered, then we were driven home next day. I spent a very strange night in bed with a boy who was too frightened to make the first move. Weird, how everything changed when the news came through. When they found the body in the pond.'

'What was your reaction?'

'Shock. And guilt. I wondered if a few of us had chased her off the premises, and she bumped into someone nasty in the woods. We'd given her short shrift. Like an annoying kid sister. It was group-think, pack behaviour, something like that. One or two of the girls were well off with her, and it took hold of us . . . I do remember she was wrecked, really daffy and annoying. When someone insulted her, she just said, "Cool!" She was such a dweeb. I really envied her nose ring, though. I complimented her on it.'

'Sorry, I don't get it,' Slater said.

'Get what?'

'You said you were frightened. That's why you changed your identity, gave yours to a dead girl, and ran out on your life. You were feart. Feart of what?'

She swallowed. 'There was a phone call,' she said. 'Not long after. Told me exactly what to tell the police. That I wasn't to mention anything about Daisy Lawlor. That I wasn't to say a thing about Rafferty Landing other than being at the party and then the lodge. Or I'd end up the same way.'

'What kind of voice?' Lomond asked.

'A man's voice. Polite. Definitely Scottish, hard to tell what accent. Maybe young, maybe old.'

'Did you recognise it? Any ideas?'

'None at all. But I did what I was told. I didn't contact anyone about it – not even Ursula, incidentally. I assumed she was told the same. But when I found out later that Daisy Lawlor had been stabbed . . .'

'It didn't cause her death,' Lomond said. 'Tests showed she had taken a lot of drugs that night. They might have been enough to kill her on their own. The wounds were administered post-mortem, not long after she died.'

Galbraith nodded. 'I heard that too. But I couldn't go on with my life after that. I got scared – panicky. Maybe I thought I was responsible. I don't know. It was the crisis point I had to reach to turn back. Rock bottom. And my dad was worried. He was scared for me. He . . .' She wiped away sudden tears. 'He saw me right. He put a plan in place. He thought that the only way to keep me safe was for people to think I was dead. Whether it was the drugs or my career or the person who had threatened me – he sorted it out somehow. Dad kept me safe. I'm here now, alive and well. And clean. It's down to him.'

'That's nice,' Slater said contemptuously. 'Now let's talk about the other dead girl with a very close link to your good self. Emer Ross. Tell us about how she ended up in the car that ended up in Loch Lomond. Who put her there?'

'I don't know anything about that,' Galbraith said flatly.

'Because we might end up charging you with murder,' Slater said, 'seeing as you asked about charges. That's what happens with dead girls being forced into cars.'

'So,' Lomond said, 'the car had crashed into a shale wall by the lochside. One side of it was mangled. But I wonder if the crash didn't cause the car to go into the water immediately. Maybe the crash was staged, then the car was shoved in later . . . According to the report, one tyre was deflated.'

He shared a look with Slater.

'As I said, I don't know anything about that,' Galbraith responded. 'I was told where to go and what to do, and I did it. I'd been threatened. My name was linked to a death, possibly a murder. I wanted out of drugs. I wanted my life back. Not my old life . . . I wanted freedom. I wanted out of the spotlight. It was making me sick, anyway, long before that girl died. I was playing at being the party girl. It was disgusting. Then someone ended up dead. I was scared, my family was scared, my dad was scared. I promise you I don't know anything about how Emer Ross died: I had nothing to do with it.'

'And everyone who did is dead,' Slater said. 'Funny, I just don't believe you.'

'All my dad ever said about it . . .' She hesitated. 'All that was ever said about it was that there was a guy sorting it all out. Dad did mention a name, but it was obviously false.'

That thunderbolt, again. Lomond's face twitched. 'Give us the name,' he said.

She shook her head. 'It's silly; there's no point. It's clearly made up.'

'Give us . . . the name. Please.'

'John Smith.'

43

Ursula Ulvaeus waited for the crowd to calm down, and changed her stance, her voice, her tone, dropping everything down a notch. The lit candles all around lent a strange animation to her angular features.

'I deplore the violence we've seen on the streets here,' she said. 'And I don't want it happening again. No one wants that. The police have failed us, but the violence, the attacks on police cars – we have to draw a very firm line. We're noisy . . .' the crowd responded . . . 'we get in their faces . . .' she grew more forceful . . . 'and we *are* angry. But not violent. Never violent. That's their game, not ours. So we're going to keep making a noise. We're going to raise our fists – but never throw them. And we're not going to stop until that animal is locked up for good!'

'She's good at that, y'know,' Lomond said. 'Should be a politician.'

'A politician, eh? I can see that,' Slater mused. 'Just when I was starting to like her, tae.'

'So now we've marched from the west end to George Square,' Ulvaeus continued, 'thousands of us, to show this so-called Ferryman that the entire city is watching and waiting. He'll no longer be allowed to prey on young people who want to do the thing that some men fear most in women: express themselves. And create art, without fear and without prejudice. He's a small man, a twisted man, and a man whose time is up.'

The applause was thunderous as she stepped down from the steps of the memorial, with the stone lions impassive on either side of her and the City Chambers at her back. The torchlight flickered over the stonework and the faces of the women surrounding her. Even the minders flanking her were women, both tall, muscular and stone-faced as they scanned the people in the front rows of the crowd.

'We on?' Slater asked.

'Yep.' Lomond clicked off his phone and opened the car door.

Ulvaeus and her two bouncers, having passed through a phalanx of men in hi-vis vests, were heading across the road from the cenotaph to the City Chambers. Seeing the two policemen standing in their way, one of the minders approached them.

'Police,' said Lomond, brandishing his warrant card. 'Ursula Ulvaeus, I am arresting you on suspicion of the murder of Daisy Lawlor . . .'

Both the minders instantly enfolded Ulvaeus; one even raised her hand to shove him away.

'No, you don't, sweetheart,' said Slater, his broad smile doing absolutely nothing to disguise the tension and anxiety he felt. 'Unless you want to be lifted as well?'

'You actually looking to cause a riot?' the first minder said. 'We'll have your car on its roof in ten seconds.'

'Ursula, please get in the car,' Lomond said. 'Let's see if you're as good as your word. Get in quickly.'

'This is a joke. It really is,' Ulvaeus said. She gestured for her minders to let her through. 'No handcuffs?' she asked Lomond.

'No. You're co-operating with the investigation and what you tell us this evening can help us put this guy away. But you are under arrest, and anything you say can be used against you in a court of law.'

'I've heard my Miranda rights before,' she said, shrugging. 'No blanket, even? No armed officers? At least a walk of shame? C'mon, you can give me that.'

'You wish,' Slater said, with undisguised contempt. 'Get in.'

★

343

Ulvaeus took a sip of water. 'How did you get round the back of the war memorial? I have a security operation that doesn't let people close.'

'You don't control everything,' Slater said, leaning towards her from the opposite side of the table. 'We have an arrest warrant for someone, we arrest them. Anyone who gets wide about it gets arrested too. We did give you a police escort. Not everyone gets that.'

'I'm very flattered.'

'Do you mind if we ask you something now?' Lomond asked.

'Sure.'

'We've spoken to a lot of people over a long space of time about what happened at Rafferty Landing twenty-five years ago. There're so many alibis, and most of them fit together. But one element of that weekend still makes me . . . curious.'

'Oh?'

'Yeah. It's the bit where you and Lana Galbraith take off to the hunting lodge the day after the party, with Donald Ward and Torquod Rafferty. Tell me about that.'

'There's nothing to tell you, inspector. I was invited to a hunting lodge by a cute rich boy. At least I thought Donald Ward was rich. Turned out it was his friend who had the money. It seemed like a fun idea. It *was* fun for a while, with Donald. I think I broke his heart. For maybe two weeks. Then he moved on with someone else. It was nice. They were nice boys, those two.'

'Tell us about the drugs at Rafferty Landing.'

She drummed her fingers. 'I'd rather not.'

'Thing is, that crowd . . . even Torquod and Donald, the bad boys of the Friday party . . . they weren't part of the drugs scene. Most of the young people at that party were well-adjusted youngsters. They thought they were streetwise, knew the score. They didn't.'

'You could be talking about teenage life full stop,' Ulvaeus said.

'Not when it comes to you, though,' Lomond said. 'There were a lot of drugs at that party. Several people said they were supplied by you. Eccies and hash, mostly, though you had something called pink champagne. Expensive gear, they tell me.'

'I don't have anything to say about that.'

Slater leaned forward. 'Where'd you get the stuff?'

'I don't know what you mean.'

'Is it the same stuff Daisy Lawlor was full of when she died? If it's what killed her, then the person who supplied it has a lot to answer for. If she was still alive when she was carved up . . .'

'*Carved up?*'

'Oh aye. Didn't we tell you? She had some funny wounds. We're sure she got them after she died. Some of the cuts make us think that whoever took a knife to Daisy Lawlor might be same person who took a knife to the lassies we've found in the Clyde. The ones you've been causing havoc about.'

'Wounds,' Ulvaeus said. Her chin trembled.

'We want to know the connection,' Lomond said. 'It's possible you might know the Ferryman. It's vital you tell us the truth about that weekend, help us rule people in or out.'

'Or,' Slater said, 'it might actually get out that Ursula Ulvaeus, big feminist hero that she is, has a link to the killer she's been kicking up hell about. I reckon that would make your career as a big crime-fighting rebel look a bit dodgy.'

'You're blackmailing me,' Ulvaeus said, in an unsteady whisper.

Her lawyer protested, but Lomond answered: 'No – we're giving you a chance. Tell us everything. Let us know the truth. I think we're very close to finding the Ferryman. You can get us closer. We could collar this guy in the next twenty-four hours.'

'I got the drugs through Lana,' Ulvaeus said, her hands linked to stop their trembling. Her voice was hoarse, and strangely delicate for once. 'She knew a guy in rehab . . . hell of a recruiting ground, when you think of it. A built-in market. I forget what he was called, and I don't know what he looked like. He wasn't involved in the party, before you ask. But I do remember Daisy Lawlor. She arrived with some miserable dabs of speed from the folk she'd been partying with. She looked like a . . . greebo, is that a word people use? Bit trampy. Needed a wash. Hippie type, but not fully committed. Bit too polite. I remember her eyes. Glazed, they call it. I remember Lana telling me her eyes looked the same as a sniffer dog's that's been too long on the job.'

'You spoke to Daisy?'

'I spoke to her . . . and I sold her drugs. A lot of them. She said she was looking to buy some to take to the festival that weekend. In actual fact she ate most of them, though I didn't know that until she collapsed. She'd overheated. Someone took her to a bathroom to put her in the shower – they actually doused her in cold water. She came back for a little bit, then went spark out again. That's that. I didn't see her again. But I know Torquod and Donald disappeared for a while. Someone asked what had happened to Daisy and they said she had left the house with someone. Donald and Torquod had called in – a friend of theirs who was supposed to be fixing the problem. He took drugs off us all, like it was a bust. He said something about the police being on their way, and that put the fear of God into everyone. I flushed four hundred pounds' worth of eccies down the toilet. I was pretty pissed off about it, I have to tell you. Next thing I know, the guests have gone, and Lana and I are staying over. The next day we were driven to this spooky old hunting lodge. It was weird. I was with Donald, but . . . he and Torquod were preoccupied. That's the word. Worried about something.'

'This friend who showed up and took away the drugs,' Lomond asked, tugging at his shirt collar. 'What do you remember about him?'

'Oh, I don't have to remember too many details. I can tell you his name. He's Torquod's lawyer now. They called him Griz at the time, like Grizzly Adams. But his name's Gerald Finlay.'

'Why didn't you tell us this before?'

'I didn't want to incriminate myself,' Ulvaeus said. 'And I just have. But let me tell you something. I'm no traitor. I was young and I didn't want to go to jail. Whatever happened to Daisy Lawlor, it wasn't my fault.'

'Has anyone ever threatened you about that particular case, Ursula?'

'Ha!' Here, tears spilled down Ulvaeus's cheeks. 'I get threatened on a daily basis. But I can't remember anyone at Rafferty Landing threatening me.'

'That's been a help,' Lomond said gravely. He sat back. Ulvaeus's eyes were downcast. She didn't look defeated, couldn't look defeated, he suspected. But something had irrevocably changed.

44

'You look nervous, Mr Finlay,' Slater said.

'I wouldn't have said so,' the big man said.

'Take as long as you like to answer the questions.'

'Let's just get down to business,' Finlay said, squaring his shoulders in a comically pugnacious fashion. 'I don't have all day.'

'Don't worry about the time,' Lomond said. 'We want to ask you about Rafferty Landing.'

'Oh yes?'

'You know it?'

'Of course. I've been friends with Torquod Rafferty for years. Regular visitor.'

'How about the summer of 1995?'

'Long time ago.'

'Did you know Torquod then?'

'You know, we're going back into ancient history here. I can't remember exactly when I met him. School days, early teenage years? When you've known someone that long, you forget the first meeting.'

'How about June the thirtieth, 1995?' Slater asked. 'There was a big party at Rafferty Landing. You invited?'

'There were lots of parties at Raffety Landing.'

'How about the one with all the trouble?'

'You'll have to be specific.'

'I'll jog your memory. Daisy Lawlor. The one where she died.' Slater clicked the mouse; on the screen, the dead girl's image appeared. A faded photograph that might otherwise have avoided notice or much comment in family photo albums, Lomond thought; a big broad smile at sunset somewhere – he'd been led to believe it was Glastonbury a year before her death – with the light catching her nose piercing. Long hair, no make-up, still glowing.

'Don't know her,' Finlay said.

'So,' Lomond said, 'you're indicating to us that you were not at the party at Rafferty Landing on June the thirtieth, 1995, the weekend that Daisy Lawlor was found dead in the boating pond to the west of the house?'

Finlay linked his fingers, tight. 'I don't remember – I can't answer that for sure.'

Slater snorted. 'What, your best mate has a big party, with actual telly stars present, and a lassie dies around about that time, her body found in the lake a couple of hundred yards from the house, and you can't *remember* that? You must go to some interesting parties.'

'I do.' Finlay grinned, his hands still locked tight on the tabletop.

'What was your reaction when you heard someone had died at Rafferty Landing that night?' Lomond asked.

'I'm sure I was very shocked.'

'I'm sure you were, too,' Lomond said. 'When did you last see Daisy Lawlor? Was she alive or dead?'

Finlay turned to the lawyer at his side, a stern young woman in octagonal glasses too delicate to be perched on such a severe face. She merely shook her head.

'I . . . have no comment,' he said.

'Daisy Lawlor was full of drugs when she died,' Lomond said. 'There was a strong batch of ecstasy on the go that night. Stronger than she was used to. Had she been overheating? Drinking too much water? It was a very hot weekend. Middle of a heatwave. Hottest since 1976, they said.'

'Wouldn't know,' Finlay said.

'Do you have any recollection of Daisy Lawlor being in any kind of distress or trouble at that party?'

'I have no comment.'

349

'Did you get her out of the house?'

'No comment.'

'Did Torquod tell you to get her out of the house? Did you have that kind of relationship? Him giving you the credibility and opening the doors for you, while you pay the price by acting like his fixer?'

Finlay chuckled at this and simply shook his head, glancing towards the ceiling in mock exasperation.

'Did you fix the problem?' Lomond asked.

'No idea what you mean.'

'Did you get rid of Daisy? Meaning, did you throw her out . . . take her into the woods? Dump her in her tent? Is that where she died? Did you throw the body in the pond after you checked on her later?'

'No comment.' Finlay leaned back in his seat and folded his arms tightly against his chest.

Lomond paused a moment. 'What if we told you that we have witnesses who saw you escorting Daisy Lawlor away somewhere when she was getting out of hand? And that was the last time she was seen alive. What would you say to that?'

'Nothing.'

'Witnesses have identified you as the last person to be seen with her,' Slater said. 'Did you know about the knife wounds on her body? Was she alive or dead when she got those cuts?'

'There's no point continuing with this line of questioning. I'm not going to answer this.'

Slater jabbed a finger at him. 'And what if we told you that the whole house of cards on the cover-up is coming down? That we have a signed statement from a police officer saying that someone at Rafferty Landing knew exactly what happened to Daisy Lawlor? That we know that Lana Galbraith is still alive? That we've spoken to her in this very room?'

At last, a flicker of unease. 'What? Lana Galbraith?'

'That's right,' Slater said, 'the wee darling from the telly. You remember?'

'Of course I remember. She's dead.'

'She's alive, pal. She was at the party at Rafferty Landing. So were you. She helped get all the drugs in, so Torquod could impress his mates. Her and Ursula Ulvaeus, the lassie causing chaos in the toon as we speak. According to them, you were the guy who helped "take care of the problem", in inverted commas. The guy who fixed things. That was your job even then, wasn't it?'

'No comment on any of that.'

Lomond gazed into Finlay's eyes. 'Did you kill Daisy Lawlor?'

'No.'

'Did you knife her?' Lomond continued. 'In the back, across the throat, beneath the breasts, just above her hip on the right-hand side, and in her vagina?'

Finlay shook his head.

'Was that a yes or a no?'

'No.'

'Did you dump her body in the lake and hide it underneath some overhanging bushes?'

'No.'

'Did you do this to make sure she was exposed to the elements?'

'No.'

Lomond's voice was still neutral. 'Was she dead or alive before you used the knife?'

'No comment.'

'Do you still have the knife, Mr Finlay? Do you still use it today?'

'No comment . . . no.'

'Are you the Ferryman, Gerald?'

'Christ. No.'

'You're the only suspect over Daisy Lawlor's death,' Slater said. 'Every witness we've spoken to has told us that you were the guy who steered her off the site. It looks like you had something to do with it, Gerry.'

'I didn't . . .' Finlay said, shoulders quivering, on the edge of some terrible eruption.

'You didn't?' Slater sneered. 'Looks like you totally did, to me.'

'Did you use the knife to make sure she was dead?' Lomond asked neutrally. 'Or to draw attention away from the fact that she died full of drugs, which were sourced from your friend's party?'

'She collapsed. I made a phone call,' Finlay said. His linked fists could not still the tremor in his hands. 'After that I left her. In her tent. I hardly even put hands on her. That's all I did.'

'Tell me about it, son,' Lomond said. 'Every detail.'

'Lana Galbraith's drugs guy knew someone. He said he would fix the whole thing, cash in hand. So I made the call. I was told to leave Daisy Lawlor in her sleeping bag, in her tent, and he would come and sort it out the next day.'

'Was she dead when you left her?' Lomond asked.

'I can't be sure. She had had a fit or a meltdown . . . I don't know. She was comatose when I made the call. I couldn't find a pulse.'

'Didn't you have a brainwave at that point?' Slater asked, slapping his forehead. '"Hey! Let's call an ambulance!"'

'I thought she was already dead. And we'd have gone to jail. All of us. The guy who came to sort it out must have done the cutting. I don't know why.'

'Did you see him?' Lomond asked. 'This man?'

'No.'

'Did you get a name? Nickname, anything? Anything at all?'

'I got a name.' Finlay sat back, drawing a hand over his stubbled head. 'But you won't like it.'

Slater emitted a long sigh, and threw his pen onto the table. 'Go on then,' he said. 'Hit us.'

'John Smith.'

45

'Redway,' Slater said, as he pulled up at the gates set in the pristine, whitewashed wall, waist-high and speared with iron. 'You ever get that feeling, gaffer? You know the one I mean.'

'Aye. Had it several times in this gig already.' Lomond got out of the car. 'I know not to trust it by now.' As he bent to examine the intercom system in the gates there was a solid click, and they swung open.

'In you come, gents,' said a voice.

'Don't you want to know who we are?' Slater called.

'I can tell a polis man from half a mile away, mate. Front door, straight up the path.' There was a dry chuckle, then the intercom closed off with a rasp as a handset was replaced.

They walked up a driveway paved with red stones which split an immense garden in two. There were several out-buildings: one was a summer house, another seemed to be a red-bricked shed, and the next was a greenhouse. As they passed the final structure, a squat building set to the western edge of the property, a chemical scent triggered childhood memories in them both.

'Reckon there's a pool in there?' Slater asked.

'I reckon there is.'

The house itself was on two storeys, the walls washed white under a black slate roof. 'You don't often get places this big in this part of town,' Slater said. 'You wouldn't even know it was here, driving past. Man must be loaded.'

'He makes porn. It makes money,' Lomond said, pushing the doorbell set into the black storm doors.

Rab Cullen was fifty-three, but might have passed for ten

years older, with what remained of his hair shaved tight into his scalp. His large blue eyes were magnified by his glasses. He was short, maybe five foot four, and wore a black polo-neck pullover. He had a frank look about him that Lomond instantly distrusted.

'Mr Cullen?' he asked.

'That's right. Who wants to do the introductions?' He rubbed his hands together and chuckled. The smile changed his face, but not necessarily for the better.

★

Cullen led them through a gloomy lobby into a broad, bright kitchen, with a large patio window looking out onto a bare lawn.

He sat on a high stool opposite the two detectives, across a breakfast-bar peninsula. 'Well?' he said finally.

Lomond said, 'We're here to talk about some of your clients at Redway.'

'There're lots of them.'

'One of them was murdered recently,' Lomond said. 'Her name was Roya Van Ahle.'

Cullen nodded agreeably. 'Oh aye. Cracking lassie. Redhead. The legs – that was the trick with her. Could have been a ballerina.'

'But she ended up working with you,' Slater said.

'That's right,' Cullen said brightly.

'I want to know about the relationship between you and the Cesar and Romeo's team.'

'Yeah? Start-up, isn't he? Mr Cesar. Or is that his first name? I can't remember.' Cullen chuckled. 'It's straightforward – I package the films, he sells them. My fees are low, but I make sure the performers get a decent amount. He came to me, if you're wondering. I do loads of work with MyGirl and CamJack, and they're doing really well. I've heard it called "elevated porn".'

'This is your main line of work?' Lomond asked.

'I'd say it's about sixty per cent, probably not as high as you imagine.'

'What's the rest?'

'All sorts. Weddings, student films, stuff for professional production companies . . . even showreels for people who want to work on TV or appear on reality shows. A kind of digital CV, if you like. Social media, as well. People make a good living off wee clips on apps. That's the way it's going now. My job is, I shoot things that look good. Doesn't matter what it is. I gave up being fussy a while ago. When the serious money came in.'

'Porn isn't exactly on the same shelf as weddings,' Slater remarked.

'Oh, you'd be surprised,' Cullen said. 'There's all sorts goes on. I've done boudoir shots for women to give to their husbands as a wedding present. Straight up. Naked as the day they were born by the end of it. Don't need much persuading, some of them. I've seen some sights. They want to remember what they looked like when they were young and beautiful. I helped them take their wedding lingerie off before their husbands did.'

'How did you get into this line of work?' Lomond asked.

'I asked my careers officer about it at school.' Cullen cackled, then saw fit to point out: 'That was a joke, by the way.'

'No flies on you,' Slater said. 'So you decided one day you were going to shoot dirty films?'

'I was trained as a cinematographer, and that's what I am. I have some credits to my name – underground films. I shot a project that got into the pictures for a couple of weeks – stand-up comedian wrote and directed a film about being at school in the seventies. *Balaclava*, it's called. You might have heard of it.'

'I'll look it up on the internet,' Slater said.

'From there, I helped a photographer light a shoot he was doing with some models. This is about twenty-five years ago, just afore the millennium. From there I found out about a film company that needed someone to make their digital films

355

look better. The market was just broadening out. Streaming wasn't a thing then, but DVDs were doing well. Lot of money came out of that. I worked with them, found out they shot porn movies . . . And I saw how much they were selling for. I stole all their contacts, formed my own company, and here I am.'

'Did you shoot the video of Roya and Watt?' Lomond said.

'I did – it was right here, in my studio downstairs.'

'We'd like to look at the raw footage as well.'

'Not a problem. I can give you the lot.'

Somewhat surprised that he hadn't had to resort to arguments or threaten court orders, Lomond said, 'What's the workflow? You shoot the material bespoke, for Cesar – then what?'

'It goes out to a production company for editing. If I've the time, I'll do it myself, but I was busy that week.'

'What's the name of the company?'

'It's not really a company – we send it out to students based at the College of the Moving Image.'

'My daughter goes there,' Lomond said. He blinked. 'Students do it? Edit movies like that?'

'Yeah, and they do it for absolute peanuts. Quite skilled, some of them. Cost-effective: they get paid; I don't kill myself with the outlay.'

'Even pornography?'

'Sure. They do the lot – it's a skill in big demand. Good editing's something you don't notice – or shouldn't notice, if it's done right. They learn how to edit in cumshots, they can edit anything. Music videos, video blogging, home-made movies, porn . . . They do it well, and they get paid. As they should. I do the real stuff, which is making the set and the performers look good. No amateur-hour stuff here. None of your clip-site nonsense. It's all for paying punters.'

'Have you ever worked with either of these women?' Lomond brought up the images of Aylie Colquhoun and Sheonaid Aird Na Murchan – handout images, from their own modelling portfolios.

'That one,' Cullen said immediately, pointing to Sheonaid. 'The mermaid girl. Her. She was done in as well, was she not?'

'She was "done in", yes,' Slater said, labouring the term. 'How did you know her?'

'Same way I knew the other lassie. She came here for a shoot.'

'A photo shoot?'

'No,' Cullen scoffed. 'You not been listening? A film. Porn.'

'Same as with Roya?' Lomond asked.

Cullen nodded. 'Aye. Same performer she was with, as well.'

'Watt?'

'That's right. Big lad.' He grinned.

'How did that come about?'

'Same way. She went through Cesar – answered an ad, I'm guessing. She'd been on CamJack – I'm sure I saw her. Mermaid thing. Kink, if you ask me. But that wasn't part of the shoot, unless you count a bit of diving.' He chuckled, then grew serious for a moment. 'She had the most gorgeous underwear for the shoot, that lassie. The mermaid.'

'Was she confident? I mean, did you think she'd appeared in that kind of material before?'

'She was quite shy before we started. Most of the lassies shooting that kind of stuff are first-timers or amateurs. It's good money, for what it is. There's a lot of it about, but not a lot of good stuff, if you know what I mean.'

'What do you mean by shy?' Lomond asked. 'Reluctant? Uneasy?'

'Just shy,' Cullen said. 'I've got ways of warming them up. A couple of glasses of wine never goes amiss. Plus, I think she liked the boy, Watt. He's a nice kid, for all that. That's a boy who could make a million. But anyway . . . these shoots sometimes take on a life of their own. They're the best ones. Lightning in a bottle. You'll see when I give you all the footage. Everything. Nothing to hide.'

'When was this shoot?'

357

'About five . . . six weeks ago? Late summer. Maybe early September. It was a bright day outside. I threw open the windows to get some natural light in. Golden hour. It looked brilliant.'

'Did she get paid on the day?' Lomond asked.

'Yeah, cash in hand. Good amount of dosh, as I say. She didn't hang about afterwards.'

'Did she leave with Watt?'

'She left alone, so far as I know. Watt left a bit later. Stayed for a drink, talked about a few other projects.'

'Mind if we have a look at the studio?' Slater asked.

'Not at all. You curious, mate? Quite a big market for police porn, believe it or not. Same with firefighters and nurses. The army's a good one. Men and women. People like a uniform.'

'Classy stuff,' Slater remarked.

'What? Classy? Compared to a lot of the stuff out there, that's exactly what it is. Nobody's coerced. And they get paid well with me. I make no promises, and I take no advantages.'

'Don't kid us on,' Slater said. 'You're a grubby wee pornographer. You can sit in a big house and give us the pish about cinematography and light balance all you like. You make dodgy films and take advantage of people.'

Cullen just laughed. 'And there goes a hypocrite. You look like a lay preacher. Someone in the kirk, you know? I can see you reading a lesson on a Sunday.'

'I'm not anything like it,' Slater said.

'Just a puritan, then.'

'Eh?'

'You know and I know that everyone at this table has looked at porn at some point. Maybe even recently. Maybe even today.'

'Last time I saw it, it was a film you had shot, with a lassie who got her throat cut a few days later,' Slater said.

'That's fuck all to do with me. You can call this a dodgy business all you want, but it's everywhere, son. Don't be naïve. You know that yourself. If you don't use it, you're in a minority.

People paying through the nose for the real deal is more honest than a two-minute snippet for a clip-scraping site. With me, at least the money's flowing in the right direction. And there's an art to it, like it or not. It's not for crackheads uploading videos for a couple of quid.'

'Who do you deal with at the college?' Lomond asked.

'It goes through an official email address, comes back from one sender. Funny name. Minto, something like that. Minty?'

46

The city centre came at them like a series of hurled knives as Lomond and Slater drove over the expressway.

'Sheonaid's on-off boyfriend, back home,' Lomond said, 'mentioned she wanted a loan of a fair bit of money. He could only offer fifty quid, and she took it. He said this was unusual for her.'

'You saying she was being blackmailed as well?' Slater's face was set.

'It's a good reason for someone putting themselves at risk in that way.'

'You reckon our man's blackmailing them? Is that how he's getting close?'

'Aye. Remember Aylie as well – according to her mother and her pal at the club, she was short of money, looking for ways to make more. Maybe she'd branched out from MyGirl into Cesar's as well. According to Cullen, they agree to star in a film, they go to Redway, he shoots it professionally, and they get cash in hand. Hardcore stuff. Then someone blackmails them.'

Slater chewed the side of his mouth. 'Normally I'd say you were on the money, but look at the stuff they did off their own backs. Is jumping into stuff like CamJack that much of a stretch? Strip clubs, nudie modelling, swimming about only wearing a tail . . . God forgive me . . . plus, their families and boyfriends knew about it all. It's a step up, sure, but it wasn't like they led totally secret lives or anything.'

'It's a big step up to having sex on camera. With a stranger. That's not necessarily something they'd want to broadcast to friends and family. It wasn't their art. I could see a woman wanting to be painted in the nude . . . remember what Cullen said about wedding shoots? How they looked when they were young and beautiful? That was Roya, for sure. She knew the value of her looks. She was more up-front about it than the other two. It sounds like she was going to branch out, use what she had, try to make a fortune out of it . . . but it was a different kind of drive for Aylie. She was into the burlesque side of things, the vintage clothes. It was her passion. It's not my thing, never will be, but that was her art. And Sheonaid . . .' Lomond sighed. 'Basically that lassie wanted to be a mermaid. Anything else was just a medium for it.'

The bitter, bile-black irony of how she died. The water roaring in her ears, her blood staining the water before the light blinked out for good. Lomond clenched his fists. 'So yeah. They had to fund what they did, but this was more desperate. They dropped down a level – even past the level of MyGirl. They went a grade lower. Sheonaid and Roya, for sure. I wouldn't be amazed to find out Aylie had done the same. It was down to blackmail.'

'There's a link. Sheonaid and Roya had the same partner: Watt. And he didn't talk about Sheonaid.'

'We didn't ask him about her. We didn't know, and neither did he. He was close to Roya; Sheonaid might be a coincidence.'

'Come on. Biggest murder case this country's seen in years. You'd slept with a victim and put it on film, and you're saying you wouldn't remember?'

'Maybe he was scared of the connection. Didn't want to incriminate himself.'

'You don't think it was him?'

'He checked out for Roya. We'll see about Sheonaid.'

Lomond's phone rang. It was Smythe. 'We've got something new in. Sheonaid Aird Na Murchan's disappearance. An old dear had set up a video camera looking out onto her street to try and catch the postman doing something dodgy. And . . .'

'You've got footage for me?'

'Aye. Looking out across the road, facing the bus stop where Sheonaid was picked up. I'll ping it over to you.'

Lomond opened the attachment. It was a video clip, taken at night, in unusually sharp clarity. It showed the bus stop opposite the one from where Sheonaid Aird Na Murchan had been picked up on the night she died. They saw a tall figure with short dark hair and spindly legs dart over to a rubbish bin near the stop and pick up a plastic bag that was lying on the pavement beside it. The figure rooted around inside the bag, gave a thumbs-up, then walked off briskly.

Lomond came back to the call. Smythe went on: 'OK – the person in the video looks like they're signalling to the bus stop across the road. We know Sheonaid was there at this time, so it could be that the signal was to her. Some kind of exchange? A reason for her to be at the bus stop? It looks like a female, very distinctive, about six feet tall or just under. And a female was blackmailing Roya, according to her partner.'

'I know her name,' Lomond said. 'Minette Carruthers, also known as Mint Carruthers. She's twenty-two years old, studies at the College of the Moving Image.'

'You want us to pick her up?'

'We're just about there already. Should have her in two minutes. Stand by.' He hung up.

They saw the college ahead, a long, squat building.

'Told you a lassie was involved,' Slater said smugly. 'Told you.'

47

'Oh,' was all she said, when Lomond and Slater appeared in the room of the editing suite, startling her.

'Aye – "oh",' Slater snapped. 'Stand up.'

'I'm kind of busy here,' Mint said. She turned away from them and started typing. Before her, twin screens – massive, each the size of Lomond's television at home – went dark.

'Get up and stand back from the computer. Now!' Slater gripped the edge of her chair, pulling it back from the desk.

'Hey!' Now she stood up, face turned from disbelief to fury. 'That's my main project! Don't touch it!'

'No one's touching anything until our techies show up,' Slater said. 'This is a crime scene now.'

'Someone going to tell me what I've done?' Mint folded her arms in defiance.

'You tell us,' Lomond said. 'You're under arrest for black-mail. You have the right to remain silent. Anything you say to us can be used against you in a court of law. Do you understand what I've just said to you, Mint?'

'Blackmail?' She laughed. 'What blackmail?'

'Blackmail involving Sheonaid Aird Na Murchan, and Roya Van Ahle.'

'I don't know anything about blackmail . . . ah. This is about . . . this is the money in the bag.'

'Eureka,' Slater drawled.

Lomond paused. 'When was this?'

'A couple of weeks ago . . . I was asked to pick up some money in a bag, and wave to someone in a bus shelter. Then I had to drop it off.'

'Drop it off where?'

'Another bus shelter, round the corner, maybe half a mile away.'

'Who told you to do this?'

'It was a message that came through to my phone . . . number unknown. They showed me a clip that I made a while ago. Me and a boyfriend. Something daft I uploaded to a website. If I didn't do what they told me the clip would get sent to my family.'

'This message is on your phone?'

'No, it self-deleted. It was on a messaging site.'

'So you were forced to do the money drop, or the person involved was going to release a clip of you having sex – that's what the message said?'

She nodded. 'It was going to be sent to my dad,' she said softly. 'Normally I wouldn't care, I'd have told them where to go . . . even fronted up to it. But my dad hasn't been well.'

Slater pointed to the console, the racks of camera equipment, the wiring, the recording booth. No one else was in the editing suite. 'You do extra work in here?'

'I don't have time to do extra work. I've got coursework to hand in.'

'But sometimes you guys do extra work in here, is that right? Editorial work?'

Mint shrugged. 'Sometimes.'

'What kind of editorial work?' Lomond asked. 'Films? Documentaries? What?'

'Various stuff for outside companies . . . we do it for experience, but sometimes they pay us.'

'What have you been paid to edit?'

'Well . . . there's some stuff for Redway, with a guy called Rab Cullen. It's not dodgy or anything – well, not illegal. You know. It's a bit like MyGirl.'

'We know all about Redway,' Slater said. 'How much of their stuff have you handled?'

'Bits 'n' pieces, just over the past year.'

'Just you?' Lomond asked.

She nodded. 'I cut together one or two packages . . . Rab was quite happy with them. Said there might be an opening for me once I graduate.'

'Did you recognise anyone in the videos you edited?'

She shook her head. 'Why are you asking me this? I haven't blackmailed anyone.'

Lomond pointed to the console. 'Can you get me some examples of editing you did for Redway?'

'Sure. If you'll let me get to the keyboard?'

'Delete nothing,' Slater said. 'I'm watching you. And don't forget – we're going to pull this place apart, so we'll find anything you do delete.'

'I'm not going to delete anything! Jesus!' Mint sat down huffily. She hit the keyboard hard, face set. 'OK. There's a list of files there.'

'That one,' Lomond said, pointing. '"Selkie" – that one at the bottom.'

Mint clicked on the file. A window opened, showing some video footage. She went full-screen, and a series of title lines appeared. *Deep Dive*, the film was called. *A Redway Studios production.*

'Who did the graphics?' Lomond asked.

'They were already packaged by the time the footage came in.'

Sheonaid Aird Na Murchan appeared, walking through a hallway Lomond had stood in less than an hour before. The room was cosily lit, accentuating the red and golden hues in Rab Cullen's hall. *Golden hour*: that was the phrase he'd used.

'You edited this?' Lomond asked.

'Yeah.' Mint sat up straight, chin thrust out proudly. 'Cut in some music, too. First rate job, the guy called it. Paid me well, too.'

'How did the work come to you?'

'Through our course leader. Martin. There's a list he gives us to do.'

'Martin?' Slater frowned.

'Yeah. Martin Granger. In fact it's here . . .' She minimised the video, where Sheonaid Aird Na Murchan was talking to a young man dressed in a suit at a long counter, presumably a maître d', a confident, smiling man Lomond had been talking to quite recently – Watt.

Mint opened a file with names attached. Lomond immediately marked the names: *Aylie*, *Sheonaid* and *Roya*.

'Right,' he said. He nodded. 'This is it, now. This is it here. What happens? You pick in and get work? You get sent the files?' His heart was pounding so hard it seemed to distort his voice. 'Did Siobhan work on this?'

Mint shook her head. 'No. Don't worry. She wants to work in journalism, not this kind of stuff. Flat no. True believer. She didn't want anything to do with it.' Mint turned to Lomond and smirked. 'She's a *good* girl.'

'Just let me see what's on there, please.'

The reel opened up. There, in front of a camera, her face almost glowing under bright lights, Aylie Colquhoun spoke. 'Hey! I'm Aylie, and I'm here to tell you about what I can offer Cesar and Romeo's . . .' She clapped her hands. The image cut abruptly to Aylie doing her fifties housewife thing, hair tied back, but dressed only in her underwear – vintage, surely: conical, outsized, with a thick girdle. Then another shot, Aylie in bobby sox this time, and nothing else. There was a brief black screen and a crackle of light – some digital interference – and then the image changed again.

'Hi! I'm Sheonaid, and I want to show you what I can offer Cesar and Romeo's.'

She wore the black one-piece swimsuit – swimwear, not beachwear. She clicked her fingers, and then she was performing a backflip from a high diving board, straight into a lagoon-bright swimming pool. Incredibly, the camera followed her all the way down, through the white slashes and muted thunder of the water. Then the shot changed, and she breached the surface in super-slow motion, the water spreading across her forehead and face before she was slowly, painfully born, rising all the way beyond her shoulders and bare breasts. There was no sign of a mermaid outfit here, none of the graceful aquatics that had seemed so poignant, so numinous, in the MyGirl footage. Then the image shut down – again with that curious fleck of light.

'You worked on all these?'

'That's right – for Cesar's. Or CamJack, that was the other one.'

'Not on MyGirl?'

'Nah, that's done professionally elsewhere. Bit beyond my pay grade. And Martin's.'

The image on the screen changed again to Roya Van Ahle, looking over her shoulder, crying out, as a man with his back to the camera thrust into her. Then came the edit, the swift cut to black, then the white flicker near the top of the screen.

'This was compiled for you?'

'Yeah. Showreel, I think it was called. To show me what I'd be working on for Redway – for Cesar's, and CamJack.'

'Scroll back a bit,' Lomond said.

'Which bit in particular?' Mint said, grinning. 'The last one, I'm guessing?'

'Don't be smart,' Lomond snapped. 'Go back to the bit in between the footage . . . after the first edit, between Aylie and Sheonaid.'

Mint wound back the digital footage, her finger relaxed on the black wheel on the control panel. 'It's just a black screen, an insert,' she said.

'Wait . . . pause. Now. On that,' Lomond said.

'What? The interference?'

'It's not interference.' Lomond turned to Slater and pointed to the mark.

With the image paused, the white shooting star had turned into a long dash or comma. At the left-hand edge of the screen, it had a kink in it, a nick.

'You see it?'

Slater stood stock still. '*Could* it be interference?'

'On a digital image? Maybe if it was a video tape. Nothing has a flaw in it with digital stuff. If there is, there are tools to remove it. Am I right?'

Mint nodded. 'You can fix pretty much anything. Like if you've got an old photo with a crease in it.'

'Scroll it forward to the next edit.'

'God, you're *intense*,' Mint giggled. 'You weren't like this at your house.'

Lomond felt the blood drain from his head. *At your house.*

In the fade to black, there was the white star streaking across the top. Frozen, it was exactly the same as the image in the first edit.

'Same thing,' Slater said.

'Could have been the same image, cut and pasted in,' Mint said.

'And is Martin Granger usually that sloppy?' Lomond asked. 'Does he leave mistakes in?'

Mint shook her head. 'No. He has a bit of a stick up his arse for that kind of thing, if I'm honest.'

The third cut, after Roya. The same thing: stark black with the white scarring.

'It's his signature,' Lomond said. 'Absolutely no doubt. *Look* at it. Now think of the wounds in the neck. Tell me it's not the same. The nick at the end. Maybe it looks like an M. Martin Granger, that's the name. That's him.'

'Jesus,' Slater said.

Lomond turned to Mint. 'Is he here?'

'No, he finished at lunch. Had a job to do, he said.'

Slater pulled out his phone immediately. 'We'll have him in two seconds.'

'We've got him now. Martin Granger, 88 Watson Mews, Kilbardie. Drives a '19-reg Volkswagen Passat.'

'How d'you know this?'

'He's been at my house,' Lomond said hoarsely.

'You mean our course leader . . . Martin Granger . . . is the fucking *Ferryman*?' The mirth had dropped from Mint's voice.

'He compiled a list from lassies who sent videos to Redway Studios. All three of them needed to make some extra money – fast. They were being blackmailed. Maybe he already knew them. Maybe he knew their videos before, from MyGirl or even YouTube. He probably knew Roya and Sheonaid because he follows Erskine Copper around. Copper painted Sheonaid, so that's one more link. Once he found out about them, he blackmailed them.' Lomond turned to Mint. 'He used you to make the drops. Probably he had already made contact, offered to pay the fee for them. White knight type. Then, when he had their trust, he picked them up in a stolen car and took them back to his house.'

'Well, he won't be doing it again,' Slater said grimly. He was dialling Gartcosh.

Lomond turned back to the screen, pointing to the video timer at the corner. 'This reel has a bit more to it, Mint. Run it on, please.'

'OK . . .' She clicked the mouse.

The image changed after Roya's brief, disturbing appearance.

'*Hi! I'm Siobhan Lomond. This is a showreel of my work so far as a video journalist. I hope you like what you see!*'

Wearing a smart blouse, her hair high, lots of make-up, a long skirt and her best shoes. She clicked her fingers, like the Cesar's girls, and the image changed instantly to black.

The white scar at the top.

Lomond's knees buckled. He sat down heavily on the spare seat beside Mint. 'Whit's this?' he said, out of breath.

'It's part of her showreel; we all have one. Martin said we should each compile a showreel.'

369

'Then what's it doing on here?' Lomond said. 'With that other stuff?'

'I . . . I don't know.' Now Mint looked aghast.

Lomond got up, the seat rocketing away behind him. Slater, still talking to control, looked round, alarmed.

Lomond fidgeted for his phone. He found Siobhan's number and dialled.

The line was dead.

He tried another number; that diverted to answerphone.

Then he called Maureen. 'Where is she?' he said, trying to keep his voice under control. 'Siobhan, sorry. Where is she today?'

'She's at uni,' Maureen said. 'Said she had to finish her show-reel or something. What's wrong?'

Siobhan

48

This is how it was done.

You wait for ages at the burger bar before the text comes through from Mint.

Hiya – change of plan. Can I get you at the bus stop?

What bus stop? you text, feeling a wee bit irritated by Mint by now, but still young enough to tolerate it.

The bus stop opposite the Conservatoire, silly! x she responds.

It's a fair walk, and you're thinking of jacking it in – you don't have time for this. You're not even sure why she wants to speak to you today, when she's editing the Ulvaeus interview. Probably wants something. She always wants something. *She's got to go; not a friend; always on the take; a weirdo. Dad was right about her.*

At the bus stop, an ancient car – plum-coloured, Fiat, a J-reg, made well before she was born – stops, prompting angry blasts from a bus at its back.

Squeaky descent of a hand–cranked window. 'Siobhan?'

Squinting through the window: Martin. You feel a sudden leap. 'Hi!'

'You looking for Mint? She's coming over to do a shoot at my place.'

'Oh. She said she was meeting me here . . .' Then you check your phone, and there's a message just this second in: *Going to Martin's. Photoshoot. Might be beer. Can catch up there? Don't want to go on my own.*

'She's heading to your house?'

'Already there – the daft bugger's taken a taxi.' Another angry blast from the rumbling beast at his back. 'She said she wanted to do some more editing in my suite.'

The rain billows in and out of a bus shelter that is no shelter at all. 'Sure. Why not?'

In you go, into the J-reg plum-coloured Fiat that looks surprisingly well kept inside, with a new pine scent air freshener dangling from the rearview mirror.

'Thanks,' you say. 'It's been an awful day. I've wasted so much time waiting for Mint. She's dragged me all over the place. I thought she was heading to the college to finish some editing on our project.'

'Nah, she wrapped that up this morning,' he says. 'Your interview with Ursula Ulvaeus came across well. You're a natural on the camera. You ask better questions than Mint.'

'I'm not sure about that,' you say diffidently – although privately you'd thought it had gone well, and for once you didn't dislike how you looked on camera.

'Don't be so hard on yourself.'

Down Union Street and the buildings seem to shuffle along with the traffic. Then you head over the bridge to the south side. Over the Cart Water and further out. All too soon, more greenery than sandstone, no roofs, then the odd barn, and then after one right turn, you're bouncing along a single-track road, at the mercy of the suspension in a car produced in the nineties.

'Did you borrow this motor from your granda?' you manage to say.

He smiles and doesn't respond. He's focused on the road. Then he jerks the wheel to the left. 'Christ!'

'What is it?' But you've heard the impact, felt the explosion, even felt the car sagging. The car is out of control, as if it was slithering on the ice, and then a tree comes round, up close enough for you to make out the elephant skin bark. It hits your side of the car and your shoulders jerk.

A slight impact, a kiss; you aren't hurt so much as shaken.

'Are you all right?' He looks shocked. He shakes your shoulder. 'Siobhan, are you OK?'

'I'm fine.' You laugh. 'Is this a crash? Am I a survivor? Have I got hysteria?'

'Oh my God. How do you feel?' His hands, on your shoulders, your arms: quick, concerned.

'I'm fine, I'm not hurt or anything. You braked just in time. What was that on the road? I thought I saw something just before we went over it. Looked like a shark's fin.'

'Yeah, I saw it, but not fast enough. Some idiot left something on the road, a spike maybe. Wait there. Try not to move. You could have whiplash.'

'I'm fine. I'm just worried how you're going to get the car moving now.'

'Don't worry about that – I think it's just a blowout. There's a spare in the back.'

He eases the car away from the trees. Once he's put on the handbrake, he gets out and bends down, out of sight for a while. You gaze out into a lonely, wooded trail. You get a fright as he reappears while you're feeling inside your coat for your phone.

'You believe that?' he says, holding up what looks like a bent metal railing, a sharp edge pointing towards her like an extended middle finger. 'Burst the tyre like a bullet. Could have killed us. Someone's done that deliberately.'

'But . . . we're in the middle of nowhere.'

'I drive down this road all the time.' He hurls the misshapen iron totem far away into the browning ferns and bracken by the roadside. 'I reckon someone doesn't like me coming this way. There's a farmer up hereabouts, he stopped me once. Said it was a private road. Could you come out and help, please?'

'Sure.' You get out, but in truth he doesn't need much help. The jack, the wrench, the nuts and bolts, and finally the spare tyre is in place. He tuts at the crumpled bodywork. 'It's going to be five hundred quid, at least, to get that beaten into shape. Probably easier just scrapping it. Not my favourite, this car. Just as well.'

'Where'd you get it, anyway? I thought you drove a VW.'

'I collect vintage cars. Run them about, make sure they get used. God knows why. Power steering, stereo systems, satnavs, airbags . . . I have to admit, there's a lot of good things about modern cars.'

The rain comes down harder. 'Mind if we get back in? I'm getting soaked.'

'Aye. I'm just about done.' He replaces the wrench and other equipment in the back, then rolls the burst tyre off into the undergrowth.

'Shouldn't you keep that for insurance or whatever?'

'Nah. Farmer can deal with it, if he's so keen on bursting my tyres.'

You both get back in the car.

'I can't find my phone,' you say – and you're sure now it's not where you left it, the usual button-hold inside pocket in your raincoat.

'Oh, right – did you maybe drop it when we crashed?'

'I don't think so. It's not like the car flipped or we had a head-on or whatever.'

He peers at your feet. 'Hang on . . . is that it? I think it's there.' And he reaches down under your seat, close enough to touch your leg, if he wanted. 'Got it.'

He brings the handset up into the light.

Smashed. Splintered down the middle and snapped length-wise – ready to fall to pieces. If mobiles could bleed, this one had already bled out.

'Oh no!' You snatch it from him, try the button – nothing.

'It must have fallen out of your pocket. Maybe it went down the side of the seat.' He pinches his nose. 'I am so sorry, Siobhan. It's all my fault. You insured for it?'

'No,' you say. Tears in your eyes. Thinking of all the photos.

'You got your stuff backed up?'

'I guess, but . . . I still had a year to go on my deal.'

'Hey, never mind – I promise I'll pay for a new handset.

You can retrieve data off smashed phones, it's easier than you think.' He grins. 'Now, I think we'll get you a nice cuppa tea back at my place.'

★

Slater gripped the edge of his seat. 'Gaffer, maybe stop the car and I'll drive. It's . . . my car, gaffer.'

Lomond ignored him. Trees scrolled past them on either side. Blue lights ahead of them. Squad cars, on their way. Above them, the helicopter, arcing away to the south-east.

'Gaffer.'

'Leave it,' Lomond said, teeth set. 'Just leave it.'

Slater swallowed and tried to relax his shoulders. The engine roared. 'We should leave it to the boys. Take a step back.'

'No chance.' It wasn't clear if Lomond was talking to Slater or anyone. 'Maureen doesn't know yet. Maureen . . .'

49

It feels a little bit wrong to be going into your course leader's house.

It's a bungalow, but a big one, at the very end of a street which backs onto a farm, miles out of town.

Why did we go down that wee road? you wonder. You can hear the muffled roar of a main road, though you can't see it as you get out of the battered old car. Surely it would have been easier to feed off the main road than go down that leaf-clogged track? It was a short cut, but an awkward one.

You go through some open gates and you're on his driveway. The neighbours – spread out along the estate, all old houses, these – would never know he had arrived.

'This isn't where we were for the cheese 'n' wine thing,' you say, unbuckling your seatbelt. 'Where are we?'

'Barrettstown. This is my wee holiday house. Just a couple of miles up the road. I do some filming here.' As you get out of the car, he tings a fingernail off a brass sign that reads *The Whileaway*.

'You left Mint in your house by herself?'

'Yeah. Why – don't you trust her?'

'It just seems a bit weird. I don't know what she's playing at. She mentioned she wanted to meet for a burger . . . then you tell me she's got a taxi out here.'

'My fault.' He holds his hands up. 'I told her to get a taxi – I had an appointment I couldn't get out of. I should have planned this a bit better.'

'Then you come along and give me a lift. I know you've got a better studio out here, and Mint raved about it, but . . .'

You swallow. There's that faint, pulsing alarm, that steady unease. 'I don't get it,' you say finally.

He looks agitated. He bends his head low, and whispers: 'Listen. I'll level with you. I don't mind students wanting to be sociable and I was happy to host the cheese 'n' wine at my house – you all came to that. But Mint . . .' He sucks in a breath between clenched teeth. 'I think things can tend to get inappropriate with Mint.'

'Well . . . maybe don't invite her to your house, then.'

'This is different. It's for an art thing. I'm an artist, I don't know if I mentioned it to you?'

'I think you said you did photography in your spare time.'

'I've done a bit of that,' he concedes. 'But art is my thing. Painting. Did I not tell you? I'm self-taught. All the bad habits. I agreed to paint Mint, but, end of the day . . . I need someone here with me when I do. A chaperone. I'm a married man, you know.'

'I get you.' And you wonder: *If contact with her is inappropriate, why are you looking for it?*

But this is the stuff of gossip over a glass of wine or two, in the future. So you ignore that faint alarm. He unlocks the door, and you step over the threshold.

★

Lomond pulled up beside a row of squad cars parked untidily in a quiet rural street with old, handsome houses. He yanked the handbrake, got out, and ran towards the officers piled up at the front door.

The battering ram was comically small and compact, like a doorman you might have had four or five inches on but knew not to mess with. After one single blow, the front door was sprung, and the high-vis vests poured in, bellowing.

'Every single room, every single corner,' Lomond said. 'We're looking for a basement, a trap door, somewhere with a swimming pool.'

Catching up with him at this moment, Slater had never seen such a blank, lost expression on the DI's face before.

'A bath won't cut it,' Lomond hurried on. 'That's not grand enough. He needs something bigger.'

Shortly, a young male officer with the chiselled look of an action figure emerged. 'Sir – this house is clear. We've even been up in the loft – there's no one here, and no sign of a basement or a pool or anything like that. We've called him – no response. His wife is away at her sister's with the kids. October week.'

'They must be here somewhere,' Lomond muttered. 'Somewhere hidden.' He chewed at a thumbnail. Then he slammed both hands against a door with great force, startling the men and women in uniform around him, and sank to his haunches, hands still touching the white door.

Slater laid a hand on Lomond's shoulders. 'It's all right, gaffer, we'll have him soon. It'll turn oot.'

Lomond straightened up, his face to the door, and tried the phone again.

*

'I cannot believe this,' he says, turning his phone to you. 'She's done a runner.'

A message from Mint. *Had to go – Ursula called. Demo starting Sauchiehall Street, taking DSR-PD150 camera. That OK? Mx*

'What . . . she just left the place unlocked?'

'Well . . . I gave her a key to get in. And she obviously locked up. Well, now I'm fed up and I'm cold. Coffee?'

That doesn't sound like a bad idea.

Moments later, you're sitting in a compact little kitchen with a view out onto a large, well-tended lawn with loose yellow leaves flying across in the wind and rain. Above, there's a thick line of trees bordering the property, in the process of undressing for winter.

You set your cup down. 'I'll level with you here, Martin. You're a good teacher and you've been a big help to us. I've enjoyed this module more than anything else I've done. But I wonder if all this stuff, open house and whatever, is a bit . . . inappropriate, to use your word?' You raise your hands, cutting off his shocked response. 'I'm not saying there's anything dodgy going on. But you know and I know, if a lecturer or a course leader gets too close to his students you're asking for trouble. And I'll be even more honest with you . . . the more I spend time with her, I'm starting to think Mint is trouble. I don't think she'd hesitate to drop you right in it if she thought it'd help her in some way.'

You're doing this for his sake, for his protection, and maybe for Mint's, too. You try to see the good in people where others would only respond with cynicism and innuendo. You think he is decent; you detect no flirtation in his interactions with you or any other young women in his classes. You see his vulnerability, and you can imagine Mint's vulpine features, giving evidence before an employee tribunal or a civil court or even a criminal one. *And that's why I felt I couldn't continue my studies . . .* And you worry about this, not just because you are good, but because *he* is good, so very good, at doing this to people.

'She's a climber. And I use that word neutrally,' he says. 'She wants to succeed. I recognise that in her. I encourage it. She's not a rich kid. And she's not as wise or as switched on as she thinks. But I want to help her. Because . . . well, I've had a bit of success in life. All this . . .' he gestures around the kitchen, the patio window, the garden outside, 'all my own work. I've been lucky. I've sold some art, worked in film, TV, photography . . . I don't have a mortgage to worry about. But I used to be a kid like Mint. I came from nothing, and there weren't opportunities. I had talent but no one was interested. No support. No exam results. I had to start from scratch.

'I mean, you're from a good family, they'll back you up,

encourage you . . . Some kids have nothing. They have to hustle. Cut corners. Maybe even bite and kick a wee bit. Anything to get ahead. I recognise that. I respect it. And I want to be a person who can be there for them as they make their way in the world. The guy who gives them a hand. If that's inappropriate, then I'll walk away. I've never done anything in my working life to jeopardise anyone's safety, anything like that. I may get taken advantage of by the Mints of this world, but the Mints of this world are tomorrow's leaders. Maybe it's a risk worth taking.'

'Sure, but . . . maybe next time, don't give her the keys to your house. Free advice.' You make a dismissive gesture as he laughs in your face. 'I'm just saying.'

'Point taken. Maybe you're right. But I've got an instinct for these things. Mint's a hustler, but she's not a wrong 'un.'

'I hope you're right.' You sip at your coffee, distracted for a moment by a police helicopter making a slow sweep over the top of some farmhouses, visible through a gap in the trees. 'They've been up there for a while.'

'Wonder if someone's missing,' he muses. 'Anyway. Fancy checking out the darkroom?'

★

Lomond stood away from the house, out on the pavement. He didn't want to set foot on the grass of Granger's front lawn. Unholy ground. Some of the neighbours had come outside, alarmed.

The dial tone of his phone pressed into his ear echoed through his blood. Finally, Maureen answered.

'Hello? What's up?'

Lomond took a deep breath.

★

'This must have cost you a fortune,' you say. The red light outlines everything. You haven't seen a darkroom outside of old movies. 'Is it even necessary now, with DLR and all the digital stuff?'

'It is for me. I still use film rolls. It's not even retro chic – I just prefer the hands-on element. You have to know the past as much as the present. My old man taught me that. Never get too big. Never . . .' His face goes blank for a moment. Then he smiles. 'Anyway. I need my hobbies. Same with art. You can do just about anything on a ten-inch tablet these days. Not so long ago, you'd need canvases and half a craft shop. I've also got canvases and half a craft shop. Are you into art?'

Still the alarm doesn't break through into shrieking life. Why would it? You know this person. He's been in your life for a year. And he's not standing anywhere near you. There's a door at your back, and an unlocked front door behind that.

'Not really. How about we sort out this reel? I'll need to think about getting back home. I think we were ordering in pizza tonight.'

'At your dad's house?'

'At my mum 'n' dad's house, aye.'

'No problem. I can drop you off. Don't think your dad took it too kindly when I was over the other night.'

'No, but . . . Well, polis's daughter. Whole world's full of villains if your work is trying to catch them. You know.'

He nods. He does know. 'OK then. I'll let you have a quick look at the other studio before we get started.' He flicks off the red light and guides you back into the corridor. 'It's in here,' he says, gesturing to a door to the right.

You wait for him to unlock it. 'Lot of expensive gear in here,' he says, putting on the light.

You step inside, and you can't help but say, 'Wow.'

It's a swimming pool – not huge, maybe twenty feet in length, along one whole side of the house, enough to have a few strokes, turn, then go again. It has that clean, briny smell of a spa pool rather than a chlorinated fungus factory. But the appearance is what gets you. The walls seem to drink in the light, which emanates from lamps in odd places – the corners, burrowed into the walls. It's a dim place, only a notch or two above the darkroom. There is no natural light.

He shuts the door behind him and locks it.

To the side of the pool, there's a blank canvas on an easel, and a workbench with various brushes and tubes of paint.

'I've a proposition for you . . . would you be up for a modelling session? It's not nudes, nothing dodgy. I just want you to sit on that sun lounger over there, in front of the pool.'

He touches a control at the wall; the light changes from warm peach to stark blue. Lights in the pool also blaze on, full glare, giving the water that electric effect of a holiday swimming pool after dark.

He steps forward, wringing his hands somewhat diffidently. You can't quite make out his face in the gloom. His glasses reflect the pale blue wraith light. He has the faintest smile on his lips, a suggestion of teeth. They reflect the light, too.

Unconsciously, your hand goes to your bag.

Then you remember.

'Hold on a minute, Martin. I'm just going to call my dad.'

'What?' he barks.

You pull out the phone. You haven't even switched it on. You do so now.

'But your phone was smashed, wasn't it?' he says, voice ricocheting off the walls. 'I said you could use mine.'

'No, I've got this one. I just remembered – it's a burner phone Dad gave me. Polis's daughter, right? Just in case I lost mine. He told me to keep it in my bag. He said the Ferryman does something weird to the phones of the lassies he kills.'

You see the missed calls – eighty-one of them. All from Dad. Frowning, you hit the button to reply.

He answers on the second ring. 'Siobhan!' he screams, loud enough for anyone in the room with him to hear.

'Dad, what's up? Listen, I just wanted to check in about dinner tonight . . .'

'Where are you?'

You didn't even hear him move. Perhaps he'd taken his shoes off. Maybe he knows how to move that quietly. His hand closes over the phone, but before he can get a grip you snatch it away, and the bells are clanging loudly now, you know everything, and you're running around the side of the pool.

'Dad!' you scream. 'I'm at Martin Granger's house! Barrettstown. *The Whileaway*! It's called *The Whileaway*!'

He catches up with you, teeth bared, spitting obscenities, and he grabs your phone and then it's in the pool. You see the light of the handset flicker and die as it sinks. A hand closes over your face, fingers raking your skin, and you pull away, running, screaming.

He's laughing now. He doesn't try to chase you. He seems pleased. 'Where're you going? There's nowhere to run. Just do what I say. Take your clothes off and kneel down. Or I'll cut your legs off.'

His drool is an electric blue snake, trailing off his chin, and he has a knife in his hand. He keeps low, low centre of gravity, ready to spring or swipe. You run around the pool. He follows you, gibbering, shrieking. It's a sound of infernal delight, the glee he can show only to you, here and now.

'*Take* your clothes *off*,' he bellows, 'and *kneel . . . down*!'

You run for the door – it's locked tight, there's hardly any reverberation as you batter at it. He aims a huge cut at your shoulder – missing, probably intentionally. Wants you to lurch, and it works. His hand closes round one shoulder. On instinct, you barge him aside, much easier than you'd think.

There is one place you can go.

You jump into the water and the crash smothers everything for a second or two, your visual field suffused with the eerie blue glow that gives your skin that alien tone, the way it was intended.

You can't touch the bottom, at the centre. Deep. That's good.

'You want me, come in, freak!' you scream from the surface. 'You scared of a bit of water?'

He pauses at the pool's edge. Hands by his sides, the knife pointing to the floor. Then he removes his glasses. He opens his mouth wide.

He holds the blade horizontally, then clenches it between his teeth. He exaggerates the bite; you hear enamel clashing with steel.

It even slices the ends of his mouth. Chelsea smile. You see his blood. He doesn't flinch. He simply walks down the steps into the water, and dives deep. You see his ghostly shadow, his corrupted light, streaking towards you. You strike out, mad strokes, to the other end of the pool.

He hasn't taken a breath. He turns and his legs scissor and as he passes through a blue beam under the water his eyes glare at you. You flail back up the steps, clothes dragging, water cascading off you. He almost gets you then, knife a pale blue arc an inch from your calf muscle. Then he's after you, incomprehensible ravings and sheer fury.

You seize the blank canvas and hurl it at him – then the easel, the paints, the brushes, everything to hand. None of them hit him.

'Get away from me!' You back towards the door; it's hopeless. He's grinning, laughing at you, blood curling down the sides of his mouth.

'Take your clothes off and kneel down,' he screams.

Then the door crashes open at your back. It knocks you off balance; you land on one knee. You stare at Granger; you're both confused.

Big men in high-vis pour in, shouting.

Then your dad's there, and you're sagging against him, crying.

He's strangely calm, though you've never been hugged so hard in your life. Swallowed by his coat, the way you were as a wee girl. The stitch in his cheek tickling your temple. 'It's all right, love. Everything's fine. It's OK. You came through loud and clear, didn't you? Just in time. You're fine.' You bury your face in his neck.

'Where is he?' That's Slater. You've always found Slater a bit rough around the edges, a bit too quick to make off-colour jokes. Your mum isn't a big fan of Slater, either. But you're pleased to see him.

'What do you mean?' says your dad.

'He's gone – where is he?' Slater tears around the side of the pool. 'Where'd he go?'

One of the wall panels at the far side of the pool is slightly ajar.

50

Lights, on either side, flashing blue. Other traffic blocked and backed up, the main artery of the city in stasis. The Kingston Bridge, spotlit by a helicopter. The beam centred on a man standing on the crash barrier, looking down into the black water. On either side of him, the glittering cityscape. Thousands of lights, thousands of windows, thousands of phones.

The man had a knife to his own throat. But the more immediate threat was the drop. At any moment, it seemed that he must be blown off by the wind and rain.

Another man approached him, casting long shadows in the spotlights, until he reached the barrier.

Granger looked down at Lomond. The knife remained at his own throat. 'What's this in aid of?' he shouted into the wind.

Lomond raised his hands. 'I'm here to talk.'

'I'll split you in half first.'

Lomond tucked his chin into his raincoat as the wind picked up. He felt unsteady on his feet – and he wasn't even on the barrier yet. 'Look closely. Your left trouser pocket.'

Granger glanced down at the red laser dot, quivering slightly, fixed on one of the rivets in his sodden jeans.

'Now to tell you the truth, the sniper won't kill you, if that's what you're after,' Lomond shouted. 'But they will disable you. You might fall, but probably not, if that's the entry wound. Bullet through the pelvic cavity . . . you can imagine. Not nice. Come on down, we can do this somewhere warm and cosy. Get you a cuppa tea.'

'Yeah, bullet through the pelvic cavity. I imagine a ricochet. Off the bone. Blowing your stupid face off. They won't do it.'

Lomond shrugged. 'Acceptable risks. C'mon down, Martin. You know it's finished. I've spoken to your wife and daughter. You can speak to them too.'

Granger laughed. The point of the blade had pierced his skin. Blood, diluted by the rain, trailed down his Adam's apple in a pinkish trickle. 'Now why do you think a person like me would give a single fuck about that? My daughter's a block of wood, but not anything like as useful. And my wife . . . daft as you like. Imagine being married to a serial killer and not realising! Perfect wife material, you might say.'

His knees quivered. Lomond flinched in response. Granger stood on the middle slat of the barrier, with his shins braced against the top, but all he had to do was pitch forward a little.

The helicopter came closer, revolving sightly, buffeted by the wind. The updraught threatened to tear Lomond's coat off; he signalled for it to back off, angrily.

'Funny if it crashed, eh?' Granger said, head tilted back, staring up. 'Some finale, that.'

Lomond began to climb the barrier.

'Behave yourself,' Granger said.

'This isn't very dignified, pal, I'll give you that,' Lomond grunted. He lifted one leg over the side and straddled the uppermost slat while Granger still stood on the second, the top one tight against his shins. For a moment or two, Lomond was the more vulnerable to falling, and absolutely did not look straight down at that moment; he focused instead on the Broomielaw, on the glass-fronted businesses down by the front, and the lights of The Ferry. It looked as if there was a band on. People were queuing outside, at any rate.

'Look, we both know you're not going to cut your own throat,' Lomond said. 'I think you want to talk me through it. I think you want to explain yourself.'

'I don't have to explain anything to anyone. And if you want this to be some big showdown – no problem. It's going to end with me putting this blade right through you. It'll only take a second. If the last sound I hear is you screeching, then I'm happy with that.'

'Nah,' Lomond scoffed. 'It's not your style, all this. I think you take your work more seriously than that. So come into the station and talk to us. If you want to make me your big baddie, fine. But if you knife me, you'll just get another polis in my place, then another, and another. C'mon, it's freezing up here, son.'

'Maybe,' Granger said. 'Or maybe I take my chances and jump off. What do you reckon? Think I could survive that? Big drop into the water. They say it's like hitting concrete above a certain height. Maybe we'll both go.'

'I think you would have done it already if you were going to. Are you coming down?'

'Nah, I'm taking my chances. I'll jump.'

'With a knife to your throat? Come down. Don't cheat yourself. First things first, put the knife down – nearest safe and convenient spot. Hey, I sound like a driving instructor. Mirror, signal, manoeuvre . . .'

'Shut up.'

'Then you step off the barrier, and we walk over to the car. No dramas. Well . . . it's a bit late for "no dramas". But you see what I mean.'

'I don't want to go to jail. Don't you have professional negotiators or something? Why have they sent you?'

'If we'd sent negotiators, you'd be more likely to do something you don't really want to do.'

'For an idiot, I suppose you're clever.' Granger turned, and let the knife go. It flared once, in the beam of light, then plunged straight down into the dark water.

'Good knife,' he said. 'I'll miss it.'

'Right. Next step. Off the railing, pal.'

'No. I only did that so I could keep both hands free.' Granger turned to face Lomond. 'And now, we're going for a swim.'

Lomond's knees buckled, as if struck from behind. 'Whoa!' He lurched to the side, and instinctively reached out and gripped Granger's arm. 'Sorry.'

Granger jerked away, snarling. But only so far.

His left hand was cufflinked to Lomond's right.

'It's a cracking trick, that,' Lomond said, grinning. 'Everybody says so. What d'you reckon?'

'You fucking . . .' Granger turned; then his face went completely blank.

He stepped onto the top of the barrier and leaned forward into space.

At his right-hand side, Slater caught him by the shoulders as he fell. Lomond and Slater dropped to their knees; Lomond's elbow locked and he cried out in pain, face pressed to the metal.

'No, you don't,' Slater hissed through clenched teeth. 'Swimming's cancelled.'

Other hands arrived to help Slater heave the dead weight, and the pressure on Lomond's arm, shoulder and back eased. As he was hauled up, Granger stared into the wavering beam of light from the helicopter above as the rain bulleted through it in white sparks, his face expressionless. He might have been at the end of a rope. The moment his back touched the roadside, officers in uniform swarmed over him.

Lomond's keys jangled as he handed them over to Slater. His cuffs were unlocked. But he remained on one knee, even after the uniformed scrum a few yards away began to revolve towards the flashing lights.

'What's up?' Slater said. 'You posing for the cameras? Superhero stance?'

'Give me a hand, you idiot,' Lomond growled.

'What for?'

'I've done my back in!'

51

Lomond leaned back in his seat, without wincing. *God bless ibuprofen.*

'Did you get a good shower?' he asked. 'That's the best thing, after the cold and wet, I think. Well, a bath's better, but, you know, we're kind of restricted here.'

'Shut up,' Granger muttered from the other side of the interview table.

'No, *you* have the right to remain silent,' Slater said.

'You too, baldy. Shut up.' Granger glared at him. Slater only smiled.

'You should be glad you didn't go into the water,' Lomond said. 'Been there, done that. Had an ear infection after it. And it tastes like you'd imagine. Anyway, Martin, for reasons I don't need to spell out, my part in this investigation is over after our informal chat here. There's a conflict of interest, given that you made things a bit personal, and I can't risk prejudicing this case. Another couple of officers will be along to talk to you soon.'

'She squealed,' Granger said suddenly. 'Oh God, she squealed. She was the worst of them. Guaranteed. Absolutely yellow. Screaming in terror. You must be proud.'

'Course I am,' Lomond said, shrugging. 'She got away. She's fine. You failed.'

'There's no failure, really. Unless we want to talk about how long it took you to find me.'

'Tell me what I could have done better, then. Tell me where I went wrong. Now that we've sorted the "who" bit, I'm happy to go into the "why". You can tell us as much as you like.'

'I wanted to get caught,' Granger said. 'Getting caught is part of it. I knew it'd happen eventually. Couldn't do it again and again and not get caught, could I? Polis are a joke at the best of times, but they can put two and two together eventually.'

'How many people have you killed in total?'

'I've never killed anyone,' Granger said, turning to stare at his lawyer. If irony had a physical quality, it would have oozed from his mouth at this point. 'You'll have to prove otherwise.'

'Here's what I know, top to bottom,' Lomond said. 'In the mid-nineties, you were already active . . . as an artist. You called yourself John Smith. You were pretty good, and you had big ideas, but you didn't have prospects. A teacher spotted you, years ago. Thought you were a bit dark in your interests, but you had talent. He wanted to help. You were from a broken home, dodgy background. Your da . . . whoa. In prison for assault and battery, on your mum.' Lomond stared at him. 'Among others. I'm sorry about that. That's awful.'

'Shove it,' Granger said.

'Anyway, you're very enterprising. You make connections. Some of them through your da. Total wide-os. That isn't quite you, but you speak their language. You've got brains. You know how to do a deal, you're known as a guy who gets things done. So Finlay, who knows somebody who knows somebody, drafts you in in desperation after a lassie collapses at Rafferty Landing. He wants you to get rid of her. You're the kind of guy that can make that happen. She's unconscious but still alive at this point. Rafferty thinks you're going to take her off the premises and leave her at a bus stop or in a hospital entrance. But you don't. You watch her die. Maybe this gives you ideas. A sense of power, maybe. I'm guessing. However it came about, she turns up in the pond, carved up. By you. That's where you make your mark for the first time. This one.'

Lomond brought up an image on screen. A putrid wound in something that looked more like torn upholstery in a landfill than human flesh. 'This is an old photo,' Lomond said. 'You're a photographer, you'll know this is analogue stuff.'

'Very interesting,' Granger sneered.

'So you mutilated Daisy Lawlor's body and hid it in the pond. Whether you got paid for it or not, and just who paid you and how, might never be known or proven. Unless you fancy telling us.'

'I just . . .' Granger chuckled and shrugged his shoulders. 'I give up with you guys, I really do.'

'From there, there's a big gap. Now what were you doing in all those years, I wonder? That's a question for later. We do know you kept painting. That's your passion, you would agree with that.

'You make contact with Sir Erskine Copper, and Sir Erskine Copper's basically a big daft auld pussy cat. He's very fond of himself and he'd make a twenty-episode podcast of his own farts and call it art, but there's a reason people take to him and listen to what he says, because he's one of the best living artists in this country. And he thinks you're a talent. He actually funds you – he buys your paintings, cash. He says he's never met you in person, and that might even be true. He *is* just daft enough to have behaved exactly the way he said. His bank account shows cash withdrawals that made their way to you. We don't know how, yet. He sets up sales to other people, he *loves* your stuff. But he can't persuade you to step out from behind the curtain.'

Lomond took a sip of water. His hand was steady.

'Now comes the really weird bit. Daisy Lawlor's death is subject to a massive cover-up – I mean, top-to-bottom, people involved left, right and centre, funny handshakes, you name it. People who don't want Torquod Rafferty or Lana Galbraith's name attached to a massive scandal. Things are a wee bit complicated with Lana. The upshot is, they decide to fake her death by swapping her for another dead girl. You get a chance to see another poor wasted lassie out the door, though at least this time you don't get to carve her up. Again, other than the name "John Smith", which must have seemed funny the first time

I heard it, I haven't got much to link you to that. But these cases weren't exactly your thing, were they?'

'And tell me. What's my thing?'

'Slitting women's throats and watching them bleed out. I think you might have painted with it. That bowl we found beside the pool . . . Makes me wonder.

'You planned this last part of your career very, very carefully. In real life, you find it easy to get good jobs. You're a self-made man: educated, a lecturer in film and TV studies, with a special focus on documentaries. You were sharp when it came to the internet – quite far-sighted. You saw the way things were going and you were in there, fast. Short films, that kind of thing. Students liked you. Trustworthy – a bit too close to them, for my liking, but never any suggestion you went over the score.

'You're earning great money, you're married, you've got a daughter, you've long punted the mortgages, and if you were a normal guy, you'd have one eye on retirement by now. But you've got these other interests nobody else knows about.'

'Here it comes,' Granger said.

'Film and TV work leads you into the world of streaming. There's money to be made off bespoke services for certain types of content – I don't need to make suggestions or insinuations here because it's patently true: we've already proved it. You worked for Claymore Films. You worked for MyGirl. You were bespoke editor for Redway Studios, which put out stuff for CamJack – all under the radar and off the books – and this is how you selected the three lassies you killed.'

'You're an awful blether.' Granger folded his arms and glared at Lomond.

'No need to be upset,' Lomond said, 'we're just having a chat. If I get anything wrong, tell me. So you select the three lassies – you've already seen two of them through your editing and production work for MyGirl and then Cesar and Romeo's and CamJack. Hey, you were even a customer, for a while, though we're pretty sure that whatever you watched, you viewed through a dodgy VPN. Always thinking ahead, Martin. Always.

'You were an adviser for MyGirl when they set up. Technical side, at first. You modelled it on other subscription sites, and it seems that you had the idea to aim for a classier clientele, with classier content. But then there's stuff like Cesar and Romeo's, which is very different. All roads pointed to Redway. All three girls made porn for easy money. That told you they were desperate. So you started the blackmail campaign.'

'Like *Coronation Street*, this,' Granger said, delighted. 'Twists 'n' turns.'

'They were working-class lassies. They didn't have the option of, say, talking to daddy's pals in the polis or fancy lawyers or Holyrood or anything like that. They could only rely on themselves. But they also had families. A proud maw, a grieving da and wee sisters who looked up to the eldest and adored her. That was the three lassies you chose. That was why you chose them. They couldn't keep their heads above water.'

'Pun intended?' Granger asked, tittering.

'So – they paid up a little at first, which is how you knew you had a mark. Then in order to put them in the killing zone you threaten them again, but this time you make it known that they can pay off half of their debts by making sexually explicit films. Which they do. Some of it's nasty stuff. BDSM, all kinds of things. Degrading, to my mind. You put them through it. You really wanted to humiliate them. Break them, almost. And you got someone gullible in to make the cash pick-ups – it's Mint, and we know it's Mint. She was very useful to you, and as far as I can tell she didn't even know why, half the time. Just following orders, it seems. That's her story anyway. Again, we might never be able to stick anything criminal on her. But we'll gie it a good go.'

'An idiot,' Granger said, nodding. 'Loud-mouthed, narcissistic, take any opportunity going, and I mean *any* opportunity going. I was going to top her last, if you were thick enough to let me get away with bleeding your daughter out.'

Slater threw back his head and laughed. 'This is great! *You're* psychoanalysing people – you!'

'I could psychoanalyse you, you fucking ape,' Granger said calmly. 'Wouldn't take too long, though.'

'Ape, was that? You just called me an ape? Hey, I wasn't the one swinging off the top of a bridge a couple of hours ago, mate. It was on the telly and everything. If I'm an ape, what does that make you? King Kong?'

'Here's the part that was very clever . . . Well. Not clever,' Lomond corrected himself. '*Sleekit* is a better word. You made contact with them, separately – not as a blackmailer, but as an interested party who'd seen their work. You told them you liked what they did, professionally, and you could hook them up with other producers through Redway . . . They could make good money, you said. Coincidentally, this money would cover the blackmail. So they accepted. And you even made money yourself, a kind of commission. They were all absolutely stunning, beautiful lassies. In another era they might have been beauty queens.'

'Maybe. Or they might have been sacrificed to Crom, if you go back far enough,' Granger said. 'Might have ended up on a ducking stool. See if they float or not.'

'Never considered the human sacrifice element,' Lomond said, making a note. 'That's a great suggestion. Anyway, you get talking to them, and because you're very charming you find out about their worries and problems. You're very good at doing the favourite-uncle "I'll sort this all out" act. So that's what you do. You swoop in, the big hero, and basically you make the pay-off on their behalf – as a favour. So you've helped to offset a scam that you created. Great stuff. And the end result to all this planning is that they end up getting into a stolen car with you, late at night, to take part in a wee art project. Their silence was the killer. They kept it to themselves.

Shame, guilt, relief, a nasty wee blend. If they hadn't, we might have caught you before you touched any of them.

'Then, you drive the backroads – a different one each time. Outside the city. You set up a trap that punctures your own tyre. There's a minor, staged accident – and that's a big risk: you could end up with four wheels in the air and a serious problem – but it lets you distract them, steal their phones and smash them. You know fine well the phones are a key bit of evidence. Once you've changed the tyre, you take them back to *The Whileaway*, a lovely name for the studio you've got hidden among the millionaires' houses and farmers' fields out in Barrettstown.'

'I'll miss that place,' Granger said. 'Wonder what'll happen to it?'

'We can tell you what's happening to it right now,' Slater said. 'It's being taken apart, inch by inch, by clever gadgies in white overalls. They're good at finding evidence. Blood. Hair. Semen. That kind of stuff.'

'You make it sound so romantic,' Granger simpered, and laughed.

Lomond continued: 'We think you entice the women into your pool house to pose for paintings. Despite what happened with my daughter, I'd agree with the forensic view that the dead girls didn't know what was coming. You made them kneel; you approached from behind; you grabbed them under the chin, then you very quickly make the cut. Except you leave that wee kink at the end, your signature. The same signature on the paintings. The same signature you left on Daisy Lawlor's body. The one I saw on your videos. That's been a wee fantasy for you your whole life, I bet. Did you practise that signature on school books, or on folders at college, or maybe use it as a graffiti tag somewhere? We'll find out, Martin. There's nothing about you we won't find out.'

'You can find out, but you won't understand.'

'What's to understand?' Slater said. 'You're a pervert. That's it.

In your head you're Picasso, but you're just a creep, mate. A sleazebag. You get off on killing lassies. It turns you on. It's that simple.'

'You're that simple.'

'This is a waste of time, gaffer,' Slater sighed. 'Leave him to Smythe and Tait. Game's over. Let's go for a pint. We've got him. What's to learn? What can he tell us?'

'I can tell you this much,' Granger said. 'The point to learn is in the art. I'm an artist. I have urges. Every artist has urges. I wanted to combine the two. I have an image that I can never quite forget, and it's always been in my head. I don't know how it got there. Maybe I saw a film poster or a book cover as a child. It's a woman lying back in some water. She's bleeding. That's the image I can't forget. The one I want to make last for ever. And . . . I've done that. Jail, death, whatever . . . you can't take it away.'

'Interesting,' Lomond said. 'And you also used some of the blood in the paintings, is that right?'

'What paintings?' Granger said, deadpan.

'Oh, the ones you painted right after killing the girls. You had them shipped out to Erskine Copper. Your masterpieces, you called them. They might still be in storage now, if his wife hadn't smelled a rat. Maybe he's more involved than we suspect. I think he was just a batty auld luvvie whose attention wandered too easily. Svengali complex – he can't be the young buck, the up-and-comer. So now he wants to be the guy behind the next guy.'

'Erskine Copper . . . is innocent,' Granger said. 'With innocence comes naivety. If I can say or do anything decent at this point, then I'd say don't put him in any cells.'

'He'll explain what he did, and why he did it, under oath in a court of law,' Lomond replied. 'Regardless, he did take receipt of three paintings in recent days – paintings recently completed by you. He can't quite remember. Might have been a few weeks or a few months ago, he says. Sir Erskine isn't a good one for details. But his wife is. She called us about these new paintings, on top of the collection she already told us about. The ones Sir Erskine Copper had removed from his house, the minute he found out the mysterious John Smith might end up being a wrong 'un. Not forgetting the painting of Sheonaid Aird Na Murchan you did. Did you contact her direct off her website? Dox her through her videos? Maybe you painted her once, to get her trust. To lock her in. Anyway . . . did Sir Erskine mean to hide the paintings? Damage limitation? Or did he want to make sure your work was kept safe, even if you were in the jail? Art's an investment like anything else. Even if it's by serial killers. You know that, right?'

'And I'll keep doing it. The art.' Granger nodded. 'There'll be a market for it. Bigger than you realise.'

'You won't make a penny,' Slater declared. 'You won't get away with a wee proxy or shady dealer holding on to the cash for you, either. I swear to God – you won't be selling any art while you're alive.'

'I'm not interested in selling anything,' Granger said. 'See what I said about understanding? And you being an ape? You're proving the point. I don't want to *sell* art, I want to *make* it. And I'm good at it. And those works will stand.'

'What . . . the paintings?' Lomond cocked his head. 'Seriously? What were they called? "The Blue and the Red and the Yellow". Striking, I'll say that for you. Or they *were* striking.'

Granger cocked his head. 'What?'

'They're in shreds, pal. Those paintings are matchsticks. Being swabbed. In wee plastic bags. Being looked at by much cleverer people than us apes. Did you use any blood in those paintings, by the way? I notice you didn't answer before. If you did, we'll know. Soon.'

Granger's face fell, but not for anything like long enough. 'I can make more art. I can get it out there. There are always

ways and means. I've got a good sponsor, plenty of money. Private collectors will want it. There's a market. And imagine what it'll do for my other work. When we're all in our graves, there's only one of our names will still be spoken of in the future. It won't be yours.'

Lomond sighed. 'We've got, I'd say, three cold cases involving missing lassies from the past twenty-odd years that we're going to reopen. Women picked up at bus stops, never seen again. Students. Young. Beautiful. Might have been you. Might not have been you. We'll find out. You are a person of interest. We're going to check your every move from those days to this. Congratulations. You've got yourself some attention.' The inspector clapped his hands. 'Well. That's you all done. Incidentally – just on the off chance we don't speak again: Slater's right about you. I'm not interested in how much you try to pretend that what you did was clever. That there was some intellectual angle to it. You are a pervert. Paraphilia, that's what the psychologists call it. That's at the heart of this. Not any artistic impulse. Just a perversion. You're just a grubby, filthy wee guy. No better or worse than a tuppence ha'penny sex offender cutting about in the bushes. Any attempt to dress up what you've done as some kind of aesthetic, something creative . . . nah. You're lying.'

'Prove it.'

'I will. This is just a theory. But we'll find out for sure. The facts will speak for themselves.'

'You going to paint me a picture of that?' Granger said. Then his face transformed, lips peeled back, eyes bulging. He hooted and shrieked like a monkey and snorted.

Lomond's voice was level, revealing nothing of his shock and revulsion, as he said, 'Oh, by the way, we found the knife. In the river. Score one for the dive team, that wasn't easy. Just as well we had them on stand-by. We'll see if it fits in with any other throat cuttings or crimes of that nature. We've got you, son.'

401

Granger giggled, then said, 'Miaow.'

'Whether you planned to get caught or not, I think you'd rather still be out there, doing what you were doing, than squared away in here. But that's not an option for you now. Good job, eh?'

'I'll keep making art. That was always the goal. You'll never stop me.'

'I have stopped you. Past tense. You're done. I'll see you in court, Martin.' Lomond got up. He left Slater to say the words. 'Detective Inspector Lomond has left the interview room.'

52

Lomond stayed long enough to watch the team celebrating – Slater and Tait, slapping each other a little too hard on the back, both of them hugging Smythe a little too close, if you were watching with curious eyes, as Lomond always did.

But he left before anyone could call for a speech, having already been embarrassed by the arrival of Drummond and Sullivan for a photo opportunity.

No one saw him leave, and he ignored the calls as he walked up the street. Always best to leave while most people at the party are smiling, he thought, as he hailed a taxi.

Mr Flick drank up and left the pub at Lomond's back. He passed very close as Lomond stood on the kerb outside and the yellow eye of the hackney cab bore down on him. Lomond was alert to his proximity and frowned at the retreating back.

Mr Flick glanced back, nodded, and moved on.

'Here,' the taxi driver said, glaring at Lomond briefly in the mirror as the cab rattled down St Vincent Street, 'you heard they caught that bastard? Yon Ferryman?'

'I heard they did,' Lomond said. 'About time as well.'

'Here, that Ursula Ulvaeus will need to go and whinge somewhere else, eh? What a pain in the arse that is. Brought the city to a stop! I agree with what she said, but I mean . . .'

'She'll definitely find something else to moan about,' Lomond said. 'Can't blame her, can you?'

Soon enough, the windy driveway was ahead. The lights were on in the hall, and two faces appeared at the window as the taxi pulled up. He waved at them as he paid up: his wife and daughter. *All the chickadees home.*

Lomond got out of the cab and smiled.

Acknowledgements

Many thanks to my brother, James, for his invaluable insights into police work, and once again to Dr Stephen Docherty for the medical stuff. Any errors, omissions or exaggerations in any of these areas that cause police, doctors, pathologists or killers to snort, splutter or sniff are all down to me.

Once more, thanks to my wife, children and other members of my family for enduring all the typing in the background. Thanks also to Justin and all the team at Kate Nash for their heroics, to Alison Rae at Polygon for all the support and advice, and special thanks must go to Nancy Webber, the Pele of editors; there is an art to editing a manuscript, structurally as well as cosmetically, and Nancy is an artist.

And, finally, I'm very grateful to you for reading – speak soon.

Polygon

AN IMPRINT OF BIRLINN LIMITED

Head over to our website to find more
Birlinn books across fiction, non-fiction, sport,
poetry, children's books and academic history.

You can also sign up to our newsletter. Keep up
to date with all our new publications, launch events,
author interviews, special offers and much more.

http://birlinn.co.uk/birlinn-newsletter/

Follow the link or scan the QR Code below:

Explore Scotland with our app, Scotland-by-the-Book,
a new tool for readers at home and around the globe with
an interest in Scotland. Find out more on our website.

https://birlinn.co.uk/scotland-by-the-book/

Follow the link or scan the QR Code below: